At first he felt snared in a rainbow of reflections shot through a rapidly spinning crystal.

Colours etched a bright, acclerating circle, dazzling more senses than the eyes, hissing in the ears like an entoiling moonweasel, swathing the tongue with their imperious glancing flavours, whipping the skin with a fugitive sensation.

He knew who he was, what he was, where he was; so Kendric who had been Wrathman of Rule, assured himself.

He had gone into the gate willingly, as he had done once before. On that first occasion the gate, a mere mist of rainbow overarching a rock, had spit him out senseless. He remembered little of that passage, other than acquiring an aching body and groggy mind.

But this gate he had come to as a man of power, however reluctantly gained. He came as one who would pass, no matter the barriers. And for his effrontery, the gate welcomed him with open, unhinged force . . .

Also by Carole Nelson Douglas

SIX OF SWORDS
EXILES OF THE RYNTH

and published by Corgi Books

KEEPERS OF EDANVANT

Sword & Circlet 1

Carole Nelson Douglas

CORGI BOOKS

This is a work of fiction. All the characters and events portrayed in this book are fictional, and any resemblance to real people or incidents is purely coincidental.

KEEPERS OF EDANVANT

A CORGI BOOK   0 552 13306 X

First publication in Great Britain

PRINTING HISTORY
Corgi edition published 1988

This book is set in 10/11 Times

Corgi Books are published by Transworld Publishers Ltd., 61-63 Uxbridge Road, Ealing, London W5 5SA, in Australia by Transworld Publishers (Australia) Pty. Ltd., 15-23 Helles Avenue, Moorebank, NSW 2170, and in New Zealand by Transworld Publishers (N.Z.) Ltd., Cnr. Moselle and Waipareira Avenues, Henderson, Auckland.

Printed and bound in Great Britain by
Cox & Wyman Ltd., Reading, Berks.

For the three white ladies
who could not stay

Citydell

City of Edanvant

The Wood
Between
The Walls

Black
Tower

Spring

The
Women's
Keep

Edanvant

CND

RETURNING POINTS

A man came to Edanvant as the setting sun's last light polished the swollen brass bellies of the marketplace ewers to the color of blood rubies.

He was a thin man, whose lance-long shadow stretched far even for the hour of sunfall and who wore the chill of oncoming evening in the drape of his dark cloak. He stalked, as one dazed, among the twilight-quenched stalls, staggered, then lurched against a tent prop.

'Be wary, fellow!' snapped the metalsmith, busy covering her ranked pewter wares for the night. She paused, a work-hammered woman with sinewy arms and tight face, to regard him. The cast-iron features loosened into surprise, then reflected a spasm of fear.

'Your pardon, Lordling. I didn't notice . . .'

'Notice?' The man's deep voice vibrated with incipient offense. 'Notice what?' He drew up his cloak-swathed form, further elongating a height that towered well near seven feet. 'What have you noticed?' he demanded.

'You are one of them,' the smith answered, her eyes growing leaden in the sun-snuffed demilight. 'We mean you no disrespect. But they keep to their fortress since their return and bother us as little as is possible for those whose very existence nettles us. We will not welcome more of your kind — though we must abide it. We have lived well enough without Torlocs for too long.'

Other vendors had gathered, the fading sunfall's dull vermilion turning their faces and figures into an angry red clot against the burlap-draped silhouettes of the stalls behind them.

7

'They,' the stranger repeated, ignoring the woman's other words. His shoulders — broad but sharp, and tipped to one side like a scale that is weighted with an invisible burden — straightened. 'My kind,' he savored as much as said. 'Then I have come . . . home at last. To Edanvant.' Every word oozed irony.

'Edanvant, yes,' the woman answered boldly. Bitterly. 'Your home only because we townsfolk dare not contest you and your ilk. Do not disport with us, Torloc; you walked through our city gate and into our marketplace, our midst. You know where you are; you are ambitious to play lordling of it.'

'Gate . . .' The man pressed a long, thin hand to his eyes, as if reading the surface of his palm instead of the dimming scene before him. 'Of course — the gate from the Inlands! It must have spat me here, as a failing fire spews out cinders.'

'We know what you bear,' a merchant across the way conceded. 'We'll not bar your way. We'll not aid you, either.'

'What I bear? You know that?' Surprise brought the man a long stride toward the merchant. The fellow, as rotund as one of his hip-high wine amphoras, quailed. Then the stranger stopped abruptly in midstep, as if chained by one ankle to the ground.

Behind him, the smith had ignited a torch. The rising flame inhaled air with a voiceless howl, its red glare dancing ill-temperedly over the townsfolks' somber faces. The smith's voice became contemplative, nearly evoking a tale-teller's tone.

' 'Twas ill enough eons ago when the Torloc dames ran roughshod over Edanvant with their seeresses' powers,' she said, 'as we've heard at our grandfather's knees. The legends say the Torlocs left, all at once. Years became decades and our hope became certainty. We thought all that talk about Torlocs mere legend, but, even so, considered ourselves well rid of you, all of you.

'Now you men — once ordinary, unmagicked folk at least, to hear the old tales — return one by one, bearing your foreign talismans. Get yourself back to our Citydell then, with the rest of your sorcerous kind,' she suggested bitterly, glancing up along the rising main road. 'Rule over us as before. But expect no liking from us.'

The man remained frozen in midstep, his jaws seemingly soldered shut.

'Go then,' he ordered at last, his voice rising in the disdain they expected of him. 'Remember what I am, and get to your houses and your tangled byways. Leave the broad road to me.'

'We go because it is our time to go,' came an answering voice, softer than the whisper of weepwater tree branches, yet carrying far and strong. The young braid-crowned basket-weaver, rebuke in her insightful eyes, gathered her nimble-fingered children, then wafted them between her stall's high hunched shoulders into the twilight beyond.

The others left then, slowly, in groups. The smith was last to leave, passing her torch near the stranger's impassive face as she went. He winced.

'Good even, Lord,' she said in mock civility, and, bowing defiantly, vanished into the shadow-thick byways.

He waited, the man, until he could hear none of their departing steps nor see their fading lights. Stiff fists unclenched on the cloak, letting it part with an audible, relieved sigh of fabric.

Then he gathered himself and took the second step he had halted so abruptly. His left foot scraped across the cobblestones as a flint scratches steel, pulling listlessly until it joined his forward foot. But his bootheel struck no sparks and the evening remained half lit.

Limping painfully, the Torloc lord edged himself toward ancestral towers he had never seen, bearing a burden that was all too visible even in the oncoming dark — himself.

The blind basketweaver sat on her marketplace stool. A fat afternoon sun amused itself among the threads of sheer silver braiding her hair while the woman's knuckle-swollen fingers swiftly wove loose reeds into a rising circle shape.

Near her placidly swollen figure the basketweaver's children, surrounded by young of their own she had never seen, wove

9

with nimble-fingered skill. Some stacked baskets or counted glittering round black lordlings into a strongbox.

The marketplace buzzed with the come and go of hard- and soft-shod feet, with the murmur of bargaining voices and the high-pitched pleas of children for a tongue-sweet. From a distant stall, the shatter of the crystal-caster's orbs mingled with the whine of the herb-poacher's calls.

'Torlocbane for fending off talismans! Don a brooch of brush and forgo the touch of magic.'

Scents of Spicemullen and roasting songbirds on tiny spits entwined into a single slightly rancid but reassuringly familiar odor. The blind basketweaver smiled as her fingers flew through their time-endorsed patterns.

'Weave your basket another four rounds higher and I shall buy it.'

The basketweaver cocked her head. She had heard most sounds this world had to offer, even after she had stopped seeing its sights, and this voice was a new one — female and aged, but not infirm. Not in the slightest infirm.

'Why need you a basket so high and wide?' the basket-weaver inquired.

'Perhaps I go calling, and would bring a greeting gift.'

'Then you are new to the market.'

'Nay, old to the market.'

The voice had grown cryptic and amused; the basketweaver no longer liked it. She detected a rustle of garments, many long garments of some supple, rasping material, fluttering in the breeze.

'You are not alone,' she diagnosed.

'No.' There was a silence, then, 'Your hands pause.'

'I was simply wondering where you go calling.'

'I hear they call the place Citydell. No, stop not weaving, woman! We are in no hurry, but your profit will be higher if you work consistently.'

The basketweaver's plump, sun-ruddy face had gone as white as her hair. Misshapen fingers tightened on stiff reins of reed, malforming them.

10

'I feel your shadow,' she told the unseen woman. 'It brings a chill to my old bones.'

'Not so old as mine.' Thin, papery fingers lifted the unfinished basket from her grasp. 'Here, your pay.'

Something smooth, icy, and round dropped into the basket-weaver's reed-callused palm.

'What coin do you pay in, stranger? It feels like merely a stone — some small, chill stone.'

'We come from another place and bear none of your coinage. There such a token is highly prized, though it is but a small, chill stone, as you perceive. Coldstone, they call it. Some say it forms from certain women's tears.'

A small, clear stone flashed to the cobblestones. The basket-weaver's open palm trembled. 'You are a Torloc dame—!'

'I am a Torloc seeress, weaver, and you see better than your fellow townspeople. Tell me the way to Citydell, but tell me first whom I will find there.'

'More of . . . your kind.'

'Many?' The question, like the voice, was suddenly sharp.

The basketweaver shrugged. 'More than enough for us. When the men began returning, well before my birth, we thought the city should be choked with them, as it was before when Torlocs lorded and ladied it over us all. But they came in only a trickle, these men, the last when I was yet young enough to be vain. I remember seeing him standing at sunfall not three steps from where you pause now.'

'Many?' the voice insisted.

'My hands . . .' The woman spread her knotted fingers. 'Times two.'

'And — few — women among them? No . . . seeresses?'

'They are men only, save that they are Torlocs and thus not "only" anything. Oh, why do you come? There will be no peace in it!' The soft voice grew anguished.

'We come because we must, for reasons most people come, even those who are not Torloc. We have no place else to go. Finish the basket, woman.' The curved reeds were thrust into the basketweaver's hands. 'I would not further postpone a long-delayed — reunion — with our kind.'

Stiffly, as if the sun had decided to cast ice water instead of warming light upon her hands, the basketweaver forced straight-grown stems into a complex circular intertwining. She moaned quietly once, then wove the last strands tight.

'What is your name?' she asked as the basket levitated from her worn hands.

'Finorian,' said the seeress in her dry old voice. There came another rustle as the Torloc woman bent to the ground. Something lay again in the basketweaver's hands. The object was small, warm, and so smooth it felt oily.

'Amber,' Finorian explained. 'In some lands, of which I have some knowledge, it is said to have a beneficial effect on swollen joints. The afflicted roll it between their fingers until their bones grow eel-supple.'

'You only had a coldstone,' the woman worried with a slight shiver.

'In some lands, of which I have knowledge, it is said a Torloc seeress once shed amber tears. Much is said, but what can be done is more important. Good day.'

The blind basketweaver no longer heard the clatter and call and bustle of market. She heard only the subtle rustle as a flock of silent figures brushed by her.

When they were gone, the bloodied late sunlight struck her like carmine lightning, warming her head and hands and heating the tiny stone cradled in her palm. It felt hotter than a lump of fresh-boiled sugar candy. Her fingers lengthened, then clenched into strong, youthful fists.

'Why me?' she whispered, 'Why was I chosen to ask? And worse, why was I chosen to *tell*?'

The Torloc Eldress walked on, trailed by twenty-some raven-haired women whose uniform height of nearly six feet was beginning to draw every eye in the market.

Even the crystal-caster, a figure as globular as his scrying devices, paused in juggling his glittering orbs to watch them pass. Silence formed a train behind them through the marketplace and up the long, cobblestoned street.

Citydell's enormous bulk commanded a gradual rise, all of its ten towers snaring the setting sun's ember-dark rays.

'Wait here,' the Eldress instructed her flock. Her long, pale fingers tapped a rough-cut geography of green borne on her breast like armor plate. The thin slab of emerald faded and grew dark. The seeress winked out of view just as the sun fell fully behind Edanvant's jagged-cut rooftops.

Inside the massive, ten-towered edifice, the sun's faint ruby gleam sifted through windows shaped from lozenges of clear coldstone. A sinuous, premeditated harmony shaped the vast spaces of Citydell's great hall. On the floor far beneath the soaring windows a fire paced the blackened maw of a fireplace, roaring. It illuminated a spare room, sparsely populated.

The home-come Torloc lords, their torsos and limbs draped in the reptilian glitter of linked mail, sat around a huge, carved trestle table. A few folk of Edanvant scurried behind their high-backed chairs, passing platters heaped with food, and refreshing opaque metal goblets with anonymous liquors from ewers as opaque.

The Torloc lords loomed tall in their high chairs, long men used to being perceived as such even when seated, men in their prime not used to sitting perhaps. One leaned forward, mailed elbows screeching across the tight-grained wood, a medallion upon his chest flashing sun-bright for a moment in a glancing blow of firelight.

'We are new to the ways of talismans,' he said, 'but the Eye beneath us is older than our kind. Its iris shifts to green. I believe some season changes for us.'

'Medoc,' another chided, a man shrunk into the shadow of his chair. 'Edanvant is ours again, as it always was. What should change? Who would challenge that?'

Servants came and went, quietly, filling the goblets if not the eyes and ears of their lords.

The fire hissed and broke a thick log's back. It collapsed in a shower of sparks and charred pieces, ripe-scented as incense. Something other crackled in the room, some assembling presence.

'Greetings, brothers.'

She stepped from the shadows of the soaring pillars, a figure, harpstring long, lean and pale. Suddenly she seemed the oldest

13

thing in the ancient hall, more venerable even than the icy, coldstone windowpanes now shining obsidian with utter night above it all.

Mail chimed as men moved to clutch dagger hafts or goblet stems according to their natures, although the woman before them carried nothing more than a somewhat incongruous basket. Only one man remained chair-bound, motionless as the dark that obscured him.

'Finorian!' The man called Medoc stood, straightening to his full seven feet, his long fingers clutching the gilded medallion that hung near his heart. 'You have left Rindell and Rule?'

'There is little left of the Rindell and Rule we knew to leave, Medoc. I see you have found Edanvant on your own. I am surprised you have not sent for us.'

'Obviously there was no need,' said the seated man, leaning forward. 'We could rely upon you to come.'

It was the old seeress's turn to show surprise as light limned the sitter's grim features. 'Orvath!'

'Orvath,' he answered. He was a young man who looked early aged, a vigorous man who seemed too-soon-sapped, an angry man willing to carry his grievance as a cudgel. 'And I who was last to leave Rule, and last to come to Edanvant — with least — speak now for the rest. I am first among them. Why are you here?'

'Why should I not be here? It was agreed upon many, many years ago, which are as nothing to a Torloc, that we should seek our separate ways back to Edanvant and find each other again.'

'Look at us.' Orvath's hand swept the gathered company. 'How many Torloc men left Rindell in Rule, left other Torloc havens in other lands before Rule, in search of Edanvant? How many?'

'I am . . . aged, Orvath. My mind does not cast numbers into prophecy. Many men left. Many. None returned.'

'How many perished on their fruitless quests?' Orvath's low voice hissed in counterpoint to the fire's spitting flames. 'How many died in alien lands on alien swordpoints, clutching alien talismans that served them not?'

14

Finorian shrugged frail shoulders, a gesture that lifted the parchment-thin slab of now-bright emerald decorating her breast.

'My business is the future, not the past.'

'We,' Medoc interrupted. 'You spoke of we. There are others with you? The women of Rindell?'

'They wait . . . without. I came to strike a truce within.'

'Truce! Well admitted, Eldress.' Orvath leaned forward to hammer one fist upon the table. 'You have brought *all* the women of Rindell with you, then?' His dark eyes asked a question his lips had not formed.

Finorian turned her impartial gaze indirectly upon him. Her eyes were cataract-scarred, moon-white, and disconcerting.

'Not . . . all. One remained behind.'

'One.' Orvath sat back into the darkness of his chair.

'Finorian lost a lamb along the way?' Medoc questioned dryly. 'You are no longer as omniscient, then, as you represented yourself of old?'

The Eldress shook her white-locked head. 'So you might wish, brothers. But 'tis not my flaw. It was our youngest member, a silly girl dawdling beside a woodland pool to spy her own reflection. She found instead a wounded Wrathman of Rule, and dallied to assist him while a long-sought gate opened at last without warning and swallowed our settlement. I was able only to instruct her briefly before the gate gobbled me as well.'

'Rule did naught for us Torlocs but drive us into solitude,' Orvath said. 'Since when have Torlocs in Rule aided Wrathmen?'

'Since she did.'

'Which Wrathman of the Six was it?' asked a hawk-nosed man across the table. 'Wrathmen . . .' His voice dwelled nostalgically on the word as a smile tugged at his lips. 'I'd forgotten about those overgrown ancestral sword-wielders for the Six Realms . . . They were a breed as rare as ourselves, although only mortal.'

'The Wrathman from the Marshlands,' Finorian answered.

'Ah, Grandival.' Medoc's features relaxed into a grin. 'I remember—'

15

'No, you do not remember this particular Wrathman. He was Grandival's successor and his name was Kendric.'

'Grandival . . . gone?'

'Dead,' Finorian intoned a bit triumphantly. 'In your long travels, you have forgotten how quickly the spark flies from the adamant flint of human longevity. Long dead.'

'And what of this Kendric?' Orvath demanded, quaffing from his goblet, draining dark wine into the darker shadow of his being. 'Is he dead by now also?'

Finorian was so still that her breathing seemed to have stopped. Even the great emerald on her breast ceased to rise and fall.

'It is possible he survived,' she conceded finally.

'Then her mercy was not for naught, your silly young one who was left behind. Methinks she was a kinder breed than some Torloc dames have become.' Orvath leaned forward again. 'What was her name?'

'Irissa,' Finorian hissed, as if breathing an incantation. 'Irissa.'

Orvath blinked, his face blank and confused. He sank back into shadow again. 'I thought—'

'It was not she, Orvath. I said this one was young, and you are old, all of you, though you do not look it.'

'We are young enough to choose our own future, Finorian,' Orvath answered. 'I think that does not include being at your behest any longer. If you and what women you have pried from Rule wish to join us here in Citydell, there is room and work enough to occupy you. We men are willing to welcome our long-lost. But we are no longer willing to serve the whims of a seeress, whatever her powers or however ancient they may be. We have and hold our own powers now.'

This time the men's hands moved in unison, each clutching some fugitive glint upon his person — a ring, a dagger, a medallion, a chain. Orvath's figure remained motionless and dark within the shoulders of his chair.

'What talisman do you bear, Orvath, that makes you so bold?' Finorian asked.

'None!' The man burst from the shadows at last, lurching

from the chair, his knuckles white upon the carved falcon claws that fashioned the ends of its broad armrests.

Orvath half hurled himself to the table, grasping its edge for support.

'You *know* that, Finorian! You know you sent me on a fruitless quest to a vile land rife with alien stone-bought magic in search of a talisman that did not exist! All I found was a dead demon at a gate. I wrested one thing from that dark force — myself, or what little is left of that self.'

Orvath straightened and moved toward the Eldress, labored step by labored step, half of his body raging forward, the other side dragging, as if an afterthought.

'You knew before I even went,' he accused again.

'I knew we needed something more than one aging seeress to see us all through a gate to our lost home of Edanvant. That is what I hoped you would find on your quest.'

'Nothing. I found nothing. I who left Rindell last, for sentimental reasons, came last to Edanvant, with least, and with no sentiment left at all.'

'Yet you speak for the others.'

'It is all that is left to me. Besides, the city folk do not fear me as they do the talisman-bearers. I can . . . move, in my way, through the city. I assuaged their fears, hired their young for servants in our fortress. But' — Orvath's harsh face softened into mockery — 'nonmagical work always propagates, and Citydell was long abandoned. We could use more eager hands to plump the pillows, polish the goblets, sweep the cinders from the hearth.'

'You offer us much,' Finorian said sardonically, twisting the empty basket gently in her hands. 'But Torloc powers spawn naturally only within the females among us, and the rare silver-eyed ones at that. If you turn your hard-bought talismans against us, against myself, I will break them like the toys they are.'

'Toys?' A man across the table flung a golden comb to the tabletop. Its teeth gnashed the wood like fangs.

Before Finorian's slight figure a fence of Torloc-high golden bars sprang up as if rooted in the polished stones

17

at her feet, tangling the auburn firelight in their tall prongs.

Finorian's lips curved into a scimitar of scorn. Her blank eyes blazed brilliant silver for a moment. Gold bars melted and ran eel-supple to the floor. Jaws snapping, the creatures writhed across the stones to the Torloc lords before shattering into random sparks.

'Let her taste the Tongue of Flame,' a rash voice urged.

Once said, it was done, a dagger of hurled light fell — though none saw whence the threat came, perhaps not even blind-eyed, all-seeing Finorian.

Smoke eddied in a corner of the fireplace grate — subtle, soft-shaped wisps of lavender and amber hue. Like reeds the airy filaments twined into an interlacing pattern, then wove a vaporous path across the floor to Finorian's hem.

While she watched impassively, the vivid smoke circled into a long, lean form, then coiled further to encompass the Eldress. Hissing, it wreathed her, writhing higher, its colors spinning, until it was close enough to swathe her throat. Her hands moved then on the basket, too late. Through the smokesnake's transparent form, the emerald touchstone faded to sallow impotency. Finorian's skin bleached whiter than her hair.

Her eyes, rolling in her head to repel the sending, began blinking blindly. Every breath she took slipped a faint mist of snakeskin down her throat. She coughed roughly.

The Torloc men watched, frozen by the spell's uncoiling form. Finorian's hand rose not to her touchstone, but her throat. Coughs racked her almost-flat form. Her wrinkled eyelids squeezed shut on her empowered eyes, while from their corners, glinting down her face, came the speeding flash of small, wet droplets. None there had ever seen tears fall from Finorian's face. Most had never seen a Torloc seeress's tears.

Fast as they fell, and dim as that echoing chamber was, no man could fail to see that the Eldress's tears fell not as legendary coldstones, but as solid, smoke-black gems. They fell and fell, clucking like gossiping tongues into the bottom of the blind woman's basket.

Then the smokesnake and Finorian's figure twined into one,

18

wrapping the Eldress in a diaphanous shroud of acrid mist and shuddering silk.

'Very well.' Her smoke-scarred voice cawed from the roiling center of the storm. 'Keep your Citydell. Edanvant is nothing without those in whom our hereditary power slumbers. We women shall keep that power alive and to ourselves, men of Edanvant. Look to your own powers.'

Air quieted suddenly. Seeress and smokesnake both had vanished. On the ground where they had coiled, a humble basket sat, abrim with a shining array of small black stones. The firelight picked swirling threads of rainbow color from the gems' dark facets.

The men came slowly over, their clicking mail reflecting a subtle multicolored sheen within its own black interweaving. Orvath bent painfully to scoop up a handful of midnight pebbles. In the palm of his good hand they weighed heavy as iron and lay as cold as ice.

'Iridesium,' Medoc marveled. 'Finorian shed tears of pure metal.'

'Of magical metal,' Orvath reminded him, his fist shutting on the sparkling hoard. 'Of metal native only to Rule, which has served us men as mail for generations. Iridesium. Even the material of our defense is hers to command!' he raged. 'We fight the women now for our lives as well as our talismans.'

A thoughtful Torloc pulled on the brush of beard at his chin. 'Did we battle our way to Edanvant for so long only to end by warring with our own kind, and with the weaker of our own kind — our women?'

'We will war longer,' Orvath predicted. 'You forget how long-lived our kind is, how long-lived Finorian has been. Women have always hoarded the inborn powers among us. But even Finorian grows old beyond surviving — the smoke-snake repelled her — and there are no seeresses to succeed her, only ordinary women. And even they can betray.' Orvath's eyes flared with bitter memory. 'In quite ordinary ways, these ordinary women.'

'As we were once only ordinary men,' Medoc said pointedly.

19

Orvath met his eyes — dark, level gaze to mirroring dark gaze.

'Now we shall have to be extraordinary men,' Orvath rallied the others, 'to keep what is ours, our hard-won magic and our right to be first in Citydell.'

'Perhaps they will leave now that Finorian has tasted the fiery lick of our power,' suggested the bearded one.

'Perhaps. Perhaps not.' Orvath's weary body tightened to a phantom of its youthful resolve. 'But we will keep them out of the city of Edanvant, with our talismans. Even Finorian was no match for the merest lick of the Tongue of Flame.'

'Perhaps we are not either.' Medoc looked grave.

Orvath straightened and, with a brush of his good foot, sent the blind woman's basket skidding across the smooth stones on its side, scattering Iridesium stones like ebonberries, like years, like bitter memories hardened into dark unhappy motes, into midnight tears.

CHAPTER ONE

At first he felt snared in a rainbow of reflections shot through
a rapidly spinning crystal.

Colors etched a bright, accelerating circle, dazzling more
senses than the eyes, hissing in the ears like an entoiling
moonweasel, swathing the tongue with their imperious
glancing flavors, whipping the skin with a fugitive sensation.

He knew who he was, what he was, where he was; so
Kendric who had been Wrathman of Rule assured himself.

He had gone into the gate willingly, as he had done once
before. On that first occasion the gate, a mere mist of rainbow
overarching a rock, had spit him out senseless. He remembered
little of that passage, other than acquiring an aching body and
groggy mind.

But this gate he had come to as a man of power, however
reluctantly gained. He came as one who would pass, no matter
the barriers. And for his effrontery, the gate welcomed him
with open, unhinged force.

Vibrant colors looped into blindingly bright rings all around
him. They wove themselves into a rainbowed canopy and
pressed nearer until he was bound by ropes of light — shackles
of crimson, azure, bronze, silver, violet. The interwoven
colors weighed upon Kendric like white-hot Iridesium mail.
Having netted him, they pressed closer, until all the scintil-
lating hues merged, tautened, grew silver, then gray — and
became utterly black.

He no longer knew where he was. Across his back the great
longsword, which he had manufactured in his mind as twin
to the original he had borne in his homeworld, grew less heavy.
That was the eeriest sensation, to feel the massive sword as

he had always felt it, with some inner sense, and to feel it lighten, fade perhaps, under the impress of the night-black rainbow gate.

Out of the darkness swirled a parade of visages, all dazzling, some dangerous. They shared his past, and many had wished that he had no future. Some were dead to his homeworld of Rule; others had ranged the world he had just left, the fierce Inlands of Ten. All leered from the roiling dark.

A mist-veiled woman with tilted lavender eyes flourished a gold-embroidered skirt like a cloak before her face. Brassy gilt stars adorning its hem spun loose to shower Kendric with spinning, lethal blades. He dodged the illusion, knowing the sorceress Mauvedona dead. But still . . . her spelling stars twirled on, past the edges of his eyes.

An icy male face, frozen with power, loomed into being on the black slate of the gate. It melted, the features oozing into those of an ancient Torloc Eldress of his acquaintance.

'Dead, too, Finorian?' he challenged the changing darkness, hoping an answer — or the lack of it — would prove whether he watched reality or dream. 'Dead along with Delevant in the depths of the Inlands' Cincture?'

In a chill dark moment of nothingness, another face formed. An amber-bearded man with spring-sky-bright eyes embracing flecks of blue and yellow both at once nodded sinisterly, playing the gracious host even in uninvited circumstances.

Geronfrey! Kendric tensed, his fingers flexing toward the featherweight of his longsword. Something prevented him. His hand hung heavy, as if all the weight of his sword had drained into his left arm and paralyzed it.

A white shadow, if such a contradiction can exist, cast itself against the bottomless black the gate had become. It swirled smokily, taking lazy, boneless shape around eyes of feline green, their dark vertical slits swelling even as he watched. Geronfrey's image shone bright, small and malevolent in those twin dark mirrors. Then the mage's likeness vanished, fast as a wink, almost as fast as the white presence faded with a winking out of its own bottomless green gaze.

A new visage flared into life — a savage, long-toothed,

ape-like face burred with coarse hair. The scent of rotting meat invaded Kendric's nostrils as he faced one of the Inland's lethal lemurai.

This time Kendric instinctively grasped the sword hilt riding his shoulder, not to be restrained, even by himself. His right hand clasped icy shape — not substance. His left hand, he realized then, itched to release its hold on a solid piece of the surrounding unseen and unseeable dark, but something stopped it.

Then he knew. He knew whose hand he held and why. He recalled that some force had sought to separate him from the Torloc seeress, Irissa, in just this way in the first gate they had attempted to cross some time before. Had sought — and had succeeded.

A Wrathman's ire surged into the dark, coursed to every far-flung extremity of Kendric's seven-foot-high frame. And in the broad stream of that anger, that resistance, sped the tenuous drifting strands of whatever magic he had mastered, however small.

Force compressed him. He felt his fingers entwined with those of another, and felt the infinitesimal giving of that hand-clasp. He and Irissa were separate in the gate, despite their conjoined hands, despite their resolution to remain together on leaving the Inlands of Ten for this magical journey. The gate took whatever attempted passage on its own terms and engaged the trespasser in single, inner mortal combat.

He could not rely upon Irissa's inborn, superior powers here, Kendric knew. She fought her own unseen battle with the gate. He could only hold on to what he held — a mere, invisible memory of her presence, her hand.

And that hand burned; its flesh stung like nettles. He could feel the gold circlets on their five-ringed fingers sizzling into their skins. Those sorcerous inherited rings of Delevant's that could not be removed by might or by magic were altering now, melting and burning, burning, burning . . .

White-rimmed eyes of silver-gray reared up. A huge albino wolfish face, extravagantly fanged, snarled before Kendric's eyes, even its tongue seared frost-pale. A howl

23

whose wildness matched the fierce predatory mask echoed somewhere near.

It took all of Kendric's considerable physical strength to keep faith with the simple handclasp that had taken two into the gate, that would see two step out of it. He called upon the inner strength, so seldom tried, that arbitrary alien well of magic within him.

The cloaking blackness whipped away in great folds. A wash of crimson like a silken lining rippled around him. Etched upon it for a fleeting moment was the figure of a huge white owl in flight, talons curled, wing feathers fanned, hooked beak emitting a horrendous shriek before it vanished against a new wave of faint saffron.

The colors felt lighter, cooler now. Kendric wanted to reach out and grasp a thinning haze of blue-violet, touch its subtle surface . . . He was reaching for the sky, for an amethyst-shaded underbelly of distant cloud.

He looked around. He stood in a place other than the Inlands. Beside him stood the Torloc seeress Irissa, her right hand still linked with his left, but gently now, as if the tremendous trial of the gate had been a dream.

Before them both sat a huge, lean-haunched beast with a feather-crowned head and the great round expressionless eyes of a hunting bird.

'It's only you.' Kendric reached his free hand toward the fierce yet passive owlish features. 'Only the Rynx,' he marveled, 'who guided us through peril and now follows us through the gate.'

'No petting, we beg you.' The huge creature minced backward on slender, strong wolf's legs while the feathers on its head fanned impressively. Its double-pitched voice dipped into a lupine growl. 'We saw much in the gate,' it added in the plural self-reference it always employed. 'But nothing so dire that we need our feathers ruffled.'

Kendric's large hand withdrew quickly. 'I merely wished to see if you were . . . real. Within the gate, I thought I saw many wonders and some dangers—'

'I *know* what I saw.' Irissa was shaking her long dark hair

24

free of the gate's lingering webs, not looking quite real yet either. Even as Kendric watched, strands of light — cerulean, red, amber — snapped out of existence. Her long, strong fingers flexed within his grasp, as if sentience were just returning.

He looked to their still-locked hands. The rings, the ten rings that had been wedded to each finger and the thumb upon his left hand, her right, the stolen magical rings that dying Delevant had conferred unwanted upon them . . .

Irissa was the first to free and raise her hand, studying her fingers. All but the middle one were ring-bare. On that, the longest finger of her right hand, a braid of metal bands seemed to writhe still around each other like armored snakes, weaving a single, solid-metal circlet. Center-set astride the band posed a large new cabochon that reflected all five colors of the now-conjoined stones in turn.

Her gate-dazzled voice trembled as she spoke. 'We have held . . . and the rings have merged in the gate! Yours?' Irissa looked at him expectantly.

Kendric raised his callused warrior's hand, the left one. He, too, had been freed of the five rings when they had forged themselves into a single thick band around his middle finger.

'Five,' he mused, waggling liberated fingers and too shaken by overmuch magic to do more than make light of it. 'Finorian always said it was not a harmonious number. Now we each have five-made-one. And speaking of that elusive Torloc Eldress, who called us hither with some tale of dire danger . . . where is she?' Kendric gazed around with tawny eyes as alert as a hawk's. 'I fancied I caught an appetizing glimpse of her within the gate. I would be most sorry to miss her now that we have come so far.'

Irissa laughed, joyous at safe arrival, bewitched by the accomplished wonder of Kendric's presence, toasting the bright light of a gilded sun with the wave of her jeweled hand. Colors danced in the revised ring's single-domed cabochon.

'Finorian called *me*, not us,' she reminded him. 'I doubt she returns your yearning to see her face. A gate cannot change human nature, nor Torloc prejudice.'

Anxiety briefly shadowed Irissa's features before they brightened again. 'Let us not worry about uncertain receptions! At least we were not separated in the gate. At last you will no longer complain that ringbands hamper your battle readiness. And if I must be ringed,' she added, 'I would prefer my baubles to be consolidated, like this . . . but as for where Finorian is, or even where we are, I know no more about it than the Rynx.'

Kendric fixed his piercing gaze on the unruffled creature before them, realizing that within the gate he had glimpsed the beast fractured into its two disparate elements. It seemed whole and wholly composed now, giving them its mute, undivided attention.

'And how did you survive the gate, my fine furred and feathered friend?' Kendric asked. 'Do you regret leaving the Inlands of Ten for an alien place?'

Rustling feathers provided his only answer. The Rynx arranged itself on its belly, thrusting narrow forelegs forward until it posed like some carved ivory statue. The odd-colored eyes, one silver-gray as an overcast sky, the other as gold as the gleaming sun ever lurking behind such clouds, blinked.

'We appear to have transgressed the gate successfully,' the creature's oddly constituted voice, part rumble, part trill, responded. The great owlish head rotated backward as its curved beak began combing ruffled neck feathers.

'All present and accounted for,' Kendric agreed dubiously, waggling his liberated fingers again. 'But I cannot believe we didn't leave a piece of ourselves within the gate. It seemed a thing that demanded some toll or other. All magical things do — eventually.'

Irissa seated herself on the clover-carpeted ground. Around her, palsied pale blue stars of blossom wavered in an almost indetectable breeze. She clasped her hands over her ragged trouser knees and smiled.

'At least, Kendric, we passed this gate standing on our own two feet instead of being ignominiously catapulted from it to our knees, as we both were, albeit separately, in the first gate from Rule to the Inlands. Perhaps we're getting better at it.'

'Or gates are getting subtler.' He shrugged under the comforting weight of his shoulder-slung sword and strode protectively around his seated companions, surveying the landscape.

'This seems a peaceful place,' Irissa observed mildly.

'So does a patch of swamp-swallow in the Marshlands of Rule. Yet many bones pave its deceptive depths.' Kendric adjusted the set of the sword across his back, then set his fists on his hips. 'Well, then, is this the Torloc paradise, where all your people scampered as fast as magical gates could take them? Is this Edanvant?'

Kendric's forthright question, the hopeful elevation of his dark eyebrows, chilled Irissa. She gazed around, triumph at having navigated the gate fading.

'I don't know.' She studied the ground, the sky, the distance, her face pensive. 'The Inlands seemed fair when first I saw them, and then danger sprang from the very grasses to devour me. This *should* be Edanvant, Kendric, but what have we found in our wanderings that was as it should be?'

She gazed at the distance again, lost in this land she had never known. Irissa's dark hair shimmered on her back in the clean sunlight. Across her temples the Iridesium circlet reflected a multishaded swirl of colors in its dead black metal circumference, reminding Kendric of the gate's colorful phenomena.

He recognized again in Irissa the elegant, fey forest creature he had happened upon in the Shrinking Forest of Rindell, her silver eyes measuring shadows for unseen foes, her black hair and white skin made for melding with the dark and light of a purely natural world so removed from what he knew of worlds now that it seemed enchanted. The circlet was the last legacy of her Torloc heritage, the sole thing remaining from when he had first found her — or had she found him? — beside a weepwater tree root in a world known as Rule.

All that was two worlds away now. Kendric's tough sillac-hide boots had spurned the familiarity of Rule for a gate to a supposedly better destination, then had pushed off

27

even that new world's accustomed unfamiliarity for yet another leap into elsewhere — into this silent, as yet unrevealing place.

Kendric sat without preamble, a major commitment from one seven feet tall. He set his scabbarded sword by his side and plucked a small blue star from the clover.

'When we get there — wherever "there" is, the first thing I want is a long, hot bath,' he said abruptly.

Irissa took the tiny bloom and inhaled experimentally. 'No scent.' She sighed. 'It is a different world, true enough. What I want' — she glanced to the lap of her gray silken tunic where an undistinguished lump reclined — 'is a falgonskin pouch in which to carry this Overstone egg on a cord around my neck. It is a great responsibility to bear a thing unknown.'

Kendric leaned to peer at the oval of pale rock even now pulsing in veins of rich color. It was the last thing Irissa had plucked from the lair of the long-dead Torloc sorcerer Delevant before they entered the gate.

'I see why you call it the Overstone egg,' he said. 'Even palm-size, that pebble reminds me of the unmoving, dead daylight moon the Inlanders called the Overstone. Except . . . this one looks alive,' he warned.

Irissa's fingers curved protectively around it. 'It is rock; yet it is fragile in some deeper way.'

Kendric frowned. 'So are we all. I told you not to take it.'

'There's no harm in it,' Irissa insisted, 'merely inconvenience.'

'When we are bound somewhere we do not know, in a world we are not sure of, that is harm enough.' Kendric flexed his knees and looped his long arms around them. 'This is a lulling place, I grant you . . . quiet. Listen, I hear no chatter of birds nor even the scuttle of small wooded things.'

'And green,' Irissa noted wistfully. 'Finorian always said our true Torloc world would be green.'

They stared together at a sweep of verdant, flower-dotted meadow ended only by the farther line of spreading forest. Sunlight fell warm; grasses bowed, softly pliant. Kendric surveyed the sky, looking for a daylight moon or other out-of-place phenomenon. There was none. Beside them, the Rynx dozed, shutting its unmatched eyes. No trill of running water interrupted the stillness. Even the wind was so mild the grasses moved with haunting silence, like slender green spirits of themselves.

Kendric discarded the scentless flower. 'I do not like it,' he said.

'Of course you don't,' Irissa answered cheerfully. 'You like nothing new or different, and you understand nothing until you part it with the blade of your sword. Part these grasses; you will only engage simple earth.'

His big hand swept aside a silken tress of long green grass. 'I know it all seems as idyllic as a shepherd's song to his goats. Why then did Finorian hail you here so desperately?'

'Perhaps she merely wanted company.'

'Not mine.' Kendric snorted. 'I have never seen a Torloc whose motives were not as veiled as a Torloc seeress's eyes.'

'Never?' Irissa fixed him with her gaze's undiluted quicksilver.

'Not fair.' He matched her look. 'You are an exception. You can do what no Torloc woman of power − including Finorian − has ever done: look direct into the eyes of another and even into your own mirrored gaze. You have passed beyond the Far Focus your kind must face to draw upon its deepest powers, beyond that arduous trial into—'

'Perhaps it is the human in me. And not a ''beyond''but a ''beneath''.'

Kendric's hands juggled air while he searched for the right expression. He ended with a shrug.

'Our road consumes itself when we take a path of speculation. You have grown as riddlesome as Rule ever was.'

Irissa balanced herself with one hand on Kendric's knee as she rose, the Overstone egg cradled in her careful palm. It was not heavy, but utterly inconvenient, as she had said.

'Mayhap I could carry it,' Kendric suggested.

'No. I would have it, thus I should caretake it.'

Kendric pulled a small tanned purse from the baldric slashing diagonally across his chest.

'Here. This pouch will tie around your sash.'

29

Irissa slipped the pale, egglike thing into Kendric's offering and attached it. She looked around, as if free for the first time to do so fully.

'Green, everywhere, not ebbing like the Shrinking Forest of Rindell, but spreading. It is exactly as I always pictured it.' Doubt darkened her silver eyes. 'But I wish we saw some sign of habitation.'

'We won't if we remain here speculating,' intoned the Rynx without opening its eyes.

'Onward, then, until we spy a reason to stop,' Kendric directed them. He rose, slowly, like a mountain, Irissa and the Rynx moving with him.

So they set out, a tall woman, a taller man, and a creature of clearly muddled nature. In minutes their forms had faded into the bland, empty landscape, and the new world drew its distances shut upon them as softly as a sigh.

CHAPTER TWO

Kendric and Irissa walked in the dazzle of an eternal noon; even time seemed uncommitted in this lovely, vacant world.

It was impossible to tell from the sun's placement in its vast, sky-blue bezel whether day ebbed or night drew nearer. Thin clouds skated so high they seldom cast shadows on the ground below. A rainbow's gauzy bands spread like dissipating scarves wind-pinned against the sky's airy dome.

The party of three kept silent as they walked — the Rynx because it never spoke unless it had something to say, Irissa and Kendric because they had much to say and were afraid to say it lest they ruin something intangible.

Lithe grasses brushed Irissa's tattered silken trousers. She walked the grassy swells of this place she hoped was hers, mulling the Torloc roots she had clung to through three worlds. They had given her little sustenance. The women of Rindell had taken the gate from Rule without her, and the men had long before vanished on their separate quests for Edanvant, leaving the women behind.

Finorian accused the absent men of abandoning the community for adventure and self-aggrandizement, yet she promised the women reunion with them someday. Why reunite with the dispensible — or seek those who have not sought you? Irissa knew why she did it — because Edanvant would answer all mysteries and end all doubts. Because she longed to belong again. Because she was Torloc and because Edanvant was Edanvant.

Yet even as Irissa anticipated reunion with the Torlocs, she knew that Finorian would not welcome Kendric into that select company. The rest would follow the Eldress's lead. They always did, including her mother, Jalonia . . . Irissa's thoughts tolled a name she had not recalled in many months, a woman who had been as denied to Irissa as the sight of her own image in a mirror. If her mother remained an uneasy fog figure, Irissa thought with swelling panic, what of her never-seen father, who could very well wait mere footsteps ahead? If the men and women had reunited in Edanvant, surely he would be among them.

She had not even a name to give him, her embarrassment reminded her − or to give any Torloc man other than dead Thrangar of Rule. Irissa had never spoken with a male of her kind, and was eager to, she decided − perhaps someone other than her father first, she hedged nervously. A name surfaced. Olvarth . . . ? Orvath? Of course the name eluded her. Torloc blood relationships, always casual, were all but forbidden to a seeress. No wonder the aloof, long-lived Torlocs, who knew each other so little, were disliked by humankind.

Torlocs had not been trusted in Rule, where she had been born and reared. Torlocs had not been trusted by Kendric, among others, who had found Irissa just as the women of Rindell had melted through a sudden gaping gate, marooning her among those whose powers were inherently human.

Irissa had been as one blind, and Kendric had served as a somewhat cranky cane while they traversed the Realms of Rule looking for a gate and finding the limits of Irissa's untried powers. They had found the gate, but Kendric had been severed from her in midpassage; Irissa had come alone to a land much like this.

This time two confronted the alien beauty around them; this time Kendric was not an untried man of power who denied his unwanted gifts, but one who had learned to face his fear of using them; this time they had managed to keep together. This time, Irissa told herself, they would find what they sought.

'What now?' Kendric asked with his usual blunt practicality.

Her reverie thus ended, Irissa glanced to the man measuring his longer stride to hers. Kendric pointed wordlessly. Far ahead, looming like a not-quite-submerged rock from a placid emerald sea, a rough edifice of stone broke bold and black from the rippling grasses.

'It . . . it reminds me of Rindell Keep.' Irissa, still memory-snared, smiled to recall her home in Rule.

'Not much,' Kendric objected. 'That was a modest pile of mortar and stone, before it melted into the mist and Finorian with it. This looks to be a hard, haughty fortress, well polished and ready to reflect back as much trouble as faces it.'

'Nonsense.' Irissa would hear no doomsaying on the brink of paradise. 'A warrior always reads danger where only the words peace and quiet are scribed. The structure simply looks deserted, nothing more sinister than that . . .'

'Looks deceive.'

Irissa, in her relentless optimism, was already striding through the whispering grasses, the Rynx at her heels. Kendric shrugged his sword into firmer place upon his shoulders and followed. It was, after all, her land supposedly.

Although the daylight still seemed the same, the mere passing of time must have modified its quality. As they neared the fortress, they saw that the structure cast a thick, dark shadow. It was far taller than wide, now that they saw it close up, and exquisitely refined in form — more tower than castle, thus more oddly situated for that reason.

'There is nothing here.' Kendric turned to view the washing, wind-hissing grasslands around him. 'No rise of ground, no water, no reason to build a bulwark in such empty landscape.'

'Yet care went into it; see how the stones are buffed in counter directions.' Irissa indicated the facade, where polished black rock alternated with dull charcoal-colored stones, producing a checkerboard in the round.

Kendric went close enough to pass his palm over the sun-bright surface.

'Cold!' He retreated, shivering. 'As if it had sat in a Furzenland streambed for decades.'

The Rynx trotted near, tilted its snowy head, and tapped its ebony beak on the tower. The stones resounded, high and delicately, like a plucked harpstring. The sweet twang sped skyward and dissipated.

33

'A singing tower! How wonderful. Is there an entrance?' Irissa circled the structure, running long fingers over the stones and leaving a ripple of melody in her wake. 'Here! The stones change their tune.'

She stretched and bent in turn to shape the long and short of a doorway, her questing fingers striking deep bell-like rumbles from the basalt.

' 'Tis solid rock,' Kendric objected.

'It seems so, but is an illusion.' Irissa's laughter trilled in melodious counterpoint to the bass grumblings of the stone beneath her hands. 'Look.'

She stepped forward, laughing over her shoulder at Kendric, to embrace the rock, to enter the rock. And it took her — her right leg to the thigh, her right arm and shoulder, the spinning tendrils of her hair, the right edge of her face.

'Irissa!'

But her smiling features sank into the rock as into a vertical night-dark patch of swamp-swallow. Kendric was left staring at the place where the last gray trace of her bootheel had vanished.

His white-knuckled fist struck the swallowing stones. A deep-bellied sound rang into the still air, like a pealing knock. There was no answer from within. Irissa did not step forth again.

'We must follow,' Kendric told himself as much as the Rynx, which sat unruffled behind him.

'You, not "we",' the Rynx corrected. 'We do not enter constructions shaped by humankind.'

'Humankind made this?' Kendric snorted in disbelief. His fingers strummed the stones despite his revulsion at their icy surface and guttural moaning. 'There must be a hinge, a break — something . . .'

'More of humankind than you think,' the animal interrupted in its double-toned voice.

'You lived within Delevant's Maw in the Inlands of Ten,' Kendric accused.

'An earth-made cavern, not of artificial manufacture.' The Rynx seemed serenely unconcerned about its defection in time of crisis.

'Very well then; sit here and record my folly!'

Kendric gathered himself to hurl his body at the stone. Amazingly, it gave like gauze before him, veiling his perceptions and then turning as midnight dark as had the gate itself.

Kendric recoiled from his headlong rush, startled by glimpsing a tower of white light opposite him. It enclosed a shadow — a shadow of himself, complete to the aggressive slant of sword hilt over its shoulder. Even as he recognized his own silhouette, the luminescence dulled, softening the sharp shape into an indistinguishable form he knew for himself only by assumption.

A motionless Irissa stood beside him, rapt with wonder — or fear.

He touched Irissa's arm. Her silk tunic sleeve snapped at the contact as a small blue spark winked in the twilight inside the tower.

'What — is this place?' he asked.

'I don't know,' Irissa whispered, as if they were not entirely alone. 'But I think — I think there is no bottom to it.'

Kendric lowered his gaze. Only deepest, darkest black met his eyes, a midnight column of endless lightlessness that shot straight down from where he stood. His senses reeled at contemplating their sudden, unsensed pinnacle.

'Can we leave as we came?' he asked hoarsely.

'I hope so, but . . .'

Irissa's voice trailed off. She seemed spellbound by some force other than the sheer nothingness they stood by a toe's-length from. Kendric regarded the dimly-seen stone opposite them.

He saw his own reflection still, now all in white. Perhaps his entrance had etched a swath of remnant daylight on the dark inner rock face. He saw a phantom Irissa as well, a ghastly pale likeness shining like a shield emblem on a rectangle of sleek, black stones opposite them, as if the inner walls were lined with obsidian mirrors.

Their remote counterparts struck Kendric as horribly unnatural, as fey reminders of a pale sorcerer with access to a Dark Mirror and its secrets. One secret that Kendric alone kept was a remembered semblance of Irissa caught within Geronfrey's elusive mirror. He had seen her stare at him from the silvered glass, the Shadow Irissa, even as he had shielded the real one unseeing in his arms.

'Can we leave?' he demanded again, more urgently.

A third figure swirled into being on the midnight mirror, its height halfway between the disparity of theirs, its shade a murky gray. Kendric squinted skeptically at the image.

He saw a soldier etched in midblow, a sorcerer caught in midspell, a beast frozen in midcharge. It raised a dagger . . . a hand . . . a horn.

The singing tower shuddered until its stones ground out a disconsonant wail.

Kendric answered with a sharp keening of his own — the rasp of his great longsword hissing free of its bindings. No light danced along the naked blade, which pierced the darkness and vanished halfway to the hilt.

Kendric tightened one hand around the other, refusing to believe his senses. Mere air, no matter how dim, could not swallow half his blade. Yet he saw it impaled. The sword's weight increased by the instant, as if all the emptiness below them had become material and hung from it. Seeking to withdraw it, he found the blade mired as in stone . . . or bone.

'Irissa — can your eyes lighten my metal?'

Even as he asked, glancing at her motionless figure, he knew he requested too little, too late. Irissa dallied in some spell-net flung by her opposite image. She could no more help him than she could help herself.

His own pale reflection, as slow-moving in the tower's inner lassitude as he was stolid-thinking, aped his wide-based battle stance and hefted a broken blade.

The solitary man-beast that had appeared between Kendric and Irissa's opposite images snorted, smoke crowning its amorphous head. It came leaping from the wall, swirling on the empty air around the flesh-and-blood Kendric and Irissa. The apparition was ghost-white and smoke-wispy, yet the bellows of its hollow breathing struck dissonance like ill-rung bells from the walls all around.

36

Kendric's hands tightened on the sword hilt, pulling until his shoulders cracked and the blade finally sucked free of dark, empty air.

The thing that singly surrounded them sometimes seemed a man mounted on a bearing-beast, next a bearing-beast wearing ceremonial saddle garments that fluttered in the wind of its coming. Then it was a robed sorcerer who walked on four hooved feet with a dagger raised before his forehead like a helmet spike.

Kendric's heavy sword cleaved air, smote it, chopped it into tendrils of smoke. Limbs of illusion — semiman, demi-beast — severed and shrank and churned until they rose and reassembled again.

Kendric turned around the anchorage of Irissa, who stood still and dark as death itself. His blows defended her, and himself, but offended nobody — if indeed someone specific fed the sending that seethed around them both.

Iron-shod hooves clattered on the dead air flooring the bottom-less chamber. A long, twisted scimitar of smoke slashed past Kendric's shoulder. It seemed a company cavorted round him now — many beasts and as many riders, cutting as they came.

'What magic is this,' Kendric bellowed, 'that multiplies even as I slay it?'

Something in his voice, perhaps desperation, shook Irissa from her bespelled reverie. She blinked, her silver eyes dull.

'Your blade but feeds its powers,' she warned. 'Even the hilt-light has been darkness-dampened. Use . . . the magic native to the tower.'

'Black magic?' he retorted, huffing as his sword halved a rider's torso only to see the bisected figure sprout four hooved feet and the bearing-beast grow another man upon its back.

Around them the stones droned with monotonous dread.

Irissa clapped her hands to her ears. Her eyes saw only the pallid reflection of herself that seemed to be dangled before her from a distance by an unseen hand.

'I feel myself spinning thin,' she said, 'and that Shadow She fattening on my passivity. Help yourself, Kendric, or none shall save me!'

37

Grunting agreement, he hacked apart a whirlwind of smoke and saw it disperse into a new swirl of attackers. In all his blows, he had not once felt the satisfying shock of metal biting bone or heard the dull thwack of weapon striking target.

The creatures whined as they spun around him. Beside him, Irissa's solid form smeared into the dimensionless darkness that formed the tower's core.

Tower magic. Inherent magic, he crooned to himself like a battle dirge while he dueled shape-shifting phantoms. Curse that whining, Kendric thought, gritting his teeth to mimic the grinding stones.

He paused, letting his sword return to his side.

Whining, buzzing, singing . . . Sound. Sound was the tower's inbuilt magic! Then he would let the sword croon a countermelody to the magic that beset them.

The sword lilted in his tighter grasp, nearly humming with the cleanness of a new, more confident stroke. He thought of sound, of attacking with sound, and heard the sword answer. It struck on a sweeping glissando of rough music, like finger-nails scraping taut strings. Every segment of its motion held a tone — a noise of rushing air and fire-hardened steel. Every blow piped a note. Sound. All motion was sound. All sound was . . . motion.

Singing, the sword clove airy adversaries. It buzzed into them, vibrato shattering them into chords and then into single notes. Truncated attackers drifted toward unseen depths, sliced and stung and sung hither and yon until they gleamed as dust motes do in the rich baritone thrum of a bar of sunlight.

Around Kendric, the tower stones performed a cappella. His ears could finally detect each block's keynote, could hear their interweaving alto and soprano. The sword in his hands, in his ears, executed a series of self-indulgent basso runs. Fragments of smoke faded into blinks of failing light.

Darkness fell back around them like a profound drumroll. Kendric had never known a thing so impenetrable could be so welcome.

Across from him his brother image impaled his sword in the shining dark at his feet and faded away. Kendric blinked.

The gray specter in the walls saluted with a lifted fist . . . knife . . . horn — and vanished to the neck. Finally the watching eyes winked out, like patches of sky hiding behind a sheet of storm cloud.

Irissa sighed at her reflection drowning slowly in the wall's darkness. 'One last thread. Sever it.'

Her sister image glimmered palely in the gleaming wall, a bright girdle around its hips spawning a tail of mist that bridged the distance between the two and webbed Irissa's hands.

Kendric's sword cut the air on a single horn note, sliced illusion in midcast. The thread severed with the sob of a high harpstring breaking. Recoiling, it lashed the ebbing likeness of Irissa back into the glossy night of the inner walls.

Kendric and Irissa stood alone, on a floor that was not a floor, ringed by the dying vibration of singing stones.

Mere withdrawal in the face of such phenomena struck Kendric as insufficient.

'Can we leave?' he asked a third time. Now he heard the unconsidered music in his voice, the humble ending upswing of a question.

Irissa, half-ensorceled yet, repeated the chillingly uncertain phrase that had been her earlier answer.

'I . . . hope so—'

'*We* try, then.'

Kendric grasped her arm and stepped backward in one rough stride, perhaps a longsword's length. He didn't pause to think that he might pull Irissa off her feet, only that she must come with him.

Sunlight blessed his tensed shoulders, blinded his eyes with twin drilling blades of brightness. His ears, assaulted by a discordant parting wail, interpreted it as musical stones being rubbed the wrong way. Beside them the Rynx sat, displaying its maw in a decidedly unbirdlike yawn.

Irissa was blinking and brushing her clothing, as if she'd returned from somewhere dusty.

'Why didn't you come back out at first?' Kendric wanted to know.

39

'I was . . . surprised. It was so unexpected within.'

'Unexpected to you. I knew from first sight that this cursed tower boded nothing but danger.'

'It's not dangerous! Not in itself, anyway. I remember little of what happened within—'

Kendric made an inelegant sound but forbore to remind her of what he himself would as soon forget. Somehow the sorcerer Geronfrey had secreted something of Irissa in the Dark Mirror from which Kendric had once rescued her. He had never admitted what he had seen afterward — the chilling duplicate shade of Irissa moving in its own shadow world. The image had haunted the blankness at the back of his eyes ever since.

Now, he'd seen that dark visage stir again on a tower wall in what might be Edanvant. Yet how could he disenchant Irissa when her quest's desire was within plucking distance? He would watch for traces of Geronfrey, though, from now on, he promised himself. And if he saw that simulacrum of Irissa again, he would kill it. The sword thrummed seeming agreement as he resettled it upon his back.

Irissa turned to study the tower, still refusing to see anything in Edanvant as ominous. 'It's, it's . . . an entertainment. A mere architectural fancy. Made to amuse.'

'You mean Torloc-made?' he began doubtfully.

She nodded eagerly, grateful for understanding.

The tower's truth as only he had seen it was far more sinister, but Kendric resolved to muffle any misgivings behind his habitual note of skepticism.

'And if we had stepped farther into that inky piece of solid swamp-swallow . . . that "fancy" had no floor!' he grumbled. 'We could have plunged to Rule knows where, perhaps down to the Swallowing Cavern itself.'

Irissa dusted her palms, sending the conjoined gemstones on her finger into a riot of flashing colors. 'If we had stepped into it, I think we would have entered another amazing place, at least at one time.' She sounded completely herself again. Certain.

'And now?'

Under the Iridesium circlet holding her dark hair from

spilling into her silver eyes, Irissa's smooth white forehead wrinkled.

'That aspect of it is gone,' she admitted. 'This tower was made to be harmless, even wondrous. The makers are gone. What remains . . .' She blinked as if to remember, and cocked her head as if to hear.

'Yes?'

'What remains is not enough to support even good intentions,' she finished briskly. 'It is magic without its core. If we had stepped onto it, into it, there would have been only nothing — and whatever cared to seep in and claim that nothingness.'

Kendric turned to the black tower soaring like a charred tree spine above them, remembering the reverse images of themselves and that mixed-form, half-engendered other that he had perceived and Irissa had not. 'It is evil, then.'

'It is magic bereft of the good intentions of its maker. Call it evil if you like.'

She was walking away, the Rynx rising to follow her.

Kendric stared again at the windowless, doorless tower. He stood in its exterior shade and contemplated the deeper, darker shadow it cast within. A vagrant breeze strummed a low warning whine across the black stones. Kendric turned; in moments sword-long strides had taken him alongside Irissa, out of the shadow.

They paced along the edge of a thick-treed forest too congested to enter. Primroses of every color bloomed at the tree roots like drops of imaginatively hued blood; ropes of violet, coral, and golden blossoms garlanded the dark, vine-entwined trunks.

Irissa smiled to see Kendric bolt toward each new variety of flower, pluck a bloom, and raise it to his aquiline warrior's nose. But his inhalations were suspicious, not appreciative, and he cast each dainty blossom away, his face puckered as if it had sniffed decay.

'No scent,' he reported at the silent interrogation of Irissa's raised eyebrows. 'What kind of place is this, that is all sight and no smell?'

She shrugged and walked on, seemingly unconcerned. 'Perhaps it so overcomes the eye that nothing was left to amaze another sense.'

The Rynx trotted alongside them, unconcerned as well. Having as it did a bird's head, smell was its least keen sense. But it would miss the presence of red-blooded prey, Kendric guessed. As yet he had spied no rustle in the woods, no skitter or slither in the grasses. Not even an insect paid court to the ubiquitous flowers.

Kendric paused, detecting the faintest tremor in the ground, even through the thick, sillac-hide soles of Rule at its most prosaic.

'Wait!'

Irissa and the Rynx stopped and turned inquiringly.

'That . . . sound . . . do you hear it?'

Even as he asked, the distant tapping grew louder and came faster. 'Hooves!' Kendric asserted, the fervor of the horseman stirring his voice.

They froze, waiting, the Rynx hunching into a hunting stance, Irissa and Kendric ready for flight but more eager for another's capture. Irissa pictured a wild, bounding lorryk herd spilling over the brow of the rise ahead. Kendric saw a more docile beast — satin-tailed and maned, saddled and bridled. With some patience and a firm hand . . .

The thunderer pounded into sight, first a pale scimitar of horn, then tossing head and mane, sleek body, churning legs and knife-edged hooves.

It saw them. Nostrils flared, eyewhites flashed, all the shimmering motion of mane and tail coiled to rest along its muscle-sculpted neck and hindquarters. Bracing four hooved feet, it lowered its long-faced head so the horn-tip showed lethal, and waited, exhaling rhythmic gusts of air.

The Rynx suddenly relaxed into a seated posture, recognizing possible prey as too big for anything but an equal foe. But Irissa and Kendric stared in wonder, natural wonder, at a bearing-beast dappled gold and silver, shining in the sunlight and naked of any constraint.

'Perhaps it would respond to me,' Irissa speculated in an anxious hush. 'Like the lorryk.'

'Nimble-footed ninnies.' Kendric dismissed the Inlands' herd-running lorryk. 'This beast is of another, single-minded kind, closer to the bearing-beasts of Rule, deep enough of chest and high enough of wither to bear even an Iridesium-mailed Wrathman . . .'

He was approaching it, his big boots soundlessly crushing the grasses, his attention fixed on the restless black eyes set into the creature's head.

'It's not a bearing-beast of Rule, no matter how it looks so,' Irissa warned. 'It carries only one horn, Kendric, and that honed for goring; you'll never tame it.'

She followed in his bootsteps anyway, speaking as levelly as he. Almost unwillingly, the two were drawn to the waiting beast, who churned the turf impatiently with one forefoot from time to time. They came close enough to congratulate themselves on their skill; then the creature snorted, wheeled, and danced as far away as it had been before.

Again Kendric followed the gold and silver lure of its form, moving so subtly and quietly that even Irissa hardly saw him do it. Again the beast allowed him near enough to taste satisfaction, then minced just beyond reach.

Kendric straightened, disgusted. ' 'Tis a canny creature, and it has played this game before. I'll not follow it humpbacked from hill to hill.'

'Why not use magic to capture it?'

'How? Wish a saddle and bridle onto it?'

'That you can do later,' Irissa said calmly. 'For now you need to contain it.'

'I could conjure ropes to hobble it, but that would only make it useless to both itself and me. Were we not in need of finding your Torlocs, I could spare the time to maneuver it into some woodsy corner where I could catch it.'

But Irissa was not listening to him, nor even watching him or the beast that had captured his attention. Her silver eyes gleamed with concentration, focused on some inner landscape. Across her puckered brow the black metallic Iridesium circlet

43

flickered with rainbow hues — red, violet, green, blue. It seemed to take slow wing, lifting a twin of itself from her forehead, expanding wider as it went.

Kendric saw it then, a giant shadow of the circlet suspended in midair and silently nearing the wary bearing-beast. By the time it had reached the creature, its circumference yawned like a giant maw. It hung momentarily over the unconcerned beast, then plummeted to earth around it, striking the grasses with a snake-like sizzle.

The creature, alerted, spun and raced to the circle's edge, its slashing hooves striking the bright confining rim of Irissa's magic. Sparks flared horn-high — soaring magenta and cobalt bolts. The creature snorted wildly and wheeled to test the circle's opposite perimeter. Again mere contact generated a flock of flying sparks. The beast galloped to midcircle, reared on its hind feet until it towered high as a young tree, then rammed its front hooves to earth with a defiant thump. Head and horn lowered, sides heaving noisily, it watched them.

Kendric's forefinger paid the black metal circling Irissa's forehead the awed tribute of wary touch.

'All hint of color vanished,' he marveled. 'Only dull black metal remains visible. The incorporeal Iridesium in it now scribes yonder creature.'

'I know . . . Quick, tame your beast! My iron-made circlet binds tight without the cushioning balm of its natural magic.'

Kendric needed no further urging. The lure of quiescent bone, muscle, and gleaming hair sang too loudly through his veins. A bearing-beast — to replace long-lost Willowisp. This one would weave its own whimsical name, too, out of thin air; it was smoke and sunlight, muscle and mist. Beauty at its most balkish.

He set his five-foot-long sword on a pillow of soft grasses and stepped over the Iridesium curve, glancing down to see a chain of living sparks hissing between his boots. Then he was within the enchanted circle, alone with the alien bearing-beast, so close he could discern the nervous tremor of its body.

'Here.' Kendric extended his hand, palm up.

Well-warmed human scent wafted to the sensitive nostrils.

44

Kendric edged closer, crouched for any necessary spring, planning his motions — a foray inward, a fist clenching a hank of strong, silky mane, then himself hurling over the glossy back, any which way. Knees tightening, hands moving to the well-muscled neck, his body clinging by any means until he had proven his right to ride . . . If only he had a bridle—

A loop of supple black ringed the startled muzzle, twisted itself over the horn and ears in turn, and trailed three feet of rein on each side.

Kendric twisted his head over his shoulder. Irissa stood smiling behind him, a single filament of her dark hair taut between her fingers. It vanished as he watched, and the magic-made bridle became black leather.

Kendric's plans changed. He would advance without warning, grasp the reins, mount . . . Thought became action. His fingers twined firmly in the bridle. He swung himself upward — and found his legs hitting ground, the beast churning sideways, and his hand caught in a loop of leather connected to a lowered and thrusting spiral of alabaster horn. He wrenched his fingers free only in time to spring sideways and avoid milling hooves.

They circled one another in the ring, each intent on catching the other in arrears. Around and around, until the sun seemed to be spinning in the sky. Always Kendric sought to take the beast sideways, to leap astride it. Always the beast strove to keep Kendric dead-center in the circle, an easy target for its hooves or its impaling horn.

Kendric stormed it again, so suddenly that he rejoiced to feel himself vaulting the bare cradle of its sun-warmed back, which as suddenly slid away. Hard turf met him full length as he landed on the beast's other side. He grunted and rolled frantically, hearing the ground pounded in his stead, pausing only when a fencing dazzle of sparks flared before his eyes. Then he regained his feet and resumed the struggle.

He and the beast matched wills for what seemed like hours. Once his inward leap brought him briefly astride the twisting body. He caught the reins taut in his hand, felt the ripple of stubborn muscle between his knees and inhaled the first smell this new world had offered, the conjoined sweat of man and beast.

45

Then he was plummeted earthward again to dodge hooves and horn, to wish for a saddle even as he knew it would only further madden the animal.

'Kendric!' Irissa's voice sprung from someplace outside the hard and jaundiced green circle of trampled grass and rough-breathing man and animal. 'I'm releasing the beast.'

Sulfur fumes flared in the still air; smoke momentarily curtained them. Then Kendric stood watching a banner of flying gilt tail as the bearing-beast cantered back over the meadow from where it had come. A black leather snake melted into the green grasses. At his feet a rim of charred vegetation scribed a perfect circle.

'Why? I almost had it,' Kendric complained. A veil of shimmering iridescent color rose around him and wafted softly over Irissa's head. He barely heeded the phenomenon. 'We would have had a four-footed beast at our service again.'

Irissa's fingertips circled massagingly at her temples. Above them, the Iridesium circlet's black surface pulsed again with its phantom rainbow coloration.

'I could no longer contain the creature, Kendric. Odd how this metal of Rule keeps its magic no matter what world we wander.' She saw his disappointed eyes. 'Besides, the animal was beyond taming,' she consoled him. 'It would have fought to the death before it would serve any other creature, even a human one.'

'Magic!' Kendric wearily lumbered over. 'A come-and-go squire, always whining a thousand excuses when it wishes to be in someone else's service.' He cast himself down upon the grasses. 'For a moment I thought . . . this place would not be so bad.'

Irissa sat beside him. 'The air is pleasant, the sun warm. Nothing has moved to harm us.'

'I'm not so sure of that.' Kendric's eyes narrowed. 'But does it feel like — your home?'

She looked startled. 'Perhaps that's why I search for my kind. I know not the feel of true "home". Rindell in Rule was ever represented as a foster home, a temporary shelter and one not oversafe at that. This place has shown us no dangerous side; perhaps that is as good a representation of "home" as one can ask for.'

She watched Kendric pluck a palm-sized purple blossom, raise it to his face, and then hurl it away at the lack of odor.

'What is "home"?' she went on thoughtfully. 'Did the marshes of Rule seem like that to you?'

His ale-blond eyes puzzled as they turned to hers. 'No. I never grew to love the stink of murkweed, the taste of marshwine, or the slurp of mud. We needed no bearing-beasts in the Marshlands, only boats. So . . . no, there is no place I call home over another. Or rather, no place I call home.'

They fell silent for a while. Kendric leaned back on his elbows and waited for his breathing to smoothen. Irissa rested also; drawing upon magic was as wearing an action as debating questions of mastership with an untamed bearing-beast. Beyond them, in a patch of verdant shade beside the wood, the Rynx dozed with slitted eyes.

'It makes a taciturn travel companion,' Kendric observed.

'Would you prefer a talkative cat with as many complaints of the journey and its direction as it has whiskers?'

Kendric grimaced. 'No. Don't remind me of *that* one. Felabba.' He laughed to consider Finorian's old white cat who had traveled — and talked — with them in Rule. 'No palavering cats here, anyway.' He glanced skyward. 'And at least this place has no ever-overlooking eye.' He glanced around. 'Yet I do not feel this world is unaware of our presence.'

'All places and things are sentient, in a sense. It is their brand of magic.'

'My brand of magic is what I can see and hear — and smell.' Kendric grasped a sheaf of grasses. 'This vegetable hair of the earth is fine enough for a four-hooved beast like that elusive one yonder to eat, but we require more solid sustenance. Let us walk until we spy some habitation, for surely all this beauty is not wasted on mere air and one wild bearing-beast.'

47

Irissa smiled to hear Kendric admit at last the loveliness of the landscape and rose with him. Behind them, the Rynx stoically fell into step. They began descending the next rumple of hill, over which the single living thing they had yet seen in this land — the gold-and-silver-coated bearing-beast that would not bear — had appeared . . . and as quickly, vanished.

CHAPTER THREE

'I cannot abide it any longer!' The baldric hung with useful Inlands tools clattered to the ground atop Kendric's discarded fowlen fur vest.

While Irissa and the Rynx observed with polite wonderment, Kendric sat and began tugging off his boots.

The party now rested in shade, the forest's tangled trunks and limbs finally having thinned enough to allow them under its boughs. Once admitted, they had found the first of the wood's secrets — a rock-formed grotto surrounding a perfectly round pool.

'There may be devouring water-things in it,' objected Irissa. 'Remember the flesh-fins?'

'I care not if an Outer Abyssal sea slug has taken residence in the place; the travails of our journeys wear upon my skin like itchweed.' One boot wrenched off on Kendric's last word. He screwed up his face and pulled at the other.

The Rynx, sitting by the still pool, bowed to study its owlish reflection before tilting back its feathered head to swallow a beakful of water.

'We find the water exceedingly cold, swordsman,' it offered. 'A fine vintage for drinking but somewhat unsuitable for bathing.'

'You dragged me across the length of the ice-bound Cincture — twice — yet now counsel me to avoid the cold of a woodland pool kind enough to cast itself in my path?' Kendric rose to wrestle off his tunic. 'Watch my sword,' he instructed Irissa, his voice muffled by a welter of twisted arms and half-divested tunic.

The great blade was the one item Kendric had removed with

care. It lay naked atop its scabbard upon a bed of olive-green moss, its silver point protruding over the water so a mirror image trembled beneath it, as even still water will waver slightly.

Kendric contrary was nothing new to Irissa; she settled on the soft moss, knees tucked up and arms crossed over them. She also had seen the Wrathman bare before, his long arms and muscled chest notched with the pale souvenirs of his warrior's life. One of those angled scars across his side, the palest, had knit itself shut on the first unveiled application of her silver Torloc eyes.

Yet there came a time in Kendric's hasty, unthinking disrobing when he moved behind a stand of screening bushes, whether for Irissa's benefit or the Rynx's or his own, it was difficult to tell.

So Irissa sat solitary guard upon the sword that Kendric viewed with the same emotions as he had once regarded magic in general — whether her inborn variety, or now, his own magic unexpectedly acquired from her. He looked upon them both — sword and sorcery — with an uneasy emotional marriage of wonder and distrust.

'May Ronfrenc's bones rest in waters as chill as these!'

Irissa heard the splash of Kendric's plunge before he voiced his reaction to the icy water. She couldn't see through the leafy screen between them, but could picture him, and that was even better.

'Is it deep?' she inquired mildly.

'No.' He amended that. 'To my neck, which should be sufficient to drown a Torloc dame.' The water roiled, lapping at the bank beneath her feet.

'But cold.'

'C-cold enough.'

Silence held for a moment, then came enough plashing to indicate a saber-toothed beaver litter at play. Irissa studied the swordtip and its longer reflection in the water. She remembered drawing the original of this great sword from the murky depths of Rindell pond at the request of a wounded Wrathman whose name she had not even known then.

Now Rindell and Wrathman were firmly in the past, if wounds were not, and she and Kendric knew each other far beyond the outer limits of names.

Irissa leaned forward, her reflection hovering indistinct in the shaded pool. She could face that false image now, yet still shied from it, keeping her silver eyes shuttered.

Once, two worlds away, a sorcerer whose name still fell heavy between Kendric and herself had tempted Irissa with a dark, sleek mirror called from a distant pit. That brief bow to human vanity had cost Irissa dearly. No longer self-blind, she still avoided her own image. Old fears, slain, reseed themselves as new cautions.

Yet, the sword . . . Irissa smiled, an expression the water below her dutifully repeated. Her fingertips tested the clear liquid — so chill it seemed to leech the blood right out of them. Her thumb rubbed the water-blanched tips as she stared at the naked sword, willing its length to stretch towards the water, into the water.

A phantom extension snaked slowly into sight until the pointed tip dimpled the water's glossy, fluid skin. Irissa leaned forward, swathed in concentration. Her silver eyes measured the metal, and the magic-made extension of the metal. Then they warmed it, slowly at first, so the steel grew rosy before turning a bright blood-red and then burning so hot that color could not contain it. Glowing white, radiating a double power, the shadow of the sword struck the water, which exhaled a sudden mist of steam. Water roiled, boiling wildly around the swordpoint.

Irissa's fingers plunged in, plunged out again, rosy at the tips that had been snow-white. She laced her hands around her knees and kept her eyes on the sword as a wide ring of water bubbled with a rising unquenchable heat. The warmth spread insidiously, colorlessly, only the water's silent, secret, deep, bubbling laughter a token of its progress.

She hung over the steam that misted from the swordpoint, her long straight hair coiling into a hundred snaky tendrils. She smiled and waited, looking like a rather impish sorceress tending some boiling cauldron of potions.

51

'This is not so bad,' Kendric shouted over the bushes. 'One becomes quickly used to the water's chill. Or should I say, one becomes used to the hardships of life on the march? Irissa? Are you keeping watch on my sword?'

'Of course. But perhaps you should leave the pool now, before you catch a chill.'

'Nonsense.' Water splashed exuberantly. 'I've just grown accustomed to it. In fact, this water seems tepid enough to bathe a babe in; it's all a matter of discipline.' Kendric began singing some spirited ballad, his deep voice resounding off the sheltering rocks over the repeated sound of thrashing water. The splashing stopped. 'Although . . . there is a strange sizzling to it, an almost — it sounds like it's . . . Irissa!'

The water roiled as if a wounded sea slug fought for life within it, lapping upon even the moss at her feet.

Irissa's eyes lost contact with the sword as she scrambled back from the impinging wavelets; its sorcerous extension vanished. She looked up to see the bushes' uppermost fringe parting and a flushed, wet, and angry Kendric peering through it.

Water rained from the rattails of his hair and the lobes of his ears, and slid down the arched profile of his nose to drip incessantly to his lips. He sputtered out the surfeit of it, searching for words within the damp indignity of his not insignificant person.

'It will cool now,' Irissa predicted, standing yet also edging away. 'Don't stay overlong; I would use it while the water's still warm . . .'

He shook his head, bedewing her with hand-me-down droplets, and turned, wordless, churning through the bushes back into the pool of warm, gently bubbling water.

Night did visit this place, or at least an evening. Irissa and Kendric sat near the pond, the shade of a distant sunfall casting cool semidarkness over them, their clothes still clinging to drying bodies. There was wind as well as twilight, a soft, nearly invisible thing that stole through the branches above them. Only when they were wet did it make its timid presence felt.

They had no fire. Despite the faithful company of Kendric's flint and steel, any wood he gathered was green, its inner whiteness streaked with viridescent ichor. Having been balked in his urge to deal with fire, he had turned to battling its opposite element.

Kendric was wiping his sword blade upon his discarded fowlen fur vest, certain that water spots would mar the steel.

'There are none, I tell you.' Irissa combed her fingers through her uncharacteristic curls. 'Only a simulacrum of the blade actually touched the water; I'd never let water oil your steel.'

'Still, it seems a trivial use of magic. The world spends half its time fretting over the large evils misused magic may do; I think it is in the small things that magic most goes awry.'

'Did you not prefer your water warmed?'

'That is not the point. I could have made do with it as it was.'

Irissa laughed. 'But I could not.'

'You could have learned.'

'What? For teaching you magic, you repay me with hardship — and unnecessary hardship at that?'

'If we are to travel alien worlds, we must learn to make the best of what we find.'

'And so I did. Kendric, your sword is magic — both in its original forging, and more so in the mind-forged replacement you made on Ivrium's carmine desert sands. You cannot unloose it, or the magic within it — or yourself. 'Tis like trying to outpace one's past.'

He pulled a pouch off the undonned baldric beside him.

'I know that. Even a marshman knows better than to walk backward; that is when swamp-swallow pools spring into one's own wake to suck one under. I wonder . . .'

'Yes?' Irissa waited, struck by a serious tone in his voice.

'I wonder if this bread survived the gate still edible.' He offered her a dry, dark hunk and tore into his portion with strong teeth.

Irissa sighed at Kendric's usual retreat to practical matters. She ignored the bread to chew on the future. 'I know my people are here,' she insisted. 'It is only a matter of journeying far enough.'

'Journeyed we have.'

'But not far enough.'

Kendric leaned upon an elbow, running his fingers through his wind-dried dark hair. 'What if there are no Torlocs? They all could have perished in their journey, you know. Didn't you say the men of Rindell had left one by one, never to return? Perhaps they couldn't. You may be the last Torloc in more worlds than our old Rule.'

'No!' Irissa's fingers fisted on her thighs, her body as well as her mind refusing the notion that she had quested so futilely.

Kendric had finished gnawing his tough bread; his palm held only crumbs. He reached over his shoulder for the Rynx, but its white form had melted into the forest's evening shadows while they talked. Gone hunting, he hoped, for more than stale breadcrumbs. He turned back to Irissa.

'Irissa, what if this is not your Torloc paradise; if neither Torlocs nor anything else vaguely human reside here; if that coltish bearing-beast is sole lord and master of this land? If we never find another gate, even one leading backward? If we abide alone, with the Rynx, in an empty place overlooked even by legends? Where does your quest take us then?'

She was silent for long moments, under the light of the brightening sickle moon, which claimed its own reflection in her Iridesium circlet, in the luminescence of her profile, the quicksilver strands of her hair. None of that moved now, not even with her breath.

But her hand settled across his, light as windthistle, the warm metal underbelly of her new-formed ring chiming against the stone-cold, jewel-set dome of his.

'Then we quest no more, except for the powers within ourselves.' Comforting him eased her own inner turmoil.

He considered it, sighing. 'I have always been the last, and — most of my life — the least. The last of the Six Wrathman to sentry Rule-that-was. Halvag the Smith had no other offspring than I, and my mother had died on my birth, thus insuring my precedence. I am used to standing by myself, as you are not.'

'No,' she agreed, 'but I do not stand by myself.' Her smile was a slim, white sickle in the night, as if her lips reflected the moon itself.

'Then you regret no gates.'

'And you regret no magic.'

They were questions spoken as facts. Their answers came wordlessly. Kendric couldn't be sure whether his hand had touched her shoulder to draw her to him, or she had merged with the dark and sank upon him, like a cloak. Their lips met serenely, with formal unspoken agreement. Nothing stirred in the night-silent woods but the rustle of silk and wool upon each other.

In the morning, the Rynx took up its selfsame post at the foot of some flower-vined trees. Before its neat, snowy lupine paws a pile of raw bones lay in crimson-dewed disarray.

'Then there *is* animal prey here!' Kendric squatted over the ruddy bones, prodding them into nearer semblance to their original configuration. 'Some four-footed, furred creature, I think, perhaps a fox—'

'Poor thing—!'

Kendric's eyebrows paved a straight, severe road across his forehead as he glanced up. 'Poor Rynx; and poor us if we were forced to forage for it.' He stood, still studying the scattered bones. 'If there are beasts we cannot see, then perhaps there are Torlocs we can see — eventually.'

'It *was* a foxlike thing,' the Rynx said abruptly. 'With thick fur of midnight green. It was fast, clever and — tasty.'

'Flesh-eater!' Irissa accused indiscriminately, stomping away.

Kendric remained to ask the sometime-hunter's question: 'Where did you find it?'

'Yonder.' The Rynx's head turned indifferently over its shoulder. 'Many such creatures teem and tear, inhabiting a kind of confine—'

'You've raided the Torloc's chicken coop!' Kendric accused,

laughing. 'Feathers will fly! That breed likes to loose nothing. *If* this is Edanvant, *if* there are Torlocs and *if* the absence of animals in this wood is because the Torlocs are containing them. I'll expect you to show us where "yonder" lies if we do not find habitation or at least some cultivated edibles soon.'

'You would not like it,' the Rynx answered, 'and she less.'

Reminded, Kendric discreetly swept the mangled bones under a swell of vines just as Irissa returned with her sensibilities under control.

'I suppose we could try eating roots, berries, leaves, flowers—' he suggested to both her and the Rynx as a compromise.

Irissa adjusted the Overstone-bearing purse at her waist, ensuring it was positioned opposite the shortsword that hung at her right hip.

'They might be poisonous,' she objected, finally admitting the possibility of danger into her long-sought paradise. 'If ever borgia needed a vineyard, this is it. Besides, I feel . . . I sense that we shall not be alone for long. There is something ahead, something Torloc.'

'Not another of your deserted Torloc towers? Is this your famed Torlockian architecture — buildings that melt or fall away from our very feet?'

'I am not responsible for all things Torloc,' Irissa pointed out, 'merely myself.'

The Rynx ignored their word-jousting, trotting ahead to vanish over the next rise of meadow. Irissa studied the woods as they walked along; all was as silent as before, except to her inner ears a sharp, wounded bark echoed and sounds of scuffle haunted the blossom-studded underbrush.

Kendric was wrong in saying that no scent prevailed here, Irissa decided, inhaling the perfume of death distilled down to an art, the death of sentient life, of artless magic. Its rank outpouring underlaid all the surface visual beauty around them, as the reek of sour wine can flood from the neck of a carved-coldstone decanter that windows only rubicund beauty.

They walked all that day, ignoring the indiscreet protests of their stomachs, unwilling to turn to the land until forced to. Evening came again, the arboreal green around them darkening to black as red stilettos of sunfall pierced through the trees.

'You are quiet,' Kendric observed.

Irissa merely pointed ahead, to the thing that had risen into her vision even as her thoughts explored the uncustomarily dark depths that had occupied them all day.

'By . . . Finorian's chin hairs! It *is* Torloc!' Kendric's voice fell away as he paused to marvel, caught again by the eternal entrapment things Torloc held for him, alluring and repelling at the same time.

Torloc the construction was, to its ten vaulted towers that ringed the sun-blushed core of the castle stretching skyward before them. Torloc in the Iridesium gleam of ornamental metalwork edging window frames and in the rainbow-hued falgon's-eye glass that formed peaked windows like massed soap bubbles. Torloc to its clear coldstone foundation circling the edifice in an icy crystal band, a bracelet around an extravagantly bejeweled, ten-fingered, sky-pointing hand.

'A rather large residence to hold one straggling band of Torlocs,' Kendric commented.

'Perhaps *you* were expected,' Irissa answered. 'Oh, it looks like a vision seen in Finorian's emerald touchstone! And, oh, to see them all again, even Finorian, to eat Dame Agneda's cooking, sink into a copper tub sizzling with fire-heated water, to don a clean gown, to smell fresh, garden-grown herbs . . .'

Irissa's run-down bootheels dug into the sturdy turf despite themselves; her walk became a trot and then lengthened into a run.

Kendric kept a more dignified pace beside her, a smile stretching his worried expression too thin to clothe his features any longer. He pictured food other than some stale bread-crumbs — wine. Or beer even! Spring-cooled brown beer, foaming at the conjoined mouths of tankard and drinker . . . clothes new-woven on some Torloc dame's loom; the breed did not do everything by magic. And directions. Directions to the haunt of the headstrong bearing-beast, which soon would play a lady's palfrey around the Torloc castle's crystal base, giving docile rides to all who wished . . .

The Rynx, infected by their malady, spurted ahead, its feather-tufted tail waggling behind it ludicrously for so ferocious a blend of predators.

The three drew up before a diagonally woven Iridesium portcullis. Irissa and Kendric had never seen so much of the magical metal lavished on one application, had never witnessed the full play of the swirling rainbow shades imbuing its black surface.

'No wonder they sought this place, your people.' Kendric's voice throbbed with new respect. 'What they were in Rule, in what was left of Rindell, was a mere reflection of their achievements.'

'It is more than I ever imagined,' Irissa exclaimed. 'More . . . magical.'

'A not unpleasant place, for a dwelling,' the Rynx contributed, sitting wearily on its haunches.

'But how do we enter?'

Kendric's question received a grating answer. The metallic barrier ground slowly upward, casting a long, predominantly red shadow into the courtyard within.

A sound came in rebuttal — the slither of Kendric's great sword from its scabbard. Irissa reached for the pommel of her own weapon, her fingers curling into a fist as if to restrain herself from an assumption of ill will in the Torloc thing before them.

They walked together under the still-elevating portcullis, gazing upward at an almost magically fluid interweaving of the strips of phosphorescent metal. The space beyond unrolled as quite ordinary to the eye — sheer stone wall faces interrupted by the whimsical placement of windows, exterior stairs climbing to upper levels, doors leading inward on every wall and at the top of every stair. And in every door, poised there like some portal guardian, waited a figure.

'Finorian!' Surety underlay Irissa's voice.

'Finorian.' Grim satisfaction reverberated in Kendric's.

She moved toward them, the old woman, silvery robes

flowing around a tall, thin body, her head level and imperious above the viridian slice of emerald chained around her neck.

She moved toward them from the top of an opposite stair . . . from the small arched door under that stair; from the wide double-barred door across the courtyard . . . from the high narrow door nearest them with a single bubble of falgon's-eye glass wounding its exact center.

Every door opened upon a shadowed interior. Every archway framed an advancing Finorian.

Kendric turned, confused to the point of letting his swordtip rasp across the inlaid stones at his feet. Irissa stood motionless, uncertain of all but one thing.

'Finorian,' she repeated, this time the word more admonition than recognition. Irissa froze then, shocked by her own temerity. Once she would have found the idea of admonishing the Torloc Eldress unthinkable. Yet the impulse returned, borne by a hot wave of righteous anger.

'Finorian, is this how you welcome a hard-fought return to Edanvant — with courtyard games directed against your guests?'

The multiple Finorians diminished by not so much as one.

'You are not a guest,' the Eldress observed acidly, speaking in every form so her voice became an echoing parody of itself, 'but one of our own returned. Besides, you can see through my guises to the genuine.'

'But *Kendric* can't!' Irissa exploded in shame. 'This is not what I said would await us, this is not hospitable—'

'Perhaps he would like it better elsewhere, is that not right, Wrathman of Rule? I foresaw you would aid Irissa in Rule, but I did not foresee having to admit you to Edanvant. Come, man of the Marshlands; you are used to choosing where you walk—' One arm, upraised in many mirroring forms, gestured inward. 'Choose the door that enters the keep and I shall shrink to my singular self . . . Find reality amongst the illusions and follow it.'

Kendric blinked from one Finorian to the next, bemused.

'It's not fair!' Irissa argued again, moving to meet the Eldress magic to magic.

Kendric's hand interceded. 'Back to back,' he ordered, responding to the illogical with a warrior's inbred physical wariness.

So they circled in the courtyard's central, sun-pinked eye, watching Finorian's meager figure enlarge on every side as the Eldress walked toward them.

'Here,' Kendric said, stopping. Behind him, Irissa did the same. Some string at the back of his neck — half natural instinct, half magic — tautened as he eyed one particular aperture. 'This one.' He raised the great five-foot-long blade like a steel finger to the modest door beneath a set of stairs. 'Step forward, Finorian, and show us your single self.'

'Your luck has improved since last I saw you, Wrathman.'

Kendric, concluding that 'luck' was as good a word for unspoken magic as any other, didn't argue with her.

The multiple Finorians had vanished, but an old woman stood limned against the door he had indicated, her long robes trailing the white courtyard stones as her wispy white locks dusted narrow shoulders.

Nothing had changed from the moments Kendric had first — and last — seen her, he noted. She looked as insubstantial as when she had quite literally faded from sight in Rindell, abjuring Irissa to remember she was Torloc . . .

Now the ancient seeress turned her blind eyes — silver beneath the opalescent patina of great age — toward Irissa. Not at Irissa, but toward her. She had hoarded her inborn power for immemorial years, had Finorian; not so much as a glance had been squandered on any surface that could reflect back the slightest revelation of herself. Thus had she kept great power and lost other, smaller powers more personal and therefore more satisfying.

'I see you brought your Wrathman with you,' Finorian said dryly, 'as you insisted when I called you from the Inlands. Irissa. Always obedient from the first, to a fault. And always coming last — with too little.' She looked at Kendric.

Finorian's words fell to the intervening stones like critical coldstone hail. Irissa stood bewildered, feeling forsaken. This was her kind's *home*, she told herself, which she had reached

60

at great cost. Even the urgency of Finorian's recent summons in the cup of borgia wine faded before the well-chilled reality of actual reunion.

Finorian did not seem glad to see them, Irissa admitted to herself — Kendric, understandably; he was not Torloc. But to withdraw so from Irissa herself, Finorian's only pupil, long-lost and now returned despite mortal trials . . . Something had changed. If not Finorian, then Irissa.

Nothing in the Eldress softened while Irissa studied her with clear silver — yet troubled — eyes.

'Do you? Do you see?' Irissa, stung, finally demanded. She turned from Finorian to stand beside Kendric, her eyes confronting the Torloc Eldress directly. Standing there, Irissa realized that she had always been afraid of Finorian. Always.

Sunfall's last warm rays painted youthful rouge upon Finorian's sunken cheeks and pale lips, but even that rosy light blanched at the cold, white sightless gaze of her eyes, round like coins, and, like coins, not to be had but for a price.

A frown further wrinkled an aspect seemingly fashioned from furrows already. 'See?' demanded Finorian. 'See . . . I see a Wrathman of Rule who stands alone, which is a contradiction. I see a Torloc seeress who stands with another, which is a greater contradiction. I see a four-footed, feather-eared beast that sits before a Torloc Eldress, which is an impoliteness . . .'

'Your pardon, Eldress.' The Rynx rose, stretched its lupine forelegs until its belly bowed to the ground, then straightened.

'Ah. A talker as well as a heeder, an ill aspect in an animal so oddly made. And what of you, Wrathman?' Finorian asked, as if he were an afterthought. Her hem hissed as she circled Kendric. 'How have your travels treated you?'

Kendric stiffened at the Eldress's approach. 'Not well,' he admitted. 'We are footsore, hungry, and tired — and as Irissa says, in no mood for games.'

Finorian ignored his answer and stopped before Irissa.

'Footsore, hungry, tired. Yes, all that . . . and other things.' She seemed to measure Irissa as she would an opponent. 'I am glad you came,' she at last told Irissa, and only Irissa,

61

her voice burning dry and hot with conviction. 'We are even sorer tried than you, and wearier. If you will come within, you may bring your Wrathman and your — your—'

'We are Rynx,' the beast supplied, its double-edged voice dropping low. 'And we do not abide in edifices of piled stone, Eldress, or rely on halfhearted hospitality. If we are footsore, hungry and tired, we can attend to it ourselves.'

At that the creature turned and trotted through the open portcullis into the dark of the woods beyond.

'Independent,' Finorian judged, displeased.

'Yes.' For once Kendric sounded happy to agree with the Eldress.

'Unimportant.' Finorian dismissed the retreating beast and Kendric's barely veiled antagonism with equal disdain. Her long, pale fingertips played the emerald's rough edges as if she sought some tune in it. 'When you were . . . a girl, Irissa, you looked once into the flaw within my touchstone. Once — for a mere wink of a moment. What do you see there now?'

Kendric stirred, distrustful, but Irissa had long since learned not to overshield her eyes from outer objects. Her head tilted to study the milky green stone and the faint flaw that stirred within it as imperceptibly as frost upon a coldstone windowpane.

'It has grown, the flaw!' Wonder outweighed the new disappointment in Irissa's voice. 'It is like . . . the veins of a leaf, reaching out, ever wider, to the very edges of things. It is the strength that holds the stone together; it is the disease that eats it!'

Finorian's fingers flattened abruptly over each other, obscuring the touchstone. 'Enough. It is wiser to keep stone-lore to oneself. Yes, much has changed, and you see deeper than you did before.' The Eldress couldn't resist glancing at Kendric as she added, 'Some things.' She stepped back to address them both, her voice finally finding a cordial note.

'But you must enter and accept your travelers' hospitality without more questions this night; the Rynx is right. There will be time for questions tomorrow.'

'Whose questions? Yours — or ours?'

Finorian's slanted silver eyes spun unerringly past Kendric's face as she answered him. 'That question, too, can wait till the morrow.'

She turned and retraced her steps through the door. At all the other visible doorways, Finorian's pale back departed in formation. Kendric nudged Irissa to indicate the phenomenon, then ducked to accommodate his lengthy frame to the skimpy under-stair portal.

'One small question at least,' Kendric insisted as he and Irissa trailed the Eldress into a dingy interior. 'What is the . . . magic . . . of the courtyard; the illusion of one as many?'

'An old and trivial sorcery, set within the stones. It is one of our Torloc tricks that time has forgot.' Finorian led them through a low passage lit by a solitary torchère.

The way ended without warning — in a giant, well-lit yawn of space and color that resolved itself into a great hall.

Once Irissa had stood and watched the home stones of Rindell melt from her vision into mist; now at last stones, Torloc stones, would shelter her again. The emotions of this moment rinsed away Finorian's queer discourtesy and Irissa's misgivings. The sight before Irissa's eyes told her one quite unmagical thing: she was home again. At last.

She paused at the threshold of the hall, sensing as much as seeing the white pavement beneath her feet, the pale walls soaring upward to narrow windows, whose crystalline panes reflected a rainbow's wealth of colors.

The sinking sun's carmine wake flared now, dyeing all the interior with a soft, pulsing rose shade. Although natural magic lent a twilight spell to the surroundings, the hall was furnished predictably enough — ranked wooden trestle tables and benches, high-backed chairs sturdy as oak trunks carved into almost animate designs, stools sporting pelts as exotic as Rule's not-so-mythical moonweasel fur, green rush mats carpeting the stones helter-skelter.

More greenery covered one of the trestle tables — glossy leaves piled and shredded and rolled and stuffed with exotic roots, flowers, and berries . . . the very things Kendric had lightly suggested they consume in the woods.

A scattering of Torloc dames busied themselves in the huge hall. One kept a distant loom humming near the cold, flameless fireplace. Another sewed by the unsteady light of a wall torch. And one sat at a trestle table, dark head bowed, the gleaming braids she wore looped around her ears swaying slightly with her motions.

'Jalonia!' Irissa exclaimed.

As the woman raised her head, a flickering wall torch traced the zig-zag course of one false silver strand through her night-dark hair.

'Finorian promised a reunion.' Smiling, the woman rose and came forward, her leaf-stained hands wide with welcome.

Irissa shyly extended her own. They touched. Jalonia's amber eyes brimmed into her daughter's face, then absorbed the new directness of gaze. It seemed to distress her. Her hands dropped Irissa's. Her eyes lowered as if she were a seeress meeting her own long-forbidden reflection.

Irissa had always found Jalonia's amber irises disconcerting. They had hung like twin suns over the mist of her youngest memories, as had the twin cold silver moons of another pair of eyes, until Irissa's early days reeled in confusion and eventually the moons unnaturally outshone the suns.

A slow smile froze on Irissa's face as she realized she'd never really seen her mother, had never been allowed to see *anyone* face-to-face until she had found herself so with Kendric. How could she have forgotten the isolation of Rindell Keep? What else had she forgotten — or never known well enough to forget?

She glanced away to find Finorian's shrewd old face watching expressionlessly. Irissa clasped her hands together as if they were cold, and returned her fascinated attention to her mother.

'I am elbow-deep in kitchen tasks, I fear.' Jalonia was apologizing breathlessly, as if for more than her lowly occupation. 'Life here is even more necessarily domestic than it was in Rule. Without meat—'

'No meat?' Kendric was thunderstruck. 'Then I was right. Except for the dapple-gold bearing-beast and what distant prey the Rynx can catch, we are reduced to roots and berries!'

'Life is as hard here as in Rindell,' Finorian said without inflection. 'And must remain so. Except for Irissa, I am the only truly empowered Torloc here.'

'It is the same as before?' Irissa questioned, unable to disguise her chagrin. 'All this travel and travail and we are the same as we were before? We are by ourselves, mixing magic and petty tasks? I thought Edanvant would release us from necessity, that we would *all* be what we had been before! What of the men who went in search of talismans?' Irissa demanded. 'What of those you women came here to join?'

Eyes glanced up from tasks all around the room. Silence suddenly held breathless sway.

Finorian shrugged. 'Gone on about their own business, as is the wont of men, as was always their wont — gone in search of mist-o'-the-marshes. The men! Is that all women wonder about? I am sick of answering such questions. The men abandoned us years ago — against my counsel, my will — on reckless quests for uncertain powers. Perhaps they have not fared well; perhaps they have forgotten us. Men always sunder domestic bonds. We are here as we were on Rindell. Only a few. Only women.' Her lips crescented like the sickle moon now grinning palely through one of the darkening windows. 'Only Torlocs.'

'Not all,' Kendric said.

Finorian's unfocused eyes lifted to his voice, to the alien timbre and calm certainty of it. 'You are tired,' she said abruptly, 'as are we all. We will deal with questions tomorrow. For now, help yourself to what food attracts you.'

Her hand indicated the leafy repast Jalonia had prepared. Irissa and Kendric, wood-weary and dazed beyond more questioning, did not need a second invitation. They quickly took that which most resembled what they'd been accustomed to call food in other places, Irissa and Jalonia avoiding each other's eyes as if ordered to.

'Laella will show you to your rooms,' Finorian said, indicating a tall, pale woman with weary eyes.

'Room,' Kendric corrected between bites of a green-tinted bread piled with vegetable condiments.

Again all the Torloc dames' eyes flickered up, the communal breath held.

'You are weary,' repeated Finorian. 'I have assigned rooms to you both.'

Kendric lay down his dinner and slung off his sword, resting it alongside his long right arm.

'We have . . . shared bed-bond,' Irissa intervened. She glanced nervously to Jalonia, but the dark braids fell forward over her task-bent head, obscuring her face. 'You knew that, Finorian,' she added, resenting the Eldress for forcing a public declaration of what was already private knowledge among the three.

'Did I?' Finorian's crosshatched face was set. 'I am old, and forget much,' she added blandly. 'Very well. Laella.' Finorian leaned to whisper to the woman who rustled over at her call.

Minutes later, their leafy feasting done, Irissa and Kendric were following their Torloc guide up long sets of white stone stairs in the wake of a green-flamed torch.

At the doorway indicated, too low for Kendric, Irissa slipped through first. Kendric caught his skull on the lintel, forbore to curse, and turned to light an interior torch from the licking tongue of green without.

'Many thanks,' he offered to the back that had turned on him as soon as the fire had caught. It vanished into the unlit dark even as he spoke.

He banged his head again on backing into the room, and this time swore.

'By Finorian's great toe, this is a sour welcome we are given! Finorian couldn't have found a meaner doorway in all of Rule, much less Edanvant. Or perhaps she set it to shrinking precisely for my benefit as we made our way here.'

'You are overly distrustful, Kendric.' Irissa sounded like one who admonishes another with words she wishes to aim at herself. She had collapsed on a fireplace stool and was munching doggedly on a cold, leafy leftover.

66

'Would you not be leery of a land where even the peat burns green?' he asked, studying the unnatural glow in the small fireplace, which suffused his hawkish features with lurid shadows. 'It seems that when a Torloc promises a thing, such as a "green, green, world," there is a surfeit of satisfaction. I wonder . . . I wonder what color of rain falls here?'

'Better green than the color of an inventive Wrathman,' Irissa retorted, invoking the memory of Kendric's magic-made yellow rain in the Inlands. 'Oh, Finorian is right!' She leaned over to pull a boot off a swollen foot. 'We must save our questions for the morning, when much will become clear.'

He was silent for a bit, which Irissa, ever-optimistic, took for agreement.

'One thing will not become clear,' Kendric finally said, his voice oddly controlled, 'on the next or any other morning. And that is how we are to fit into yonder . . . jewel-box of a bed.'

Irissa turned. She had noticed the curtained aperture of a bed; she had noticed nothing beyond the soft promise of its presence.

Now she stood and measured it with her eyes. 'Oh . . . it's not only short but narrow.' Her face hardened. 'Finorian was trying to teach us — you — a lesson, I fear.'

Kendric laughed and sat upon the high mattress of some sweet-smelling stuff. His hand punched a depression next to him.

'*More* greenery — dried — inside, I'd wager.'

'Perhaps I could . . . stretch the bed. Or you could—'

'Too trivial an application of magic,' he said, looking mock askance. 'Perhaps Finorian did us a favor.'

He pulled Irissa down beside him into the cozy bed linens and intently eyed the leaping emerald-flamed torch, impaled in its wall socket. It winked out, a sadly unluminous example of the trivial application of magic.

CHAPTER FOUR

Sensation brushed Irissa's closed eyelids. She struggled up past dreams far too subterranean to remember, through the dark and watery place that required crossing to reach the brighter yet more ponderous world of consciousness.

The flutter breached her eyelashes — dancing, burning, spinning. Myriad light motes fled to the chamber's perimeters, splashing the white stones with such bright dots of crimson, cobalt, and vivid green that the walls and floor seemed to be bleeding gemstones.

Across from her curtained sleeping niche a peaked window shone daylight-white. The many crucibles of its round panes performed a rainbow alchemy as sunlight invisibly slipped through the glass-clear coldstones to don its many-colored guise within.

Irissa turned her head. She was alone in the bed, wrapped to her chin in some weightless coverlet, warmed to her toes, more comfortable than she had been in months.

A stab of alarm prodded her fully awake — Kendric was gone.

On a table beneath the window lay Kenric's great sword. Abandoned. The word reverberated warning in Irissa's mind. Kendric would not have left his weapon behind had any evident danger threatened. Still, he had left; and unless impelled to, she and Kendric had not been parted since they had joined forces in Rule.

Irissa forced bare feet from the bed's nestlike warmth onto a rug of thick, evergreen-dark fur, then onto the tepid white stones beyond.

At the window she stretched for the latch, then split the

bubbled panes wide open on the morning. Butterfly-bright light motes streamed over her skin and flickered away, melding with the broad, translucent bands of a rainbow arching the farthest pinetops.

Her fingertips stroked the homely, leather-bound hilt of Kendric's sword, marking its presence, his absence. Her own sword lay beside it. He must have left the room, left the sword, left her, for a reason.

Turning back to the room's clean, white comfort, she stumbled and glanced down. Her worn, gray boots from Rule stood toe-to-toe with her. She remembered rising to strip off her clothing in the lingering liquid-emerald of last night's magic-doused torchlight and leaving her boots any which way in the dark after finally working off the journey-stiff leather.

Now her torn trousers lay neatly folded on a chest and her travel-stained boots stood upright, decorously paired. Her lips curved ruefully. Someone had straightened her boots before leaving. Someone who felt secure enough to leave, and to leave her alone. If Kendric felt safe, why shouldn't she?

Home. The word tolled a single, mellow bellnote in her mind. On a windowside table a brass basin and ewer radiated big-bellied conviviality, winking warmly together in the sunlight.

Droplets from an earlier laving still dewed the basin's sloped interior; when Irissa poured a new stream the water warmed her touch. Had it been heated by the everyday mortal magic of sunlight sifting through a window? Or had Kendric, clandestine lover of small physical comforts, chafed the brass with his shy sorcery? It was more intriguing to speculate than to know.

She elevated a serpent-shaped Iridesium comb whose back boasted an imposing bristle of upright scales spraying sunlight into an unfurled rainbow fan. Inset coldstones winked at her, the gems not polished round as mined coldstones were, but tear-shaped. Once her own tears had fallen coldstone-hard; she wondered if they still did now that she could look at things directly.

Perhaps she should think of something sad . . . But her

thoughts refused to produce a suitably tragic subject as she drew the jeweled comb through her fingertip-long hair. Its plowing teeth separated the black strands into filaments of raw color, drawing natural highlights into threads of undiluted green, gold and blue. Irissa impulsively wished for a mirror, as ordinary women often do.

The morning's magic chilled again. Of course there was no mirror. This was a Torloc place — at last, inhabited by Torloc women — and she was not ordinary. Though seeresses were ever a minority, their needs would overrule the unmagicked majority's yen for sops to ordinary female vanity. No mirrors. But — Irissa glanced around — this solitary safe awakening alone was luxury. This was a time and place for privacy, peace . . . and reflection.

Yet questions began to prick the skin of her complacency. Where was Kendric? The answer was not urgent, but it was of interest. Where was breakfast? And, of course, she must reacquaint herself with the other Torlocs. She had been too weary to pay them more than scanty notice the previous evening, though they had seemed less than welcoming themselves. Irissa had much to explain.

Her mother, Jalonia, for instance, would expect some explanation of her travels. As would Finorian. Finorian would expect more than explanations. She always had. Irissa sighed less happily and began drawing on her travel-worn clothing. Yet, for once, some explanations were owed *her*. Where were the Torloc men they all had sought so long? Old questions could be as unsettling as new ones. Where was Kendric, for that matter? An unanchored dread claimed her. She might need him, even here. Perhaps especially here.

She tied the green silken sash into a sling for her shortsword. Then her face paled — though she had no mirror in which to confirm it — at another seeming defection.

Gone! The Overstrong egg, which she had looped at her waist for security's sake . . . it was gone! She must not lose the talisman, sick surges of inner panic told her, although she didn't know why. Lost? No, now she recalled . . .

Irissa ran barefoot to the bed to lift an indecently overstuffed

70

pillow. Ah, safe! The pale stone reclined in a deep dimple of mattress.

Large enough to fill her palm, it felt oddly light for its size — and oddly warm. Its dully opaline surface pulsed with a gathering of faint colors. Irissa's nail traced one meandering vein as she slipped the thing into its pouch and tied it securely at her waist. She bent, grunting, to pull on her neatly mated boots, and smiled again, not bothering to seek the cause of a returning serenity more palpable than summer sunshine.

At last she stood upright, feeling competent to face Finorian and explain herself, which of course would not be sufficient for Finorian. Perhaps the sword would be. Irissa paused again by the two blades, one so extravagantly long, the other ordinarily short.

Irissa reached to don hers, but paused, wondering why she felt it necessary to arm herself in her own long-lost Torloc home, among her own people. It was a plain weapon meant for blunt business, not like the mind-forged sword she had made in Rule and embellished . . .

Her silver eyes narrowed against more than the white daylight. Some unseen inner blaze flared high. In the room, water lay mirror-still against the curve of brass and a light wind stirred the forest-green fur, revealing a paler, borgia-shaded undercoat. The comb's coldstone teardrops seemed to tremble in their settings.

A glowing daggerpoint of green pierced her sword hilt from within. It waxed emerald and fattened into a smugly outsized, cabochon-smooth jewel of cat's-eye intensity.

'There.' Irissa sounded self-satisfied as the gemstone appeared. Her palm polished it familiarly before she set the sword at her hip, looked one last time around the room — regretfully, and pushed out the door into the hall beyond.

Three high peaked windows of falgon's-eye coldstone lit Irissa's way through the long, empty halls. Finally she found a stairway cut like a stepped mountain of salt against one white wall, with a swagged Iridesium chain for a wallside handhold.

No one seemed about until she came again to the great hall.

71

There the high-set opposing rows of arched coldstone windows changed light motes into flocks of songless, rainbow-shaded birds perching on the bleached weepwaterwood rafters far above.

Daylight clad the hall in its full measure of magic. The wild glancing haze above filtered through the distance until the hall's white stone walls gleamed milky, as did the pristine floor where green rush mats lay scattered like oversized fallen leaves. Even the simple wooden furnishings wore a greenish tinge, as if cut and fashioned before their time. No dirt or disarray aged the place. Across the vast room, the Wrathman-high fireplace spoke with a mouth of pure white marble, its deep throat barely blackened by the tongues of uncounted fires. Yet it all felt old, irretrievably old. And used.

Nothing familiar to Irissa's life from Rindell occupied the area, other than touches of Iridesium metalwork − that, and the sight of her mother, Jalonia, sitting alone at the long trestle table, shelling peas.

Irissa found herself reluctant to announce her arrival, to disturb the uneven balance of alien and familiar that met her view. Jalonia looked up first, with the common amber eyes that labeled her a mere Torloc and not a Torloc woman of power, as her only child had been marked from birth by her quicksilver eyes. Mother's and daughter's eyes had never met fully that either could remember.

Now Jalonia's regard burned brighter, washed by common tears that would fall into no gemstone guise, and by an odd blend of wonder and worry.

'Your eyes, Irissa! They no longer evade mine, as a seeress's must. You risk their powers in the miniature mirrors of mine—'

'No.' Irissa stepped nearer and smiled reassuringly. 'My powers no longer ebb and flow at the happenstance pull of where I look. When I gazed only where I was allowed, to preserve my power, I lost nearly all of it. Now I look where I will and see what I can.'

Jalonia's head shook in uncomprehending wonder. 'Even a seeress who has undergone Far Focus must veil her sight from the thoughtless drain of others; you are brave.'

72

Irissa smiled again, at herself. 'I have not been brave, but foolish, and that permits one to take risks.' She edged nearer the table to study the white willow baskets heaped with shelled peas and splayed pods, like a shy young child who finds mystery in the commonest of adult activities.

'You never were one to stand and watch.' Jalonia's leaf-stained hands spread apologetically. 'The farther we Torlocs migrate, the deeper we become mired in ordinary tasks. So few of us are left who can accomplish the extraordinary ones . . .'

Irissa's own hands spasmed helplessly. She had spent little time with her mother, even in infancy. Irissa's childhood had become an aloof, sideways affair of protecting powers she had not yet learned to use; even a mother's doting eye was to be avoided as a pitfall. Now, ironically, she found Jalonia's evasive gaze difficult to bear.

Irissa's polite, uneasy smile deepened as she thought of Kendric's honest, dubious regard. His were the first eyes she had read from without and within, the first step toward shaping her lonely heritage to the call of a new future.

'Your journey seems to have agreed with you,' Jalonia noted, her quick fingers snapping peas as perfect as jade beads free of their pods.

Irissa popped a few free-rolling ones into her mouth and sat abruptly beside her mother.

'Nothing has agreed with me, and I'm the better for it. Have you seen . . . Kendric?'

Jalonia's work stopped. 'Ah, your Wrathman, as Finorian calls him. He does not strike me as belonging to anyone but himself. His name is Kendric, then. There was little time for introductions last night.' Her eyes grew softly distant. 'It is strange to see such a one here, among these lonely stones. Strange to see a man, a breed we Torloc women have found to be faithless—'

'He is not my Wrathman,' Irissa interjected hastily. 'You are right. He is not even a Wrathman anymore, now that we are free of Rule. And, of course, he is not Torloc.'

'Men are more like to men than Torloc is different from

73

mortal.' Jalonia's dark eyebrows rose emphatically. 'But the greatest difference, I think, lies between men and women.'

This was one mystery Irissa felt uneager to discuss with Jalonia, for reasons even a seeress couldn't delve.

'You take an interest in him because he and I are bed-bonded,' she declared cautiously, twisting empty pea pods in her fingers.

Jalonia laughed and shook her dark-haired head. 'I take an interest in him because he is interesting, the first interesting phenomenon to cross our threshold in years, or in what seems like years. And' — her face grew pensive — 'I like a man — anyone — who can say no to Finorian.'

'I have,' Irissa answered.

'Have you? And would you have before your path crossed his? He is strong, this Kendric-who-belongs-to-no-one, in ways far deeper than the obvious. I am not sorry you two are bed-bonded.'

Irissa found herself flushing. 'It was . . . accidental.' Jalonia's golden-brown eyes widened to liquid lorryk-gaze dimensions, so Irissa rushed to explain. 'No one ever told me that my maidenhood was the threshold to some man's power, not even Finorian!'

Reading only confusion in Jalonia's eyes, Irissa realized she had committed to explaining something her mother had never known enough of to ask. She was a novice at reading others' eyes, Irissa realized; even knowing one Kendric could not make up for a lifetime of ignorance.

Irissa braced herself to walk the unwanted road she had rushed onto. 'If a magically empowered man had been first to lay with me, he would have won full share of my Torloc powers. I never knew that until we — Kendric and I — came into the under-mountain keep of a Rulian sorcerer who desired my Torloc powers for himself.' Irissa shivered. 'He courted me, as a keep cat would woo a mouse. Geronfrey, he was called in Rule, but I think he calls many worlds home, and he was not used to being denied . . .'

'My poor child!' Jalonia's eyes flashed ire. 'I didn't know . . . and Finorian never warned you—?'

'No. But then, we were suddenly separated by the gate. Perhaps she meant to.'

'So Kendric saved you from this seducer, this ambitious sorcerer? He intervened and spirited you both safely away?' Jalonia's voice warmed with certainty.

Irissa winced at the tart taste of forthcoming honesty on her tongue. 'Yes. And no. I saved myself — and endangered both of us in that world and the next one, as well. I . . . divested myself of my peculiar value, which the village maidens call virginity and treasure for less material reasons than my variety of it. I . . . seduced Kendric.'

'Well.' Jalonia sat back and stared at her daughter. 'I don't believe it!'

'It's true!' Having given painful testimony, Irissa resented being gainsaid. Her cheeks flared cherry-red. 'At least I was the one to gain most by it.'

A smile was quirking the corners of Jalonia's mouth. 'And he didn't know what was at stake — and why? You were indeed sent into the world ignorant, my girl, to think you can use a man so.'

'A man would have used me!' Irissa retorted, 'and even for common reasons men often use ordinary women so. If my mere . . . condition . . . was of such value to Geronfrey it seemed that Kendric would not complain of it.'

'And of course he did not.'

'He did.' Irissa squirmed upon her stool. 'He railed. He raged. He refused to understand how desperate I was — and I did not mean to convey my gifts to him! I thought him unmagicked. Immune. I thought him the safest possible repository of these . . . two-edged . . . powers of mine.'

'And has he proved to be?' Jalonia asked gently.

'For me, yes. For himself . . . that remains to be seen.' Irissa's eyes grew troubled. 'He has no native love for magic.'

'Then it is fortunate indeed that he at least bears love for you,' Jalonia concluded with maternal briskness, her honeyed eyes twinkling.

'That is . . . speculation,' Irissa answered doubtfully. 'Necessity drove us together from the first; necessity has been our bedfellow ever since. I do not regret it, but neither of us have chosen . . .'

Jalonia sighed. 'I chose. I chose Orvath. And Orvath chose. He chose to follow the men on their quest for talismans. Although, like Kendric, he relished riding Finorian at cross-grain, when she asked him to take a gate he took it gladly.'

Jalonia idly shook her fist, loose peas rattling in it like coldstones in a Rulian merchant's purse.

'There was no "accident" in our coming together — or in our coming apart,' she went on. 'Simply choices made, and choices lived with. I wish—'

'What?' urged Irissa, questing behind her mother's melancholy in hopes of answering her own uncertainty.

Jalonia smiled and patted Irissa's clenched fist as it lay on the tabletop. 'I wish because I have no power, no magic. What such a creature wishes is of no consequence.'

Irissa felt a wish spring unbidden into her mind. She wished she had seen — could see — her father.

There were so many mysteries to her parents, she realized, mysteries she'd never thought to mull before. Finorian had always seemed to be answer enough. She had insisted on it. Finorian had always insisted on having all the answers.

Irissa didn't know what to say to Jalonia, so she turned away from the chasm's edge of confidences, running her fingertips over the oiled wood before speaking.

'I recall only glimpsing a man or two from my childhood at Rindell; I was kept well away from them because of their mirroring Iridesium armor. My — father, I suppose, must have been there once.'

'He left before your birth, although he knew I was carrying you.' Jalonia's voice was brittle. Peas scattered furiously from her long fingers into their basket and tears burnished her amber eyes.

'Then my childish eyes must have seen Thrangar,' Irissa mused, nervously sidestepping the pain in Jalonia's words because it provoked an answering, unassigned pain in herself. 'Thrangar, the only Torloc Wrathman among the Six of Swords. He was expected at Rindell before the sudden opening

76

of a gate took you all; later, we found him dead in Geronfrey's antechambers. Why did that gate open with so little notice? Why was Thrangar, why was *I*, left behind?'

'You ask questions twin to those I have asked for twenty years, since Orvath left,' Jalonia burst out. Her hand clasped Irissa's wrists, not tentatively as the night before, but firmly, urgently. 'Oh, child, I had so little to do with you when we both were younger. I was *allowed* so little to do with you. How can I answer your questions now?' The anguish in Jalonia's eyes hardened to topaz honed on the dulled edge of swallowed anger. 'No one could — or would — ever answer mine, either.'

But Irissa, once begun, could not contain the questions that crowded behind her potent silver eyes.

'Why do you all accept these questions as if you did not deserve answers? I have quested through many worlds and have found that things are not always as they are told to us. Why do you all sit and mourn and munch upon your lot like sheep? If we Torlocs have truly come to our ancestral place, why have we still not found the men who went ahead? That is the question we women should ask — what of the present if the past be barred to us? I thought if we came to Edanvant, all would be answered. Our kind would be reunited.'

'And so we are.' An age-darkened voice spoke dry and cold behind Irissa, with the haste of timely interruption. 'It has been some time since I have seen you, child,' she added ironically. 'Give me your eyes.'

Irissa spun to face Finorian, surprised, her hand curling around the pommel of her sword. 'Gladly.'

'Not so directly!' Gnarled fingers shaded Finorian's blind-white eyes from something she sensed rather than perceived. 'Is there no subtlety in you, Irissa? I hoped you had learned at least that in your travels.' Her concluding sigh rasped like a sere leaf across the stones.

'I was not taught by the subtle, save for yourself.'

Finorian laughed softly. 'Perhaps I was not subtle enough in those days. Come, I have things to show you.'

77

She turned unerringly to face a farther door. It was hard to remember sometimes that Finorian's outer blindness veiled an inner acuity of vision beyond mere seeing, that she had mined her considerable powers within through years of tunneling into the darkest caverns of her mind.

'But I wish to know where we are!' Irissa said, not moving to follow the Eldress. 'Is this indeed Edanvant, which we Torlocs sought so ceaselessly for so many generations? At last can we rest, knowing this for our homeworld, for ours?'

'This is Edanvant,' Finorian answered. 'More than that I cannot say.'

'But — what do we do here? If we have nowhere else to go and cannot go on, if this is not what was promised, if the men have not preceded us here, what are we to do?'

'Survive,' Finorian vowed, her voice thrumming like the dying plucked cord of some taut-strung harp. 'And we shall do it far better with you than without you. I will lead you to the Circle.'

Irissa hesitated, looking back to Jalonia, whose head had bent back to her work and whose dark braids swung silent accompaniment to the rhythm of her motions.

'Surely some magical means could make these tasks easier,' Irissa suggested again in an undertone, loath to leave her mother at her humble work, although Jalonia — being unmagicked — had never done any but humble chores.

'No mere kitchen work for you, girl,' Finorian promised harshly. 'For you it will be harder. Now come!'

Irissa finally rose and followed Finorian's inflexible figure through a white stone passage dim only because it drove deep within the unlit portions of the castle.

'What of your adventures in Rule when you were stranded — and later?' Finorian inquired calmly in the dark passage. 'What did you learn when you were away from me? When you were alone?'

Irissa paused in the shadowy tunnel. Ahead of her, Finorian's pale upright figure seemed to emanate its own aura. It stopped also.

'I learned that one can learn nothing alone,' Irissa replied.

Finorian stood still for a very long time. Then the faint flutter of her gown resumed and Irissa followed it.

'This is a noble lesson,' the old woman finally commented. 'And untrue. We who hold the power of Far Focus are always alone, for we alone can alter what is and what may be. There are no partners in such powers. Not even you and I.'

Finorian turned, her blind gaze drilling into the stone directly before Irissa's cheek. Some shape sizzled into the darkened surface then, formed of converging iridescent lines like Iridesium.

Finorian's projection assumed a bizarre configuration, demanding attention. Irissa's fingers traced the image until they knew its shape. A boot! A boot like the one she had lost in the dark pit under Geronfrey's mountain, and that the Rulian sorcerer had returned to her, the gesture of a mage supremely confident of his artfulness. But Irissa had bested him — 'betrayed him,' was how Geronfrey had phrased it in his pride and his ire. And he had appeared in a new guise in the Inlands to menace both Irissa and Kendric. All that history was reflected in the Iridesium outline of the boot Finorian had conjured on the passage wall.

'How do you know of that?' Irissa demanded. 'How do you know what transpired in Rule in your absence? Or elsewhere?'

'I have mastered Far Focus, too, child,' Finorian answered. 'And more conventionally than you. There is much I know of your adventures: how you joined forces with Kendric the Wrathman, how you were courted by — and disappointed — the sorcerer Geronfrey; even how Felabba, my old cat, served as your sometime guide . . .'

Despite the lack of light, Finorian discerned the shock upon Irissa's features. She laughed softly.

'You are needed here, sore needed, girl. If that discomfits you, we are all sorry for it. But you must rest and restore your powers. Even I am not totally . . . immortal.

'I think only of the good of our kind,' Finorian added. 'A Wrathman of Rule, no matter how many gates he blunders through or whose bed he rests in, is not of our kind, or our concern. If you remember that, Irissa, you will accept better what must be done here.'

Irissa's fingers slipped into the cold metal grooves of Finorian's inlaid boot. She focused suddenly on the metallic glint, her silver gaze burning white-hot until the metal ran molten and flowed into another shape — it was a sword, a great long Iridesium sword set at an angle into the rock, half-raised as if in reluctant threat.

'You do not know everything that transpired, Finorian. I saw that in the first gate, when you tried to wrest Kendric from me. I saw it when you hailed me here and tried to deny Kendric's new powers even then. Bed-bond is a more potent partnership than all the powers of Torloc and sorcerer—'

'You infantile fool!' Finorian dashed pale gnarled hands to her temples, shaded her blind eyes in the dark as if from a blow bright as lightning. 'To lavish your gifts so, on a mere marshman . . . has this not already altered all beyond changing?

'I care not what tawdry powers your union has bestowed on one such as he. I would have wed you to Thrangar, a Torloc and a Wrathman, if Wrathmen so enamor you; then the magical gifts you conferred with your maidenhood would have gone to one equipped by birth and nature to use them. To a Torloc! They are wasted now; better to have armed your sorcerous suitor, Geronfrey—'

Irissa would have retorted even more hotly then, but Finorian's hands lowered as her eyes leadenly moved across the engraved Iridesium sword.

'The blow that is raised is as good as delivered. What is done, is done. What has been given, is lost.'

Ageless melancholy echoed in Finorian's voice. The old woman turned her back on Irissa and diminished into the utter darkness, became one with it.

'If I am so useless to you, to myself, then why did you summon me so urgently? What do you want of me?' Irissa interrogated the dark.

'Felabba.' The sound reverberated hollowly, more whisper than word. Finorian's voice grew even more remote. 'I want you to help me summon Felabba.'

CHAPTER FIVE

The emerald pommelstone of Irissa's sword glowed torch-like through her fingers. She fixed her eyes and thoughts upon it until they coaxed its feeble illumination strong enough to guide her through the dark alone.

No side passages distracted her from the path; unlike Finorian, the way at least was straightforward. Grimly amused, Irissa followed it. At one time Finorian's veiled sayings and cryptic orders had commanded Irissa. Now they seemed unneccessarily pretentious.

An oblong of soft light opened windowlike in the darkness ahead. When Irissa finally stood within it, she sensed she paused deep within the castle's hidden heart, and even deeper within the Torloc mysteries Finorian protected so fiercely. She stood in a doorway leading to a rock-walled chamber.

And she was no longer alone.

Twenty Torloc women sat in a circle, solemn, gray-garbed, on the dank stone floor, their long hands linked, their bowed faces obscured by the swag of their braided front locks.

In their midst stood Finorian, although Irissa knew instantly that no handhold had broken to permit the Eldress entrance into the cirle. Irissa had never seen this many of her kind gathered so ritually, had never guessed that it might be possible or even routine. She felt she saw for the first time something that had always been, and that had always been concealed.

'Welcome to our Damen Circle.' Finorian's voice, wrung dry with irony, echoed off the wet stones. Her fingertips framed the slab of lucent emerald covering her breast. In the farther darkness unlit by the circle of green-flamed wall torches, beads of moisture huddled near enough together to produce a melancholy dripping, drop by unseen drop.

Irissa shivered, but stepped forward.

'What is this place?'

'Not so much a place as a process.' Finorian's pale robes swept the stones at the circle's inner edge, brushing by the still, draped forms. 'These Torloc dames are all descended from seeresses, though they themselves hold little power. By their vigil, I can focus my own powers elsewhere and sometimes draw on deeper potencies possessed by those who are no longer here.'

'Have . . . we . . . always had such things?'

'Always,' Finorian answered. 'Few knew of it. Few know at what cost we keep the world green around us, or the waters fresh and untainted by other, elder magicks. Few know how our Damen Circle maintains a wall of force to keep our enemies from pressing in on all sides and crushing us to a tiny vanishing pinprick in the center.'

'Enemies?' Irissa said doubtfully. 'Even in Rule, our enemies were more humankind's indifference or ignorance than specific persons. Do we have enemies in Edanvant, Finorian?'

The old woman waited, her silver-white eyes blank, her lips folded. 'Perhaps. Perhaps we have enemies beyond Edanvant,' she admitted softly.

'Then is it worth—' Irissa gestured to the interlocked women, 'worth keeping?'

'It is ours!'

Irissa thought about it. 'We Torlocs seem unadept at keeping what is ours. From my earliest memories, I knew the Shrinking Forest was living up to its name, lessening with every falling leaf. Is it enemies who diminish us — or ourselves? Even you seem unwilling to name our bane. Perhaps we should lay no claims . . .'

' ''Perhaps'' is not a word for a seeress. Your travels have made you indifferent to your kind.'

'Were I indifferent, I would not be here,' Irissa said quietly.

Finorian stood silent while Irissa paced the Circle's outer perimeter. The women of the Circle were concentrating so deeply that they ignored her footsteps. In the empty ground at their centre, fashioned of inlaid stones, was a malachite eye within a pentagram within a six-pointed star, obviously the focus for the Circle's power.

'Tell me how it works.' Irissa's tone poised precariously between request and command.

Finorian's lips worked, then she began rattling off an emotionless explanation.

'It works by simple strength of numbers. The Eye of Edanvant can show us what transpires at a distance if something Torloc resides there. The Circle draws forth that vision and sends forth other powers. Most Torlocs, even the men, have dormant powers that can be drawn upon by a true Torloc of power. Melyconial there — look up, woman—!'

A dark head raised to shock Irissa with the sight of off-coloured eyes. One studied Irissa with amber honesty, the other, silver as a seeress's, veered in another, evasive direction. Irissa began to comprehend the fear and hatred her argent-eyed face had stirred in the people of Rule.

The woman's facial anomaly seemed to well please Finorian.

'She is changeling-born,' the Eldress went on. 'Within the womb her budding powers were choked off by some change in the life of she who bore her. It is impossible to know what. But now Melyconial anchors the Damen Circle and provides a slim thread of power that, when linked with others' untapped magic, permits me to hold back the enemies of Edanvant, or to reach a derelict Torloc in another world, or even to summon a Guardian.'

'Felabba.' Irissa frowned. 'Why do you want her?'

Finorian bent her frost-whitened head to the Eye. The green iris faded and grew translucent. The natural bands of light and dark green in the stone became the foliage of a wood. Something stirred within the empty forest. Something wove around stalk and trunk and branch, a great thick rope of multicolored smoke. What it touched, it choked.

Leaves dropped ashen to the forest floor. Twigs snuffed out

83

of existence; branches broke into powder, striplings snapped and huge trunks shriveled to charred faggots.

'That is a small sending our enemies have loosed within the wood,' Finorian said. 'Oh, it slithers at the limits of our land, but there is always a chance that someone will loose more like it — or something worse.'

'But what can Felabba do here that you or I cannot? She is a thing of Rule—'

'She is a thing of more than you perceive,' Finorian corrected sharply, 'and she can do much if she will. But what she is remains my business — and hers. It may be that these powers we fight cut too close to our own and we need a magical ally. Enough of questions. Will you help us? Will you lend your powers to our Circle so that I may reach back to Rule and awake Felabba?'

It seemed a simple enough request, and Irissa felt a sudden secret longing to see the cat again. She edged nearer the women. 'What do I do?'

'Break into the Circle; touch hands with two and slip between them.'

Irissa bent to place her hands over a clasping pair. It was as if she had touched the mind of a falcon or some other huge, mythically primitive beast. Power surged through her, barely sentient. It pulled her down to sit between the other Torlocs — legs crossed, hands linked to theirs. It welded her to the Circle. She looked up at Finorian and knew that only when the Eldress released her, could she break free.

That return to Finorian's control seemed oddly unimportant now. All Irissa could consider was the enduring elder spirit of her kind, which she sensed as some dark bottomless well unsilvered with present power. She and her enhanced powers were merely the bright, passing glance of sunlight on its surface. And Finorian, Finorian was the light-riding reflection of an unseen figure above, leaning down to draw water from the well.

The Circle became a mental path. Irissa's eyes turned inward. Her mind chased itself through unfelt reaches until it found the voice of Finorian.

'Felabba, who is Guardian, return. Return to Edanvant, from which you sprang. Overleap many worlds and endless time; eschew gates and the notice of Those Without. Come to us. We call you.'

The Damen Circle imprinted its outer semblance on the inside of Irissa's eyes, so she saw a slow, silent spinning of Torloc faces before her — the faces of anonymous Torloc dames, both met and unmet; the face of unhappy Melyconial with its eyes at odds; the ice-carven face of Delevant the fallen, and the visages of many Torlocs of power — dead, gone, or simply forgotten, which was all much the same.

Her own face flitted past, white with seriousness. She felt banded by an inner circlet whose power she had never discerned before. Into that circumscribed new inner world sprang something from a previous world — a lean, sharp, white slip of memory made incarnate.

'Felabba,' Irissa whispered in tribute.

'Felabba,' the word came back.

The memory turned on them all with burning eyes of feline green. 'No,' it said.

Finorian was suddenly there, in the forefront of Irissa's mind, prodding, urging, railing.

'Yes! Our need is great. We know not what they might do!'

The figure of the cat, the memory of the cat, leaped lightly from mind to mind, until it made a complete circle. Irissa could feel shock tighten the hands linked with hers as each mind sank momentarily under the slight but ancient weight of an undeniably feline form, however metaphorical.

It ended in the center of the Circle, a curl of lean mist wreathing Finorian's ankle.

'Come to me!' the Eldress demanded in a tone even Irissa would have hesitated to challenge.

'No.' The answer sped around the Circle. Stiff lips, long silent, cracked to mouth it in a voiceless echo. 'No.'

'You have no right—' Finorian argued.

'Neither have you,' came the answer, more felt than heard. 'Worse, you have no wrong to right.'

A chill swept the Damen Circle. Irissa felt icy beads pearling at her temples. A presence, white and inviolate, bounded from their conjoined minds.

Irissa's hands, suddenly free, touched her forehead. A harvest of tiny coldstones fell from her brow to her palms, as if a jeweled headband had broken. She stared at the glittering handful, then looked to Finorian, who hunched like a tree stump in the open space. Irissa cast the coldstones dice-like onto the damp floor, where they shone starrily in the semidarkness.

'Finorian, I am not sure I can lend my powers to you if Felabba cannot. If you need me no more—'

'Need?' Finorian's silver eyes bent inward. 'Take your needs above, where they can be more simply met. She would not come, It is not a harmonious sign.' Her hand waved indifferently, dismissing Irissa, dismissing the Circle, dismissing more than anyone could apprehend.

The Circle filed away together, stiff and tired, down the long ill-lit passage, trailing the faint pulse of Irissa's emerald hiltstone. Finorian remained behind.

At the entrance to the great hall, Irissa caught Melyconial's wrist as she went by.

Questions flared in the mismatched eyes, but the woman said nothing, lingering with Irissa in the shadowy passageway until the others had moved on.

'Why?' Irissa demanded. 'Why the Damen Circle?'

Melyconial's eyes shifted, separately it seemed. 'Custom.' Both spoke in whispers, with metaphorical glances over their shoulders.

'Custom has reason,' Melyconial added. 'Despite all Finorian's promises and all our meek conformity to her wishes, we have arrived at Edanvant with no more than we had before. There is nothing here for us. If we cannot find our kind, at least we could settle in some more welcoming world where we could mingle with humankind.

'But perhaps some among us *can* find our kind . . . and do not wish to.'

'Who?' Such heresy shocked Irissa.

'I have some scrap of sight,' Melyconial conceded. 'I have

. . . in the Damen Circle . . . seen more than Finorian might suspect. We are not as lost as she would have us think. When we first arrived, at dusk, we saw a city with common folk in it. The others have forgotten that glimpse, but Edanvant is not as empty as Finorian tells us.'

'What do you mean?'

'See for yourself, seeress,' the woman mocked. 'Your silver eyes are to be the salvation of us all, as Finorian would have it. ''When Irissa comes . . .'' she'd say, and say and say, until we all sickened of it!'

'What did she want of me?' Irissa asked in bewilderment.

There was no answer in Melyconial's embittered eyes.

'What does she want of *you*, of the Damen Circle?' Irissa asked on. 'Why did she summon Felabba? And why did Felabba not come?'

Melyconial shrugged. 'You are the seeress.'

'Are you not . . . disappointed that we have not found the Torloc men?'

'The men have escaped!' Melyconial seethed. 'Escaped our inbred powers, which decay; escaped the weariness of cleaving to a way that works no longer. Be glad you have not found them, Irissa of the Green Veil! One service at least Finorian performs for us that is better than magic — she keeps us to ourselves, for that is all we women are fit for after long years of having nothing to do but wait—'

'She keeps us from the men—? Why?'

'Use your eyes,' Melyconial intoned stolidly. 'You have the vision for it.'

'This is more like it.' Kendric, seated with his broad back to the table, nodded approval that evening while he surveyed the lamplit great hall, which was filled with a full complement of Torloc women busy with a range of domestic tasks.

Squat Dame Agneda spun spider-fast by the fireplace, an activity that promised new clothes for Irissa, who had spent half the day convincing the dubious old woman that trousers and tunic — not a flimsy gauzelin gown — best met her present needs.

87

Jalonia still commanded the large trestle table, reading now in some gilt-edge tome. Odd-eyed Melyconial passed among them with a tray, distributing coldstone goblets filled with a fiery wine the women called Spicemullen. Finorian had not yet returned from the place of the Circle.

'What did you discover in the woods without?' Irissa asked.

Kendric's eyes clung to Jalonia, although he answered Irissa. 'Only what we saw before — flowers, trees, and little else. I did see signs of the passage of a large beast — perhaps the one-horned wild bearing-beast. But it could have been the Rynx. Otherwise, you Torlocs apparently have the place to yourselves.'

'Yet we have "enemies",' Irissa mused. 'An interesting paradox.'

'Enemies!' Kendric mocked, leaning his elbows on the table behind him. 'So you say Finorian says, and you know how I heed the sayings of Finorian.'

'She is said to be our wisest woman.'

'And yet she cannot so much as call a cat,' he scoffed, for Irissa had recounted the morning's events on his return. 'Even I could do that.' Kendric's fingers snapped. 'Here, kitty, kitty . . .'

Something stirred the hall, a breath of wind or a certain breathlessness among the women in it. Torchlight flickered low, the deep emerald flames dampening to a light, poisonous green emanation.

'Hush; it is ill to jest about such matters,' Irissa cautioned. 'I felt the prowl of something through my mind during the Circle calling, even if Felabba would not come.'

'What does that wily old woman want with so irritating a feline, anyway? Well left behind in Rule, if you ask me, with her unasked-for advice and my original sword.'

'I don't know.' Irissa stared across the hall, her eyes netted by a bright-threaded tapestry on the opposite wall. Night had darkened the windows high above, but the jewel-toned weaving shed its own luminescence.

'Perhaps *that* was the beast you saw,' she added. 'In the tapestry.'

They stared upward, jointly recognizing the gilt-and-silver-embroidered creature around which all the other beasts cavorted.

'The bearing-beast that wouldn't bear,' Irissa noted.

Kendric nodded glumly. On either side of the creature, which was portrayed in midprance, a man and woman stood in garments stiff with decoration. Around the trio grew a silken forest whose leaves amost seemed to tremble in the emerald-green torchlight. Amidst that silkwork forestation dozens of animal faces peered out, bees and butterflies flitted, birds perched, treemonks scaled, insects crawled and snakes slithered.

'The thing's a woven bestiary,' Kendric remarked, 'and most of the creatures caught in it are far more succulent than the leaf-filled bread Dame Agneda prepared for my explorations this morning.'

'Why did you leave without me?' Irissa finally plucked the thorn of his disappearance, which had nettled her since rising.

Kendric shrugged evasively. 'You slept, and I did not.'

'You wanted to see Edanvant through your eyes alone,' Irissa said perceptively. 'You do not accept this place on face value.'

Caught out, he became blunt. 'No. Do you?'

'Yet you feel less threatened here than anywhere else we have been. Why else would you leave behind your sword?'

'Oh, yes . . . safe.' Kendric sighed gustily. 'A most unpleasant feeling, safety. I feel more secure with insecurity. I had my long-bladed dagger, so I left the sword; it seemed, for the first time in my life, redundant. Often when it rode my shoulders raw I ached to be rid of it. Now I find such freedom chafes me as well. Your Torloc world is too safe, Irissa. And too empty. Where have the beasts that inspired that long-ago tapestry gone?'

'Perhaps our enemies — the ones Finorian fears — have taken them.'

He considered that soberly. 'Then perhaps I would like to meet your enemies.'

Irissa smiled without answering, rising to borrow one of

Dame Agneda's long, silverlike needles, said to have been carved from the hollow wingbones of a dwarf falcon nestling. However obtained, its sharp white tip sewed swiftly through the tough falconskin fragment from which Irissa fashioned a draw-necked pouch.

'Another thing more trouble than it's worth, like certain cats,' Kendric grumbled as Irissa returned to slip the Overstone egg into its new, neck-hung sling. It plummeted the full length of cord to nestle hidden in the valley of her breasts, hidden deep within her tunic — but not before all eyes in the hall had glimpsed the milky flash of its smooth surface.

'I thought Torloc seeresses scorned magical talismans?' Jalonia had risen, drawn by a glimpse of the alien object.

'But not magical beasts,' Kendric put in. 'First there was Felabba, the loquacious feline from Rule. Now, I've encountered a one-horned bearing-beast in your deserted forest, and it evaded my capture as if slicker than the thread that embroiders it into yon tapestry.'

Jalonia stared over her shoulder at the wall, the ring of one fore-braid shadowing her pale cheek.

'We reclaimed that ancient tapestry with the keep, Kendric. We ourslves have never seen such a beast in the scant two years we have been here. Perhaps it is woven from mere fancy.'

'Mere fancy does not throw me,' he answered sardonically. 'So Irissa and I alone have been blessed with a vision of this beast? Surely, it can't have posed for your ancient embroideries. There must be many such. No beast evolves from one alone.'

'We've never seen it or its like,' Jalonia insisted. 'The forest is empty of all but earth-sprouted life. Perhaps you saw an emanation from Irissa's magical talisman . . .'

'It may not be magical,' Irissa objected.

Jalonia grew silent, head bowed, eyes downcast. Then she looked up, warning in her eyes. 'Your father left on a quest for a talisman, a distant, secret thing that promised power. If he found it, it had no power to return him.'

Irissa and Kendric stared at her, frozen by her words, by her sorrow-haunted presence, for different reasons.

'The past, Jalonia?' Finorian's words came breathlessly, as if she had arrived just in time and must trip over herself verbally to do so. She rustled into their midst, emanating a chill in the very breeze riffling from her flowing robes.

'There is no profit in the past. Why mourn the absence of he who abandoned you, as all of his sex have abandoned all of us? Men consider only themselves, not the future we women have always borne. And our future here is worrisome unless I can summon help. Your daughter's stubborn will compromises her powers. Join the Circle below; our defenses wither.'

Jalonia, her eyes ripe with mute reservations, melted wordlessly away with the other women. Finorian regarded Irissa and Kendric for a long moment, then whirled from the room again.

'Circle?' Kendric asked alertly.

'That is how Finorian concentrates her power, how she tried to call Felabba today,' Irissa explained. 'She draws on the presence of a score of Torlocs. She had hoped I would make that unnecessary, but I am not ready to exercise my powers against enemies I have never seen.' She rose wearily and moved to the stairs leading to the upper chambers.

'Interesting,' Kendric granted, following her up the white stone steps. Now that the hall had emptied, it had lost its allure. 'Finorian must be concentrating much power if she keeps this Circle working day and night. She won't say what enemies threaten us here?'

Irissa shook her head, waiting until their chamber door had closed behind them before answering.

'If you found no outer enemies in your explorations today, Kendric, I found none here. And no . . . friends, either, except for my mother. It is strange how they keep to themselves, how diminished I find them. I do not remember feeling so . . . apart from my kind before.'

'I'll tell you what is strange.' Kendric had gone to the window where the coldstone shutters still welcomed the evening with wide open wings. Stars gleamed through the treetops

91

and through the gauzy multicolored shawl of rainbow arching the dim sky.

'What is strange?'

He turned, the night's faint luminescence casting his figure into undifferentiated shadow.

'You, Irissa. You come into this place without question, without even noticing . . .'

'What is there to notice?'

'Your mother, for one. Jalonia.' He spoke the name reluctantly, as if fearing what it invoked.

'She is the most effacing of creatures, is that what you mean? That I am not like her?'

An impatient sound broke from his unseen lips and exploded on the empty stones between them.

'You *are* like her — that is what seems so strange. Exactly like her! Irissa, you and she could be sisters, twins of the same womb! There is no . . . age . . . between you.'

'She is my mother. That is not a lie, I feel it is true—'

'Then Jalonia is a lie. Have you not seen? Have you not seen that you, she . . .'

Lost for words, he stepped closer, perhaps hoping to find them. In the greenish light of their chamber's single torch, his worry-drawn face startled Irissa.

'She has always looked like that,' she tried to explain. 'I *think*,' Irissa amended conscientiously. 'I did not see her directly for most of my life.'

Kendric's eyes shut momentarily. His fist thrust into the boarskin purse at his belt.

'You, whose whole power is built on seeing inner realities, and I cannot make you face this small outer one that looms so large. See, Irissa, I will make a mirror for you; then look into it.'

'A mirror?' The word paralyzed her. She knew that seeing her own image could no longer threaten her. Still, the ghost of herself from the black tower haunted the back of her mind.

Kendric had drawn something from his purse that shimmered like a small silver fish. The Quickstone. It was his own personal talisman, the only remnant of Irissa he had found after they'd been separated in the first gate. Once a coldstone tear shed in joy, in Kendric's possession it had transfigured itself to a cabochon of reflective silver.

Now it sparkled tiny between his fingertips as he pressed it unthinking to the wall, as his hand sketched a narrow oval in the air. Where his hand moved, the Quickstone flowed, spreading thin as silver leaf, washing the wall with a swath of pure radiant argent.

'Look at yourself, Irissa; see that self as it stands.'

She hesitated. 'I don't need to look,' she finally demurred. 'It is too bright; perhaps it will harm me more than Geronfrey's Dark Mirror—'

'It will harm you more to evade it.' Kendric thrust her between himself and the mirror he had made, as if using her as a human shield. His hands on her shoulders forced her to confront herself.

'Exactly alike, Irissa,' he whispered, worry and wonder mixing as uneasily as oil and water in his voice. 'Jalonia looks not a moment older than you. She's alike to the tips of her hair and her fingers . . . except for the eyes.' His voice dulled. 'She is not burdened by the seeress's silver.'

A silver seeress stood in the mirror, silken gray clothing shimmering like molten metal, hair more pewter than black under the Iridesium band restraining it, eyes double-silvered and fresh-minted. Yet beyond the enhanced silver image stood the truth of Kendric's words — a young Torloc woman who could have as easily been Jalonia as her daughter, Irissa.

She saw it finally, she who had been forbidden her own reflection for most of her life and thus took others on surface value. She was the very image of Jalonia. That realization required a tremendous mental leap sideways. Irissa knew her mother's semblance, knew the look her mind conjured when she thought of Jalonia. Now that separate expectation lurched toward her own self, its very unselfness pressing against her body, smoothing some vague image of utter individuality Irissa had always treasured of herself. She felt as if her

93

identity had been wrenched inside out. Staring at herself in another's guise, Irissa felt the added weight of Kendric's heartfelt revulsion at what she was.

'You do not know yourself, your outer aspect,' the wise old cat, Felabba, had said in Rule once. And had been right. Now Kendric questioned that aspect, and thus questioned all that had happened between them, even their union.

'What manner of thing are you, you Torlocs?' His emotion-laden voice sank low under its burden. 'I come to your home of homes — to meet yourself in your mother. Where are the gray hairs among you, save Finorian's? The wrinkles, the caring? Where is respect for one's elders when all generations merge into an eternity of ever-youthful faces? You are sorcerer-folk, Irissa, all you Torlocs. You can evade the scourge of sun and wind and the turns of time itself.'

'She is my mother! I *should* resemble her,' Irissa exploded defensively, even as she glimpsed the terrible wrongness Kendric found in the fact.

Kendric's eyes, so like Jalonia's in their brown-gold honesty, met Irissa's in the Quickstone's sleek surface.

'Resemble, perhaps. Mirror, no. And not forever,' he added wearily, stretching his palm out to the mirror. It flowed from the wall like a samite train, dwindling into a tiny teardrop congealed in the cup of his hand; Irissa was left staring at blank white stones.

Kendric's hand, weighted by the ring their passage through another world and gate had forged, left her shoulder.

Bewildered, Irissa continued to confront the spitting image of herself. The ageless face reflected in the mirror of her mind offered no answer. Only time and much thought could reconcile the eerie sameness that had screamed for Kendric's attention and had completely eluded Irissa's since she had reunited with the women.

'I'm going to study these woods by moonlight,' he said gruffly. 'Perhaps some native night creature comes to them, after all.' He paused by the door. 'Perhaps there is something natural in Edanvant. If I could find one natural thing . . .'

He was gone, leaving the room still lit, with its unnatural accoutrements gleaming in the torchlight, with his mind-made sword shining ice-dagger clear in the moonlight, with a Torloc seeress standing as blindly as her kind in the center of it, staring deeply at nothing.

CHAPTER SIX

The night woods hung like a black-green mantle over Kendric, rustling as he passed. It seemed ready to drop upon his shoulders, only restrained from engulfing him by a patient, invisible hand. Moonlight tipped the leaves silver-gold and seeped through the sieve of blurred rainbow bands streaking the nocturnal sky.

Moonlight and rainbows might seduce another; this night they repelled him, tainted by a kinship to things Torloc. Rule and its inhabitants, he remembered, had cherished no doubts about Torlocs. He laughed harshly, aloud, to think that he had thought to shed the prejudices of his people and his place so easily.

Knowing one Torloc well, he had forgotten what all Torlocs represented — unnatural power, unnaturally extended life spans, cryptic ways paved with the stepping stones of fearsome magic.

He walked briskly, relieved of the daily burden of his heavy sword, certain that the landscape was safe enough to justify carrying only a long-bladed dagger. This new sense of security unnerved him; it gave him no means of exercising his instincts, even his reluctantly acquired magical one.

And Kendric needed instincts now, when reason recoiled at what he couldn't help seeing. Irissa was . . . not as he was. She was born of long-lived stock, as he was born of a long-boned kind. She had been teethed on magic, and had — without trying — passed it to him as one would a platter at a table.

He winced to recall how lightly he had cast the Quickstone mirror upon the wall to confront Irissa with her disturbing likeness to her ageless mother. He had come a long way in

96

his use of magic, yet he knew that anyone Torloc — Irissa herself, the never-satisfied Finorian, even the satisfyingly absent cat, Felabba — would tell him that he still had farther to go than he had come.

Yes, the thought comforted. There was that. Who was to say that humankind was not unnaturally short-lived, that his kind were not revoltingly disparate from their forebears? Perhaps if he didn't know where he went, if he was uncertain why he went there, he should try harder. It was not, he reminded himself, Irissa's fault. Hers least of all, born as she was, reared as good as blind among those who depended upon her to remain true to themselves. For her sake, perhaps, he could conquer his sense of isolation and strangeness, of an unease that had nothing to do with physical courage. None of this was her fault.

His thoughts had cooled to a manageable simmer. He walked a world not his own; perhaps he should explore it before judging it. He had spent most of the day learning the limits of the forest, first swinging away from the castle and looping back again to maintain his bearings, then striking off in distant directions before turning back again. So Kendric already knew much of the wood's ups and downs and ins and outs.

He whistled moodily in the empty night, knowing no bird would yodel answer, and walked rapidly, stretching his long stride to its fullest, not stopping to question this or wonder about that. From time to time he crossed a clearing, within which rose fanciful edifices that reminded him of the single black tower. He had avoided these by day and did so doubly by night. Despite their deserted look, he had no doubt that dormant magic inhabited them still. They posed no danger in an active sense, but a wise man would do well to skirt uncertain pockets of forgotten magic, even in an apparently secure world.

It was a world that was his now, by choice, he reminded himself, however much it was not what Irissa had expected. And Torlocs themselves were not as he had expected. His own mother had died at his birth; he had never thought of her until now. Yet he knew if she were to appear before him she would

97

have aged decently, with silver threading her hair and worry treading the well-worn paths of her face.

'Mortal,' Irissa had called him from the first. And neither he nor she had needed the implicit warning in that epithet. He had dealt death in his time, and in his time would bow to it.

As for Irissa . . .? As always with Irissa, he dueled a disembodied fear as one would an invisible enemy. Someone must stand by her among these kin who were not really her kind. Kendric paused. He had walked far and should be turning back. Irissa, he knew, would fret over his prolonged absence, and had worries enough.

Ahead the woods thickened and — propelled by the same restless frustration that had driven him this far — Kendric thrust his imposing form through it, mindless of briars, unfearful of meeting any living thing that could harm him.

He met a wall. A smooth, black metallic expanse cool and contained to his touch. Kendric froze against it, stretched, let his fingertips explore outward and upward. Wall, all wall, as far as he could feel, or could see, or could sense.

A wall. He stepped back, baffled. Man-made, he would say, save that it appeared to be seamless. Then magic-made? And, if so, by whom? Man or magic, Finorian had never mentioned that either waited at the boundaries of Edanvant.

Kendric laughed, untroubled that any should hear him. It seemed a most effective wall, high and curving outward to discourage scaling. Daylight would tell how high, and how curved. He reached his hand to it, stroked the cold metal as he would a favorite mount's belly. He could almost feel the surface swelling and sinking slightly, like a bearing-beast's sides.

A wall. It smacked of danger. And deceit. Now *that* he could deal with! It whispered of places beyond here and people unknown in those places. It promised the end of paradise and the beginning of something much more interesting.

Kendric laughed again and slapped the wall temporary farewell, turning to retrace his steps through miles of beneficent wood. The world around him remained empty of any sound but the crashing of his boots and the persistent, cheery off-key hum that accompanied him all the long way back to Irissa.

Dawn flourished her gauzy raiment, arched her back into a rainbow, and relaxed into a warm blue glow.

Crashing through the woods with real weariness now, Kendric found himself nearing the Torloc stronghold at first light, his stomach waxing eloquent at the idea of another leafy repast. 'Greenery,' he growled to no one in particular, and smote some tender beech shoots out of his path.

Then he stopped and narrowed his eyes. He had breached his way into another clearing; a rough-shouldered hump of fallen stones anchored this one — saw-toothed remnant of one of the bizarre edifices that customarily played centerpiece of any bit of open ground.

These stones held none of the mystique, fell or benign, that swathed unfallen towers. The upcropping was simply a gray pile, perhaps two Wrathmen high, a jagged, unclimbable miniature mountain. Kendric could not quite see its summit, but he could certainly see what perched alertly — sat — atop the inhospitable stones.

'What are you doing there?' he asked, never being one to leave an interesting stone unturned.

'I don't know.' She — there was no doubt about that, though Kendric doubted many things at the moment, including the veracity of his eyesight — lifted an arm draped with a sweep of fur-edged sleeve as if to examine it, herself, her surroundings. 'I don't know. Is it morning?'

'The very crack of it,' Kendric confirmed, coming closer. 'How did you get up there?' He eyed a foot daintily clad in a pristine ermine slipper.

She sat above the level of his head, perhaps eight feet off the ground, and seemed to relish her superior position. His quick eyes had discerned no telltale disturbance in her lavish gown to explain her ascendance of such a rough seat.

Fur a foot wide bordered her skirt hem, which heaved gently in the breeze as if its albino bearer still lived and, sleeping, merely curled around her feet. She was dressed all

99

in white — no, she *was* all white, from her long silvery hair to her parchment skin to the pewter-set opals that ringed her neck. Only her eyes were not white, but broad gilt aureoles surrounding a tiny black pupil; true gold — not yellow or amber. They glinted as magically and metallically gold as Irissa's eyes shone true silver.

'You are not Torloc,' he half accused her.

'Oh, no.' She laughed agreeably, the low rumble of it replicating the purr of a very satisfied cat, a sound he had never thought he missed until now.

He joined her in laughing, snared by an earthy, inexplicable delight. Her presence rang brooklike in the morning, animated the inanimate woods. If she was magical, and he could not doubt it, she was benign magic incarnate.

'Do you — do you . . . want to come down?' he asked.

She thought, tilting her head and regarding him unblinkingly. 'Perhaps I should.'

He reached up as her arms reached down, the magnitude of her trailing sleeves pelting over him like heavy snow. She was not real; she would melt from his grasp or turn into a cloud, he predicted to himself, always the safest recipient of bold prophecies.

Yes she seemed a harmless illusion. Kendric enjoyed at last sharing this lifeless woodland with something sentient, even if it was only and obviously a spirit.

Yards of fur-trimmed cool silk brushed by him, rustling as it settled. She stood beside him, her raiment curling into elegantly devised folds, the sharp passing impress of long, strong fingernails withdrawing from his shoulders.

'You're still here,' Kendric marveled.

She sighed. 'Yes. It is a pretty place. But lonely.'

'You say the word as if you know it well.'

Her eyes burned molten gold in the pale crucible of her face. Even in deep shade, an airy whiteness clung to her. Kendric thought of frost etched in a thousand furred strokes on a winter windowpane.

'Lonely.' She said the word as a ruler would pronounce a death sentence on a subject. 'Ah, my friend, I am as lonely as a wailwraith.'

Fear's first feathery tap on the shoulder iced Kendric's good cheer.

'That is a legend from my old world of Rule,' he said sharply. 'This is another, a new one. There are no wailwraiths here, and you said you were not Torloc.'

Her face tilted again, regarding him with a bright, calm gaze. 'There are wailwraiths everywhere, and loneliness haunts even more places than that.'

'Who are you?'

'I cannot tell you.'

'Why not?'

'I do not know.'

Her utter simplicity began to weigh upon him. 'Why are you here?' he demanded.

'Because . . .' Her face grew so sad that he began to believe in her again. 'Because there is nowhere else that I can be.'

'But if you could—?'

'Rengarth,' she said, looking surprised at the way the word had leapt into her mouth, as if her tongue was intent on hurling itself toward some swallowing self-destructive pit. 'Rengarth.'

Her own surprise dismissed her.

'Thank you for your aid. I bid you farewell and good day.'

Before his slightest word of gesture could prevent it, she turned and melted into the early morning dapple of green and gold, passing through it as unaffected as a ghost, becoming a fading white figure under the thickening trees.

Kendric's shock shackled him to the spot, uncertain if he was dreaming. He moved to follow her, then glanced to the rocks. He would hate to scale so jagged a prominence, even gloved in falgonskin. He had heard a word once to describe such an apparition, he decided. Figment — a plain word that suited him more than it fit her. Having named her, he could leave her in good conscience.

Whistling cheerily, he resumed his early morning march through the — almost — untenanted woods.

'Where have you been?' Irissa asked too casually when Kendric returned to their coldstone-windowed chamber just as the palest citrine wine of morning's first vintage poured through the bubbled crystal panes.

Her face seemed as milk-pale as the woman of the woods' visage had been, and concealed worry had dulled the dark luster of her hair.

'Rengarth . . .' Kendric intoned abstractedly. 'Rengarth. It rings a bell within the thick steeple of my skull. I don't know why.'

'Rengarth?'

At their chamber window he studied the scene outside. 'Is the name familiar to you, too?'

'Yes, I heard of it somewhere. We've heard of many places in our travels, but that doesn't explain where you've been all night.'

He turned, grinning, his confident self again. Irissa sighed deep relief. She had not been certain that the Kendric she knew would — return, that Kendric would return at all.

'I've been to the edges of paradise and found a wall I would scale,' he announced with zest. 'I've been to the foot of a rock pile and met a maiden all in white.' His expression darkened. 'I've been through the great hall of a place you Torlocs call a keep, and saw another tableful of raw foliage in the preparation—'

Irissa expertly plucked the object of her greatest curiosity from the tangled threads of his answer. 'Tell me about the white maiden.'

'She spoke of loneliness — and Rengarth. Was she an enchantress, do you think?'

'All in white, like Finorian?'

'In white like Finorian, yes. Like Finorian . . . no. She was fair to the point of seeming bleached, swathed in silvery furs, and had eyes of gold . . .'

'Young and fair . . .' Irissa mused.

'I did not say young.'

'You didn't have to.' Irissa finally joined him at the window.

'When I found her she was sitting atop some fallen stones she could not have possibly climbed, and said she was as lonely as a wailwraith.'

'Hmm. Did she say lonely for what?'

He laughed. 'Not *that* kind of enchantress, Irissa. She seemed . . . lost, mislaid; she didn't even know her name. And then — *poof*, she was gone, off into the woods. Perhaps I dreamed her.'

Irissa's tone grew suddenly serious. 'Perhaps you saw a wailwraith. They lived in weepwater tree roots in Rule.'

'She was as dry as you or I, and spoke, not wailed.' He turned from the window so Irissa could see the seriousness in his face. 'She reminded me that there are many unexplained differences in this world — or Rule or any other.' His expression softened with his voice. 'Perhaps that means I should allow for unexplainable similarities as well.'

Irissa's head bowed to the bright daylight, crowning her dark hair with a sun-forged ring of multicolored highlights just inside the familiar press of the circlet. Kendric laid his hands lightly on her head, warmed them at the mutual sun-glow of natural and unnatural substance.

'I have been thinking,' she said. 'I have always seen the world from inside a small, protected ring of Torlocs. I question all that is outside that circle, and nothing within it. Perhaps I look in the wrong direction for answers.'

'And I look in the wrong direction for questions. That is what you get for linking fortunes with a mortal.'

The last word fell innocently from his lips, but she looked up to verify that impression. Kendric was smiling down at her, quite undisturbed.

'Peace, Torloc,' he offered. 'I pride myself on getting along with at least one of every breed.'

'Is that all that drives you — pride?'

His eyes sobered. 'I have met a vision that reminded me that there is more loneliness in the world than antidote to it. So let us repair to Dame Agneda's flowery breakfast and exchange suspicions with Finorian, for a change, instead of with ourselves.'

Kendric had not exaggerated. They descended to the great hall to find an unscented but floral array of comestibles. Rose petals floated in a clear broth that seemed suspiciously vegetable in origin, and plump green dumplings sat Kendric's plate like paired cabbages. A salad of diced lions-mane weed stems was mixed with lavender leaves and indeterminate dew-gleamed morsels as vivid as baroque gemstones. Even the soft white cheese that slumped in a communal brown pottery bowl smelled oddly redolent of earth.

They ate together at the long trestle table — the Torloc women, their eyes veiled by custom if not cloth, keeping their gazes fixed to their plates. The two who had most recently joined them remained somehow apart, and Kendric's oversized knife and two-pronged fork clattered more than he wished.

He seemed to loom in their midst like the proverbial sore thumb — bigger than they, broader than they, more aggressive than they, a single noisome 'one' among an array of differing but staunchly united fingers.

Finorian commanded the table's farthest end, white-miened as the maiden of the wood but less ingratiating.

Kendric's fist hit the table as he stood his fork upright. A rabbitlike munching all down the long table stopped. Torloc faces froze. A puzzled Irissa, beside him, glanced his way; across the table Jalonia's mirroring face reflected a sudden interest that was all her own. Finorian did nothing.

'What sits beyond the wall?' he thundered amiably down the long greenwood expanse.

'Nothing,' Finorian began. Then she hesitated as if listening to an invisible advisor. 'Nothing of any importance,' she amended.

'Who lives beyond it, then?' he demanded.

'No one. No one you need trouble yourselves about.'

'What wall is this?' Irissa demanded, anger at her own ignorance dividing itself equally, if unfairly, between Kendric and Finorian.

'There is a wall, as I mentioned,' he explained rapidly to Irissa, speaking loudly enough for them all to hear. 'I found it last night. High — higher than the lone black tower in the woodland clearing but as ill-summoned, I think. Impervious. Impossible to scale, I would imagine.'

'You imagine right this time, Wrathman.' Hostility underlined

Finorian's words. 'How quaint, an imaginative man of Rule
. . . But all your imagination or might cannot conquer that
wall. It is maintained by the power of my Damen Circle.'

'What lies beyond it?' Irissa asked.

Finorian's white head shook. 'It matters not. What resides
there? Much that is unknown, and much that is evil, that
reaches out for us as salt water erodes the shoreline sand.'

A murmur had started among the subdued women, a
murmur of distress.

'This is Edanvant,' Irissa went on, her voice ringing louder
than even Kendric's had. 'Our home, our refuge. Yet you
reach for power and convene Damen Circle and weary us all
so in our own defense that nothing remains but a hollow safety.
You speak at enemies, yet hide behind a wall of evasions. What
have we to fear beyond the wall Kendric has found? Whom
have we to fear?'

Murmur hardened into mutter; even Melyconial Odd-eye
rolled her good orb around until it focused on Finorian with
single-minded demand.

Finorian stood, the emerald on her breast glowing bright
borgia-green. Her long, age-crooked forefinger straightened
enough to point accusingly at Kendric.

'That! That is what we wall out! The voice of dissension
and doubt. He is not one of us! He is not Torloc, nor female,
nor honestly magicked. In him fester the seeds of our
destruction. He is why Felabba failed to answer the Damen
Circle's call, why even Irissa's powers falter before the
presence of such a taint, which has accompanied her like the
reek of rotten meat . . . I was wrong to tolerate him among
us; at the first opportunity he goes sniffing for walls and the
evil beyond them—'

Kendric had stood slowly, as if to make a more obvious
target of what was unconcealable from the first — himself.
The impassive mien he had adopted at the start of Finorian's
denunciation had given way to a towering anger his full height
only accentuated.

One by one the women turned their eyes from Finorian to
Kendric. He toted up their mass defection indifferently,

noticing that across from him Jalonia's face blazed with a decidedly un-Torlockian blend of excitement and admiration.

He didn't know what Irissa's face revealed, and suspected it was little. But someone stood beside him, having risen with him.

Finorian heeded the wordless pull of all around her and stopped speaking suddenly, her finger still aimed toward him, heart-center, like an unreleased arrow. It shook, with either emotion or age, yet he credited her with the weaknesses of neither quality.

'Doubt, you say!' he answered. 'Your mouth is as blind as your overhoarded eyes.' He cast the fork to the table, where it trembled on two-tongued prongs that tasted deep of soft, green wood. 'It is not *my* doubt but yours that erects walls in a world already thick with impassable woods. It is *your* doubt that weaves human bodies and magic into circles, that hoards power and calls on distant Guardians. And your doubt that seeks to accuse itself in another's person.

'I will see that wall of yours again, Finorian, and scale it, if I can. I will see the other side of your fear, which is more than you allow yourself — or anyone else — to do. What kind of safe retreat is this vaunted Edanvant, where we must chew upon your meek grasses, as upon a cud, and you Torlocs hide half your days in musty deep-boweled chambers so that you may hide the other half of your days behind some distant wall?

'A Torloc paradise, no doubt! Well, I am not Torloc and I am not to be contained by walls, however persuasive. My magic may be second-hand and thrice-undone, but I've mind enough to know yours shrinks within as it expands without. Keep your walls and your blessed heritage. And your cursed greenery! I can promise naught but that if there's a wall I'll try to scale it.'

Finorian's arm lowered slowly to the table, where her fingernail balanced on the wood like a knifepoint. 'Go then,' she said, her voice low and calm. 'Try my wall. You were never meant to come here — or to go from Rule, for that matter.'

'I go as well,' Irissa warned.

'You have no reason to leave,' Finorian argued.

'If Kendric goes, I have no reason to stay.'

A Torloc breath drew in — one, among many Torloc dames simultaneously.

'If you go now, with him,' Finorian pronounced heavily, 'I will never allow you to return.'

'If I had not gone with him before, I never would have come here.'

'You do not need him anymore.'

'You are wrong, Finorian, more wrong than a Torloc Eldress has a right to be. Besides . . .' Irissa smiled ironically. 'Perhaps he *is* my Wrathman, as you have said yourself from the very first—'

'He is death, as all men are!' the old woman screeched.

Irissa had no answer, but as she turned from the table she saw the amber eyes of Jalonia adrift in a clear salt sea of tears.

Kendric and Irissa left the great hall together in silence, and climbed the mountain of stairs to their chamber, feeling each step as a foothill.

They said nothing as they gathered their meager belongings from once-assigned places in the room, the items already at home there as those owned them were not — and would not ever be after this.

Kendric finally threw his implement-laden baldric to the mattress, where it sank deep in the cushioning of dried grasses.

'The accommodations were crowded here, anyway,' Irissa noted from the window, where she was braiding her forelocks for the journey and watching the forest dim at the sun's last, long-distant light.

Even Kendric's stoic ears could hear the threat of tears in her tone. Guilt choked his throat; Irissa was turning her back on what she had sought so long, and he knew himself as cause. Yet she had not even stopped to question if it was necessary to leave so near to nightfall.

'Why is there a wall,' Kendric puzzled stubbornly, 'and why did Finorian not tell us of it?'

'We will have to find out.'

'Irissa . . .' His back was steel-straight when she turned

107

to view it, but oddly vulnerable without the customary slash of sword across it. 'You need not go,' he announced gruffly. 'I am the sour note in all this Torlockian harmony — the odd man out. You wanted to join your people and you have. Stay, and I will go and let you know, somehow, what sits the other side of Finorian's wall . . .' He turned then, his mind made up, his expression mastered, his voice encouragingly certain.

She was standing in the middle of the chamber, watching him with the full, uncurtained serenity of her silver eyes, direct as lightning.

He paled. 'These are your people; I cannot be responsible for rending you from them.'

'You cannot be responsible for the slightest thing I do,' she answered gently, 'except if you decide what it is I should and should not do. You have made your choice, Kendric; allow me to make mine unquestioned.'

There was nothing to say. He slung the baldric over his shoulder with a sigh, hefted the longsword from the table, and waited while Irissa took one last look around the room. Her glance seemed to bestow a silver glow around each object it touched. Kendric saw a parting fondness in the phenomenon that he could never share and jerked open the door, eager to be out.

Jalonia stood on the threshold, her hand raised to knock, her eyes not yet ready to enter. He surprised a tangle of emotions in their amber depths, not the last of which mixed pride and sorrow. She stepped suddenly near, her hand upon his sleeve, searching his face as if it should be familiar.

'I have not heard anyone apply the rough edge of his tongue to Finorian since Orvath left.' Kendric's raised brows made her voice lower further. 'Irissa's father,' she explained. 'My . . . we were bed-bonded. He left shortly after Irissa had quickened within me. My revelation was followed fast by his announcement of departure. No one ever consulted me,' she added bitterly.

Kendric made ready to say something consoling, his ears reddening at being gifted with such a sweep of unasked-for confidences.

'Still your tongue,' Jalonia ordered warmly. 'Your eyes and sword speak even better for you. I am glad to have seen you here, in these halls, even if only for a short time. I am glad—'

Kendric saw Irissa's arrival behind him reflected in the wary softening of Jalonia's eyes.

The woman smiled, and he began to wonder how he had ever thought her the twin to Irissa. She was sad beyond saving, like the white woman of the woods. And she was older than he had thought.

Jalonia licked her lips. 'Irissa . . . daughter. It was good to know you again. When your — father — left to dare some gate, before you were born—' Jalonia's warm eyes chilled and her gaze dropped. 'I never thought to accompany him,' she confessed.

'You could not,' Irissa consoled her mother, yet sounding as authoritative as Finorian. 'One cannot take another unwilling through a gate, and if I was in the womb I would serve as barrier, for I could not be queried as to my will.'

'No?' Jalonia's smile grew rueful. 'Perhaps we all under-estimated you even then. But I never saw Orvath again, and expected to never see you more, either, after you were marooned in Rule.'

Irissa felt this too-keen reminder like a knife. How forcefully she was severing herself again from the Torlocs! 'It is only a wall, not a gate, we cross,' she hollowly reassured her mother for Kendric's sake. In her heart, she knew that any Irissa who returned would be another person. This time her choice, not necessity, caused the breach, and she forsook them for the companionship of a mere mortal, and a hated man at that.

'It is the same,' Jalonia echoed sadly. 'Gone is gone. I am glad that this time, at least, I am not dissolved away in some net of Finorian's weaving without saying good-bye. I am glad, too, it is choice and not mere chance that separates us, that I now know—'

She did not finish saying what she knew, but spun away and slipped into the embrace of the hall's shadowy arms.

Kendric turned to shut the door behind them. Irissa stood

109

against its already closed surface, her finger at the foot of a meandering tear track down her cheek. She touched her wet fingertip to her tongue, then glanced at him in surprise.

'A coldstone forms . . . so slowly, but—' Her tongue darted to her fingertip again. 'It's sweet, not salt-sodden.'

His tracing thumb swiftly dried her cheek.

'An omen then, for scaling walls and bidding Torloc paradise farewell,' he said with searching eyes, as honeyed as her single tear. 'Sweet sadness. Sweet farewell. I've had enough salt from Finorian, and all of it rubbed the wrong way, to last me a lifetime.'

Irissa smiled as Kendric wrested the green-flamed torch from its wall socket. Together they moved into the shadows of the long, dark hall.

CHAPTER SEVEN

'How will we climb a wall as smooth and high as you say?'

'You will have to scale me like a treemonk and then scale the wall.'

'How can you jest? We have no food unless it grows along our path, nothing to carry us but our feet, no sense of direction but our curiosity.'

'Perhaps the dazzling bearing-beast will appear again. I can tame it, then we'll mount it and overleap the wall in one bound.'

'Finorian is right in one thing,' Irissa complained, stopping to lean against a tree trunk and shake her foot until a sole-trying pebble dislodged itself. 'Your imagination has overgrown your height.'

'My imagination or my magic?' The smile in Kendric's voice widened to reach and find dawning reflection in Irissa's face. 'You forget that, mighty Torloc seeress. We both have magic; why worry about ordinary problems?'

'The wall is magic, and well-cast magic, too. Apparently no one has broached it − except possibly the Rynx, whose very form is magical, or the white woman you met in the wood, and she may be a phantom. We are mere flesh and blood, yet choose to hurl ourselves against the iron will of Finorian, buttressed by the invisible steel of a Damen Circle.'

'But Finorian needed you to complete the Circle, which proves she has little trust in her own powers − at least against whatever lies beyond this wall.'

'It was Felabba she really wanted,' Irissa reminded him. 'I have a feeling Finorian had tried − and failed − before, to tempt Felabba here. I wonder why? Felabba displayed little

111

inclination to use whatever magic she possessed, though she was a — dear — companion.'

'Felabba, in person again. What a near thing.' Kendric shuddered for effect in the forest's lukewarm darkness. 'Absence makes your memory grow fonder. Just imagine that thorny-footed feline mincing after our every step, calling out unwanted advice, warning us that failure makes a fourth in our party . . .'

'You sound as if you miss her.'

'I? Rule forbid! I'd as soon languish for the Tolechian Plague.' Kendric forged through a thicket of chest-high seedlings. 'The only quality that makes this place paradise to me is the absence of conversant animals. Other than the Rynx.'

Irissa stopped in her path behind him just in time for a recoiling fan of greenery to whip her lightly across the face, which she took as admonition for leaving all she knew behind for a plunge into the unknown that called Kendric. The night was young but darker than its years.

'The Rynx!' Irissa gasped in guilty regret. 'Kendric, we can't simply move on and leave the Rynx behind!'

'Why not? 'Tis an independent creature, no more anxious to link fates with us than we with it.'

'But the Rynx came to Edanvant on our invitation; we have a responsibility—'

He caught hold of her arm without warning, so she wobbled momentarily off balance.

'I know what forces pull you back, even as we forge forward. Irissa, we are all responsible only for ourselves, or so a certain Torloc seeress insisted not hours ago,' he pointed out. 'Qualms will never help us overleap a wall, or our own nicety.'

'You're right, of course.'

Kendric's grip relaxed. 'You agree with me?' he inquired dubiously.

'Of course. Only—'

'Aha!'

'Only . . . I saw something, behind you, through the other side of the clearing. Something as pallid as moonlight.'

He whirled, all his instincts quickening. 'The bearing-beast!

The sweet, wily grass-eater come to munch itself right into our hands . . . Quick as you can be quiet, let's steal upon the creature—!'

Irissa knew better than to quarrel with a huntsman gripped by quarry. She grasped Kendric's tunic in the almost-dark of the shaded thicket and followed its unflagging tug. They emerged into a moon-rinsed clearing where even the grasses had been worn low and ripples of velvety blue-green moss upholstered the ground.

Jewel-colored mushrooms sprouted atop the moss like uncut rubies and sapphires lolling on a jeweler's prize display cloth. In the clearing's center stood a tall, many-limbed tree, an empress among trees, its age-gnarled roots encrusted with the careless, gilt glitter of fallen leaves.

Neither could see the tree's top, but then their eyes never tried to. Their gazes fixed instead on the figure of a man perched on the first of many great limbs fanning from the tree's hoary central trunk.

The gems studding his pale leather boots twinkled as he swung his feet. Scallops ate into the long ends of his sleeves, which fluttered in the wind like a confederation of albino leaves, for he was white-garbed from tow-head to blanched boot-toe. He also sat in danger of altering his harmonious lack of color, for he was happily biting into a bright violet toadstool of awesome size culled from a supply upon his lap.

'Wait!'

He stopped midbite at Irissa's shouted alarm.

'That might be poisonous,' she warned.

In the moonlight Kendric's face looked greenly sick. 'Now I know what Dame Agneda has been mincing into her leafy dishes for color all these days.'

The man sighed and shook his head, the hair of it so bright white a blond it resisted moonsilvering, as his pale tights and tunic did not. He shone like some night-escaped sun spirit.

'Poison!' He ruefully contemplated the mushroom's domed skull. 'No such salvation for me. I come from a breed that sniffs poison with every sense. Believe me, Torloc lady,

113

nothing lethal grows in Edanvant. It must be distilled to destroy.' His silver-white teeth decapitated a mushroom head plump as an Outer Abyssal pear. Rivulets of crimson juice meandered down his unbearded chin. 'They knew how to cultivate mushrooms, the ancient Torlocs. Try some yourselves.'

Kendric, horrified, glanced to his feet, where gaudy rings of obscenely oversized toadstools squatted in clusters.

'You mean someone *cultivated* this unnatural garden of horrors?'

They gasped in unison as the man bounded to the ground, landing lightly as a moth, his smartly tattered garments rustling around his form as he sat again with a great sigh of settling fabric.

'Nothing is unnatural to a Torloc,' he reassured them, selecting mushrooms as he spoke, 'except nature as it is found raw. These have gone wild, but were once tame. Here, young seeress, sample this fine Borgia-blood Egg — the flavor is truly delicate, so mild . . .'

Irissa was hungry enough to reach for the glistening mushroom that gleamed more deeply green than a spider's eye in firelight.

'Borgia wine can be fatal,' Kendric warned, staying her hand.

'Not if it's brewed properly,' the young man countered.

'You know much of Torlocs and of borgia,' Kendric said suspiciously.

The man's icy gray eyes twinkled like winter stars. 'I traveled much in my youth and saw even the borgia breweries of Rule when Torlocs were unrivaled there.'

'Rule!' They spoke together, Irissa and Kendric, and for once with equal skepticism.

'Torlocs hold no sway in Rule. They have left Rule to its own divisiveness,' Irissa told him.

The man looked at the ground, at the sickle of fresh-plucked mushroom caps before him. His appetite apparently had waned. When he looked up again, Irissa saw his eyes had sobered, the black pupils growing from pinpricks to a depth of brackish wells.

'Division,' he intoned, as if that one word could be more poisonous than any gaudy assortment of mushrooms. He sighed, uncoiling agile limbs so swiftly that Kendric tautened for attack at the taffeta-rasp of his motions.

'Yes, all worlds change, time passes, and even the most refined of appetites palls.' Springing up, he glanced wistfully to the bounty at his feet.

'Take these, then, travelers, for your own journey through time. They are innocuous, I promise you, and so delicate of flavor . . .' He wiped his juice-stained chin and turned toward the farther darkness.

'Wait!' Kendric's commanding baritone halted him. 'You have not told us your name, who you are?'

The man paused reluctantly, his sleeve unfurled against a white-barked tree limb, his pale-garbed body blending with the moonlight-silvered trunk.

'I can tell you the pedigree of a mushroom, but I cannot tell you that. I do not know. I only know the moonlight gentles my eyes and that it is good to talk with strangers and eat mushrooms.'

Like a phantom, he vanished with his last words, melting into the tree or the moonlight or the farther woods, leaving a crimson palm print on the waxy bark.

Kendric blinked and consulted Irissa. 'You tell me: Is he flesh or phantasm, magical or mad, threat or cipher? Did we dream this or perceive it?'

'Does it matter?'

Kendric's shoulders shifted, as if the skin under the hang of his sword itched. 'It seems unnatural to suffer these apparitions, if such they be, to come and go unchallenged by anything other than our surprise.'

'This is Edanvant; the unnatural is as at home here as magic is natural to Torlocs,' Irissa answered calmly. 'Whatever else he is, he is right; these mushrooms are meaty but mild.' Irissa had sat to consume the Borgia-blood Egg in methodical bites.

Kendric licked his lips, then bent to gather some less flagrantly colored of the caplike fungi before setting his sword aside and sitting beside her.

'I thought at first I should grow green from Dame Agneda's provisions and require pruning; now I must fear growing gaudy!' But he began eating the palm-sized mushroom heads, eventually leaning his back against the light-barked tree. 'They make a hearty meal,' he admitted at last.

'The dun-colored variety you favor is called "Fool's Cap," I believe.' Irissa took a mottled orange and crimson toadstool gabled with as many peaks as a village mayor's house, broke it into edible portions, and chewed thoughtfully. 'He was young, our mysterious woodsman, yet spoke of traveling into Rule in his youth.'

'Doubtless he is as "young" as Finorian or Felabba, which in Torloc terms means as old as the mountains.' Kendric discarded a lemon-colored outer rind, his contented expression souring over. 'He seemed old enough to be capable of remembering his name.'

'So did your white lady of the dawn.'

'Yet, she too was exceedingly coy . . . Well, unnamed walls await and at least we have food of a sort upon our stomachs.' Kendric pulled Irissa up from the velvet-carpeted earth, which she already felt loath to leave.

He filled his various pouches with toadstools, carefully choosing the least vibrantly shaded varieties. 'Who knows when we shall see anyone, elusive or not, or real food again?' he said direly.

'Are we near the wall?' Irissa wanted to know.

'Close, as best as I can tell in a wood so wild.'

They walked slowly under trees set at staggered positions seemingly calculated to impede their progress. Brambles rose up to nip at their booted feet, then twined higher to snag their trousers and tunics, both fresh from Dame Agneda's loom, although woven in the same silken gray for Irissa and sturdy blue for Kendric as their former attire, hence feeling more like old clothing too stubborn to wear out than new. Kendric elbowed the briars aside, careless of small stings.

'The path seemed less thorny on my previous exploration,' he ventured. 'Mayhap Finorian's Damen Circle meet and sits on pins and needles now, to our discomfort.'

116

'Or Felabba has finally answered Finorian's call with some sharp reminders of her own,' Irissa added.

But the night was ebbing; daybreak trickled through the higher branches. Birds would have been calling the dawn down from its rainbowed retreat to earth, had there been any birds.

Kendric studied the flowers unfurling to cup their portion of sunlight and sniffed the air despite the futility in this scentless paradise.

'I think we come near the wall,' he said.

It leaped up before them in answer to his prediction, a high, curving sweep of unadorned Iridesium that reflected the sky's perpetual rainbow in its dull black surface.

'So much metal,' Irissa marveled. 'It must be natural-built. Or was once. Why does Finorian need sorcery to maintain so imposing, so forbidding a wall?'

'Rule knows.' Kendric's hand greeted its cool sculpted surface. 'Who built it, I wonder, and when?'

'Torlocs,' came a familiar answering voice, half buzz, half rumble.

They whirled to find the Rynx behind them, prone among the close-set trees, its eyes opening one by one to mirror in turn the dimming gray of the ebbing night sky and brightening gold of the morning sun.

'Torlocs built all that stands upon this land,' it went on, 'with hands and eyes, with might and magic.'

'Where have you been?' Irissa asked, refusing to be distracted by another sudden appearance in this wood.

'Here. There. Hunting.'

'And have you found food enough?'

The great white owlish head nodded sluggishly. 'Enough. Our thoughts are muddled. Time hangs heavy in this wood; we find ourselves pulled in new directions, sometimes opposing our instincts. We range far and feed on alien things.'

'Have you been beyond the wall?' Kendric asked hopefully.

The Rynx's eyes widened momentarily. 'Perhaps. But you dare not pass the wall; there chaos rules and you would . . . you would . . .' The creature drifted to sleep in the soporific sunlight already lancing thin blades through the tattered leaves.

'It is sated,' Kendric whispered to Irissa, 'as large beasts often are after feeding. Apparently it gorged last night.'

'On what?' she demanded. 'Mushrooms? There must be beasts of prey hiding from us in this forest. The Rynx found one before.'

'If they have done this well so far, we'll see no sign of them. We have not even sighted the dappled bearing-beast again. Come,' Kendic urged, 'the Rynx is well able to feed and fend for itself, as you observe, however mysteriously. You are better for not knowing the details. Leave it to the woods it is content with; we have other business. Climb to my shoulders and see if you can spy the top of the wall.'

Despite the able boost of his hands, Irissa found Kendric made a thankless ladder, with few footholds to offer. At last she balanced precariously on one of his shoulders, flattened her palms on the wall, and leaned back to study the Iridesium arching over her like a curled, scornful lip.

Her hands flared back. 'Kendric! It's warm! The wall is warm.'

'Even morning sunlight lingers on metal, and despite its magical properties, Iridesium is mere metal at base.' His hands tightened around her boots on his shoulders. 'What matters most is: what do you see?'

'Nothing.' A pause unwound, during which Kendric could hear the wind softly snoring in the treetops behind him. Perhaps it was the sleeping Rynx.

'This wall is . . . hotter than sun-warmed. And — Kendric!'

He lurched backward as her weight shifted suddenly. 'Don't move!'

'I didn't,' came Irissa's tension-strangled voice. 'The wall did.'

'The wall moved?'

'Only a bit. It . . . heaved under my hands like the withers of a winded bearing-beast and then I jerked back. Oh! Again. Kendric, I think the wall is . . . breathing!'

'I wonder if it sings.' He tugged on her trouser legs. 'Come down, then, before you discover it converses. What are our chances of surmounting it, whether it heaves or no?'

118

She leaped down, momentarily breathless. 'The higher it soars, the more it overarches us. Perhaps we can burrow under it.'

'I was not born to be a mole,' Kendric grumbled, fanning his hands to demonstrate their unsuitability for digging. His eyes cast around in search of a solution, returning reluctantly to his hands and the ring upon it. 'Perhaps we can wish ourselves through it.'

The expansive gesture he made as he spoke hurled the dancing glitter of the ring-set stones against the black metal. Where the dazzle touched, it sizzled. Where it burned, it ate. A small portion of the wall's slick face now bore pockmarks. The wind, or perhaps it was the wall, emitted a sturdy sigh.

'Perhaps we already carry a key,' Irissa suggested.

Kendric's fisted hand raised the ring to solitary prominence upon its central finger.

'But which of the five stones turns it?' he wondered. Then his deep voice began tolling the lessons of the stones they had learned in the Inlands.

'Sandstone,' Kendric said uncertainly, watching a copper cabochon grow molten at the word, then then fade. 'But sand will not scrub away a wall of metal. Gladestone . . .' A dull, olive-green gem blazed emerald bright. 'But the glade stands at our back, not our front. Perhaps the Lunestone—' Silver flashed like the wink of Irissa's eye, had she ever been frivolous enough to wink. 'Or, better, the Shunstone!' This last was a plain, colorless stone whose surface did not so much brighten as shift. 'The Shunstone might force the metal from itself, might make a door.'

He bent his gaze to the Shunstone, concentrating on it without asking Irissa's advice, his mind commanding the metal shrink away before them until a Wrathman-high hole ate through to its opposite side . . .

'Kendric!'

He looked up. The woods all around bowed away from him, trees straining sideways until their lower limbs swept the ground. Grasses parted at his feet and drew back horizontally in a perfect circle. Even the strengthening morning sunlight seemed to rebound from his head. And Irissa, Irissa clung to the backward-driven trunk of a tree, hair and clothing whipping behind her as if in an irresistible wind, although for now there was not even a zephyr ablow.

His right thumb hastily clouded the ring's surface. Everything snapped violently upright again with a relieved hiss of wind. Irissa catapulted against Kendric like a bag of lumpy peat, taking both their breaths away.

The wall swelled visibly and shrank again, the sound of its motion like a groan.

'No Shunstone,' Kendric agreed, forestalling Irissa's reaction. 'That leaves nothing but . . .' He studied the obsidian stone that beamed blacker in response to his glance upon it. 'That leaves the Nightstone of Reygand, who was called Geronfrey in another place and may still be.'

At his back, he felt Irissa's voiceless, interior objection to the mere mention of their foe's name. The longer he lingered by the metal skin of a wall that matched its respiration to his, the more he dreaded passing through it. He touched the black stone to the black wall anyway.

To his eyes, the metal began melting, like night, into endless, disembodied darkness. He saw the subtle rainbow coloration shrinking, drawing away from the central darkness. He saw the metal thick as velvet soften to a pulsing liquid shimmer. It panted now, the substance of the wall, taking quick, sheen-enhancing breaths.

Kendric gulped his own gigantic breath as if he were a swimmer contemplating a plunge into some tarry sea. Then he reached for Irissa's wrist, drawing her into his wake as he forged through that thick, viscous midnight, the prow of his extended and beringed fist cutting a path through its unfelt depths and length.

How many steps he took Kendric could never say. He felt the metal peeling away from the edges of his body, sensed the safe place behind him in which Irissa walked untainted by the touch of whatever flowed past them. It must not reach Irissa, that he sensed, even as he knew that the floating darkness harbored no immediate danger for himself.

With mutual gasps of hoarded breath, they burst into the land beyond the wall. It exploded back at them in waves of raucous screechings and the stench of death and decay, of birth and striving. Daylight shattered the dark, lit the endless landscape of tattered forestation, shaped the forms of thronging beasts, sparkled from the surface of fetid ponds and litter-choked streams.

The scene ahead was populated so thickly it seemed to swell before their eyes; treemonks swung and screamed as hawks swooped down to squeeze them in their talons; green-furred foxes ran before the goad of large, white-fanged pursuers; birds complained in every note of nature's scale, out of tune and hoarse. Shaggy bearing-beasts thundered before the stalk of huge hunting cats spotted orange and black.

Irissa and Kendric stood and watched, feeling mute, motionless, naked. They turned back to see the wall looming smooth and curved behind them, like a giant, black toothless smile, a metal mouth forever closed to them.

The land before them fell away, into deeper and deeper distances, although a low black ridge defined the farther horizon. Above their heads, beyond a wide-limbed tree, the sky lowered with blue-black clouds; no delicate-hued rainbow would have been strong enough to cast its colors on that frowning opaque expanse.

'This place reminds me of a certain trench dug round Sofistron's lemurai pit,' Kendric said grimly, recalling a less favorite adventure. 'If you will hold my sword, I'll climb this grandfather of a tree and overlook the land.'

Before Irissa had prepared herself for the sword's weight, Kendric had thrust it her way. She saw why he forbore to lay it on the ground. Rancid, pale fruit lay all around the tree, while small scrawny-necked birds strolled among the rotting matter, pecking fitfully.

Kendric leaped the ring of rank fruit to stand beside the cart-wide trunk, then hurl himself at a branch. He was up treemonk-nimble, scaling branch after branch until they grew so thin Irissa feared his brunt would snap them.

His descent was sudden, hailed by a shower of sallow fruit

121

and the thrashing scaled form that fell to earth with him. Irissa drew her shortsword, the pommelstone winking alarmed emerald green without benefit of her summoning thought.

She tossed it to Kendric as she saw his ringed hand gaping wide and white. The other hand delved busily, wielding the dagger blade for foray after foray into the lizard's tough hide.

With the sword Kendric now had room to retreat from the flashing saw of teeth and still inflict damage. He thrust it daggerlike until his attacker finally rolled onto its scaled side, briefly cawed surrender, and lay still.

'Not a pretty creature, is it?' Irissa surveyed a mottled brown hide and eyes of lackluster egg-yolk yellow. The body stretched as long as a small child; webbed feet curled shut on lethal claws.

'No knightly notice given of its intentions, either,' Kendric agreed, breathing raggedly. 'Just lying along a limb, brown as bark, and then all hot, putrid breath upon my face and claws playing my body like a harp.'

Irissa surveyed the scene around them, which roiled with the ceaseless motion of bird, beast, and insect, all intent on seeking prey or evading prey-seeker.

'This must be where the Rynx found food! It sleeps now just on the other side. Strange it did not direct us here since it knew . . . And how did it pass the wall without a talisman?'

'It's never been one to share its secrets — or its magic. Besides, I regret no bounty from here. I would not feed a rabid lemurai a creature from this side of the world.' Distaste lent Kendric's face an expression of pure revulsion. 'Mayhap Finorian spoke true: we do not want what waits this side of the wall, and now we cannot return. That stink . . . of hide and hair and rot and foulnesses impossible to number! A scentless blossom would seem a boon of great price right now.'

Irissa plucked a brindled flower growing on a single rubbery stalk. It oozed sour ichor. When she stooped to smell it, acrid powder discharged into the air.

'A scent strong enough to overpower a moonweasel,' she decided, dropping the shriveling blossom atop the thin skin of decaying vegetation that carpeted the ground around them. 'Lies there anything ahead of us besides regret, do you think?'

Kendric laughed shortly. 'The dark ridge beyond is another wall, the twin of this one. The walls define a wide trench that sinks toward the middle into utter darkness, then the ground rises again to meet the opposite wall.' He scanned the unappetizing landscape. 'A long stroll it would be, and perhaps the next wall will not answer to my ring.'

'We can try to go back . . .'

'And give Finorian reason to crow? No, not even if the wall behind us were to lie meekly down and make itself into a road for us to tread. Let's aim for the other barrier — and let whosoever rules this place protect whatsoever steps between us and it.'

He reclaimed his sword after wiping hers blood-free on the anemic grasses and returning it. They began a downward trek into a land that seemed the ragged, putrid ghost of the one they had renounced.

'Who *does* rule this place?' Irissa speculated. 'Could it be the white lady you saw, and the man we both witnessed? Are these woods home to them?'

'Mists-o'-the-marshes rule nothing,' Kendric answered. 'And they were wailwraith-phantasmic, I swear, perhaps some guardian spirit of the place. Though if sheer insubstantialness were enough, they could lace their ways in and out of the breathing walls a thousand times easier than our stubborn bone and blood would beat a path through, talismans or not for a key.'

'They are most welcome to this feral world beyond the wall,' Irissa said feelingly, batting clinging insects from the tendrils of her hair. 'I hope your pining for the sight of game has been satiated.'

Within an hour, Kendric's nostrils had been gifted with enough odors and his eyes with enough sights of a varied but universally dangerous-looking animal life to make the emptiness of Edanvant seem divine foresight.

'Is this still Edanvant?' he asked Irissa once as they ducked under the resin-dripping branches of a disease-splotched tree.

'It could be. It could be that—'

'That what?'

'That *this* world between the walls is part of the defensive magic Finorian weaves with her Damen Circle. There is such futility to these creatures; they seem at odds with everything but the air they breathe. They stalk, scream, chase and hide perpetually. And the hungry way they look on us . . .'

She could not describe the disharmony that ate into her very bones, but moved faster into the deeper landscape, as if sinking farther into an unhappy land at least obscured viewing the full extent of it.

Slap! Kendric pressed a stinging insect to its death upon his neck. Blossoms floated in the rank water alongside their path, a death's head design neatly drawn on each of their central upright trumpets of nacreous petalwork.

Wind seemed loath to stir the surface of this land. An animal reek hung heavy as fog in the still air; even the air seemed jaundiced, sulfurous to breathe.

Irissa took the lead, striding forward despite the drag of unhealthy broken webs and stringy foliage on her hair, the suck of rot-soft ground at her boots.

'It reminds me of my birthplace,' Kendric said with dour satisfaction. 'The Marshlands of Rule, where I spent so many worthwhile hours dreaming of escape. The ground must rise soon,' he promised, failing to discern any sign of that blessed eventuality.

They came at last to a cool circle of pool where the twilight-dark shade was untainted by the scum of fallen petals that had graced all the watery surfaces they had seen so far.

Kendric bent to run his fingers through it, and smell it, then nodded reluctant approval. Irissa crouched gratefully beside him, splashing droplets to her face, bending over the pond's near-black surface until the braids looped around her ears pulled loose and trolled the water.

'Bitter,' she observed, nevertheless continuing to wet her parched lips.

'I would not bathe in it,' Kendric conceded with illogical nicety, 'but it seems drinkable.' His eyes, ever watchful, sought the shaded thicket around them for the pupil-glow of beastly observers. Red, green, and gold glimmered starlike as Kendric detached his sword to stand it like a watch-companion beside him. But the many twin gleams remained unmoving. He guessed that he and Irissa were among the larger creatures of this land, and that the hidden wild things knew the sniff of steel.

'Don't overdrink,' he cautioned Irissa, glancing down. She hunched over the pool rim yet, strangely still. Her bracing fingers, fanned alongside her, looked fungus-white against the dingy poolside mosses. He could not see her face, but even as he watched, the widening circle of ripples at her knees melted away and the water lay heavy and solid, a still sleek sheet of darkness.

He saw Irissa's face now, the expression frozen. He saw *through* her cloaking hair, through bone and skin to view the face itself — nay, the *reflection* of that face in the coal-dark water. The image expanded as he looked, widening like a ripple, the eyes' soft silver glitter enlarging, pulling apart — everything in the face swelling, stretching until it met the edges of the pond, no longer resembling Irissa or any human visage, until the round dark maw of the water seemed to be an open mouth screaming . . .

His sword struck liquid, cleaving it as through oiled skin. Some tension in the water, in the air, in Irissa and himself broke and released them all.

The image of a Dark Mirror floating into darker reality before Kendric's eyes shattered at the blind instinct of his sword stroke. It was only brackish water, after all, he saw, reflecting shards of himself as well as Irissa. In the relieved aftermath of fear, he felt foolish for having pointlessly thrust good steel into sluggish water, roiling in fact what Irissa had once stirred inventively with magic. A sword made a ludicrous spoon.

Kendric withdrew the dripping blade and looked down. Irissa's coin-round eyes were turned up at his, her face water-lily pale.

'I thought I saw — something — in the water,' he explained

125

gruffly. 'A reflection of my own idiocy, no doubt—'

She pointed mutely at his sword, her finger as formally indicating as Finorian's, he thought for some unreasonable reason. Then he looked down at the weapon.

For a foot from the dripping tip, wet red blood oiled the blue-steel blade.

CHAPTER EIGHT

While red, green, and gold beast-eyes lit the shadows, Kendric paced and Irissa repeatedly wiped her mouth with the back of her hand. The ring upon her finger flayed the heavy air with crimson, gold, azure, and white rays, but neither of them noticed it.

'Have I *wounded* the water?' Kendric demanded incredulously. 'Or something within it?'

He glanced to a bed of green moss dyed brown with dried blood. His blade rode his back again but he felt no safer for it. They remained by the pool only because a known perplexity seemed less dangerous than the world's worth of unknown perils surrounding it.

'The water — tasted — brackish, but seemed everyday enough.' Irissa wiped her lips again, glancing at the back of her hand, which shone white and unblemished in the woodsy twilight, despite her worry to the contrary.

'And whose face was it — that I saw reflected and thought was yours? A wailwraith's? A sending of Finorian's meant to dishearten us and send us scurrying back to the safety of her skirts? Or something else sent by someone else — someone from farther than beyond the second wall? Someone — something — worse.'

Irissa shied away from unsaid implications. 'I only saw the dark water and my hand's reflection in it,' she insisted hopefully. 'Likely this — incident has done no harm—'

Kendric's face reflected a number of expressions, none of them enduring long enough to commit him to a single emotion.

'It's only that we near the opposite wall,' he said. 'What if the ring upon my finger no longer plays key to our needs?

127

Or if the joint hostility of this whole, hidden hostile land rises up to meet us with more than watery faces?'

He paced away, his steps taking him alarmingly close to a pair of glinting crimson eyes. The eyes edged back, but Kendric didn't notice his small victory in the face of a larger and more dire possibility.

'There was sorcery in the water,' Irissa conceded, her voice dragging with reluctance. 'Perhaps it wasn't Finorian's.'

'Whose then?'

She nodded into the thickness of the woods. 'Those beyond the wall.'

'And we go there, naturally.' Kendric's exasperated laughter drove several sets of eyes back a pace. 'Then we make for the wall, and stop for no one.'

'And nothing,' Irissa amended, checking the hang of the sword at her hip. Its emerald pommelstone gleamed gently, echoing the green pairs among the undergrowth-veiled living eyes surrounding them.

'This way, then.' Kendric committed to a wall of nearly black forestation and barged through it. Eyes all around blinked out, flashing open again on an empty clearing, on a round black eye of pool so still it looked carved from basalt and on a Wrathman-wide, Wrathman-high swath of trembling greenery.

Kendric brooded as they walked. He paced a dread prospect — that Geronfrey moved upon this world like wind upon water. That Geronfrey still coveted Irissa's powers — and Irissa — and was reaching for them both. Though he'd never glimpsed the sorcerer's physical self, Kendric felt the man's powers contracting all around him — as if the weight of an invisible net woven from the very tissues of Edanvant were descending slowly upon them all. It was a good thing, Kendric thought, that he had the bulk and gift for placing himself firmly in the way of such subtle ploys as sorcery.

Their path began to lead steeply upward. Irissa climbed in Kendric's wake, lagging enough to avoid the accidental blow of the sword protruding beyond his bent back. She nearly crawled herself, scrambling over the slick turf and its hailstorm

128

of dislodged pebbles, under the acrid-scented fronds of giant ferns, past mean squat bushes with fire-tipped branches angled to snag clothing, hair, skin, and even eyelashes.

They burrowed into the vegetation, as into a tunnel, endless and green under a gauntlet of whipping branches, losing themselves in mutual though separate tangles of forestation and unwanted thoughts. Small insects invisibly buzzed and bore; things slithered out of sight but not out of sound, stirring the fallen leaves until it seemed they shook with an ague and hissed a warning.

Irissa began to itch − all over − infected equally by the real and the imagined. Ahead of her, Kendric's large form clambered faster up the growth-clogged slope; she surged forward herself, seeking to outcreep her crawling skin.

A slice of sky, pale and airy blue in contrast to the heavy evergreen world around them, smiled over the artificial knoll of Kendric's shoulder. Beyond loomed a black wall, abrupt as daybreak and tall as false pride. They straightened slowly, their bodies still wed to the curve of their long stooped passage, their minds beginning to expand to draw in the open air.

Around them, grouped as formally as the women of a Damen Circle, pressed an assortment of animals − slack-jawed, slavering, drooling, panting, waiting, watching, alien, unfriendly, fourlegged crouching beasts.

Irissa and Kendric drew themselves full height, partly because their cramped spines demanded it and partly because they sensed it expedient to confront an enclave of four-footed beasts on the traditional human two.

They faced bramble foxes furred in midnight green with sharp clever faces and lolling pink tongues; bears as big as bearing-beasts attired in ragged orange coats with accidental necklaces of uprooted striplings around their shaggy necks; great forest-dappled cats whose long, sullen faces held hungry red feline eyes; long-eared otters with complacent expressions countered by the uneasy unsheathing of nail-long talons; small, pink-haired treemonks whose fifth hands at the end of their supple tails squeezed nervously around their own blue-ringed necks; snakes scaled in nature's Iridesium that flicked forked

129

tongues and tails at rhythmic intervals; shaggy solid-colored bearing-beasts with lowered single horns.

Irissa pointed out the herd. 'Like the creature you sought to capture!'

'Like, but totally unlike. These are ignoble beasts,' Kendric answered even as the creatures' positions shifted.

The animals formed an enclosing circle of fur and hair, fang and claw and almost-human menace. Kendric and Irissa turned slowly to view them, revolving tightly around each other like the hub of a wheel that hopes never to meet its rim coming or going.

Tongues all around them hung out, pink, blue, orange, and black, producing an erroneously amiable impression, as if all those animals had loped, run, trotted fast to arrive at just this spot in time to bid Irissa and Kendric a fond farewell before they breached the wall.

'There is no tameness in them,' Irissa said, her voice shattering the spell of the animal circle. 'Not in any of these beasts.'

'None,' Kendric agreed, slowly stretching his arms over his shoulder to draw his sword. It swung free in a great overhead arc, but not a whisker flinched or an ear cocked at its sudden pointed presence. Impassive, the animals waited; the combined heat of their panting made it seem as if the very air gasped for breath. Behind them, the wall's dark metal sides heaved rapidly.

'There is no fear in them, either,' Kendric added, flexing his elbows so the longsword he held two-handed glinted along its five feet of sleek steel. Not a beast started, not even the smallest root-shrew sheltering between the ground-scraping front tusks of a hair-hooded boar.

They sat and stood together, shoulder to haunch, tusk to jowl, large and small, prey and predator, in joint animal judgment, mingling odors and angers that seemed to stretch beyond time and distance.

Irissa reached out a hand — her right, beringed hand — to scribe a tight circle, her eyes seeking eyes, seeking the merest chink of docility. She willed them weary, beseeched them

130

friendly, searched for a single tremor of uncertainty among them, an instinctive whinny or whimper or purr.

There was none, only the heated exhalation of their breaths, their even, empty eyes, and the rhythmic quiver of their panting bodies as they waited, waited for one of their number to take the lead, make the lethal leap, begin the sudden fatal inundation, fell and kill, rend, devour . . .

Irissa and Kendric crossed glances for a dangerous instant. Their heads shook imperceptibly. There was no arguing with such mass animal force, not with words, not with steel. And magic? They looked away, each exploring the inner reaches of ready magic, stunned into separate action by the enormity of the mute animal challenge around them, divided and conquered.

Kendric licked his lips and tried to concentrate on his sword, his mind-forged sword, that should do his will, whatever that would be. Fire? A burning blade as Irissa had once made it? Or icy — icy steel that would freeze with the mere wind of its passage? Either element fled the overeager grasp of his mind. He was too worried by that bear that swayed from ponderous foot to foot, by that nearer serpent whose supple tongue flicked silent admonitions.

Irissa was no wiser or readier. The hot, heavy, beast-laden air seemed to fetter her mind, and magic built its foundation there. Her senses quailed at the multitude of voiceless animosities pressing upon them, as if a thousand phantom teeth already had her in their pointed grasp. She saw and heard and felt their wrath — the chains, the burdens, the beatings, the maggot-clotted food, the hunts, the chases, the headless pups and gutted kits and skinned litters; the fires, the floods, the cast stones and arrows . . .

Her fear-slicked palm pressed upon the sword pommel her fingers refused to curl around. Even as all her limbs went watery and the ring of creatures appeared to tighten on her, she felt the stone warm and brighten to her touch, almost seeming to swell in her hand, in her mind, until a faint greenish illumination found its echo in a hundred circling animal eyes and the ground beneath her feet reached for the sky — or at least a misty wisp of cloud spun down or a scarf of ground

131

fog arched upward . . . lengthened, stretched . . . yawned to display a pink ribbed mouth set with whole ranges of white-peaked teeth . . . glittered green below the ears . . . bared all its fangs and hissed like a snake.

Dumb as beasts, Kendric and Irissa stared at what her pommelstone had birthed, a white curl of a cat who lurched to splayed feet, unkinked a long, skimpy tail, and arched a spine rough-notched as a stair.

The fur shone more yellow than white, knotted in places so a crown of cowlicks framed the wedge-shaped face that was all mouth and eyes and feline wrath.

'Wakened,' the cat growled, 'from a nap of many years, and for what?' She turned contemptuously in the center of the gathered beasts. 'I have seen you all before.' Her green gaze, pointed as a needle, seemed to stab each eye in turn. 'All. Be off with you — off!' Assorted animal eyes winced. 'Off about your revolting business.'

They disbanded, slithering, stalking, and melting away. The treetops rustled with the sudden abandonment of flocks of birds Irissa and Kendric had never even noticed. The very leaves surrounding them seemed to withdraw until the two stood alone with one beast only, with the rangy old housecat who had settled on her bony haunches to wash sleep-slit eyes.

'Felabba!' Irissa rebuked fondly. 'You didn't heed the Damen Circle's call — or so we all thought. You didn't come. Or did our danger bestir you?' She was beginning to sound deeply affected.

The cat sniffed, or seemed to have. 'It wasn't that which woke me — your magic or mortality. It was *him*.'

'Me?' Kendric foundered in a sea of sputtering denial. 'I'd never take blame for summoning a thing against its will, and a speaking beast at that.'

A wicked flash of green raked his flushed face. 'Great blundering . . . *amateur!* You think you can snap your fingers so lightly when you wear a ring formed of half the Inlands Stones, which Delevant the wizard gave his Torlochood for?'

Kendric thrust his left hand as far from him as possible and studied the ring mounting upon its middle finger. 'It was not

132

that! Even a novice knows that power must be concentrated to have an effect. My fingersnap could not so much as conjure a flea. Besides, that was a day or two ago.'

Felabba came as close to shrugging as a cat could. 'Let us simply say that someone must take the blame for it, and you make an excellent target; you are so hard to miss.'

'Your movements are as mysterious as ever,' Irissa said, crouching to regard the creature eye to eye. 'I thought you were tied to Rule?'

The cat paused midlick. 'The sword has been found,' she answered shortly, resuming her interrupted grooming.

Irissa's hand reached toward the flat skull, where time had carved vertical furrows into the short fur until the cat looked as if her brow frowned sideways. She edged away, leaving Irissa the cold comfort of a disdainful glance.

'Reunions,' Felabba remarked dryly, 'are overrated. Let's get on with it, then. I'm as curious as you to see what lies beyond that wall. Take us through, Wrathman-who-was, before the beasts reconsider their retreat.'

Kendric's arms had folded tightly. 'I thought you knew everything, for all that you usually *say* nothing. Why should I bestir my small, clumsy powers to conquer a wall you obviously can melt with a mere whisker-brush?'

'I am old, Sir Marshman, and must hoard my abilities around me as human dodderers husband warmth. I must save my powers until they are truly needed.'

The cat hunched into her promontories of bones, her tail limply wafting around her forefeet. Her eyes shut in slow, dozing stages, an action oddly reminiscent of human weeping. Felabba sat doing what she did so peerlessly — she waited.

'Well?' Kendric had drawn Irissa aside for a whispered consultation. 'Do you believe that bag of ill-tempered bones?'

'I think she gives you more credit for her presence than you or fact would accept. If my pommelstone birthed her, she planted herself there — perhaps when I joined the Damen Circle . . . It seemed for a moment Felabba was present; then she vanished.'

'Just like the sly old feline,' Kendric decided. 'Called by

Finorian and too proud to admit it, so she slips into your sword and makes her bow later, pretending to have had some say in the matter. Then, to confuse us, she claims *I* had something to do with it. Magical mumbo jumbo.

'On the purely practical side,' he demanded, 'how are we going to learn anything anywhere if our steps are slowed to the pace of a rickety feline who can speak faster than she can walk, which isn't saying much for either ability?'

Kendric paused for breath. A few feet away, luminous eyes of borgia-green burned through half-shut lids. Or were they half-open? As was usual with Felabba, one's perception of her made all the difference.

'She effectively banished the ring of animals,' Irissa said.

'Who may have meant no harm,' he riposted. 'We only *thought* them dangerous. This one materialized conveniently to preserve us from what may have been nothing. Oh, very well, I'll open our Iridesium gate and we shall see what lies on the other side of this wilderness.'

Kendric stepped to the blank wall, saluted it with his extended arm, and touched the Nightstone to its surface.

Nothing happened. After a long pause, Felabba sneezed.

Kendric stared suspiciously over his shoulder at her hunched form, which was turned almost deliberately with its back to the wall. He confronted the Iridesium again, squeezing his eyes nearly shut in concentration, willing the sleek black stone in his ring, willing the smooth black wall, to soften for their passage.

'Look at me!' At last Kendric wrenched himself away from the wall, giving it his back as fully as Felabba had. 'I stand here putting all my faith in a ring I never asked for, in powers as unilaterally bestowed. I no longer rely upon the old powers of wit and will and make-do, yet am betrayed by the new.'

'You are betrayed by your own doubt.' Irissa walked up to him, not the wall, as if Kendric were the more inflexible barrier of the two.

Her fingers covered the ring's face and forced his angry eyes from the jeweled surface to the calm quicksilver of her gaze.

134

'If a thing resisted you in the past, did you not wrestle with it? Approach it from one way, then another? Apply sheer strength, or mere wit, or varying combinations of both until you had achieved your object? Is not the mere act of living a series of attempts to tame difficulties, whether they be physical or objects of the mind and heart? To think, to feel is as great a struggle as to fight, to climb. Magic makes its home somewhere between mind and heart. It is a fey, deep-hidden thing and must be coaxed, not berated.

'If this were a key' — she tapped the ring — 'whose touch your fingers had lost, you would try and try again until you had unlocked its secret. Because it is magic, you let it live or die on one trial. Why do you assume that magic should be easy? It is the hardest thing of all.'

He pulled his hand from hers. 'There is no answer in it,' he said, looking at the ring. 'And this is not a matter of faith or persistence. It does not respond at all. It is merely . . . a ring.'

Irissa considered his words, glancing to the dormant surface of the stones. They looked ordinary, even false, in the full daylight. Her own ring glittered eagerly, as if for attention.

'Perhaps we use the wrong ring, then.'

Irissa stepped to the wall, seeing the faint image of herself press toward her from within it. It reminded her of Geronfrey's Dark Mirror, in which her forbidden image had floated on the ebony surface, a pale scum of form. Had it vanished when she walked away? Or did a thin skin of herself persist, still feeding on the rank water from Geronfrey's night-dark pit? She remembered the expanding face of herself she had glimpsed in the black, bleeding pool before Kendric's sword stroke had shattered its swallowing reflection. She would not, could not, tell him her fears. He had enough of hers to bear — magic, her unwelcoming world. Yet the name 'Geronfrey' hissed like a spell word through her mind, and Irissa felt like a small silver fish in a large dark pool, caught on some almost invisible thread. When Kendric used the Nightstone, had he unlocked more than a wall? And now Irissa had taken it upon herself to open another dark wall.

She watched the five-stoned ring's colors flash in answer to her mental naming of them. Bloodstone, Shinestone, Skystone, Floodstone, Drawstone — red, gold, blue, clear and plain. Which would best attack a slick black wall? Her mind sorted the possibilities.

As she often told Kendric, magic required courting. She vacillated between the Drawstone, which might pull the wall apart, and the Floodstone, which might wear it away to water. Then her hand reached out and the ring touched the wall. It was the hot gold Shinestone that had turned itself to merge with metal at the last moment.

An explosive golden aura surrounded Irissa; everything shimmered and softened. The wall caught light from the stone, burned flamelike. She hesitated at the mouth of fire, as Kendric's hand reached over her shoulder to test its heat.

Before either of them could react to the burning doorway, Felabba came stalking between their feet, setting one foot before the other in a gait part swagger and part tightrope-walk. They watched her small white shape vanish into a halo of molten gold.

'Curiosity,' Kendric predicted, 'will kill—'

'The curious,' Irissa finished. 'But this firestorm of a path strikes me as cleaner than the midnight morass we last passed through.'

They edged into the light; first their boot-toes, then their cautious outstretched hands. Warmth and color clasped them, drew them onward even when their skin shrank at the fiery rain of growing heat cascading over their heads.

It was too late to turn back; their vision reeled in a blurred gilt haze; their feet appeared to tread nothing more substantial than sunshine.

It seemed a long time before coolness rinsed the gold away. They stood at last in an ante-courtyard walled high all around with Iridesium. An ice-blue sky, clean of clouds and rainbows and everything but sunlight, formed the roofless lid to their prison. Ahead stood another gate, made of wooden timbers thick as two men around and braced with broad Iridesium bands bereft of scrollwork. It was a gate that took itself seriously.

At their feet, Felabba hefted a rear leg to scratch vigorously at a flea. Above their heads, a shuttered window clapped wide as the gatekeeper squinted down upon them.

'Poachers,' the gateman diagnosed, giving Irissa and Kendric a cursory sweep. His eyes locked on Felabba at their feet. 'Contraband from beyond the wall! Small reward for such risk, but likely tasty enough pickled—'

The shutters slammed shut. Moments afterward, a series of grunts beyond the wall and the creak of gears combined to swing the massive gates open an infinitesimal amount.

Kendric thrust his boot into the narrow space. 'Torloc hospitality,' he told Irissa in an aside. 'Barely room enough for a cat to slip through.'

Felabba's flat frame curved around the five-inch-thick timbers as if so invited. The gate ground open another few inches and Irissa squeezed through sideways, her sword held carefully aslant. Kendric waited, but the gate had groaned its last. He thrust as much of himself through as he could, then wrenched his full weight against it. A gateman's howl as the sudden action cracked the gate's jaws made Kendric grin. He walked through, broadside, into a scene that stopped him cold.

Another gate opened on the secondary courtyard's other side, opened in fact, not theory. Figures passed beyond it — passed? They walked, talked, paused, stopped, walked on. People moved beyond the open gateway. Ordinary folk — market-bound folk with empty baskets; homebound folk with full baskets encompassing plucked geese, and hog's heads, fish and eggbirds, rounds of cheese and squares of bread . . .

Kendric started for the vision — more magical than the marvels he had seen in the woods — of people and things as ordinary as his Marshland home. A pike suddenly angled across his chest.

'Sorry, friend, but your companion wears the Damen braids.'

Kendric turned to stare at Irissa.

'I did not see from the gatehouse,' the pikeman added apologetically. He was a short — a scant six feet tall —

thick-set man, who stank of onions. Onions! Kendric recalled the reek of Dame Agneda's salads and stared coldly down at the fellow, who began to back up.

'I did not see from the gatehouse,' he said again, retreating. 'Her kind has not been welcome in Edanvant in generations, unless it slip through unseen, and I dare not be the first to admit it.'

'Edanvant?' Kendric said. 'She has crossed Edanvant over, and I with her. You would stop us now?' he thundered.

The little man quailed. 'I have my gatemen.'

A half-dozen leather-jerkined men came at his words, their sweat-oiled arms gleaming like bronze serpents in the sunlight.

'I have my sword,' retorted Kendric, drawing it in one mighty sweep.

The gatemen paused until the keeper spoke again. 'The lordlings will not like it that we allowed such as she through our doors without a fight.' He meant to rally his men; instead he roused Kendric.

'A fight. Indeed a fight.' Kendric swayed from side to side, bracing his feet. 'I have tired of gates, real or rainbowed. I have grown unbelievably weary of gatekeepers. I pass, and all my party with me, or there will not be enough left of any of you to pass through a gnat's ear!'

They rushed together, the seven men from the city, the one tall man from outside their gate. Irissa watched from just inside the opening, mystified by the gatemen's disregard for her, by Kendric's obvious battle-relish. She did not fear for him, but found the set-to, like most things men of might did, overdramatic.

'Like old times,' observed a smug, cynical voice at her feet. 'He has not changed a scintilla.'

'That's not true, Felabba; Kendric has trod a road of inner change far longer and more circuitous than any outer path you or I have taken, no matter how magical.'

'Perhaps he will cleave them in two, like moonweasels,' the old cat added hopefully, sitting to watch the conflict with the concentrated stare of the flesh-eater.

'He won't if he has any hope of welcome within the city.'

138

Irissa folded her arms and leaned against the Iridesium wall, waiting with Felabba.

The gatemen rushed Kendric with wrist-thick cables flying whiplike. His great sword severed them as if they were bootlaces. The pikeman attempted to dodge the intimidating path of the sword and impale Kendric on his long steel point. But Kendric released his two-handed grip on the sword and let it lag long enough for the pike to jab inward; he caught the oncoming haft in midthrust to sweep pike and wielder against the far metal wall, where the pikeman hit and then sagged like a sack of Dame Agneda's foulest onions.

The gatemen would have run, but the breadth of Kendric's sword struck blows that slowed their retreat enough to permit more thudding strikes upon their retreating backs and backsides.

'Always able at the overobvious,' murmured the cat, Felabba, as Kendric triumphantly rejoined his companions. His sword had not even notched an ear, so he scabbarded the clean blade.

'What did that gain us?' Irissa wondered aloud.

'A peaceful pathway into the city.' Kendric bowed to let her precede him, which she did, but only after Felabba had suddenly bounded into the lead.

They stepped through the last doorway into the city, into hot sunlight and clamor. People scurried heedlessly past, some almost tripping over Felabba, so the old cat was forced to take refuge at Irissa's ankles, winding her lean form around each booted leg in turn.

'What did the gateman mean about Edanvant?' Kendric asked as they surveyed the scene from the fringes. 'He spoke as if *this*, and this alone, were Edanvant.'

'An ignorant, discourteous man.' Irissa dismissed gatekeepers in her own way. 'And now a humble one as well. Perhaps your great size encouraged him to pick any bone of contention with you that came to mind.'

But the people rushing by did not blanch or stare at Kendric's uncommon height. Instead, they stared at Irissa, at her own nigh six feet of height, at her neatly circled braids, at the

139

Iridesium circlet binding her temples, at her silver eyes. They stared, stepped back, and rushed on faster.

A sudden sagging of Irissa's tunic pulled both her and Kendric's eyes to the ground. Felabba, uninvited, was scaling the tunic silk rent by fresh rent. Irissa wrenched the animal free and, when the curled claws finally released the fabric, lifted the cat to her shoulder.

'If you must ride, do so decorously. And mind your claws in my skin as well as my only tunic.'

She could have been a blue-skinned bauble-dancer, for all the long looks and hurried retreats her person evoked from the respectable townspeople milling through the streets. The presence of a somewhat scraggly cat upon her shoulder did nothing to diminish Irissa's mute notoriety.

Yet the people's awe, fear, or simple distaste cleared a path for them all, eliminating Kendric's worry that his sword would inadvertently spear some careless stroller. Irissa cleaved the crowd as a ship cuts turgid water, and Felabba's scrawny neck leaned eagerly forward as she perched atop it all, acting as a voluble figurehead.

'A fair bazaar,' she announced into the two ears high enough to hear her easily. 'I have not been among so many ordinary folk since I was a kit. It is a most soothing experience.'

'Too bad we cannot say the same,' Kendric mumbled.

But, he also felt charmed by the commonplace market scene, by the sight and sound of shopkeepers and passersby haggling; of children quickly threading through the sluggish mob in games of childish devising: of snake-weavers and dwarf falgon-handlers putting their exotic pets through their even more outlandish paces; of jewelers' stands with their gaudy glass trinkets casting purely unnatural rainbows of color, so strong and vivid they could never be mistaken for magical gates. He inhaled happily, scenting the pungency of herbal wreaths and eggbird feed, of rosemary and roast goose.

'Goose!' Kendric stopped as suddenly as he articulated the word.

Irissa stopped also, spinning to eye him dubiously.

'Do you smell it? Fresh meat! Very well, ancient one. Prove

yourself worthy of your nose and lead us to it.'

Felabba, in the process of recovering her balance after Irissa's abrupt pause, wrapped her tail around Irissa's neck and twitched her pink nose discriminatingly.

'An inferior bird, old and gone to goiter,' she diagnosed indifferently. 'But it perfumes the air around the next curve, luring those whose appetites reside in their eyes and empty stomachs alone.'

'All these stands sell foodstuffs,' Irissa noted as they hurried along the pathway. 'Eggs and cheese and—'

'Meat,' Kendric agreed fervently, stopping at a booth decorated by the pale, plucked carcasses of edible birds. One, already roasted to crisp bronze, lay atop a table. The fowl merchant was dispensing hand-sized portions in exchange for Iridesium coins.

Kendric hopefully probed his boarskin purse, knowing only flint, steel, and a single Torloc tear resided there. 'That's the trouble with this gate-crossing,' he noted. 'No coin in your hands of whatever realm you come upon.'

He watched an overstuffed townsman open a purse as deep as the Swallowing Cavern itself and dark with a glittering black cargo of Iridesium coinage. Inside his own purse, his fingers told the shape of the Quickstone, even though his mind knew the talisman's worth was far beyond that of a few greasy strands of gooseflesh. Still, it had been a long meatless stay with the Torloc dames, and Kendric's fingers itched to oil themselves in hot fowl flesh.

Irissa, Felabba still standing watch on her shoulder, ambled on to sightsee. So far the city streets had coiled gently around and around, with meager shadowed alleyways threading between the broader curving thoroughfares.

Irissa took one such shortcut, being more curious than hungry. Once committed to the byway, she saw not only shadow, but fear and hatred settling on faces around her. Kendric's doughty escort had quelled the reaction earlier. Now, momentarily, it was just Irissa and a feeble-looking cat, so eyes and lips all around her narrowed. She put her palm on the sword pommel at her side as if to steady it from her

141

brisker motions, but the faster she walked, the closer pressed the frowning men.

They no longer were mere pedestrians. They formed a party, as if they had always been hanging back, awaiting their moment. The dark byway was no longer a street, but a passage blocked at both ends by clots of men.

Over her shoulder, the one not bearing Felabba, Irissa saw the high, familiar silhouette of Kendric's shoulder-slung sword, the gilt of sunlight on the back of his sable-haired head. He and the open-aired market street seemed a dream viewed from distant time.

Now Irissa moved through a moonweasel's maw of passage. Above her the sides of the dark buildings met in a prayerfully pointed arch; below her crowded earthen cobblestones, repaired here and there with Iridesium blocks. Ahead and behind twinkled the bright reminders of freedom; around her the looming darkness of its loss, or worse, tightened upon her.

She had no trust in magic; it did not cast well in such crabbed circumstances. Anything she evoked to hurl at her maybe-attackers could recoil on her also. She sighed and prepared to ask the oddly silent cat for counsel.

Before a word could wrap itself around her reluctant tongue, a shy, almost unfelt tug on her sleeve drew her attention to a fussy voice alongside her.

'I suggest, Lady Longitude, that you step inside my humble establishment for a detour.'

A block of darkness, possibly a door, addressed her.

Irissa felt Felabba's claws curl crablike into her skin in silent, possible warning, but it was too late. She took one long step sideways into absolute midnight. Behind her, the alleyway's quasi shadow squeezed shut into a wall of solid black.

CHAPTER NINE

Utter darkness, without even the respite of Iridesium's shifting rainbowed promise, enfolded Irissa in cavelike coolness and quiet. In its opaque black heart, a bright blue flicker stirred, leaving a worm of remembered light in its wake

The phenomenon propagated until the azure lights scribed runic shapes on the darkness and finally emitted enough conjoined illumination to reveal a squat form humped like a giant toadstool before her.

'Long journeys and the shortcuts of a gate,' the figure murmured in oddly familiar tones, 'were ever the way of Torlocs. This is one abbreviation you should treasure, Lady Longitude, for your safety's sake. Rude, ignorant folk, they are, but then, so are the masses of people almost everywhere. They carry daggers and throwing stones, you know.'

'I didn't know, but I have—'

'You have your three green touchstones to guide you, I know.'

'*Three* stones—?'

The figure giggled, sending the worms of blue light into one writhing ball of brightness. Against that glow, Irissa's eyes discerned a rotund body and atop it an equally broad hood billowed out by utter darkness and the arch, tantalizing voice.

A murky sleeve elevated to dart toward her shoulder and side in quick explanatory turn.

'There, alongside your silver eyes — they glow blue in the gloom, did you know? — two matched green touchstones that even the dark cannot douse. Pure paired feline fire. And there, a larger single eye from which your present fear shines forth unknowing . . .'

Irissa glanced down to see her illuminated pommelstone. The cat on her shoulder finally released tensed claws, causing Irissa to sigh relief. If Felabba's eyes glowed in the obscurity surrounding them, they also revealed their secrets.

'Gone a bit brown around the rims, eh, old one?' the voice asked, chuckling. Felabba meowed either agreement or denial. By the growing blue light's aid, Irissa finally had identified this mysterious speaker out of darkness. Her pommelstone faded as she named him.

'Ludborg the Fanciful, traveler in Rule and out of it when it suits his needs — how did you come to Edanvant and what do you do in the dark?'

'How do I come anywhere? On a path traveled in sheer ill luck and under a marker called wanderlust. As for the dark, it makes a fine disguise. You needed to vanish and I am not magician enough to achieve that effect but through indirection. Yet by now I think your disappearance has been attributed to the magic of a Torloc seeress, not the meddling of a lowly itinerant merchant. Blue-worms — formation!'

On his command, the wriggling threads of light elongated until they cast an eerie, day-bright azure light around what appeared to be a curtained room. They slithered to the perimeter and there took up sconce-high posts, adapting graceful S-curves reminiscent of scrollwork.

'That's better.' Ludborg rocked back on his chair — or rather, Ludborg rocked back. Irissa had not detected any supportive shape beneath his chubby form. 'Be seated, Torloc lady — and Torloc feline.'

A chair of wrought blue-worms blazed into existence. Irissa gingerly lowered herself to the illuminated frame and found herself rocking slightly, like Ludborg. Felabba leaped atop a matching ornate footstool that the blue-worms politely had etched into the air near Irissa's glowing chairleg.

'This entertainment is better than campfires,' she noted.

'Oh, I like to deploy my comforts when I am in a position to do so. So, how do the two of ye fare, and what brings you to this unhappy, thrice-cursed city of Edanvant?'

'Finorian always said our homeworld was green and

144

growing — I thought Edanvant named the woods outside the city?'

Ludborg's hood shook rather disconcertingly, until Irissa realized the high-pitched wheezing she heard was laughter.

'The woods you think to be outside is *inside* the city; the city encircles the woodlands as an unsated moonweasel coils around its prey. And it is *all* Edanvant — forest and city, much to the unhappiness of all within *or* without it. How unfortunate your Wrathman was lost on the journey; he would have enjoyed berating both sides of Edanvant and all the Torlocs dividing it.'

'Kendric plays city to your woods even now,' Irissa informed him. 'He is outside this place, in the market.'

'Outside! Why did you not say so? He must be inside! As long as there are no attentive witnessess to his movements, this I can accomplish.' Ludborg's arm, or at least the sleeve that housed it — for no limb actually appeared — swept upward.

There was a flurry of blue-worms and then, within a cablework fence of the creatures, Kendric appeared, arguing, a choice bit of goose in one hand and the other still empty.

'. . . I have none of your coinage,' he was even now conceding, 'but I—'

'Enjoy your meat,' Ludborg urged. 'No shopkeeper will contest your right to eat it now.'

Kendric glared around. 'Irissa? Where is—? What are you doing in this den of the benighted?'

'I was rescued.'

'By this?' A sharp goosemeat odor swelled as Kendric swept his hand toward Ludborg. 'From what?'

'From angry townsmen. It seems they are not accustomed to my kind.'

'Nonsense.' Kendric began consuming his provident morsel, hesitated to find Felabba's implacable stare regarding him with sharp emerald rebuke from the footstool, and leaned forward to toss some pungent slivers the cat's way.

'The shopkeeper was telling me all about Torlocs,' he went on. 'Seems they run the place from a huge, hill-set fortress they call "Citydell." In fact, the fellow took me for one of the breed and was most surprised I was not dripping with Iridesium "lordlings," as they call coins here. So why should anyone care if Irissa wanders the streets till doomsday cracks its knuckles?' He chewed robustly, swallowing most of the last sentence with his food.

'Is that true?' Irissa demanded of Ludborg.

'True enough of Torloc men, but not of Torloc dames. You will not be welcome here, with these Torloc hostilities underway.'

'The Torloc men are truly *here*?' Irissa demanded in surprise. 'I'd thought them lost. But . . . then I must see them! Besides, I can take care of myself in any circumstances,' she added, resenting the implication that she should be confined to some female enclave merely because some danger threatened. 'I need not be set aside for my safety. Whom do the Torlocs war against?'

Ludborg giggled until his robes trembled and his hood threatened to shake off his head, or whatever passed for it.

'Torlocs!' he spat out between huffs and puffs. 'Torlocs wage war on Torlocs! The men claim the city and the right of first second coming, so to speak. The women claim spiritual superiority and talismanless magic and have settled in the abandoned parklands. There wouldn't be so much domestic goose at market, my tall friend, save that the wild game have been squeezed into some Torlocless land in the middle and cannot be hunted.

'Oh, it is all topsy turvy, a veritable mess of a world. I am most − diverted − here. Diverted. Yes, that's a good word for poor old Scyvilla, always pushed from pillar to post. Yet a clever person can make a fine living here. The Torlocs at the Citydell seem fond of my future-casting propensities with blue-worms and crystals.'

The loose sleeve elevated again, almost knotting itself as it performed a series of adept motions. Blue-worms appeared and tied themselves in a matching row before falling limp to the floor and assuming a variety of arcane positions.

'The worms know all,' Ludborg intoned portentously. 'And

146

they tell me to hasten to the Citydell, as they spell it here. Or bespell it. Farewell, friends. You will find your way out without me. You have a habit of that.'

'As you have a habit of deserting us in dark places,' answered Kendric while blue-worms winked out in rapid turn. 'I well remember the Oracle of Valna.'

'Ah, Valna. Ah, Rule. Ah, every land betwixt, between, before and after — and to be.' Ludborg's voice was fading with the brightness of his worms. '. . . and now Edanvant. Our meetings are not over, no. But be wary on the streets. All is not as it seems. It never was.'

'Nor was Ludborg, if I recall,' Kendric growled to Irissa. 'Scyvilla, he called himself here, and once in Rule. Scyvilla of . . . Ah! I can never think in the dark.'

Irissa's pommelstone flared to life again as she drew the sword and held it upright. 'Be not overhard on Ludborg. If he hadn't pulled me into his dark presence, I would have been bottled in a more bruising dark in the alley outside.'

'*Och!*' Kendric crashed into something almost as big as himself. His hand felt along a wall. 'So Finorian's worst "enemy" is her own kind. I'm not surprised. I'm sure we've not heard the half of it, just as we were not told a tenth of it,' he added grimly. 'Enemies, indeed. Lucky I stumbled on the wall in the woods, and thought to look on the other side of it.'

Irissa was numb and growing number. 'The men are safe but . . . separated from the rest of us. Why should Finorian conceal their presence? Reunion was what the women of Rindell sought . . . or do the other women know nothing of it, as we were supposed to, had we not walked through magical walls? Jalonia still wonders after Orvath — perhaps *he* is not here, though,' Irissa speculated suddenly, almost hopefully. 'Perhaps he perished on the way. If he were here, if all the men were, why would Finorian be so cruel to the women as to hide that?'

'Ludborg said the men arrived first,' Kendric said, sounding satisfied. 'Perhaps Finorian doesn't like being second at table. As usual, Finorian has ringed us in half-truths cut from whole cloth. We won't know more until we ask — the men. At least I've got directions to this "Citydell", and we can finally ally ourselves with the right side in this unfortunate affair.'

'What makes you assume the men are right?' Irissa asked sharply in the dark, following his voice.

'They have not lied to us — yet,' Kendric answered simply.

He pressed on a piece of darkness scratched with faint white lines of light. Daylight painted the interior of Ludborg's dingy warehouse bright as they pushed through a curtain and into a market booth shaded from the sun but ablaze with the glory of gathered orbs of every size and brilliance, all of them lit from within by a moving blue-worm.

Would-be purchasers of this exotica formed a line Kendric had to plunge through. The crowds parted reluctantly for him, unintimidated by his great size despite their own remarkable heights, but they gave Irissa wide berth. In the street outside the booth, Kendric stopped to declaim the sign worked into a tapestried awning.

' "Ludborg the Fanciful, Scryer Extraordinaire and Far-thinker." Still a fraud,' he concluded.

'But right in one thing.' Irissa was studying the sober faces eyeing her with resentful fascination. 'I am not welcome here.'

'You are merely strange to them,' he answered. 'These yokels' everyday lives hold so little novelty that they freeze at any variation in what is customary.' He took her arm with an accompanying glower at the gathered crowds. 'Whatever conflict brews here, we need not be party to it. We are mere journeyers, and now we are bound for the Citydell, for a reunion with your long-lost kin. Blood is thicker than . . . than bloodshed. None will argue with that.'

'I will.' The cat riding Irissa's shoulder again spoke at last, springing the long way to the ground unaided despite Irissa's quick grab for her. 'Reunions, as I remarked before, are overrated. This one will be even worse.'

Felabba, limping slightly, stalked into the crowd, unconcerned

148

about shifting feet. As with Irissa, people drew back for her, but whether from awe, respect, or simply dislike of a Torloc thing, it was impossible to tell.

No gate awaited at the Torloc command post. They had found it along an endless curve of street, looming at the top of a slope that looked cliff-sharp when one turned back to study the acute inclination of one's past path.

Irissa did not look back, nor Felabba, but Kendric did. The building itself was everything he had not expected. It stood mountain-proud, higher than the castle in the forest, its citified shape defined by endless crenellated towers and windows of all configurations blazing with falgon's-eye coldstone work. Iridesium formed a feathered skin around the whole, so there was something vaguely sinister about its sleek, dark, soaring profile.

And yet it stood in full sunlit glory, a wealth of rainbows reflecting off its curried curves until it resembled a watered silk pattern, sinuous and surprising. It looked less made of metal-sheathed stone than of some unheard-of animal hide.

'Finorian sets up housekeeping in a mere hovel compared to this,' Kendric said slowly. 'The sight of it makes me fear her less — and them more.'

'You fear Finorian?' Irissa was surprised by Kendric's admission, but his amber eyes met hers quickly.

'I fear what she may do. And so, apparently, do those who call yon falgonskin gauntlet of Torloc architecture home. Perhaps we will find more than that in common, and there is naught to fear on any front.' His smile grew grimmer. 'It has been a long quest, to find this Edanvant. Now that I know Edanvant has two faces, I would see them both first-hand, no matter the right or wrong of either side. And you?'

'Whether I would or not, I must,' Irissa said, again struck by the alien look of her people's native landmarks. In Rule, Torloc architecture had bowed to human scale and style, so the building's size alone seemed awesome, and Citydell comprised what must be a small city in itself. The edifice hovered over them, the great Iridesium-sheathed wings of its upper stories sweeping groundward and supported by a forest of slender silver wires along which daylight ran in tremulous watery strings, so the courtyards seemed to be constantly weeping. The sound of splashing, hurling, falling water echoed everywhere, yet all was dry, and the effect, rather than being sylvan, was simply overbearing.

A gate as high as that leading into the city itself gaped open, not carelessly, but as if the residents had not bothered to fear whatever might approach from beyond their bastion.

'Torloc to the hinges,' Felabba pronounced, trotting smartly through the towering gates, like an aged great-aunt on an inspection tour disguised as a visit.

Kendric followed, looking always upward, as if for aerial attack. It was left to Irissa to walk in last, her hesitant footsteps seeming to stutter their way over the polished coldstone pavement.

'These Torlocs apparently neither fear nor greet guests.' Kendric surveyed the empty interior courtyard, his hearty tone of voice admirably substituting for a knock.

No one came — not a bewilderment of false Finorians, not a crew of churlish gatekeepers, not so much as a mouse to occupy Felabba's idle moments.

'Torlocs fear nothing from without, only the strangers within,' Felabba said authoritatively. 'I will be as I was in Geronfrey's hall in Rule — mute,' she instructed them.

Kendric bowed courtly acquiescence. 'To what do I owe this singular favor?'

'To my good sense,' snapped the cat, 'which is to yours as the sun to a dust mote.'

Kendric's eyebrows rose and he would have replied, save that a contingent of coldstone-sweepers, shy city youths as silent as Felabba had chosen to be, poured from the inner doorway.

The sweepers ushered the party inside simply by assiduously brushing the stones where they stood with fragrant hazel twigs until the trio found themselves standing on the only undusted surface, a threshold of carved weepwaterwood.

Inside, the dim coolness with which all awesome buildings

greet their newcomers hushed even the perpetual clatter of the courtyard's invisible water.

Irissa, Kendric, and the cat walked slowly — in a body, but each at his or her own, oddly separate pace — through a shaded forest of soaring weepwillow trunks. No trailing branches looped back to the ground; the massed wooden pillars narrowed upward indefinitely to a ceiling of burnt-peach glass fretted as delicately as a dragonfly's wing with Iridesium veining.

If the antehall seemed to stretch forever, the stairs that began at its end sliced the very concept of ascension into neat, knife-edged rows of red marble risers. Gold shimmered in the soft darkness — and silver, copper, platinum and pewter. Green gold it was, tinged with the shade of growth as rocks are dressed by living moss and richer for it.

Among the great burnished weepwillow trunks people came and went; carrying trays and huge falgonskin-bound volumes, toting cleaning utensils and message scrolls; all silent, as silent as Felabba and Kendric and Irissa. Perhaps no one spoke in these halls, on these crimson stairs, down this long, echoing passage, in this solemn room draped with samite in which the three found themselves pausing at last.

No one spoke, but someone came — many someones, marching over hard coldstone floors that everyone else had trod softly. A clatter like hail, hard-falling water drops, resounded all around. Irissa glanced up to find the sunset-tinted ceiling still serene, with no jagged holes of night rent in its eternal twilight surface, as she had somehow expected.

Kendric turned. 'That sound—'

They filled the room with their presence then, the men who strode in from the east, west, north, and south of it, the tall, Iridesium-mailed company of watchful but calm men. Their Torloc hosts.

One took their forefront as naturally as a lancepoint precedes the haft of a spear.

'You come from beyond the gate and do not respect gatekeepers,' he declared. A scroll curled in one hand, as if he'd been drawn from its perusal by the inconvenient arrival of an itinerant peat-seller or refuge-seeking supplicant.

Kendric stood as speechless as Felabba, too stunned to reach for words or weapon. Most of the men, numbering twenty or so, arranged themselves around Kendric, not threatening but intensely curious.

They were Torlocs, and Irissa found it meet that she should play spokeswoman, although the size of them, their number, their massed sex struck her almost dumb.

They were, in their way, as magnificent as an Empress Falgon, glittering and aloof, the last of their gigantic kind, and to be pitied as much as feared . . . though they would, of course, dismiss pity. Still, they stirred a chord of harmony in her bones, as if she were seeing for the first time the other side of a well-read page. She understood now Jalonia's sigh for a happier, wholer Rindell that Irissa had never seen.

'We have come from beyond your gate, and many others, in search of Edanvant, in seach of Torlocs,' she began carefully.

'Look to yourself,' the spokesman interrupted. 'You are Torloc enough for two.' He closed the gap between them in three limping strides and studied her icily.

'I believe that you have passed beyond common gates, seeress,' he said, his tone searingly distrustful, 'for even Finorian, weaver of wonders and falsehoods, would not dare to send one of her pet assistants into our midst. Only a fool would try the city of Edanvant and its fortress unannounced, and you are at least Torloc, therefore no fool.'

Irissa nodded ironically, seeking time, and more madly seeking a way to declare herself innocent of a past she did not yet understand or partake in. She swallowed nervously, loath to believe that these men, these kinsmen, meant to judge her as enemy merely because she happened to be one of the women. Yet their leader's slate-dark eyes remained obdurate.

He equaled Kendric in age and almost in height, although he was swarthier of complexion and hair, with an air of autocratic command that Kendric had never aspired to on his most overbearing days. He seemed a sober man, like the others; Irissa could not ever imagine him singing, for instance. He might play the lute in a melancholy mood, and might as arbitrarily cast it from him to the flames if its tune displeased him.

They looked to be hard men, all of them, sure only of themselves and some inner certainty that the world would take if they were so foolish as to give. And, Irissa perceived slowly as her deepest instincts stirred, they seemed to have lost something they were unaware of, yet all their beings unknowingly ached for it.

'A Torloc dame silent,' the man mocked her. 'We were told to expect no more seeresses to be born among us. You must be a changeling, then. Truly you are of a different breed, whatever you call yourself — Torloc or fool.'

The bitter scrape of calculated mockery touched fire to Irissa's inner steel. She answered him, but addressed them all.

'I am Irissa of Rindell, daughter of Jalonia and one among you — if he still lives. I am not ashamed to call myself "fool" if deserved, but I begin to think twice of calling myself Torloc.' Her voice shook with anger, not fear. The man's face altered dreadfully as she answered, until it became a mask of itself.

He stepped backward, then turned abruptly to Kendric.

'We know her lineage now,' he snapped. 'And yours?'

'Kendric, they call me,' he answered calmly, unintimidated by the men's size or number. 'Kendric, once of Rule, once a Wrathman of the Far Keep, once a rim-runner of the Inlands of Ten . . .'

The man, surprisingly, nodded absent recognition at mention of all three things. 'What are you now?' he asked.

Kendric shrugged, a motion that shifted the set of the sword on his back. The man's dark eyes fell upon it, respect and envy mating in his expression.

'I am a traveler,' Kendric answered. 'A crosser of lands and of gates. A seeker after great wisdom, a finder of some small foolishness. And, as you say, an admonisher of gatekeepers,' he finished blandly.

There was a pause. The Torloc leader dragged himself, his unbending leg trailing, back and forth in front of Kendric, as if to unnerve him. 'And the cat?' he demanded without warning.

'A stray.' Kendric glanced dismissively to the small white figure at his feet. 'It leeches onto whatever feeds it. Most difficult to dislodge.'

As if in response, Felabba leaped to a nearby table where some ebonberry cakes and cream lay set out, and began lapping at the thick liquid.

A laugh loosened the men's demeanor then. Even the spokesman smiled, or at least one side of his grim mouth twitched.

'A cat indeed, exactly as it seems.' His expression sobered. 'You seem a decent fellow, Kendric the traveler. We, too, have traversed many gates, not always mortally, and should exchange tales.'

He turned reluctantly to Irissa, whose anger had simmered while she had been first insulted and then ignored. He watched her idly, appearing to address Kendric, the other Torloc men, himself — everyone except her.

'As for Irissa once of Rindell in Rule . . . she may stay with us for a short while, knowing that no Torloc woman has slept under this skyroof in decades immemorial, knowing that we regard her kind as deceitful and deadly and the silver-eyed seeress as the most noxious of all—'

He limped slowly to one of the doors from which the men had entered, turning at the threshold for a final word. 'Knowing that I am Orvath and that she is my daughter, which makes no difference whatsoever to all or anything that I said before.'

The men swept out then, in a body, leaving Kendric and Irissa and Felabba mute in their absence.

'He is your—?' Kendric could manage no more.

Shock had frozen Irissa's face into a pale imitation of her father's rigid features. One deep breath heaved the Overstone pouch on a crest of breastbone. Absently, she curled her palm around the talisman, as if for comfort.

'I don't know what to say—' Kendric tried again.

'Say nothing,' advised the cat, Felabba.

Irissa stood dazed, shaking her head softly from side to side. Kendric eased a hip down on a nearby table edge with a creak all too reminiscent of the vanished Torloc men, watching Irissa's face veil in a glaze of horror so thick and then opaque it seemed the visage he knew behind it had cracked to the bone.

A quartet of serving girls, still so fresh from the city that giggles lurked in the corners of their laughter-pursed pink mouths, came later — much later than was polite. They escorted the party up coldstone stairs as clear as crystal cascades, down halls hung with feathered tapestries enacting scenes and stories so fabulous that even the cat, Felabba, would be hard put to outdo them, to a series of chambers high over the building's ground-dipping wings.

Irissa went numbly to the first ewer she spied and poured a thin stream of water into its brassy companion bowl, meaning to wash but instead running her fingers around and around in the liquid.

Kendric came softly over. She could almost see his face leaning above her, reflected in the swirling water. Certainly she felt his presence, the specific creak, smell, size of him. His emotions stirred as carefully as his breath over the very top of her head. She felt a warm, diffident mist hover at her temples like a veil.

'You have fulfilled more quests than you set out upon,' he said. 'That is not a small achievement.'

'I sought my people, nothing more!' she protested. 'Merely life as I had known it since a child — home . . . harbor . . . whatever one of any kind would call it. That they happened to be Torlocs is my grief,' she added bitterly.

Irissa suddenly thrust the basin away, both of her hands hurling it aside like a golden helmet. Water sprayed the fire until its crimson snakes of flame hissed; the moisture finally fell and soaked blood-dark upon a ruddy carpet woven of some silky strands.

Kendric bent to retrieve the empty bowl, holding it upon his dampened knees while seeming to search for words among the carpet's silken designs, and failing to find them.

Irissa, her emotions undammed by violent action, found them first.

'The lure that I followed — and you with me — was ever

155

false! I have been pursuing mist and delusion in my hope of reuniting with those who have learned to live without one another and would keep it that way. And now . . . I am caught in the teeth of their division, like a wild thing caged by double rings of wall. I must judge, and be judged by them, and I never wanted that! I did not cross a gate to follow a long-lost father! Or to find a mother. I would never ask that much. So why must he . . . go to such lengths to repudiate me? I ask nothing of him, nothing!'

Irissa knelt alongside Kendric, her eyes blind with unfallen tears, her hands wringing his arms as if to infect him with the same wrenching burn of emotions that wrung her.

'Welcome, that is all I sought; to be among those I was used to being among, to have things as they were before they were wrested from me by some harsh twist of chance.' Her voice grew wheedlesome. 'Is that so much?'

Kendric's reply came low. 'I don't know; it is more than I had.' He sighed as he stood, pulling her erect with him. 'Perhaps you should be grateful at least for the memory of believing in a better place, a better people.'

'I should disown the memory! It was false from the first — and I was the only one who did not know it . . .'

But she failed to finish her thought, turning instead to take the washbowl from Kendric and install it in its customary place. If tears fell to dew the inner slope, or it was only the residue of the lost water that trembled there, Kendric did not know, and was afraid to ask.

He reluctantly went to the door, knowing Irissa must duel her questions — and answers — alone this night. 'There is lodging enough for a party of twelve along this corridor. Felabba can choose her own suite—' Irissa did not smile. 'They said we can stay, and I think that we need rest before we — you — decide what to do next.'

'It was decided long ago, I fear,' Irissa answered, casting herself across the bed, her face pillowed on a coverlet embroidered with every variety of scentless flower Kendric had complained of in the forest beyond the city gates.

He paused, half of all the nameless things within him urging him to her, urging him to console with words, with all the wordless ways he had learned in these long days of wandering. Half of the nameless things rose to hold him back, to counsel withdrawal and retreat. Which urge was the more cowardly he could not guess, but in the end he turned and left soundlessly, even his creaky boots hushed.

The cat remained, unnoticed for the first time in her long and eventful life, and not enjoying the anonymity one iota.

CHAPTER TEN

'*Psst!* friend Kendric! This way!'

Kendric peered down the empty passage, wondering who in the maze of masonry he surreptitiously explored would have the gall to call him 'friend.'

' 'Tis I — Ludborg.' A piece of drapery detached itself from against a wall and skittered to Kendric's side. 'And where are your lovely companions?' it inquired politely, the hood angling almost horizontal to regard Kendric in the eye with nothing more than the customary interior void.

Kendric smiled at the notion of considering the sharp-boned and sharp-tongued Felabba a 'lovely companion.'

'Irissa . . . rests,' he said evasively. 'As for the cat, it wishes to be considered no more nor less than it appears to be, and wouldn't welcome inquiries after its well-being.'

The hood nodded solemn understanding. 'You sound in need of rest yourself, friend Kendric. Such a festy mood. Perhaps you would care to share my solitary supper.'

'Supper? I wondered if these grim hosts would feed us.'

'Come then. It is a tasty repast, I promise you. I need my strength for a crystal-casting.' Something within the hood's hard circumference appeared to wink, but perhaps that was wishful thinking on Kendric's part.

Nevertheless, he followed his spherical guide down more long and lonely halls to a room like his own, reached through a hanging brocade curtain rather than a door.

'They don't believe in privacy, do they?' he commented. 'Torlocs, that is.'

'We can be perfectly private.' Ludborg snapped his fingers — or rather, snapped something hidden within the excessive

158

lengths of his sleeves that Kendric assumed to be fingers.

A line of blue-worms sprang to light along the curtain edge, then sewed it shut against the wall with the stitches of their long, sinuous bodies. Inside the room, an ample array of foodstuffs beckoned on a table illuminated by candelabras lit with living blue-worms.

Kendric wasted no time in seating himself and selecting a trencherful of fish, fowl, hare, and pork.

'This is a splendid salad,' Ludborg offered, waving his sleeve over a wooden bowl heaped with chopped herbs and greenery.

Kendric shook his head. 'I consumed enough salads within the forest to feed a herd of bearing-beasts. Where do the city dwellers get meat, then, if the wild beasts rule the ring between these two separated realms of city and forest and cannot be hunted?'

'They raise it, and festy work it is too. Pigeons and pheasants in cages; fish in large, leaky brass tubs; eggfowls in Iridesium-wired coops. But they counted themselves lucky simply to salvage some edible beasts before the Torloc dames arrived and drove the wild creatures wilder, so to speak. Before then there was much hunting and harvesting of the forest, and the city folk waxed happier with their returned Torloc overlords. Though not much.'

'Quite a speech, but continue,' Kendric invited. 'I'm too busy chewing to do anything but listen.'

Ludborg, who displayed a reluctance to eat in public, folded his sleeves thoughtfully over the full globe of his stomach.

'There's no question the Torlocs sprang from here, ages ago — or that the common people of Edanvant had learned to live quite well without them. Then they began coming back. First the men, one by one, worn and little inclined to take up their old role of lordling. Everyone knew from legend that Torloc women bore the power; the men were mere administrators. Administrators without power become figureheads.

'So hardly a flutter was felt when one or two Torloc men came to the Citydell, or even when the dust-darkened windows lightened by magic and the silverthread garden began singing

159

its watery scales again. But more and more Torlocs came. By the time Orvath arrived — and he was the last to do so — Torlocs, with their new mastery of magical talismans gathered on their journeys, were once again lords of the city.'

'Orvath . . .' Kendric reluctantly set down a leg of spring lamb basted in mint-green foxberry sauce. 'He supposedly sought the most powerful talisman of all. A grim man; I think *I* would need . . . rest . . . if he introduced himself so gently as *my* father.'

'Orvath.' Ludborg rocked with some smugness, then leaned nearer to let Kendric peer pointlessly into the depths of his vacant hood. 'Nothing happens within a certain circumference but that I hear of it immediately. Orvath, the unloving father.' Ludborg clucked what Kendric assumed to be his tongue. 'Forgive him, for he knows not what he does. He bears fewer talismans than any of them — none, in fact. His stiff demeanor is more than bearing; he froze one half his face and body in some dire misadventure on the way here.' Ludborg's voice hushed to sibilancy. 'Some say it was an ice serpent, and froze the inner man as well as the outer.'

'But what do you here, noble gallivanter after gates, if you mislike these Torlocs so much?' Kendric mopped a hunk of black bread through the last of his goose-liver gravy.

'It is . . . profitable.'

A lump appeared midway up one of Ludborg's sleeves and slowly worked its way down, like a pumpkin in the belly of a serpent. At last a clear azurine bubble appeared; within it, gleaming bright as lightning, writhed a giant blue-worm.

'These newly empowered Torloc men put great faith in signs and portents,' Ludborg explained, 'in my crystal-casting's ability to foretell the future.'

'I'll foretell their future,' Kendric said dourly. 'Their affairs are bound to go wrong as long as they believe in things outside themselves and allow division from their own kind to slice their lives into bitter halves for the same rotten apple. What did the search for talismans bring the men but danger and regret and now utter discord?'

'You seemed to have learned lonely lessons on your journey,

160

friend Kendric. But do you not bear a talisman or two as well? What of the sword upon your back?'

'I thought you set great store by the Six Swords; surely one of their number means more than a mere talisman.'

If Ludboᵣg could ever have been described to have smiled, it would have been at that moment. 'Oh, the cunning of the straightforward, to say the truth sideways. That sword you carry is not one of the Six Swords from Rule. That is a mind-called imitation, with a soul of its own, I grant you, but a faint one.'

'A soul? You ascribe such to a sword, and a secondhand one at that?'

'What of the runes that impress its hilt, the runes hidden by your homely winding of leather? Have you ever looked upon them?'

Kendric's face grew serious. 'The runes you mention linger much against my will. I would have − overlooked − them when I conjured the sword, even in my moment of great need. But they came, like Felabba and other unpleasant things, uninvited. I can only assume they mean ill for me.'

'That I cannot say,' Ludborg said shortly. 'If you ever care to unveil them, I will read them. They come from my native land, which is lost to me − and all the worlds over. Perhaps you have heard of it; it is called—'

'Rengarth!' Kendric slapped his knee so hard that Ludborg jumped a full foot into the air before floating back into place. '*That* is the world you prattled of in Rule − "lost, limpid Rengarth." Sounds a pale, sniveling sort of place to me, that won't do anyone the elementary courtesy of being accessible.'

'Rengarth is elusive, yes, and by its own will. It does not welcome strangers. But some to whom Rengarth is strange are not truly strangers to it.'

'Now you grow riddlesome, like a Torloc seeress of my acquaintance.' Kendric stood. 'May I convey some of your bounty back to her?' He was already sweeping choice morsels into a cloth he had whisked off a nearby tray.

'Oh, that is Vilatian embroidery, done by rare blind blue-worms . . . ! Never mind, take what you must. No doubt she

161

could use cheering. Good night to you, then, friend Kendric. I must hear the tale of your travels since last I saw you soon. My regards to the — er, cat. And your lady.'

Ludborg, slightly subdued, bowed Kendric out while the blue-worms linked themselves into an ornamental loop on the wall before sealing the cloth shut again behind him.

Kendric whistled his way through the overbearing halls, replete with fresh information as well as food. So his sword had been forged in this mysterious land called Rengarth, which boasted anomalies like Ludborg, hardly a recommendation for anywhere . . . No wonder Rengarth hid itself in shame.

And the Torlocs, segregated by so arbitrary a standard as sex, turned on one another and turned a once-whole world into a sterile battleground, tearing paradise into piecemeal. The men had abandoned even unmagical instinct and now prized talismans, although Irissa's father himself had none, instead bearing a wound from an unlucky encounter with magic. Kenric could sympathize with a man bereft of what every man took for granted — personal power. Hadn't Kendric been the only Wrathman in Rule lacking an ancestral weapon to supplement the longsword ceremonially bestowed upon him?

Torlocs seemed as tangled a breed as mortals, and therefore not so different after all. These matters were more the meat of mystery than its solution, he concluded, but at least offered him something substantial to chew on.

Irissa was sleeping when Kendric leaned over her threshold; she still lay facedown on the testered bed, her boots on, sword askew, and dark hair unfurled like a fan of sable feathers over her back.

Kendric tugged off the boots and drew the sword softly from her sash. He crouched by the old cat sunk into the stark cradle of its bones before the fireplace embers.

'Some vittles for you.' The cat's slit eyes shut further. 'I doubt so much as a spider calls this fortress home, with all the city lads and lassies who scrub, dust, and sweep the halls. You'll be grateful for my foresight before morning,' he predicted in the face of the animal's supreme feline indifference.

Felabba, once so chatty, forbore to answer even the

162

temptation of food. Kendric shrugged and left the cooling morsels beside her. He went into the next room to doff his sword, sit on the broad bed, wrest off his own boots, and think more than he liked on topics less than encouraging — mainly Torlocs, talking cats who refused to . . . and magic.

Irissa awoke, hungry and not alone.

A Wrathman-high shadow loomed against the light-colored curtain to her bedchamber. In an instant, she realized she occupied a place where it was no longer safe to assume such a shape must be Kendric's.

She reached for her sword and found it absent. Irissa twisted and put her feet to the floor, starled to feel the stones cold and her boots gone.

'Who are you?' her challenge sounded more like a plea even to her own ears.

The shadow moved, showing itself to be a tall man who went wordlessly to a five-armed candelabra near the window. He spread the fingers of one hand over the candle tips; in a moment they shot flames back at his flesh — or had it been the other way around?

At any rate, a tall, grave-visaged Torloc stood in the room, his hand now cradling a chest-hung medallion and his sober features lit by the light he had created. Irissa itched for her sword, for the glow of her emerald pommelstone, burned for the opportunity to flaunt her own power among these doubting Torlocs. She saw the weapon then, on a table near a decimated pile of tidbits. Felabba was nowhere visible; Irissa was alone with the unknown Torloc.

'I am Medoc,' he said at last, his deep voice tinged with regret, 'and I am to Orvath as he is to you.'

It took her sleep-fogged mind a moment to trace the statement's antecedents. 'You are my . . . grandfather!' Irissa openly gaped. The man was the brother-image of Orvath — no wonder Kendric complained that Torloc longevity blurred family relationships.

Medoc nodded, coming to sit on the pewter-battened trunk

at the foot of her bed. Irissa moved back defensively, but Medoc simply shook his head and sighed deeply.

'I was among the first to leave Rindell when it became apparent that the other Realms wished to displace the Torlocs. Few seeresses were being born to us even then, and we could not rely on the services of Finorian forever—'

'Apparently you were wrong,' Irissa interrupted.

Medoc's face smoothed into a bitter smile. 'It was a — surprise — to find Finorian first among our returned women-folk,' he admitted. 'She was ever resourceful, Finorian, I grant her that. But she violently disavowed the male quest for talismans when I first went, and the others later. She contested our search for magic outside ourselves.'

Medoc's tone grew argumentative. 'Peoples all up and down the many gates to other worlds build whole empires on talismans. Why should not a magical kind like ourselves seek new external powers when our inbred ones were fading? Were we men to wait like chained guard dogs on the waning abilities of our womenfolk to birth daughters, a rare few of whom might be seeresses? And gates were no longer opening to Finorian's command; we wanted to find keys to return to Edanvant, hoping that here both our roots and our present lives would mesh into new harmony.'

'Finorian would say you men wished to usurp powers meant for seeresses alone.'

'And she would be right! When seeresses were many, we men could be — guided — by them. When it came down to one, well, what man wishes to trot forever at a skirt hem? No, we did not mourn the dwindling of seeresses.'

Medoc leaned forward to bestow a grandfatherly pat on Irissa's arm with a disconcertingly youthful hand.

'It was a shock to see you, Irissa of Rindell,' he confessed with a cajoling tone, 'to see a young seeress whose silver eyes had not yet paled over with the glaze of old powers, a seeress whose claim upon us is one of blood as well as magic.' The man's dark eyes slammed into hers with sudden fierceness. 'It is a shock to see a seeress who can see us back on her own terms. Orvath is a bitter man, with reason, and cannot unbend easily in the face of change.'

'This is what you came to tell me?'

'I came to tell you to leave. There is only one place for you if you would stay in Edanvant. With the women. Return to the castle Finorian holds in the heart of the forest that was once the heart of our circling city of Edanvant. It has come to more than bitter separation — it will be war between us. I cannot promise that you might not become a prisoner of it if you stayed here overlong.'

'Perhaps I am a prisoner of it already,' Irissa said softly. 'A prisoner of both your sides.'

Medoc was silent a good while. 'As long as Finorian bars us from our ancestral forest with a ring of walled-in beasts as warders; as long as our endless, bitter journey to find ourselves and our fountainhead city is tainted by old claims we no longer honor; as long as we hold the hard-got talismans we have wrested from a dozen intervening worlds, no woman of Rindell will be welcome in Edanvant. Once, when they first came, we would have welcomed them. But Finorian was unwilling to defer to our new leadership. She . . . spurned our blood-bought talismans, our right to assert our supremacy in the face of her obvious failures. We know her silence of the past two years only masks some treacherous plan to overcome us. Your being here now, which we tolerate for the nonce, may be the key—'

Irissa would have protested, but Medoc's hand rose to wave her silent. 'You should know that our talismans are powerful. We can hobble or undo any teachery you might unleash in our midst. Some of us would not even suffer your presence, save they are fascinated to encounter a Wrathman again. Some of us would—' He paused heavily, then laid a hand on Irissa's shoulder. His tone was gentle, coaxing, self-assured. 'Irissa, I do not say that Orvath will seek to harm you; I simply say that I cannot promise that he will not be tempted.'

The man stood and looked down on her. 'You are of our kind, Irissa, and I would be lying to say there is no call in that. But I fear it was never enough. You are more them than you are us, and ever were.'

165

'And if I return to Finorian?' Irissa had stood and was speaking, shouting, at Medoc's retreating back. 'If it comes to Torloc against Torloc, women against men, seeresses against sorcerers, inner power against outer — who is to say I am better off dead on one side's soil or another's?'

His head shook regretfully, but he didn't deign to answer.

'You were not worthy of searching for,' she charged as she trailed his retreat, feeling hurt turn and come lancing out of her like a spear, speaking — although she did not know it — to another man, another Torloc. 'You were not worthy of finding, none of you! If you men cannot, with all your new talismans, learn to sow peace instead of dissension, then Torlocs have no place in any world, even their own!'

But Medoc would not be prodded into conceding emotion.

'You may be right,' he said distantly, 'but it doesn't matter. This division drove its roots deep before you were born — before you were conceived even. Perhaps — had we known new seeresses could be born among us — we men might have stayed and fought to make Rule accept us as we were. But you came on the scene too late to change anything, Irissa; even if your motives are innocent, you come too late now.'

He merged with the hall's night shadows, elusive as an ominous dream that is eager to evade the light of dawn.

Irissa stood in the doorway as the heavy curtain swung shut, hearing Finorian's voice, over and over, lightly chiding, as she had heard — if not heeded it — so many times before.

'Irissa. Always too late and too little. It is your fate to step upon the bridge that is breaking, child, upon the ground that is melting . . .'

Irissa turned back to the room, perhaps to consult the old cat, but Felabba was still gone, and had been behaving mutely anyway.

Kendric, Irissa thought. His name salved her mind — Kendric, who gave Torlocs short shrift but was always and almost annoyingly fair-minded. He must become the guiding force of their quest, their fates, now, she decided. Irissa felt too torn to guide more than her own footsteps through the morass of inter-Torloc enmity in which she found herself mired.

166

Thank all things skeptical, she thought, that in a world given to producing brutal surprises, she could at least rely upon Kendric.

Daylight made even clearer the extent of Citydell's vastness and organization. Despite their mutual shock, Irissa and Kendric found it necessary to tread their way below to the common rooms again, but confronted no Torloc men that morning.

They broke their unusually long fast in a sunny lower room alongside a generous kitchen, where pots steamed and fires roared even this early. Something was always simmering, one of many city cooking-girls told them, to feed so many as Citydell housed. It was not just the Torloc men, who numbered only twenty-three, but their many servitors — the cooks and kettle-washers, gardeners and sweepers, masons and armorers.

'And what,' Irissa asked, 'do the Torlocs offer in return for all this loyal service?'

The cooking-girl wiped her floured hands on her linen smock. 'Why . . . safety, of course, as they have always done.'

'Safety from what?' Kendric wanted to know.

The girl was silent, methodically turning the huge pottery bowl balanced on her hip. Her freckled fist punched a lump of dough. 'I don't know . . . against themselves, I suppose, the ones in the woods.'

'You mean against their kind — and our kind, the women.' Irissa's eyes were very grave.

'Yes — no! I'm not your kind, not Torloc.' The girl was thoroughly muddled now, and Irissa's lips took an ironic twist as her nod released the young woman back to her kitchen duties.

'I cannot blame her for confusion.' Irissa said, sighing, when only the girl's apron strings were in sight. 'Torlocs of any sex seem only too willing to ride on the sweat of common folks' ordinary deeds while aspiring to extraordinary misdeeds.'

Her hand went to her breast, reminding Kendric only then

167

of the Overstone nestled under her tunic. 'I wonder what talismans the men have gathered.'

'None, if the Torloc in question is your father,' Kendric said.

Irissa's face froze into such anguish at the mention of the man that Kendric hastily went on. 'Orvath quested for some rare talisman, but came back empty-handed,' he explained. 'Such disappointment might explain his . . . severity.'

'He did not come back — back to Rindell,' she reminded Kendric. 'And his was not the only disappointment,' she added, thinking of Jalonia's words and face. 'He came here, which is not quite the same thing.'

'Perhaps it was to him; after all, Rindell served merely as a way station on your Torloc emigration route. Perhaps he is fortunate to have found his path to Edanvant at all, whether his hands be empty or full.'

Irissa sighed and crumbled her bread atop a remarkably tasteless paste of cooked grains. She started when a presence bounded up alongside her uninspired porridge.

'You wouldn't want this, Felabba,' she warned the cat. 'It's bland as boiled milk.'

But Felabba stared with such singular soulfulness at Irissa's food that Kendric thrust the dregs of his own portion under the cat's nose and was astounded to see her lap daintily at the leftovers.

Once finished, she washed her face thoroughly, leaped off the table, and went to a door, at the crack of which she sat, looking back over her shoulder and meowing plaintively.

Irissa and Kendric stared disbelievingly at the sight of a meek, meowing Felabba. The kitchen staff popped unconcerned heads around a corner.

'Your cat wants to go out,' said the young cooking-girl. 'Perhaps you'd better let it. This is a kitchen, after all.'

Shrugging, the travelers rose and opened the door, following the upright banner of the cat's tail through it.

'Now I know why it is called "Citydell",' Irissa announced to Kendric, who, as usual, had taken up the party's rear.

They both had stopped, surprised. Before them stretched a scene from a tapestry, a cultivated woodland of fountains and flowers and shrubbery. It extended farther than a garden, with trees massed into inviting groves and the fountains' overflow trickling into shallow streams leading to leafy dells. Yet between all the wilderness weaved the lure of coldstone paths like magical silver threads interwoven into a more conventional cloth.

'Borgia bushes!' Irissa darted to a greenery clump as high as herself, some still draped in green bell-shaped blooms with long crimson tongues, others bearing bunches of shiny red berries.

'I thought borgia berries grew green,' Kendric said suspiciously, his fingers rolling the hard fruit between them like beads.

'Only when they have been aged properly do they become benign. These are young berries — fresh, red, and lethal.'

'Only benign when old,' Kendric mused, crushing berries to bloody his fingertips. 'I was going to say they're rather like Torlocs, but then recalled Finorian.'

Irissa resisted answering, enjoying walking under the sponsorship of sunlight for a change. She surveyed the ten towers that appeared so crowded together from the street and now could be seen to outpost the garden at spacious intervals. Kendric trailed her silence, as if seeking to contract it and unable to.

'How — old — do you suppose your — that Orvath is?' he wondered uneasily.

'Old enough to have suffered enough to turn it on others.'

'So is a babe, could it talk enough to say so. In truth, is he eight-and-thirty, four-and-fifty, a hundred and—?'

'Kendric! *I* don't know. A Torloc can only speak for him- or herself. I know I have passed the turn of twenty-three summers. Orvath could be twice that — or ten times it. But he is likely older than I,' she added mischievously. 'I know at least that much is required. The child is not mother to the man.'

'Don't you people even bother counting? Keeping score of the years?'

She paused to let a bubbling fountain direct a stream through

169

the latticework of her interlaced fingers. The endless blade of water poured from the single horn of a bearing-beast likeness worked in gold and silver fretwork.

'No, no one really did mark time in years. I was unusual in that, but then I always felt I was waiting for something to happen and so measured my days in hopes of tricking it into occurring.'

Kendric had stopped under a shrub high enough to overshadow his seven feet of height, as were most of the squattest bushes here. That alone should have told him it was a Torloc garden.

'You could as well be two-hundred-and-three as twenty!' he accused. 'I would not know the difference.'

'No, I don't think you would,' she said, smiling. Her hands separated, washed by the fountain. She rubbed them along her thighs to dry, mimicking the floury-handed kitchen girl without knowing it. 'But you would know the difference if I lied about it, I think.'

He pondered that, his head weighed down by a crown of shadow. Irissa stood in full sunlight, the Iridesium circlet on her brow beaming an endless round of rainbow reflections.

The garden looked utterly alien — the plants, the trees, the blossoms even. Kendric was a man who might be persuaded to consume something as outré as borgia if he had been convinced the poison had been brewed out of it, but he did not care to see where the borgia bushes grew, and who tended them and under what circumstances. All the images around him rubbed his nature raw, even with his eyes and head bowed. Something made him raise it. He looking into the distance, his face frowning in concentration.

'Do you smell it? The scent of flowers, all kinds of flowers, mixed into a sort of perfumed medley?' Kendric stepped back into the sunlight. 'Now *that* is something I can understand — a garden filled with flowers for the sweetness of them, not the potions into which their petals are crushed. That is a — mortal — impulse.'

He bent to play his fingers across the velvet of fallen white-gold petals carpeting the cool white coldstone walk like drops of melted butter.

170

'You measure mortality to your own length, Wrathman.'
The cat, Felabba, sat regarding him gravely. He stared into
her endlessly deep green eyes and saw the brown discoloration
of great age rising dregslike in their bottoms.

'I thought you had forborne to speak.'

'You thought the flowers of Edanvant had forgotten how
to dispense scent. Conditions change, and with them our best
intentions.'

'Our? Am I to discuss moral philosophy with a cat?'

'It would be an improvement,' Felabba said, turning
suddenly to weave one careful foot in front of the other as
she walked away.

'You talk of age.' Irissa's voice was soft, regret sharpening
its tone as lemon does fish's flavour. 'There goes one older
than the moon.'

'Which moon? The everpresent Inlands one, the solitary
moon of Rule, or this one so like it?'

'All of them,' Irissa said absently, and she followed the old
cat out of the Torloc garden.

'Tell me of Clymerind.'

Orvath had sunk deep into the cushioned depths of a tree-
trunk-sized chair, only his long legs thrusting beyond its
shadow. One leg thrust; the other angled oddly.

His hand balanced a goblet at the end of his carven armrest
and it caught the light of the torches blazing all around the
great hall. The other hand lay in the valley of darkness that
night shadows cast over most of his figure.

It did not occur to Kendric to refuse his request.

'Clymerind the Wonderful . . .' Kendric called it momentarily to mind, that nomadic island of Rule famed through all
the Six Realms. 'It sank,' he said shortly.

'Sank?' Orvath rose, or at least half of him did and the other
half followed.

Although at superficial glance he appeared a fine figure of
a man, a mangling stiffness pervaded him, once one knew to
look for it. It was as if he had worn armor too long and now
could not doff the habit of it with the reality.

171

'We saw it sink, Irissa and I, from the back of an airborne cart.'

'Clymerind was doomed,' Irissa added, almost consolingly, 'for it housed a gate to Those Without. Now the five Wrathmen stand underwater guard upon that gate, and Rule, I think, goes on as it always wished to − without us Torlocs.'

'Rule was ever a meager-hearted land,' Orvath said, 'and Clymerind the only promising place upon it.'

'Rule was all the home I knew,' Irissa said simply, speaking for both herself and Kendric.

Orvath's eyes met hers, then winced away. His attention turned solely, as it had tended to from the moment Irissa and Kendric had been summoned for a postbanquet meeting with the Torloc men, to Kendric.

'You carry a sword of Rule, Wrathman-who-was, and we know that for a potent talisman,' he began.

'Perhaps.' Kendric reached to touch the weapon he had lain aside, casually near yet just distant enough to be courteous. 'It is not one of the original Six of Swords in true fact.'

'Not? It wears the very image of one.' The man called Medoc spoke. Kendric had taken him for Orvath's older brother, despite his seeming to be junior in command.

Kendric smiled sardonically. 'The very image exactly. Nicely put, Medoc. I've learned from Irissa that Torlocs are gifted with putting their fingers on the pulse of things. This is my mind-built version of the sword I abandoned in Rule − I let the original slide into lakewater . . .'

But the Torloc men were less interested in Kendric's careless treatment of his sword than his casual mention of instinctive magic.

'You mind-made it?' they demanded around the room, all at once.

'I was forced to, yes. It was either that or lay my own bones beneath several feet of red Inlands earth.'

'Ivrium's Keep,' Orvath grunted in recognition from the dark of his chair.

'Yes. In the Inlands of Ten.' Irissa leaned forward eagerly,

172

amazed to think her father had viewed the same lands as she. 'Do you know it?'

His laugh was more terrible for being unseen.

'Where do you think Finorian sent me on a wild talisman chase but through that cursed rainbow gate into that cursed world? I ranged the Inlands up and down and found nothing but hardship and a gate at last to Edanvant.' His voice lowered; still, everyone in the huge chamber heard it. 'I was young and foolish then, for a Torloc. I did not yet suspect the treachery of women. I was so deceived in them that had I found a talisman of such power as Finorian described, I would have returned to Rule and brought the women here with me then. I know better now. We all do.'

'You would have come back?' Irissa asked intently, ignoring Orvath's encompassing bitterness to seize upon the kernel of hope at its center. 'Truly, Orvath?' She felt his eyes seek her out and hold her in their corrosive grip.

'Had I found the talisman Finorian said I would, yes.' This time his adamant gaze held hers as if inured to its latent silver power — or addressing another argent-eyed seeress in her stead. His voice hardened to match, accusingly. 'Had I not found instead a trap set with ancient Torlockian bait, a trap that snapped me in its icy jaws and left me twisted to crawl my way to mortal rest. I — fell — into another gate on the way — and became the last of my kind to join my fellow Torlocs here. By accident.' The goblet waved, made to dance by Orvath's single visible flame-gilt hand.

'It was unfortunate—' Medoc began.

'Unfortunate? It was planned! They planned it! Finorian . . . Jalonia even. The women. They wanted us well gone so they could rule themselves.' Even the goblet vanished as Orvath drew it into the darkness with himself and drank.

Irissa's hand pressed her heart. Kendric glanced her way, surprised. Irissa was not one for breathless feminine gestures. She spoke again, her voice as low as her father's.

'What — was this Inlands talisman for which you risked so much?'

Orvath snorted bitterly. 'Why not tell you? You'll not harm

us. We have our safeguards. It was a stone, of course. All magic in that place was founded on stones. I see you wear the remnant of those stones upon your finger, Kendric. I'd hear the tale of it.'

Irissa's right hand, ringed with Inlands Stones her father had not deigned to notice, tightened into a fist on her breast. 'What stone?' she asked, unwilling to be distracted although his attention had already dismissed her.

'A stone, seeress! Do you know nothing? Pale, powerful, more powerful than any single Inlands Stone. Finorian called it the Overstone and said it was . . . egg-shaped. That was how I'd know it − if it was there to be found, which it was not. She claimed that it was there only to lure me from Rindell on a fruitless errand, perhaps to my death.'

Irissa's hand clenched on what it protected, a small warm oval of stone.

'Why are you so sure Finorian lied?' she wondered.

'Because she is female!' he snarled back, his Iridesium-dark gaze hot with despite. Kendric frowned, but his support was unneeded. Irissa regarded her father calmly, until the spark of his rage winked out and he subsided into his chair and his melancholy.

'And because Finorian had always detested talismans, until then,' he explained wearily. 'Because now that I see you, I see that she had used Far Focus to presee your birth. She foresaw that Jalonia carried the first Torloc seeress in many generations! She had resented we men's power in practical matters and would have none of our say in magical ones. With me − lost, she − and Jalonia − and all the rest, would have none to contest their plans.'

'I don't think so,' Irissa began, frowning to recall her mother's differing version of the events.

'What do you know of it?' Orvath spat. 'You are the creature of their machinations. I do not know how you slipped the leash of Finorian. Perhaps she sent you here to make some daughterly call on me and spy out our strengths. Perhaps you came yourself to bring Citydell down. I rule nothing out, save

174

that I do not trust you — and more, call you daughter only by coincidence.'

Irissa had paled until it seemed her hair grew darker around the frame of her face rather than that her skin had whitened. Her hand still clenched the Overstone at her breastbone, the other hand resting on her sword, though it trembled.

'I came to seek my heritage, not of the loins of a single man but of the long, weary interweaving of Torlocs with each other and the world. I have no more desire to call you "father" than you have to name me "daughter". I am Irissa of Rindell and I answer only for my own deeds.'

'And you will answer for any misdeeds you work here, seeress!' Orvath's tone made Kendric tense to stand, momentarily impelled to challenge its threat.

Irissa stood, stiffer than the man she would not call father, and Kendric thought he had never seen her so severe, so pride-hurt. He thought her carved of the substance they had been discussing — stone.

He remembered suddenly the power she contained and how lethally she could wield it. He knew not what to reach for, his sword or his latent bed-bought powers. The moment sang with pain, anger, and unused magic.

Irissa finally sat again, heavily, like her father, as if she had aged three human lifetimes in those few moments. Kendric, for one, breathed easier in the infinitely airy room and leaned near for a soft inquiry.

She shook her head mutely, as if to say 'don't worry, I fare well.' She had resolved to be silent, like Felabba, in this place of old wounds and new hurts. But her heart hung heavier than the Overstone egg, and her hand ached from encompassing its contours until she seemed to feel an uneasy, answering throb within it.

She held, of course, the very talisman he had sought so arduously. Irissa had recognized that at the beginning of Orvath's story of his quest.

She had even considered revealing that fact, offering it to him, magnanimously, to provide Orvath with a long-delayed happy ending. Such a healing gesture, she thought, would end this foolish contention between men and women of the same kind, would bind wounds and repair broken bonds.

'Here, father,' she would have said, she could even hear her voice declaiming in her mind. 'I have small need of talismans and you have no talisman but need. Take it; it is yours now. It was fated that your daughter follow unknowingly in your footsteps to fulfill at last your quest . . .'

Orvath would take nothing from her, or any Torloc woman, Irissa knew that now. The Overstone egg was hers, utterly hers, unhappily hers, for good or ill. She had never even opened her eyes on the Rindell sun when Orvath took the gate and traveled the Inlands and met the pain that marked him to this day.

None of the men would take anything from the women but surrender, she concluded, and that proud, obstinate road led both ways. Where had she led them — Kendric and herself — but to the opposite of haven, of home?

Irissa drew deep into her own inner dark, the dark beneath her veiling hair and lowered lashes, the dark behind the silver of her eyes. She listened as if she were not even there, as they all wished her to be, and let the men talk.

CHAPTER ELEVEN

'I had a dream once,' Irissa mused, 'In an ice-caught cave near Falgontooth Mountain. I dreamed of finding an egg that burned red upon my palm.'

'That was in Rule,' Kendric pointed out. The remoteness of Rule in both time and place seemed to relieve him. 'And this — egg of stone — you found keeps its coloration blessedly nondescript.'

He leaned over the article in question so intently that it appeared he sought to see through it. They shared the window seat in Irissa's light-shot chamber; setting sunlight played across the Overstone egg's smooth surface, showing no crimson infusion. Yet however lightly Kendric might mention the matter, the Overstone had changed since Irissa had slipped it into a falgonskin pouch at the Damen Castle.

'It seems heavier,' she complained suddenly.

'I warned you that we would travel lighter without it.'

'And I have seen it pulse with threads of color.'

'You talk as if it were a live thing. Give it to me.'

Kendric's steady palm curved under Irissa's; she let her hand turn, the Overstone egg rolling into his.

'I would have given it to Orvath,' she said, 'for his was the first questing for it, but—'

'Orvath is not a man to give anything to,' Kendric agreed brusquely. His hand closed on the talisman as he shut his eyes to contemplate it without recourse to the most overused sense. 'You're right. It seems heavier, almost gravid.' He grinned, his eyes flashing open. 'But for all that it is still a rock, and an inopportune one at that. Think of it as a keepstone — a souvenir of all our many wanderings . . . Irissa?'

Her eyelids had shut as well but, unlike his, were not opening again. Her entire body seemed to droop, to sink sideways into an unapparent oblivion. Only the brace of Kendric's arm kept her wedged upright beside him.

'This was how using magic first weakened you,' he recalled. 'What powers are you taxing now?'

'Not that . . .' Her voice had become as flaccid as her form. 'Kendric—' He could barely hear his name on her lips. 'The, the . . . stone. Give it back.'

For a confused moment his mind enumerated a surfeit of stones — Bloodstone, Shunstone, Gladestone, Lunestone, Quickstone. He almost overlooked the large heavy one still clenched in his fist. His fingers opened slowly, as if reluctant to relinquish it — or as if the stone were loath to release him. He dropped it back at last into the limp, white cradle of Irissa's palm. Her color had ebbed until she seemed as white and heavy as the stone. Kendric's thoughts grew thick, as if something weighed them down, too . . .

'Ah.' Irissa stirred against him, like a waking child.

The distant sunfall still burned crimson through the city spires, rouging Irissa's cheek and washing the Overstone egg in a disconcerting reflective blush.

She sat up and slipped the stone into its pouch, then dropped the pouch into its customary concealment beneath her tunic.

'If it is as powerful as Finorian and Orvath think,' she said, 'it's a pity we have no inkling how to use it.'

'I do,' Kendric volunteered.

'You do?' Irissa sounded gratified. 'How?'

'I know how to use it; lose it. Drop it from this open window to the Iridesium sea below.'

He leaned out to study dark rooftops stained blood-black, their rainbow-colored veins swollen in the fatally wounded sunlight. For a moment it looked as if he and Irissa hung high above a motionless pair of giant bat's wings.

Irissa's hand tightened around the talisman hidden near her heart. 'I dare not abandon it. Something of me has mingled with it from carrying it. When you took it, I felt as if a

178

shadow had swallowed me and I was too weary to step out of its black encompassment.'

His hand covered hers as thoroughly as her hand encircled the Overstone egg. 'I saw that. If Finorian wanted this talisman, it must be burdensome magic indeed. The Eldress is not one to change her beliefs lightly.'

'It is good, then, that I took it.'

Kendric's thoughtful face grew as heavy as Irissa's had moments before, though he had suffered no temporary loss of a talisman. 'The past is irrevocable. ''Good'' is a judgment I leave to those able to foretell the future.'

As if on cue, the curtain to Irissa's bedchamber whisked aside. Ludborg stood in the naked archway, a clear glass ball as round as he himself clasped by the ends of his endlessly long sleeves.

'Ah, just as I had hoped! Torloc lady and sword bearer. I require . . . assistants . . . before I perform my crystal-casting for the sour company below. There is nothing so skeptical as an assemblage of self-made magicians.'

Kendric folded his arms.

'Unless it is a former Wrathman of Rule,' Ludborg added swiftly, rolling into the room on invisible feet. 'But you, my remarkable friends, idle in the sun's last rays. Allow me to crystal-cast for you — merely to practice, you understand. It's been some — er — decades since I did it for magical folk, and I do it now only because the genteel Torlocs below, like most who contemplate war, don superstition along with their armor. Yet — have the crystals ever lied?'

Even as Ludborg spoke, the globe whirled in his grasp, seeming to generate phantoms of itself that stretched wider and wider. Ludborg's sleeves parted to contain the translucent images of many crystal globes — overlapping orbs that shone faintly emerald and saffron and violet along their fragile outer curves. The single blue-worm that had lit the first sphere propagated, too; a whole dancing string of them spun longer and longer, turning so fast their hue looked no longer blue but white.

'A pretty trick,' Kendric judged.

179

'Pretty is as pretty does.'

In a movement too quick to perceive, Ludborg cast away the iridescent tower of globes. They broke upon the floor with a curious soft sigh, as if all three watchers' conjoined breaths had become brittle and quietly shattered.

'Oh . . .' Irissa had instinctively gone to her knees beside the fragmentary array.

'Oh, sorceress, it is beyond the mending even of your eyes,' Ludborg mocked her. '*One* — perhaps — you might resurrect.'

She had not waited for his invitation. Already segments of the still-rocking shards were rising on their curved sides, yearning toward the pieces that matched their jagged shapes. A single patchwork globe reformed, the likeness of its animating blue-worm wiggling up from the crystal shards only as the last piece melded into place.

Irissa glanced from her work to Ludborg, although there was nothing more to see in the eternal nightfall of his hood than there had ever been. Outside, the sun had sunken into its deep cobalt bed. Inside, the room dimmed in respect; now only the tangle of evicted blue-worms on the floor illuminated it. And they were fading.

'What can you read among this ruin?' Kendric asked Ludborg.

' "Ruin" is the word, my friend,' the exiled Rengarthian answered mysteriously. 'And it is for *you* to read.'

Irissa had already elevated a curved shard.

'There is a picture here,' she said, 'forming from a mist of rainbow colors. I see a woman — a young Torloc woman. And a tall man. They stand beside some water . . . not just any water — Rindell Pool! But that pool was flooded with lakewater when we left Rule . . .'

'It is us,' Kendric said dismissively. 'These crystal-skinned globes somehow reflect our deepest memories. So you are seeing you and I as we met beside Rindell Pool.'

Irissa tilted her head to watch the image unfolding on the tiny glass shard. Kendric, despite loathing to concede it, could see two infinitesimal moving figures reflected in the silver mirrors of her intent eyes. Irissa tore her gaze away suddenly, as if unexpectedly shaken.

'It is not us,' she said, her voice far more sober than the realization warranted. 'They are *both* Torloc. And I saw a sword rise from the water and cleft them apart. The forest is empty now and melting away . . .'

'Dreams,' Kendric scoffed. 'A surface enchantment to entertain the easily distracted.' Defiantly he reached a long arm to the floor to pick up the largest of the shards.

His blunt fingers turned it this way and that. Even in the shadow Irissa blinked at the rich, dazzling colors it reflected.

Kendric laughed then and looked knowingly to the black pool that was Ludborg's face.

'Runes, aye. Yes, you like to tickle my curiosity with that. I see here only crude marks like those that deck the hilt of my sword. What magic is this to see something I have seen before?'

'Try another fragment,' Ludborg suggested simply.

Kendric, ever contrary where magic was concerned, next snatched up the smallest sliver of glass, a thing that curved between the pincers of his thumb and forefinger like a bowed needle.

'Oho, now I, too, am honored with the sight of moving images—'

'Of what?' Irissa asked eagerly. Her own shard lay empty-faced in her hand, a plain piece of broken glass.

'Of what else?' Kendric flashed Ludborg a knowing look. 'The customary man and woman — you and I, I would say, save that they look nothing like us . . . They are in some grand corridor, talking. A handsome pair, right out of a tapestry or a ballad. Torchlight-haloed lovers, I would say, pale and languid, calm and—'

'What is it?'

Kendric frowned. 'Things shift before my eyes can name them. But a shadow came. They fell, my handsome pair, each to one side, like a tree that is split by lightning or an ax. They've — melted away and I feel—'

'You feel the sharp insubstantial pierce of pure superstition, my elongated friend.' Ludborg's hood nodded once — sharply — in the direction of Kendric's fingers.

181

Blood ran down the crystal filament; it pooled rich and carmine on his broad thumb pad.

Ludborg's voice wrapped itself warmly in an unseen smile. 'You should not clutch unreality so tightly, Kendric the Skeptic; it can cut deep.'

'Nonsense.' Kendric cast away the shard, which winked bubble-bright then faded.

'Heal your wounds,' Irissa suggested, 'or I will.'

But Kendric's pricked fingertips already had found the primitive tending of his mouth. 'Not worth the trouble. I've suffered bee stings bigger.'

'A most interesting casting,' Ludborg ruminated, rising slowly.

He turned amid the cluttered shards, suddenly whirling around himself until he resembled a robed purple globe, spinning so fast the outline of his rotund figure seemed to blaze blue for a moment.

He slowed like a ponderous top. The floor was swept free of shattered crystal; the single globe Irissa had reassembled with her eyes balanced, as was its wont, between the prongs of Ludborg's elaborate sleeves.

'I am needed below,' he announced, 'but I doubt my next casting will produce the spectacular revelations of this one. It is a pity they are so underrated. If only the old cat were here; she would appreciate the significance of these events.'

'Where *is* Felabba?' Kendric asked Irissa when Ludborg had oiled his way out.

'She has been keeping herself at a distance of late. I can't help thinking she's up to something.'

'Or is as weary of our company as we are of hers,' Kendric said hopefully. 'At any rate, I will concede that the crystal-casting taught me a lesson.'

'Indeed?' Irissa's eyes glimmered in the sun's last faint light. The room was nearly dark, but each knew the other's position in it as if by heart.

'Indeed. Two handsome couples beset by sword and shadow. It is a risky world — or worlds — we inhabit, and we dare take nothing for granted, including ourselves.'

'Your meaning is as veiled as Ludborg's crystal scenes.'

'But not my deeds.' Kendric's hand reached out to the dark, as sure as a crystal-caster of what it would find.

It met, unseen, Irissa's handclasp, midway in the dimness.

'This is the highest tower in Edanvant.' Their guide gestured to a teeming river of far-below rooftops and streets, among which heads the size of cinders bobbled continuously about their business.

Irissa and Kendric occupied a needle of masonry, the Citydell's tenth and tallest tower, which wrapped around an endless spiral staircase before finally impaling itself in the plump broad expanse of the edifice's lower stories.

They stood at the remote eye of that needle, surrounded by narrow window slits that stared in every direction. Save for its narrowness of construction, which kept visitors pressed elbow to elbow and their hands clenched around the circular wrought-Iridesium railing that ended or began the stairway, depending on one's perspective, it reminded them both of Geronfrey's under-mountain tower room in Rule.

But their host and guide this time was only mild Medoc, who had dragged them from a solitary but satisfying breakfast for the avowed purpose of 'seeing the city.'

'Is it not more beautiful than the city of Rule?' he demanded pridefully.

'Everything looks lovelier from a distance, including the past,' Irissa noted.

Medoc spoke as if he had not heard her. 'Look to the north, south, west, and east, Wrathman. See how our city spreads its wings. The green beyond it is fields, all turned to agricultural purposes. Our city is a circle, you see. Continue long enough along central street and you return to where you began.'

'And that dark spot there?' Kendric pointed to a sizable blot of green set like the center of a target amid the glittering white stone and black metal that interwove into a panorama of construction. 'No heads of any size move there.'

Medoc's hands tightened on the railing. 'Inside that cursed double wall of Finorian's obstinacy, all is forest, too high to

183

show the heads within. And there are few heads worth seeing — only those of a handful of headstrong, stiff-necked women who returned with Finorian.'

'How do you know? Or do you judge on Orvath's words only? Have you seen them?' Irissa demanded.

Eyes so black they winked blue regarded her. 'We have our own minor magicks, seeress,' he reminded her ironically. 'Our talismans. They are sufficient to let us farsee to some extent, although not with a seeress's polish and evasiveness.'

'I have not seen any talismans,' Kendric noted.

'Nor shall you.' Medoc spoke sharply. 'Not with *her* present.' He nodded at Irissa without meeting her gaze. 'We are not such fools that we allow an untamed seeress among us without taking certain precautions. We have set safeguards in motion against any treachery, and beyond that, we have the common sense to keep our talismans' talents to ourselves. Unlike inborn magic, talismans are too damnably portable, and serve one master as blithely as another.'

'I have no need to steal your magic,' Irissa protested.

Medoc ignored her — perhaps for diplomacy's sake, perhaps because he no longer listened to her. He turned to the vista again. 'I brought you here to see the city, to see that Edanvant was city first and city always, and Torloc *men* built these edifices. The portion that Finorian clings to was but some . . . amusing wilderness allowed to grow awry for the people's entertainment. This is Edanvant, and if Edanvant is what you sought, you should submit to it, embrace it, become one with it.'

'And those in the forest?' Irissa's gaze still centered on the distant solid of green.

'They will give up — in time — and we Torlocs have plenty of that. Perhaps we men will let them join us here eventually, once they've recognized the folly of resisting the changes time has wrought. When we men quested for talismans, we wrenched the Torloc eternal verities into a new direction — one we made and followed. If the women, purged of Finorian's influence, recognize our right to lead in all matters, even magical, we may accept them into our city at last.'

Medoc paused, frowned, and cleared his throat uneasily. 'We are all youthful men, even for Torlocs. We grow weary of consorting with awestruck city maidens whose eyes lift no higher than the top of their own heads. They fear us, the city dwellers, and with that comes some hate, of course. They were content enough with Citydell empty and no one of power among them to direct their actions.'

'No,' Irissa mused with irony, 'the Torloc women would not fear you. Can you afford that again?' Her eyes met Medoc's with some of his own sternness.

He laughed nervously. 'You still can startle me, seeress, with the unseemly directness of your gaze. I hope that facility is not catching . . . for if we were to reunite with the women, there might be other seeresses born. That possibility gives us pause, though we are not completely averse to women of power. They have their uses, if they understand their place.'

'But the seeresses would not lead you, as before?'

'Why should they? This Far Focus was always a mystical thing. Edgy. Unreliable. Woman's work, springing from some vague well of instinct and emotion even Finorian could never explain. Our talismans, on the other hand, come differentiated for their functions. One brings light; another, darkness. One makes unseen things visible, another, the visible things unseeable. You see, do you not, the magical refinement such predictable aids permit? A seeress's magic, on the other hand, must always be filtered through herself, a most — arbitrary — medium.'

Irissa remained silent, and Medoc as well, thinking his arguments had taken hold. Kendric knew better.

'All magic reflects the nature of its bearer,' Kendric declared. 'And talismans can be lost; besides, Irissa bears potent talismans as well.' They both turned to him, amazed; Irissa's silver eyes widened with silent warning.

'I mean the ring of five stones, which she has not fully tested yet,' Kendric went on quickly, aware that she feared mention of the Overstone. Like Irissa, he had recognized it for the talisman Orvath sought. 'And she wears the Iridesium circlet, a common thing in Rule, yet it has aided her in dire circumstances elsewhere. I myself in turn bear these inward gifts you so despise, Medoc. Believe me, they make as real and heavy a burden as my sword, perhaps weightier, for only I see that I carry it and that is lonely work.'

Medoc stared at Kendric for a long while. 'Yes, we knew when you said you had mind-forged the sword that you were one of those unfortunate enough to face magic from both its sides. That is why we might cherish the hope that you — and Irissa, too, of course, should she prove herself sufficiently harmless — will remain with us, remain *of* us. You are our future,' Medoc said, addressing Kendric, 'and we do not wish to make an enemy of you.'

Irissa and Kendric shared a silence, mutually realizing that Medoc's rooftop excursion had not been uncalculated. Kendric finally released a hoarded breath.

'So we receive a welcome in Edanvant at last — from where we least expected it.'

'There is nothing for you in the forest.' Medoc gestured dismissively to the distant green. 'We men have tolerated this . . . rebellion among the women too long. Now that Finorian has imported a new weapon' — he glanced for the first time in a long while to Irissa — 'we may have to draw weapons of our own. Our talismans can batter the wall or release the beasts in a ravening flood upon the castle. The forest will become our pleasure garden again. It is only a matter of time before some factor or other forces our action.'

'These are your own kind you propose to flatten with your will!' Irissa argued ardently.

'They are misguided,' Medoc said persuasively, 'weak, stubborn, unnaturally wedded to each other at the expense of their menfolk, cleaving to Finorian and her misspent magic. We men knew Rule was lost to us, and us to it. We knew seeresses would in time come to protect only the rare fact of their own existence, not the good of all Torlocs. We knew that in a modern world magic must be quested for and fought for.'

Medoc lifted a medallion from his chest. A sunburst etched

with the figure of a horned man gave gold greeting to the sun itself.

'Quested for, fought for,' he repeated. 'And killed for,' he finished. 'Most of us came to Edanvant by bloody and bitter roads. We came here to follow our own wills, not the dictates of a seeress who knows not the smell of blood on her hands, who sits and farsees and keeps herself aloof from the affairs of men.'

'Perhaps you have been too long apart from seeresses,' Kendric interjected wryly. He turned to Irissa. 'I feel defrauded. You promised me a green world, and that it is — here and there; you foresaw a reunion with the vanished Torloc men and women, and here they both are — albeit separated; you swore an end of gates — and there are more gates between the feuding camps of your kind than ever bridged one world from another. Torlocs! Perhaps I had best leave you to yourselves.'

Kendric vaulted the railing and quickly clambered out of sight down a lacework spiral of Iridesium staircase.

'Is he . . . always so abrupt?' Medoc asked, stunned.

Irissa smiled, an odd expression to pair with the unshed tears glazing her eyes.

'Kendric is the most well-considered man I have ever known, but then—' she turned to face Medoc again, her words sharpening — 'I have known few men, and most of them power-besot. Must I add the names of talisman-bearing Torlocs to that count?'

'We do not want power for its own sake, but we will employ it mercilessly if we believe all we have fought for is endangered — by anyone. I warn you; we have means to bring a swift and deadly end to this debate, a talisman so dire even we do not know its unleashed consequences.'

Irissa faced the view. 'And any women who survive your talisman's wrath to . . . surrender . . . would be welcome here in your city, as long as they hold no inbred power. But what of those who do? You claim there is room for seeresses in your scheme for a new Edanvant. Where would one such as I fit in your Citydell?'

Medoc blanched. 'I — I hadn't thought on it. You would —

if we found you trustworthy — stay as Kendric's . . . mate, I suppose. Whatever there is in that would remain.'

'Kendric and I have been more than mates,' she answered.

'What more is there?' he asked, bewildered.

'That you ask is a measure of your folly.' She turned again to see the city coiling neatly beneath them. 'Were . . . Orvath and Jalonia wed? Or did I result from some informal bed-bond?'

'Bed-bond,' Medoc said shortly. 'Though it was a strong alliance. Orvath has dallied, the last to leave, only because of Jalonia, I think. Then Finorian urged him to depart in quest of a talisman, though she had berated the rest of us for leaving for exactly that. From what little Orvath has said, Jalonia seemed to have urged him as well . . . It was the end of much that he had considered unending. Now he will talk of nothing but the vaunted power of the mythical Overstone egg he sought.'

'And he never knew of my conception?'

Medoc's laugh was scalding. 'We men are always the last to know of such things.'

'I can't believe it has not occurred to you, any of you men, to force a seeress into a weapon for your war against the women. Is that what you fear Orvath may try to do to me?'

'Use a seeress? Why, when we have talismans? You do not understand, Irissa.' Medoc leaned inward to make himself utterly clear and spoke as if stringing words together for a child's halting understanding. 'We do not need you; we do not need any of the Torloc women! We may want you, but we don't need you. We can always find women anywhere. Oh, we do not welcome your resistance and we might be willing to make peace with you on reasonable terms, if you can renounce your magical ways and tend to what should be women's province,' Medoc conceded. 'But we do not lust for your so-called powers—'

'Not even our bodies?' she asked, a tone in her voice Medoc had never heard before and thus was not wary of.

'Oh, that. I told you that there are women in every world, and many of them willing. But it is true; only Torloc women

188

are our native kind. You hold an . . . advantage . . . in that. And perhaps yon forest-set castle enfolds those born since my departure, who are not related by blood . . .' Medoc smiled. 'So we do have some reason to sue for peace.'

'What of she who bore Orvath?'

'Why do your think I was among the first to leave Rindell?' Medoc's handsome head shook as if dislodging an enwebbing memory. 'She died in childbirth. She was one of those born with a single seeress-eye — and being half-blessed with magic became half-cursed. Orvath, thank Rule, being male, was born with a face that did not fall between the cracks of one kind and another.'

Irissa shivered in the broad daylight. Kendric's mother had been birth-lost as well. It struck her that Orvath and he had much in common, including a bitter half brotherhood in magic.

'It is high, this tower, and the winds blow chill through it,' Medoc said, his voice becoming too kindly. 'Watch your step on the long way down.'

'So in Torloc men, magic is a slumbering gift.' Kendric had been awaiting Irissa in her chamber, pacing excitedly. 'I begin to understand it all.'

'All?' she asked.

'Why Torloc men became Wrathmen — not for any love of the Six Realms, but to obtain title to a talisman, one of the Six Swords! Apparently, once possessed of a talisman, a Torloc man can draw upon the magic latent within him. And that is why Finorian called Thrangar to Rindell to come and wed you.'

'Because he was a Wrathman?'

'No, because he was a Wrathman and therefore carried incipient magic!' Kendric caught Irissa by the elbows and sat her on the trunk before the bed as if to install an audience for his reasoning. He resumed pacing.

'Think of it! You were the first Torloc seeress in decades, and Finorian knew, as did Geronfrey, that your first union would confer your magic upon the man who mated with you. She sent for Thrangar, the only Torloc man left in

189

the realms and luckily one who would accept her will.'

'Except that Thrangar was drawn aside and bespelled by Geronfrey and I—'

'And you were left to me, who, as a Wrathman, carried a magic-made sword, therefore I could, could . . .' Diffidence interrupted Kendric's performance.

'Could catch magic from me,' Irissa finished. 'That's what you did; you caught it, like a man who goes hunting bear and finds himself in possession of a butterfly.'

'Well put,' Kendric said dryly. 'If I had never borne one of the Six Swords, I would never have been able to house whatever magic you passed to me. I am an accidental Torloc. What I spent most of my life distrusting, I have become.'

'No, no Torloc,' Irissa soothed, rising to rest her hands on his shoulders and quiet him. 'I know why you left the tower so abruptly. You tired of hearing me reviled by proxy. But I cannot blame the men for distrusting seeresses. Finorian has not been completely forthcoming with us. Yet I cannot blame her.' Irissa laughed ruefully. 'The more I see of Torloc men, the less I desire to see of them. But you are truly different, Kendric, as even Medoc has the grace to recognize. You have arrived at your magic by a road utterly your own, and it is not dependent on denying the magic in another. You are lucky in that.'

'Lucky! I am cast from gate to gate, world to world. I am challenged by strangers to swordplay, beset by wild beasts, and even followed by that . . . that excuse for a four-footed creature with claws and a purr — who talks when you don't need it and won't when you might!'

Felabba had entered during his complaint, seating herself on the table near his sword and placidly cleansing the meager fur bibbing her chin. Kendric rolled his eyes.

'I'm going to explore the city from a level on which I can see things,' he said, snatching up his scabbard and sword. 'Ordinary ground! Torlocs take too lofty a view for a marsh-born man.'

Irissa laughed fondly as he left, knowing his rough humor concealed deep confusion at the interwoven complications of

190

Torlockian magic and emigration. Then she sighed, her mind already picking at the ominous threads of Medoc's discourse. She crouched with her hands on her trouser knees to put her face near the cat's.

'Is he right, Felabba? Are you merely being contrary in keeping quiet?'

The cat looked up, one paw poised midair and midlick.

'He is as wrong as ever he was,' Felabba said sourly, 'and you know it. Edanvant was better being lost. Now found at last, all Torlocs in it lose themselves more with every sunfall that casts them in its broad, bloody shadow. Why else do you think I have come?'

CHAPTER TWELVE

The men of Citydell absented themselves from dinner that evening, so balked Kendric of having his questions answered. But Medoc appeared just as Kendric and Irissa were finishing a generous pastry. He wore a long carmine robe trimmed with green fur rather than his usual tunic and its net of Iridesium mail. On his chest the horned-man medallion blazed like a noonday sun.

'You will pardon our discourtesy,' he said, bowing formally. 'Matters magical accept no delay, not even for the demands of the stomach, as I'm sure you both understand.'

'It was of matters magical I wished to ask you,' Kendric said.

'Tomorrow night, then.'

'Will I still be welcome tomorrow night?' Irissa wanted to know.

'I know that you are unwelcome because of things that came to you unasked. But this is a bitter contention and any who would straddle both sides are likely to split themselves. My advice to you remains the same.' Medoc stepped back into an arch-hung curtain, melding with it and vanishing.

'Some trick of my eyes or Medoc's magic?' Kendric wondered.

'It doesn't matter, though what the rest of the men are up to might,' Irissa frowned. 'They have some dire hidden weapon and they edge toward using it, else why would they be so concerned to protect it from the taint of my presence – or treachery, as they would have it? It must be potent magic they evoke if it takes all their attendance.'

'Medoc is most courteous to excuse the company under

such circumstances, then,' Kendric said. 'I wonder why he bothered? We have always been inconvenient guests.'

Irissa's smile was faint. 'He is more of the men than of me; yet still feels a certain obligation he is not too embittered to shirk. After all, he is my father's father.'

'Your grandfather! And Orvath's father?' Kendric's incredulity challenged the matter-of-factness in Irissa's tone. 'Surely not . . . They look the same; both are men in their prime! Orvath and Medoc must be brothers—!'

Irissa's silence was not the answer he craved. Kendric, his mind chewing anew on the sinewy facts of Torloc longevity, pushed aside the half-eaten pastry that had finished his meal.

'I had a grandmother in my youth,' he ruminated in the way of taking a circuitous conversational route to an unpleasantly near objective. 'Not narrow and cold like Finorian, but a wide, white-haired woman as soft as a down cushion − except for her hands, which were pleasantly hardened from the work of weaving bramblemats. She told me tales of Empress Falgons and other forgotten wonders. If only she had lived to know that I had seen such a fabled beast; nay, ridden upon it . . .'

Kendric turned from the empty table to face the vaulted, empty hall. 'My grandmother is at one with the marsh now, buried on the highest ground we could find, with a bramble-bush to mark the site. And your grandfather − straight of limb, dark of hair, a man like myself in every respect − lives the semblance of a young man's life here in this magic-wakened edifice in a city that rims a sorcerous wall . . . How little that is human dwells in Torlocs, after all.'

'Medoc was just human enough, if you would attribute the impulse to that, to warn me to flee from this Citydell, from my long-lived kin, from my father.'

'He warned you against your father? Why?'

'Orvath feels betrayed by life, however long, by kin, however distant − by women, however related. He might seek to destroy me, Medoc said.'

'You believe your own father would kill you?'

'Nothing so bloody − and human − as that,' Irissa avowed. 'If Orvath knew I was as traitorous as he suspects, and as

193

he suspects all Torloc women are, he might persuade the other men to use their talismans to banish me or, worse, imprison me in some magical cage. It is nothing more than the stone-keeper Sofistron tried in the Inlands. I don't think he would actually *kill* me—'

'But Orvath is your *father!*' Kendric's fist hammered the tabletop. 'I don't care how poisonous Torlocs of either sex now find each other — blood is thicker than . . . than borgia! How can you accept such cold paternity, Irissa? Warring aside, have you Torlocs no familial loyalty, no respect for the roles you each have played in the other's existence?'

'Kendric,' she rebuked him reasonably, 'Orvath had left Rindell before my birth. I was women-reared, and they rarely mentioned the departed men, considering their absence a kind of abandonment.'

'Not even your mother? Not even Jalonia, who must have waited for Orvath's return with the Overstone — or was she as eager to see him gone as Finorian?'

Irissa shrugged. 'She never spoke his name. And then, my mother took small part in my rearing once I was old enough to toddle after Finorian, so I never knew what she thought of anything.'

'Unhappy Jalonia,' Kendric said with sudden, thunder-struck feeling. 'Denied first a husband and then a child. No wonder she lives as some meek shadow hoping to avoid the attention of everything from the mightiest magic to the smallest gnat. No wonder Torloc can talk of destroying Torloc without turning a hair; nothing binds you people but separation.'

Irissa spread her hands along the table's smooth weep-waterwood planks.

'It would have been nice,' she mused, 'to have had a grandmother, a pillowed presence whose mind had stilled to patience and whose attention could concentrate on the comings and goings of small children, who could share their dreams and wonders. My dreams were always Finorian's dreams, and my childish imagination could not outdo the wonders that she could wreak . . . especially if I were derelict in my

194

apprenticeship to her or risked my seeress's vision in some secret mirror.'

Irissa's palms petted the wood, as if to straighten an invisible cloth upon it. 'I think the best part of such a person would be the memory, after she was gone.' She looked at Kendric. 'There is very little need for such memories among Torlocs. We remain, you see, unless catastrophe cuts us down early—'

He snorted. 'Catastrophe! Being born Torloc seems catastrophe enough.'

'How can we sentimentalize the past, when it is always with us? How can Medoc be to Orvath, or Orvath to me, what Halvag the Smith was to you? Torlocs do not wane as their offspring wax. We all wax well together. We are . . . more alike than different, and feel no urgency to keep or lose one another. Perhaps there is some advantage in this.'

'Perhaps.' Kendric stood. 'I always envied your search for your people, your need of them, your belief in them.'

'It has not changed, despite it all,' Irissa said, standing to face him.

His smile was rueful. 'No. But I have.'

He took her hand formally. Together they climbed the long white stair in silence. And though Irissa remained in his bed-chamber the night through, and though the magic of bed-bond resided with them, they shared the night with new invisible bedfellows, for there was a chill regret in Kendric, and in Irissa, an unease that would not name itself.

Irissa woke at dawn to find a shadow clinging to the window frame.

'Help me!' Kendric's voice urged. One arm curled around the narrow central pillar that divided the arch. His head and shoulders floated above the sill, so he looked like a drowning man barely buoyed by some turbulent sea.

Irissa ran without reservation to the window, leaning out to see what held him back. His anchor, which dangled from the crook of his other arm, was a slack white form, its voluminous garments riffling in the wind.

It seemed doll-like in his giant's grasp, yet was burden

enough to keep him from drawing himself over the last bit of the windowsill into the room. Far below them all fanned the wide black wings of Citydell's lower stories and the delicate architectural web of rooftop spines and climbing towers.

'I thought I could' — Kendric's teeth gritted as he boosted his prize over the sill — 'manage it alone.'

Irissa eased his catch onto the chamber floor, a clumsy, slack congregation of limbs and draperies. Above her Kendric heaved a relieved sigh, then hauled himself through the narrow aperture.

She turned the object over, seeking some name for it, and exposed a face as frost-white as its robes to the thin morning sunlight.

'It is your lady of the dawn!'

Kendric grunted as he sat cross-legged beneath the window. 'Thought as much. I spied a pool of white on the rooftop below even before the sun had begun to peek over the edge of the earth. It looked . . . smaller somehow, no doubt because of the distance, and feline — or at least four-legged . . . I took it for Felabba, nuisance at large, and thought I'd climb down to retrieve it.'

'You climbed all that way — in the dark before dawn — for what might have been only a piece of wind-driven gauzelin?'

'I mistook it for Felabba,' he repeated sheepishly.

'Felabba would be deeply touched by your concern.'

Kendric shrugged. 'This Torloc architecture tends toward embellishment; there were footholds enough for an army,' he said, dismissing his feat. 'Even these upper towers are webbed with narrow bridges of battlements and flying buttresses that only a pussy-footed creature would be mad enough to make a road of. I thought old brittlebones had misjudged one of its usual ambitious vaults, that's all.

'So when I descended and by the early light saw . . . her, she seemed insubstantial enough to tote handily back up.' He groaned and settled against the wall. 'Like all lovely things, there is more to her than meets the eye.'

'She is beautiful, isn't she?'

Irissa brushed back folds of snowy fur to reveal a limp white hand among the profusely trailing sleeves. Even the hand itself seemed too delicate for function, the fingers like long, pallid petals curled into exhaustion.

Irissa's efficient fingers pressed to trap the beat of life in the lily-white wrist, to find and hold it there and keep it from fading down a long slow corridor of ebbing energy. In pulling the hand from the woman's side, she unjointed a hinge of red where arm met body.

'Here's where all the blood in her has run to,' she told Kendric in dismay. 'Didn't you notice it before?'

'Wounded, by all the joints in Finorian's nose!' Kendric scrabbled over, studying the spot. 'An arrowlike puncture, yet no haft or head remains. Odd. Can you—?'

'Can I what?'

'You know. Heal her.' He imbued the words with embarrassment, as if still ashamed to call on such extravagant powers as mending riven flesh.

Irissa's face tightened as she tore away the blood-rouged white silk to expose a neat, deep well of bubbling red. She had healed enough now to take pride in it. Restoration was perhaps the most rewarding of her Torloc powers; even Kendric had tasted its subtle surcease, both as taker and giver.

Now Irissa forgot that, forgot all but the small patch of battered flesh and bone beneath her eyes. She willed herself to help in the manner in which she could most be of help — by sending her magic-balmed eyes deep into the source of suffering, meeting pain on its own alien ground and beating it back; drawing severed veins and shredded flesh and splintered bone together again; making all things whole . . .

This she did, as she had always done it, from the first time a wounded Kendric had demanded it and she had surprised herself by being able to comply. She did this, and blood stilled its flow, flesh rewove, bone reknit. And yet — it was not enough. Rent skin flowed together like milk and frost-white eyelashes stirred on cheeks where a pink blush dawned, but it was not fully done, and Irissa knew it.

'Wait.' Her hand held the awakening woman prone. 'I am not finished—'

197

But no matter how long Irissa looked, or how hard, or how deep she delved within herself to find the roots of restoration, her silver eyes had accomplished only half-healing this time. The woman was conscious, but weak.

'It is not done,' she told Kendric grimly over the languorous form. 'Perhaps you could try—'

'No, no. No, indeed. I am a novice at such things, compared to you. At least she recovers enough to speak. Tell me, Lady, how did you find yourself atop our roofs? Did you fall from a tower? Did someone stab you and throw you down?'

The woman's eyes, a gold so sunlight-pure they seemed hardened drops of honey, blinked from Kendric to Irissa and back again.

'I came . . . to warn you.'

'To warn us — why?' Irissa was astounded that this stranger should risk anything for them.

'A Hunter roams the forest,' the woman said, her eyelids and head sinking again with her voice. 'A most powerful Hunter . . .'

'There have been hunters there before,' Kendric said.

The great golden eyes opened again. 'Not like this. This Hunter seeks for you.'

'For Kendric?' Irissa asked. 'Or myself? Or both?'

But the woman was unconscious again, blood-red threads once more oozing into the subtle weave of her gown. Kendric bent to gather her up and install her on Irissa's bed.

'She looks like a bespelled princess in a tale.' Irissa gazed down on the pale sleeping figure awash in a foam of silk and fur.

Kendric was less impressed. He dusted his hands of his recent efforts. 'Bespelled princesses do not end up on rooftops with bleeding shoulders. But she did come to warn us, though why she should care what happens to you, me, or anything corporeal I cannot guess. Despite her all too human weight, I still do not credit her existence.'

'Perhaps I can't fully cure her because she *is* bespelled.'

'Perhaps. And perhaps *she* has been bespelled to lure us back to the forest.'

'By Finorian?'

'Or by this Hunter who deals wounds that will not heal.'

'What do we do then?'

'What we do now. Tend her as best we can. Few come to these lofty rooms, other than Ludborg. We can keep her presence secret and learn more later. Meanwhile, we can—'

'Pretend all is as we expected it,' Irissa concluded. 'I did not know the Marshlands bred such skilled dissemblers.'

'Perhaps it is a Torloc propensity I have contracted,' Kendric replied with a grin, reaching high to jerk the bed-curtains closed on the slumberer. 'She needs rest anyway, and is safer here than she would be elsewhere.'

'Methinks you reason like a madman — only coming to conclusions that suit you.'

'I reason like one who has learned the world is mad, not I. There is a difference, but very slight.'

They whispered now, afraid to waken their guest, and left reluctantly to mingle with the Torlocs, who seemed to revel in rejecting Irissa.

Ludborg had departed for a while, they were told when they arrived below in time for an awkwardly communal breakfast. Despite the bounty that burdened the long tabletop — rashers of baked apples, cinnamon-dusted meat pies and pastries that curled around sweetmeats as lovingly as Ludborg's blue-worms circled around themselves — the company shared only an equal unease.

Kendric studied the small courtesies Medoc extended to Orvath, hunting for the smallest kernel of deference from supposed son to supposed father. There was none; no wonder Irissa was allowed to come and go like an unwanted wraith among these men, Kendric stewed. Irissa was little to all of them, and less to the two who should most champion her. She was at best an embarrassment; at worst, an enemy.

Irissa herself refused to dwell on how unwelcome her own kin and kind made her feel. She thought of the pale lady above, who had now followed them both into the citified heart of Edanvant. She hoped that her innermost thoughts did not somehow sketch the fact of the lady's existence on some blank, talisman-magnified Torloc mind, or that the tug of her attempted healing had not alerted some latent Torloc sense. She hoped, above all, that the tension between these sullen Torloc lords and Kendric and herself would break. Her hope was not a wish. But, like a wish, it came true unexpectedly.

'Tell us, Kendric, of the talismans you carry. Perhaps we shall find you bear some in common with some of ourselves.'

Orvath's fireside invitation that evening was heartier than even Irissa could have hoped for. Kendric seemed less impressed.

'You keep your talismans to yourself; why should I flaunt mine?'

'A fair question,' Medoc intervened.

'You came seeking us,' Orvath reminded everyone in the room. 'It strikes me as meet that you take the risk first.'

As sober as a circling of ravens, the soft intermittent chime of their Iridesium mail substituting for feathery rustles, the Torloc men gathered around the high-backed chair that held Orvath.

Only Orvath sat, either a concession to his disability or his leadership. Kendric stood there, too, making his left hand into a fist so the five-stoned ring sat as high and prominent as a seal upon it.

'You know of the sword,' he began. It lay where he always left it in their company — at his right hand, scabbarded but ripe with naked possibility. Their own weapons were the jeweled hafts of daggers sheathed in scrolled alien leathers, less fabulous but more insidious.

'Here is the ring.' His fingers flexed. 'It came to me unbidden in the Inlands of Ten. Orvath knows of the Inlands, and how ten magicians there built ten magical Keeps upon the powers of as many stones, all found ages ago washed down from the icy Cincture that surroundes the habitable land.

'What Orvath does not know . . .' Kendric eyed them fiercely, uncertain whether Orvath knew or did not know what he was about to reveal. 'What Orvath and the Inland magicians did not know are that the keepstones found were mere chips washed away from a larger motherstone. That each of the ten stones had once been set in the circumference of a giant gold ring. Ten huge rings, one for every finger of a wizard swollen beyond even wizardly proportions . . .'

He had them now, in the palm of his beringed hand, on the edge of their nonexistent seats, netted by the subtle magic of storytelling. Even Irissa, who knew every word before he could say it, frowned as she listened, as if concentrating or puzzled. Kendric took a dramatic sweep away from his audience, giving them his not inconsiderable back. Mail rustled impatiently; someone who whispered to Orvath was harshly hushed.

'A giant of a wizard,' Kendric mused, turning around again to face the company.

'I lifted one of the original ringbands from its bed of icy water myself. This thick around . . .' His hands throttled a phantom cylinder of air as wide as his thigh. 'Solid gold.'

A soft exhalation of ritual greed sighed among the heavy curtains.

'Gold enough to line this hall, were it beaten thin and hammered to the walls. Ten such ringbands lie under Cincture ice still — along with the bones of their possessor, the Torloc wizard Delevant.'

A scrape stopped the tale. Orvath was standing and moving toward Kendric so eagerly his benumbed leg dragged only slightly behind him.

'That's what it was? A wizard and a Torloc? But we Torlocs have had just seeresses until now, until we defied tradition and sought talismans.'

'Behold talismans older than any Torloc in this room!' Kendric stretched his fist to arm's length and slowly swept it past their stunned eyes so all could savor the glitter of the five conjoined gems. 'The stolen stones of Delevant, the first Torloc man to defy tradition and take magic upon himself.'

Orvath stood frozen, his face as white as the wounded woman's above, though he didn't know it.

'Then it was a Torloc wizard I hurtled against in the Inlands ice? That caught me in a lethal crushing grip of cold, that reached into me and seemed to draw out a warmth I had never noticed before? That cast me aside until I rolled like a log into some crevice that cracked to become a gate and deposited me here — stiff and cold as a corpse? Finorian sent me against my own kind, my ancestor?'

'Delevant, his name was.' Irissa spoke from the shadows where she sat unnoticed. 'And what was Torloc in him or wizard in him had become evil. He had taken too many talismans, dreamed of overmuch power. He withered, cast into cold exile by Those Without for the misdeed of seeking to bring the Overstone into his world.'

'The Overstone!' Orvath's fevered eyes returned to Kendric. 'Do you have it? Did you gain that talisman as well when you overthrew Delevant?'

'The Overstone . . .' Kendric paused, not for effect this time, but to consider. Every Torloc in the room hung on his words, including Irissa, who suddenly felt as uncertain of Kendric as Kendric had felt of Torlocs.

'The Overstone is a legend,' he said abruptly, 'and like legends and reunions, overrated. I have no such thing; perhaps it never existed save in Delevant's mind.'

'And Finorian's.' Orvath turned, his whole figure suddenly seeming shrunken, and limped back to his chair. 'It would have helped, I think, had there been such a thing. I would not have felt betrayed for naught but my own gullibility.'

Silence held in the vast room. In it Kendric glanced to Irissa, but she was motionless as stone, her hands crossed on her breastbone, her head and eyes lowered as if deep in thought.

'I fought Delevant himself,' Kendric announced then. His voice reverberated with an overhearty tone, as if he boasted and knew it and felt forced to boast more. 'With this sword. He was a thing of ice and magic then, and finally shattered into pieces too small to contain either. Perhaps Finorian needed a champion to challenge Delevant and sent us both to the Inlands for that purpose.'

'If I had the Overstone egg,' Orvath said intensely, 'I would answer all ''perhapses'' with my own brand of unanswerable magic.'

202

Medoc stepped forward, a goblet held talisman-tight to his chest. 'Such tale-telling makes one weary and stretches the voice to breaking upon the rack of revelation. Aged borgia, from our own Citydell stock.' He extended the lethally distilled libation to Kendric.

One of the Torloc men stepped forward, a matching goblet in his hand, which he lifted slightly.

'To Kendric, who has wrested talismans from hostile worlds with the courage of a Torloc.'

Other goblets and voices raised, and chill, smooth borgia slid down dry throats, its native translucent green hue blackened by the night's distant torchlight.

Everyone drank but Orvath, whose hand supported his goblet along his carven armrest, and Irissa, who sat as much in the dark as her father, appearing deaf to the good cheer of the company, to the ceremony by which they welcomed Kendric of the Marshlands to their small and sore-tried fellowship.

Irissa rose slowly, accompanied by a torch-thrown distorted shadow of herself. She moved shadow-soft from the hall, hearing the voices drone on behind her, hearing Torlocs questioning and a marshman answering.

The stairs seemed endless that night; their regular white risers blinded her eventually on her slow methodical ascension, so she thought sometimes she stepped onto slices of darkness. But they led her up to empty passageways and emptier rooms. In one — hers — she found the bed emptiest of all.

She looked around the room. Surely the wounded woman had been unable to drag herself elsewhere? All was unoccupied. Even the basin water was undimpled by the ripple of evening wind. Irissa went at last to the window, which still gaped ajar, its coldstone panes glimmering in the young moonlight.

On a decorative parapet not three feet from the opening, on what perhaps had been Kendric's first foothold on his rescue mission to the rooftop far below, a large white creature sat stiller than a gargoyle on a gutter.

Its head drooped into a rich cowl of moon-silvered white fur circling its neck. Alert ears flicked partially upright at her arrival, and great golden eyes the size of moons stared unblinking on the night. A pale pink ribbon of tongue lolled out from a long nose and mouth mountainously paved in alabaster ranges of sharp white teeth.

Slim legs were power-sprung, shapelier and stronger than a cat's, but one foreleg rested elegantly askew. The long hairs feathering the foot were soaked a carmine color and the nacreous nails splayed for support like human fingers on the stone.

Impulsively, Irissa sat on the windowsill, reaching for the damaged foreleg. The animal made a sound then, part growl, part purr. Curled nails shifted nervously against the stone.

'Hush now, pretty pale wolf-cat. You are half-better and can be whole again if you'll but let me—' Irissa stretched almost too far out over the abyss of night, catching the paw in her hand as if for support. 'Now I truly know what ails you! You are made not of human bone only, but of four-footed bone as well. Let me see it, the wound—'

In the moonlight the blood blossomed old-rose brown. Irissa looked past that deception to the inner, ever-red heart of blood, through matted fur to alien animal bone. Her healing eyes cast a second stitch over her first mending, taking neat, invisible tucks in a tattered living fabric.

She leaned too far and felt the dark emptiness beneath her call. A moment more and—

From the room a strong hand curled into her shoulder, pulling her back. Outside a wild white thing fled instantly, its nails rasping stone and roof-ridges of beaten Iridesium. Astounded, Irissa watched the nimble creature spring down the rooftop decorations like a desert rockram — leaping from parapet to buttress, trotting on flashing white feet along mere razor's edges of rooftree.

It sped so fast and lithely for a moment she thought it fell . . . or flew. But the only thing aloft that night was a pearl of full moon set in a sky rinsed pale by its light. The healed creature spurted cat-certain across the lower roofs and vanished into the crenellations of darkness.

Irissa teetered on the narrow sill on which she sat, her

heartbeat momentarily faint but still soaring with the euphoria of healing. Turning to thank Kendric for keeping her from falling, she found herself instead staring full into the dark, pain-winced eyes of her father, Orvath.

Her mouth opened, but said nothing. She kept her perilous seat only by the fragile intensity of his grip. It was his good, right hand, she noticed, that held her to life and so could easily shake her loose of it. Of course there would be magic to call upon in the last spinning moments of a fatal fall, but Irissa was not sure she would remember that with so much else to forget.

Something stayed Orvath's hand, kept it fast upon her shoulder. She followed his eyes to her breastbone; the falgonskin pouch had worked itself free of the tunic during her struggle to aid the wounded beast.

Fascinated in the purely fearful sense of the word, she watched Orvath's stiff left hand reach out and cup the pendant talisman. The moon must have slid behind a cloud; suddenly it was very high and dark in the Torloc tower. Wind sliced through the open windows. Irissa felt that her entire sense of balance had shifted to the egg. The slight tug of Orvath's hand upon the cord around her neck pulled as irresistibly as tide when it commands a seaside shell.

'In all this talk of talismans tonight, you alone kept silent,' Orvath said. 'That made me curious and then . . . something less frivolous. You make an odd seeress, daughter. Your eyes look to the heart of things instead of their edges; you wear a talismanic ring. Now I see that you hide another charm—'

Orvath's crooked fingers tried to force the drawstring apart one-handed while he kept Irissa pinned to her dangerous perch.

She looked to the empty night and saw no rescuing visage on the wind, not even a bounding white furred face with reason to be grateful. She looked to the dark coffin of unlit hall beyond the gaping curtain leading to her chamber. No familiar form filled it with the silhouette of a defender. She looked to her father's fingers pillaging the simple pouch of its burden.

'It is my talisman,' she warned.

'Talismans are faithless, like much else in life, as Finorian

205

and your mother taught me well,' he muttered, keeping to his awkward task with a terrifying singleness of purpose. 'I have as much right to anything I can take as you. Whatever it is will not scream "thief" as I take it, and you are not so foolish as to do that here.'

'But it is bound to me, and I to it! I tried once to pass it on and grew faint of mind and body—'

'Then you will not miss it if your senses ebb so in its absence.' Orvath grimly sought to dislodge the Overstone egg from its pouch, unaware yet what talisman it was he so desperately sought.

'If you had asked I would have given it to you. I would have given it to you unasked once, but it is mine now, whether I will it or not—'

'It is mine if I say so!' Orvath triumphantly upended the small pouch, lowering his crippled hand swiftly enough to catch what fell as it hurtled toward the dark Iridesium shoals below. They both leaned dangerously over the emptiness.

Irissa's innards lurched with the stone's sudden plummet. The night reeled around her; she thought she sat astride a bearing-beast made of limestone, high as a mountain, with steel for a spine and coldstone for a heart. It bucked beneath her and the whole world trembled in time to the beating of her heart.

Orvath leaned into the watery moonlight, squinting at the oval stone within his palm. His eyes came to Irissa's face at last, too angry to notice how she had paled in the last moments, how only his one hand held her upright against the support of the casement.

'This is . . . the cursed thing itself! The talisman for which Finorian persuaded me to leave Rindell and Jalonia. The Overstone egg, for which I sold the flesh of half my body. It caught me so, that thing of cold greed you call Delevant. It held me and twisted until I felt its cold lodge close against me. Seared, seared by ice I was, and even when I rolled away by some merciful fluke, the cold pursued me and ate into my bones forever. Even Edanvant does not warm it. Perhaps this will.'

206

'Orvath.' Only the breathless husk of a voice remained to Irissa. She was sinking, drawn to the dark far below and unable to cling to anything but futile words of persuasion.

His hand was already releasing its grip on her shoulder as he turned to leave. 'I did not hurt you,' he said brusquely.

'Mine,' was the briefest way she could put it, and the reminder could only madden him.

His hand tightened on the tunic cloth at Irissa's throat, ripping slick silk with a hiss.

'It was bought by my simplicity months before you slipped the safety of your mother's womb. It was paid for by my betrayal, my agony both inner and outer. It is only fitting that you have brought me what I have so long been deprived of — magic.'

'Fall,' Irissa whispered. Her voice sounded no louder to her ears than the wisps of wind that slithered through the forest far away. 'Will fall . . .'

His anger and perhaps some shame boiled over together, drenching a man of ice in searing rage. His good hand clenched until the silk shrieked and he pulled her off the windowsill and slammed her limp body against the wall beneath it.

'Not enough,' she whispered, her head lolling against the stones.

But he was leaving, spelled by his new talisman, caught in its magical pull. Irissa felt as if all her inner being had rolled into one clenched ball that was slowly being sucked through her skin, until all that would remain was an empty sack of skin and bones. Nothing could save her. Magic required strength; hope required heart. Her strength and heart were broken.

Orvath turned, reminding Irissa of Kendric from the rear for several disoriented moments.

At the threshold Orvath halted abruptly.

A cat sat there, a bony white cat. The sour slant of its eyes matched the angle of its flattened ears. Some trick of the passage torches threw its shadow huge against the wall behind it.

'Felabba,' Orvath identified it at last with contemptuous amazement. 'You're far from home, old bitterbones—'

The cat swelled, stretched, reached limbs, head, and tail in all directions at once. It filled the doorway, the greens of its eyes glimmering brighter yet in the shadow its giant body cast. The shadow swallowed Orvath to the seven-foot top of him. It reached even to Irissa, who was sinking into a shadow even denser by the window.

'Give it back,' the cat thundered, nothing feline about its voice.

Orvath's stiff fingers unclasped as if on their own. The Overstone egg plummeted through air, landing on the quick pillowing presence of an oversized cat's tail. The appendage flicked gently, rolling the egg lopsidedly across the coldstones. It wobbled out of the cat's shadow and stopped against Irissa's flaccid hand.

'Leave,' ordered the cat.

Orvath, half-mad with seeing more magic than he had bargained for, ran straight through the great white form as through a door. He passed as if through mist, the retreating sound of his ill-matched footsteps scraping down the endless hall for a long time after.

CHAPTER THIRTEEN

Irissa lay in the colorless, soundless, scentless place that had claimed her the moment Orvath had wrested away the Overstone.

An overwhelming weakness enfolded her. Even the knowledge that her own father had cast her into this state was not sharp enough a goad to rouse her against an utter numbness of body and spirit.

What finally did recall her was a delicate, infinitely patient touch upon her hand. The room took on color once more, and focus. Irissa perceived again the reassuring discomfort of hard stones at her back and felt the night wind stealing through the ragged tendrils of her hair.

Beside her sat the cat, her white head cocked intently as if to watch a spider. Her paw daintily lifted to admonish some intriguing object.

Irissa glanced down. The Overstone egg touched her hand. Each of Felabba's soft repetitive pats moved it nearer. But it couldn't climb unaided the small slope made by the heel of her hand. Mustering all her energy, Irissa rolled her fingers over the talisman, grasped it — and sat up straight.

'This leech of a stone seems to suck away my senses,' she complained to herself, not expecting the cat to respond.

A crisp, unruffled voice disagreed with her assessment. 'Or rather, you lose your senses when the talisman is taken from you.'

'Taken . . . yes! Now I remember! Orvath came and—' The moments in the window frame shimmered in her mind like the shards of Ludborg's casting crystals; they assumed no order, no coherence. Irissa's ruling memory remained one of bitter disbelief in the face of undeniable fact, more emotion than remembrance, or even reason. She warily surveyed the empty chamber. 'What happened to Orvath?'

'He repented,' the cat said dryly. 'And left. In a hurry. Guilt sometimes affects people that way, even Torlocs.'

Irissa's silver eyes narrowed to accusing catlike slits. 'I feel there is more to it than that.'

'Feel!' the cat spat. 'Always your flaw, to feel first and think later; such a human failing. Think now, seeress. Set your overwrought feelings aside. Your life nearly ebbed on these stones before you could release the shield of your magic or raise the sword of your will. Why?'

'My life—?' Irissa stood shakily, supporting herself by grasping the window frame. 'I faded, yes, but didn't dream that sensation was death.' Her hand uncurled. 'It is this stone I took. If it leaves me, whether I give to another or another takes it, something in me dampens. Is it bewitched, Felabba? A thing of evil?'

As Irissa watched, the cat leaped lithely to the narrow sill, balancing over the dangerous plummet downward with bored feline skill. Swaybacked and belly bowed, she sharpened her claws thoughtfully on the hard-grained weepwaterwood before replying.

'Your talisman is the Overstone egg, which Delevant unlawfully brought into the Inlands, the cause of his downfall. It is an Outside thing; only an Outsider could say whether it leans more to good or evil — and none of those inhabit any of our worlds. But it is a powerful talisman, and you took it for your own. It is yours to carry, yours to treasure, yours to guard and yours to keep. Others will want it because it is forbidden. If you lose it, you will lose your life.'

'I didn't know . . .' Irissa studied the calm stone weighing comfortably in her palm. It warmed at her touch and throbbed to the pulse of life through her veins, its oval solidity a reassuring sensation she didn't want to relinquish. It was more than the fact that she had found and claimed the stone, that it was — by unwritten human law — hers. It belonged to her in a deeper sense. It had claimed her, too.

Irissa drew open the pouch still hung around her neck and dropped the Overstone egg within. Her voice throbbed with resolve.

'I'll leave; Medoc warned me I might tempt Orvath to treachery. I'll leave now before I tempt him to worse.'

She tied on her sword, pausing to stare out the window and thinking of the white creature she had healed before the heavy hand of her father, Orvath, had descended to wound her, wound her unto more than one variety of death . . .

'What of Kendric?' Felabba asked.

Irissa turned, astounded. 'I . . . had forgotten.' Her face stiffened. Had there been a looking glass in the chamber, she would have seen a fleeting resemblance to her father's frozen features. Despite Felabba's urgings, she could not think now, only feel. She dared not let thoughts of Kendric share an inner landscape wroth with the realization of betrayal beyond forgiving.

'Kendric has found what he never had — a home,' Irissa managed to say briskly, logically. 'He has found a new company of Wrathmen who respect his magic as well as his prowess.' She sighed. 'He may wish to linger here. He may not even miss me . . . long. No one in this iron hall has need of what I offer in any respect!'

Her voice breaking, Irissa marched to the door as if needing pointed words to goad her from the room. She turned to regard the cat over her shoulder. 'Coming?' she asked on a falsely indifferent inflection.

'No.' The creature leaped to the floor, crossed it, and bounded noiselessly atop the bed. 'I'll wait here,' Felabba said, curling herself into a tidy ball and tucking her head down on her feet. She yawned. 'It will be interesting to see what Kendric makes of this pretty turn of events. Mayhap I'll tell him what Orvath tried to do.'

'Tell him—' Irissa paused, perhaps hoping that the cat, who never agreed with anything, would protest her departure. But the animal had dismissed Irissa from her attention, from the sleepy green consideration of her all-seeing eyes.

211

'Tell him—' Irissa's voice clogged, them commanded itself, 'good-bye.'

Irissa was gone, and Felabba dozed.

The halls and stairways remained empty after Irissa's quick, stealthy passage. Orvath did not return to the great hall, but no one noticed to wonder where he had gone and what he was about. Kendric and the Torloc men continued their tale-telling jousts until the borgia ran thin in the bottoms of fat decanters and bright-eyed dawn was washing the charcoal-dark sky clean again.

By then Irissa had slipped through the city gates and faced the first ring of black wall between herself and the heart of the forest.

Irissa placed her ring against the wall, Shinestone-side-down. Dawn still quickened, so the sun had not yet showered the horizon with the extravagant gold coinage of its full-fledged arrival. The Shinestone evoked no alteration in the slick Iridesium or the stones of her ring.

She lowered her hand to consider the other gems in turn. Bloodstone, no; Drawstone — but she wanted the wall to part for her, not close. Floodstone's watery magic might take hours to wear away metal wall. Only Skystone remained, blue and clear. She touched it lightly to the wall. A tiny dot of azure seemingly torn from above expanded and ate a bright blue hole in the dark metal. Irissa stepped into what seemed like an airy bubble. Beyond its ambient curves, blackness pressed in from every side, but she walked, and the piece of sky hovered around her. On her finger the blue stone blazed sun-bright, casting the other stones into insignificance.

Then the blue dazzle lifted to paint the sky to match itself again, and the rainbow of the forest arched the treetop-patterned heavens overhead.

The ground immediately grew rough, hurrying her down its rutted slopes through ropy thigh-high weeds. A cloying dead-flower scent rose so thick from the surrounding foliage that it threatened to gag her. Nettles and clumps of thistleweed paved her way.

Irissa heard the nearby snarls and whines of feuding animals

212

debating the distribution of a dinner or a womb-ripe female. Howls and shrieks reverberated through the treetops, where treemonks swayed. And still the ground led down into darker glades and deeper shadow.

Irissa forged ahead, her sword in hand. Her other hand cradled the Overstone pouch as it swung against her chest. She only knew that her survival depended upon putting Citydell and the men and all they stood for as far behind her as possible. Felabba, for once, had agreed with Irissa's visceral instincts. The cat had forborne to disagree at least, she consoled herself.

Now she thought as Finorian had wished her to believe for so long and so fruitlessly! Citydell was undeniably an enemy camp − to her if not Kendric. Now, convinced and blinded by her own wounds, Irissa was fleeing back to Finorian, who had claimed she could not return once she left. But where else could she go? What side remained to her when the middle ground was denied her?

Even as she hurtled through the undergrowth, Irissa felt an unformed thought dragging on her heels. Was she not doing exactly what they wanted, all of them − men, women, Orvath, Finorian? Wasn't she proving them right when she still believed them wrong, proving that there was no hope of resolution for their division, that what she was − female, seeress − irrevocably committed her to one side and one only?

Questions flayed her like whip-narrow branches. For all of Orvath's raging of the women's treachery to him, his betrayal of her stalked his daughter through the world between the walls.

Kendric had seen it from the first, and said so. The thought of him whipped her to flee faster, as if harried by a voice too close to distinguish. It was the question Kendric worried like a bone: 'How can you Torlocs be so little to one another?'

Irissa was chagrined beyond bearing. More than her recent brush with death by falling and death by withdrawal of a talisman, one irksome, supposedly unimportant fact rubbed her entire spirit raw, as a tiny sand grain pressed into the soft sole of a foot can chafe the whole person eventually: her own father had sought to take by force the talisman she'd taken by chance — without even considering the danger to her such robbery entailed. He had been willing, or greedy enough, to overlook her destruction in the face of his need. And that, Irissa knew in her soul, no excuses rising to her ready mind, was unnatural. A father should not be a foe. A friend should not flee a friend. And if a father could turn on his offspring, why not a friend upon a friend? Images from the past and from a future unexpected collided in her mind. Friend — or foe? Irissa could not tell the difference any longer. She turned every issue over to its opposite side now, perhaps inured to counterfeit emotional coinage by the hard-dealing Torlocs.

So now she plunged herself into less immediate but more mortal peril. She reached the bottom of the land between the walls and began striding up weed-choked slopes, sweeping rotting foliage aside with her sword, parting the wilderness by shouldering through it as if it were a crowd. Screams ebbed and flowed all around her like blood pulsing from a wound. Irissa's fear, now far from its source, had congealed to rage against whatever surrounded her.

Let something come, fanged and clawed and fearsome. She would slice it into rags, spell it into a grimmer-walled place than this — this travesty of a world, divided into opposites—

Something whimpered at her feet as she kicked angrily through the undergrowth. Her sword stroke parted the pulpy green grasses. Among them lay a creature, one of the evergreen-furred foxes whose hides embellished dwellings in both city and forest keeps.

Small, red eyes blazed above the long, flattened muzzle, wrinkled to display edged fangs, wrinkled in fear and pain. A thick tail fanned behind it; its narrow legs looked as if wound in green velvet like certain artificial flower stems in kinder lands. Its frantic sides heaved, each ragged breath but tearing more the wound where red blood painted green fur a matted brown.

They stared at one another, equally surprised. That emotion was the only one unexpected enough to quell Irissa's random fury. She saw it for the helpless beast it was. Then Irissa went down on one knee beside it. Her voice came softly.

'Something bigger bit deep, friend fox. Rest a moment longer, and I will fix it.'

Feebly the animal tried to scrabble away. But Irissa set aside her sword while her hands infallibly parted the fur on the wound's still bleeding core. She reached deep for the threads of healing within her — and found them frayed and tangled. Sighing, she strove to banish the past few hours from her mind. Aid, she would think, and restitution. Rage made one inner-blind, barring a seeress from the storehouse of her powers as solidly as a bonewood door.

She shut her eyes and bowed her head. A thin green filament wove toward her through the darkness, then others of blue and gold and silver. The colors crept back into the darkness of her mind and twined into a rainbow cable strong enough to hang from. She opened her eyes and stared at the wounded fox's pelt, building from the will and magic within her a natural mending without.

Fur stirred as if stitched from beneath, then closed over the small chasm of once-torn flesh. Irissa sighed completion and reached to pat the fox's smoother-breathing side.

Fangs flashed white, then flushed as red as burning eyes. Irissa felt then the sudden hot charge across her thigh as teeth chattered through her flesh. She flinched back, adding her wail of indignant hurt to the shrieking cacophony around her.

The fox rolled onto its feet, gave a last lethal snarl for final measure and whisked into the camouflaging foliage, leaving only trembling leaves in its wake.

Irissa's uninjured leg accepted the brunt of her weight as a ground of gray silk sprouted a thick crop of bloodstains. She used her sword to lever herself up, reaching for the promised support of a vine-swaddled tree trunk. As she touched it, the vines slithered up the trunk out of sight, hissing warning. Pain began to drum tiny hatchets up and down her bitten leg as she balanced on the other.

She pressed her palm to her wound, almost too weary to regather her resources of healing and turn them upon herself. All for the simple act of aiding a wild thing in its misery.

What kind of world was this Edanvant, she wondered

215

bitterly, this Torloc paradise, where even the four-footed things weaned themselves on a full share of ingratitude? Her inner pain clamored for a name and finally found one. Greed. Ingratitude. Betrayal. Orvath claimed he had been betrayed and so in turn felt free to betray.

To have a betrayal, there first must be innocence, Irissa reflected as she sat down to tug off her boot and work up her trouser leg. The fox had scribed a neat pattern of punctures on her leg, elaborate as a tattoo. Orvath had lost his innocence in the Inlands along with a certain flexibility of body and spirit. Irissa had thought her innocence shed in Rule, when all had striven to use her powers as the last Torloc seeress. Apparently, she concluded, wincing before beginning the tedious work of restoring her skin to wholeness, enough innocence remained to pay dearly for.

'Where is she?'

Medoc stood politely in the archway and watched Kendric interrogate a cat.

'You must know!' Kendric insisted.

Medoc laid a cautionary long-fingered hand on Kendric's shoulder. 'Let sleeping cats lie, my friend. And save your worry; Irissa is probably exploring the city streets, shopping for trinkets. We men stayed up late last night, until we wearied of our own voices. Women can stomach neither that much wine nor that much idle boasting. Now, lad, she'll turn up again and — after holding you in thrall to suspense for some unconscionable amount of time — forgive you.'

Kendric ran his fingers roughly into his sleep-tousled dark hair. He'd collapsed upon the bed of an adjacent chamber soon after dawn, and slept until his weary senses woke. Now that new day's light already fell long and heavy with late afternoon lassitude. And Irissa was gone.

'She wouldn't have left . . . me for idle reasons. You . . . I . . . drove her away somehow. What a fool I've been.'

'Perhaps we've all been fools.' Medoc's dark eyes glittered speculatively.

'What do you mean?'

216

Medoc shrugged. 'If she is truly gone, perhaps she had reason to leave. She may think she's gathered all she needed to tattle on our strengths to the women in the woods. I had hopes the girl was not yet corrupted. I confess I found her not unlikeable, but oversure of herself, the price of spending too long in the women's contaminating grips . . .'

Kendric rounded on the man. He had learned to like Medoc during the long night of talk and wine and a more subtle self-indulgence, but the face he showed the Torloc could have blazed under the raised steel slash of a sword.

'And where is Orvath? He disappeared last night, too.'

'Of course. Why do you think we caroused so long and so loosely? Orvath casts a pall upon our gatherings, his very presence a reminder of the high cost of our talismanic journeys. He never lets us forget. We welcome his absence now and again, and never question it.'

'I question it now. You told Irissa her father might imperil her — how do I know that he has not taken her by some magical means . . .?'

Medoc's smile meant to soothe. 'You forget; that is Orvath's whole trouble. He has no magic. No talisman.'

'Then by force!' Kendric pushed off Medoc's restraining hand to pace the small chamber. 'Irissa has magic enough for two. Perhaps Orvath hopes to force her to use it on his — your — behalf. You are the worst kind of sorcerers,' Kendric accused, turning like a beast caught in a cage of his own fears. 'You charm one into dropping his guard!'

'Kendric,' Medoc consoled, stepping inward again, 'you found in our fellowship only what you were looking for. We know, having scattered to the durance of gates and alien worlds one by one for long years before coming together again here, what joy there is in simple reunion, in sharing time and space with one's kind. You are more like us than unlike us.'

'Yes,' Kendric admitted. He turned away. 'And no.' Before him the cat cocked one hazy green eye open.

'Reunions are overrated.' Its sour verdict reechoed in his ears.

Kendric turned back to Medoc, but the Torloc showed no

signs of having heard the potent reminder. Perhaps Felabba had more innate discrimination than Kendric gave the cat credit for.

He sighed heavily and again approached Medoc.

'Take me to Orvath,' he repeated, less hotly this time, but with as much determination in his voice. 'I fear he has some things to answer for.'

Irissa stood by the second black wall, regretting the absence of Kendric's Nightstone, regretting the absence of Kendric.

She hadn't paused to consider how one would recross terrain that had welcomed two with wall-to-wall challenge. She had assumed a certain independence in herself that had not been tested recently.

The wall itself remained as blandly impenetrable as before. When she presented her five-stoned ring not one of its talismanic gemstones quivered recognition. Talismans! For an instant her hand clutched the Overstone egg — powerful, more powerful than any of the ten stones of Delevant, it was said, else why would the overreaching wizard have wanted it? But she sensed with an odd certainty that she was the caretaker of the Overstone, not its wielder.

Sighing, she stared at the wall. Why not try relying upon yourself instead of foreign talismans, seeress? a mildly lashing interior voice that sounded much like Falabba's questioned. Irissa smiled. It was herself that admonished herself. She was alone now, as she had not been since a prisoner of Sofistron's coldstone circle. Then she had conceived a way out that had worked for a while. Perhaps it was again time to risk native magic.

Her fingertips saluted the Iridesium circlet embracing her temples. Bowing her head in what could have been a moment's humility, a greeting to a silent but hard-spoken wall, or simple thought, Irissa touched the circlet to the long, unseeing circling of wall; Iridesium to Iridesium, Torloc magic to Torloc magic, herself to the unknown.

Her will pushed her into the wall, more than any movement of her body. Cold-hearted blackness clung like armor to her

218

form. Her eyes saw only the midnight shoals of nowhere, colorful bolts of lightning flickering violet, orange, and azure at some great distance.

She walked the world within the wall, unsheltered by Kendric's broad protective form or his particular assembly of talismans that might have been proof against it. Her own ringstones were invisible, no challenge to the rainbow hues of metallic lightning singing a sulfurous tang into the limits of her vision.

Even the emerald pommelstone did not brighten in response to her timely thought of it. She was alone. But still she walked forward — or rather, still she walked. The wall's sly inbred trap suddenly struck her. It was a vast circle, a grander version of the oversized gold bands that had once ringed Delevant's fingers when he held full power. If she lost her direction, if she failed to pass through the wall by the shortest route across its narrow width, she could end by pacing its quite eternal length, going around and around and never knowing it.

Irissa shuddered. Her body felt no cold, nor any heat. There was nothing here to distract her and even less to guide her; no wind, no warmth, no sound, no light. Except for the arbitrary assumption that ahead was the direction in which she faced, she felt plucked from the surface of the earth and suspended in some vast, empty outer anteroom, waiting to pay her respects to a force whose name she did not know.

She had walked longer than it should take to pass through a finite thickness of wall. Or had she? Time seemed truncated here, too, with nothing sequential happening, nothing to mark it against.

Still, at least she was alone, somewhere deep within the soul of a magical metal wall. Nothing threatened, except her anxieties. No monsters stirred — not even a saw-fanged fox with a sleek green coat and an oversupply of ingratitude . . .

Irissa stopped moving, if indeed she still had been moving.

Something glimmered ahead, paler than the intermittent lightning, something misty and familiar. To see a lambent thing in utter dark was at first blinding. It seemed haloed by reflections of itself. Then it came toward her, or she came toward it. And it *was* herself. Her image.

A spired glass decanter made much of itself on a beaten Iridesium tabletop, catching the red rays of sunfall, distilling them into pure crimson as they traveled down its long slender throat, then swallowing them whole in an emerald sea of borgia.

The stopper, blown in the likeness of a flagon, lay alongside the decanter. Borgia once had oiled the glass into a glowing green sphere with its rich presence, but now had ebbed until it only tickled the decanter's midway mark, making it resemble a lethal half moon balanced on its rounded outer curve.

As naturally as the borgia filled the decanter's globular bottom, so Orvath snugly lounged in the chair that cradled him. His goblet was fashioned of glass, with bits of molten Iridesium mixed in the firing so it shone like tanslucent metal. The green had ebbed in his goblet as well. One leg, his good one, was cocked over the arm of his chair. His other leg stretched straight — far too straight — ahead.

Orvath tilted back both his head and his goblet at the sight of Kendric in the doorway to his chamber, Medoc a stern shadow behind him.

The inescapable mark of eventide on the scene caused Kendric to tote the hours likely to have passed since Irissa's disappearance. The act functioned equally as one of contrition, restraint, and resolve. Orvath, unmagicked or not, was the last of the Torloc men Kendric would have chosen to contend with. Orvath drunk was even less appetizing.

'Irissa's gone,' Kendric announced, meaning to shock the man from his self-sought inner exile.

'Is she?' Orvath drank deeply again. From the doorway, Kendric could see the fragile glass falgon's wings tremble. 'She was not welcome.' Orvath went on quietly. 'Perhaps she heeded me at last.'

'Medoc warned her that you might harbor some enmity

toward her, might try to inhibit her magic so it could not be employed against Citydell—'

'Magic!' Orvath hurled the word from him as he might have flung the goblet had he not so desired its seductive contents. He took another long draught while Medoc stepped close behind Kendric and whispered anxiously in his ear.

'Borgia makes a wicked nursemaid, telling many mad tales before allowing one to drift to sleep. He should stop.'

'Stop?' Orvath perked the keen, easy-to-anger ears of the drunkard. He leaned forward in the chair, propped up by his elbows splayed across its armrests, his face remarkably sober-looking, but perhaps that was an attribute of his malady. He could not even show surrender.

'Stop,' he repeated, subsiding back into the chair as if reminded of something. 'Aye, I stopped. When ordered. When confronted by a piece of sorcery not so much terrifying — if it had been a dragon, a soul-leech, a wailwraith, I would have set on it with my bare hands — as unnatural. I . . . believed it. I stopped.'

'What did you stop?' Kendric asked.

Orvath looked up, his handsome face crafty and therefore less lordly.

'The small oval stone. I nearly had it . . . brought to me after all, snug as a sweetmeat in pastry. In a falgonskin pouch.'

Kendric crossed the chamber in two strides and hauled Orvath from his seat by the bejeweled throat of his tunic.

'You would not know what Irissa carried had you not seen it. Where is it? Where is she?'

Orvath, drunk enough to face a man equal to his height and superior in wrath with calm, shrugged in Kendric's grasp. 'I don't know. Where it is, she is. And the other way round. I left it behind when I . . . withdrew.'

'But Irissa had a fey attachment to the thing. If it left her possession she weakened . . .'

Orvath hung unconcerned from the hook of Kendric's rage. His eyes glazed and looked sideways. 'It was easy enough to take. Where was the seeress's vaunted magic then, eh? Like taking a pebble from a babe.' He frowned. 'I don't know what

221

she did then, after I had it. I had it and saw only it. Then I saw magic incarnate rise up before me, urge me to abandon the stone.' His eyes came back to Kendric's. 'Of course I did; one reared under the voice of Finorian recognizes magic when it is not to be quarreled with. I left the stone. I left — her. They should be there still.'

'They are not!' Kendric shook Orvath impotently, further infuriated by the slack weight of this once-overstiff man. 'If you were a dragon, or a soul-leech or a wailwraith I would tear you limb from limb. But you are only a wrong, embittered man who wars with one half of your kind for no better reason than you have not learned to share yourself with anyone; you are only a father who sought to rob his daughter — I can only pity you more than I can despise you.'

'She looks like Jalonia,' Orvath mumbled as Kendric let him sink back into his chair. 'Like Jalonia but a few years ago, when I left Rindell on what was to be a swift quest for a talisman that would save us all. She begged me to stay . . . to stay my hand. To forget the stone, let the stone go. Yes, I remember hearing Irissa pleading, them both pleading — to let go . . . no, to stay. Then, now—'

Orvath's hand elevated to shield his eyes. Beside him, the goblet finally overturned, smashing to the floor in a mound of mock gemstones all the colors of melted Iridesium.

'It was evil, the thing that met me at the far end of the world beyond the gate. I fought it, resisted its icy demands even when I felt the cold of its soul weld itself to mine. I escaped, fell through another gate. I had never seen such magic, such power — endlessly old, uncaring. Until tonight.'

Kendric turned to Medoc, given pause when he saw tears brightening the man's dark eyes.

'He was . . . not this way when I left Rindell long ago,' Medoc said. 'He seeks the antidote to poison within poison,' he added, sweeping his boot through the sticky shards of glass.

'You excuse him,' Kendric accused.

'No, I forgive him.' Medoc shrugged sheepishly. 'He is my son.'

Kendric considered the statement for a long time. From

anyone other than a Torloc it would have been unremarkable. He sighed, feeling his anger dissipating like the spilled borgia. Orvath slept, his closed eyes set in maroon-circled sockets, his one good hand flexing nervously.

Kendric turned from the sight.

'Irissa is your granddaughter,' he told Medoc. 'And your son's attempt to take the Overstone tried her severely, although Orvath was too talisman-mad to see the full horror of what he did. I think . . . I think she survived. I think she fled. For her life, for her talisman that is so oddly intertwined with her life.'

'Why should she not?' Medoc sounded infinitely cynical. 'After all, her loyalty lies with her kind, and she is female first and Torloc second. We men have seen how nicely our women live without us — they show no eagerness to rejoin us now that we have the upper hand. Why should not Irissa share in that contagion and flee you? Are you better than we?'

Kendric didn't answer, going first to the window to gaze out on the red-tipped city, to absently caress the sun-warmed bowl of borgia.

'She is hurt beyond the near loss of a parasitic talisman. She has spent some time with mortals — with me — and old Torloc conventions no longer hold. She sought her people and found her parents. She found her betrayers, and they are all Torloc.'

'I thought you were coming to like us?'

Kendric turned, his eyes deliberately avoiding the chair where Orvath now snored softly.

'I am coming,' Kendric said firmly, 'to dislike myself.'

CHAPTER FOURTEEN

Irissa walked the limitless dark protected only by its lack of awareness of her. She trod a black floor she could not see, looking from side to side. One glance showed her light in the darkness. Pausing to study it, she flinched back from a dreadful sight.

The pale ghost of herself accompanied her, a mere arm's length away. Save that it was light where her mirror-self had been dark in Geronfrey's dread looking glass, it wore the same trailing gown she had then. A sun-bright circle of gold sank into the valley of its breasts, where Irissa bore the Overstone egg now.

Her heart throbbed recognition of her past self even as her legs labored to outstride it. The figure shadowed her faster movements, as if she and it were separated only by a thin magical veil but otherwise linked step for step. Did the dark within the Iridesium wall, she wondered, form a crossroads for all the Irissas who had ever, willing or unwilling, faced a dark mirror?

The pale figure came no nearer. Once perceiving or imagining that it did, she instinctively grasped the Overstone, more seeking to shield it than invoke its protection. At her touch on the warm stone, the waxy image of herself melted farther into the indistinct, less threatening distance.

Another blotch of white swam toward her from the opposite side of the thick obscurity. Irissa's head swung from side to side until her braids beat soft warning against her cheeks. Each time she looked, both figures seemed nearer, squeezing her as a gnat between soon-to-clap hands . . . But the second apparition floated Wrathman-high above the level Irissa trod!

Irissa paused, shuddering. Beneath her palm the pommel-stone dispensed a feeble, lightless heat. Dark forces sucked its power back within itself, as if a flame would beat against the candlewax and not the night. The white thing that traveled without legs came close enough to show the darkened pits of eyes . . .

Yet — the Overstone in her hand pulled with an undeniable force of its own. Irissa's fingers tightened. Some remote spell was attempting to suck the talisman from her grasp. The cord tugged on her neck now, urging her in the direction of the one who waited suspended in air. Irissa glanced over her shoulder to see the bleached version of herself close enough to merge with her.

The Overstone outdrew the Drawstone; Irissa added the weight of the physical self to the magical pull. She waded through the dark toward the brightening form swimming directly for her, then stopped.

A flutter like moonlight drew her eyes upward. The white something hovered directly above her, lethally poised. Irissa lifted her sword. Just then daylight, perhaps so summoned, clashed upon her senses as if someone had swept a curtain aside from the entire horizon.

Her arm trembled, hamstrung between striking and holding back. Thus Irissa seemed to hang from her own hostile gesture, half caught by it, or half tricked into making it. But she stood in broad daylight, beyond the wall.

Even now the hovering white form was surging above the barrier's lofty top, wide wings hurled high above its body, talons breaking its fall.

It came to rest with the dramatically violent precision of a dagger thrown from the moon. Irissa's eyes winced away from the impact, but when she looked again, a bird sat on the wall rim. Its wings, trailing like feather-scalloped sleeves, were furling against its sides again. Pewter-bright eyes stared back at her, unblinking.

'*Whooo?*' the owl inquired portentously from its unnatural perch.

'Who indeed?' Irissa interrogated herself softly in turn.

'And how?' She glanced at the wall again to ensure that she was safely through it.

Ruffling feathers rustled like parchment, but the owl's gray eyes gave it an oddly human semblance, Irissa thought.

The owl fluttered from the wall to the first fringe of woodland, where it perched upon a tree branch so leaf-laden it almost obscured the bird. A moment later its feral staring face poked back through a feathered bonnet of greenery, waiting.

'You mean me to follow you, I suppose?' Irissa asked, stepping away from the wall. 'And you will guide me safely to the women's keep? I don't suppose you speak, or offer gratuitous advice, although you may hunt mice?'

There was no answer, human or owlish.

'At least you make a soft-spoken companion,' she noted, realizing a moment after that it was something Kendric would have said.

Irissa looked back regretfully to the wall. Its rainbowed black surface seemed to tremble in her gaze, reflecting her inner uncertainty. She had left Kendric without a word. There was a wrongness in that, Irissa knew in her soul, but she felt bewilderingly reluctant to examine it even now. She was loath to tell Kendric about what had happened to her in Citydell, about what Orvath had tried to do, about her weakness — and his. Her restraint welled from something that tasted like deep shame, but whether more for Orvath or for herself she could not say.

Irissa started slowly toward the hedge of foliage, where the owl waited. She plunged into a new and less intimidating wall, but one as directionless for all that as the black Iridesium one behind her.

Trees gave way to trees, bushes to bushes, endless vistas of bobbing leaves to more bobbing leaves. Always ahead of her, almost out of sight, the white flash of wings lured her on like beckoning feathered fingers.

Felabba swept a somewhat meager tail across the tabletop, managing only to raise a few dust motes against the lurid sunset glow framed by the window of Irissa's former chamber. The

226

lavish gesture revealed the appendage's need of a dedicated cleaning rather than the cursory licks of old age.

Opposite the cat, Kendric sat silently, leaning back on his bench's hind legs, his arms folded on his chest and a by-no-means subtle gleam in his usually mellow eyes.

'Well?' he asked.

Felabba's narrow paw dabbed consideringly at scant whiskers. 'Instinct told her to flee, and I cannot argue with it.'

'Back to the forest and Finorian?' he demanded. 'You agree with that?'

Felabba studied the slow, pendulumlike lilt of one of its fine white hairs through the light-strained air until it rested on the tabletop. It was possible the old cat had shrugged, or perhaps her ancient hide simply had twitched to unseat a flea.

Kendric sighed and leaned forward, his voice lowered. 'She could have waited and told me . . . we could have gone together.'

A paw studded with anemic pink pads suddenly slapped shut on some crawling scrap of insectdom. 'There are many magicks in Edanvant — old, new; good, evil; native, imported . . . Sometimes it is necessary to face them alone.'

'Imported? Are you referring to the Inlands magic Irissa and I brought with us?'

'That — and other things you are not aware of carrying.'

'Such as—?' Kendric was frowning now, the last gory rays of sunfall painting his strong features iresome.

'Love — and hate . . . and old enmity. They make strong magic.' Felabba stared into a great distance, dreaming. She was prone to do that nowadays, and Kendric never knew whether she feigned or truly felt her detachment. Puzzled, he returned to the present quandary.

'Well, I shan't let her practice this Torloc trick of vanishing into misty air.' His palm hit the tabletop for emphasis, but the old cat — perhaps her hearing had ebbed as well — merely blinked half-shut eyes. 'I'm going after her,' he announced, his mouth tightening in anticipation of endless feline objections.

Finally the magnificent green eyes opened. Kendric usually

227

avoided studying their jeweled depths, but now he was too curious to gauge the cat's reaction to look away.

'You want to drag these old bones on another journey, I suppose? With no decent vittles to do it on, no comfort but the certainty of discomfort? Oh well, I cannot object.'

'You go with me?' Kendric, amazed, failed to consider whether he wished for such a companion.

The cat stood, her tail held unambitiously low, her furred brow wrinkled with age and the weight of its querulous disposition. 'There is something I wish to inspect on the way out,' she said, gathering her limbs to leap off the table.

Kendric rose too. 'Why,' he asked, frowning, 'did you not accompany Irissa on her flight, if you are so willing to forsake Citydell?'

The cat's irritated green glance rinsed his face like quickly flung ice-cold borgia. '*She* is not in mortal danger,' the cat replied.

Felabba landed at his feet, bracing her frail frame momentarily from the shock of descent. Then she shook her head and trotted to the doorway, where she turned to look back at him.

'I would take the low road out of Citydell,' Felabba announced. 'There are some hidden wonders I wish to see. Follow me.'

Kendric did, pausing only long enough to lash on his sword and take one last look around the room they had occupied — Irissa's bedchamber until last night. Another Torloc room revoked in heartsick haste . . .

But Irissa was not in mortal danger; the old cat who knew too much for her own and everyone else's good — and said so — had spoken.

Kendric started after the animal, relief diluting some of the bitter gall that had filled him as borgia had infused Orvath's never-empty goblet . . . No, Irissa was not in danger. Kendric paused. Sometimes the cat's subtlety acted poisonously slow upon his brain, perhaps because it took a good long way to reach it — *Irissa* was not in mortal danger; only moments ago the infallible Felabba had assured him of that. Yet the cat had implied that someone else was . . .

His boots planted themselves on the floor as his mind became abruptly aware of who was the true beneficiary of Felabba's unrequested protection: *himself*.

Ten Torloc towers loomed among the tall pines. This wood held its myriad leafy tongues save for the gentle scrub of fir needles on stone. Irissa, hushed as the world around her, tiptoed closer. The castle was what she sought, but she had first seen it before she came to Citydell. Now she saw it for what it was — a miniature replica of sprawling, ten-towered Citydell itself, a toy erected with playful power as homage to the place it mocked.

Citydell *had* been first founded, first returned to. Finorian and the Torloc dames had come too late to claim anything but a ruined scrap of their heritage. Irissa had returned later to deeper disappointment. The Torlocs' disunity tarnished their past quest for Edanvant even as their present achieved it.

Her hands fisted at her sides as if to hurl stones at the thing before her, rocks through the brittle sparkling cold-stone windowpanes, pebbles against the bright ring of coldstone foundation.

She had no one to thank for this bitter vision — or revision — but herself and her headstrong flight from Citydell. And the frost-feathered owl. Irissa's eyes sought a happier sight nearer the ground, but her winged guide had vanished into the encircling greenery. Friend — or foe, she wondered.

She swallowed hard, her body's hunger and weariness at last unquenchable. Even more unpalatable was the idea of suing Finorian for shelter now. She had been wrong to refuse Kendric the chance to urge her to stay at Citydell or to ask — tell — her that he was accompanying her back. But if he, too, had . . . Thought had become too painful, so Irissa took action, a first step toward what she had renounced not long before.

The forest did not stop her; Irissa soon passed out of its eternal shade into naked sunlight. Above her the soft shawl of rainbow unfurled its mist-woven stripes. Her burdens lightened. Surely a place over which a rainbow felt free to flourish its delicate banners would not be adamantly harsh to any cause.

But the courtyard stood empty when she entered it, with every door shut and barred, as she found when she tried them all in turn. The building decanted silence as does a crypt. No phalanx of Finorians stepped forth to challenge or confuse or reluctantly concede entrance.

Irissa stepped back, angered to the point of fury by the many doors closed to her, at her back and at her front, doors of past and future. She lifted her right hand, bare of everything but the ring. A round of colors flared between the five conjoined stones and the blank coldstone windows. The silver fire of her eyes fanned the conflagration. She drew on all the magic within her and without her, on all the magic within her grasp, be it benign or base.

A lightning storm played round the castle's coldstone foundation until it ran bright with alternating colors; wind or the simulacrum of it rattled the coldstone panes in their frames, shook the doors on their Iridesium-surfaced iron hinges. Around the edifice, windows cracked open in thunderous sequence like ice snapping in the spring, and doors, unhinged, sprung askew on the dark of their unguarded portals.

In one of them Finorian appeared, her dry locks riffling in the windless current of Irissa's unleashed magic.

'I told you that you could not return,' she said quietly.

'I have,' Irissa shouted back.

'Why?'

'Why else? I put my lot in with yours.'

'Where is your Wrathman?'

'He is not my Wrathman.' Irissa paused. 'And he is where he chooses to be.'

Finorian's hands spread wide, then settled on the emerald touchstone glowing borgia-bright upon her breastbone. 'Welcome then, if the wonders of Citydell have not quenched your loyalty to the true Torloc way, if you come to fight with us for our birthright.'

'I come because there is no place else in Edanvant I can be.'

Now Finorian paused, for a very long time, until her

fingertips trembled at the edge of the emerald and the stone itself was limned in a vivid halo of color and light.

'It is an — adequate — reason for now.' Finorian raised her hands above her head, her opaque eyes rolling up in their sockets until an even snowier white could be seen.

Doors and Iridesium-set windows slammed shut in thunderous unison, all but the one that framed Finorian as her arms swept wide.

'Enter then, and be one of us, one *with* us — against them, the men who give us naught but grief.'

It was a broader invitation than Irissa cared to accept, but she was weary and welcome no place else in Edanvant. She dropped her own arms and moved steadily toward Finorian.

A Torloc eight feet tall glowered down at Kendric with blind brown eyes. Kendric, unused to being overlooked by anybody, pushed on the unsighted one with the force of his palms.

Little happened. A creak of protest echoed in the ill-lit hall. The Torloc still stood in his accustomed spot, no readier to recognize Kendric or admit him beyond the door he guarded.

'Magic?' Kendric asked, pushing on the broad chest before him until his sinews knotted. 'Or merely stubborn with age, like all aggravating things?'

At his feet the serene cat watched man belabor soot-blackened wood. No flames flared in the narrow passage now, although gutted torches impaled wall sockets all along the tunnel. Only the light of Kendric's hilt illuminated the way, and that unquenchable flare danced relentlessly over the wooden Torloc face before it. For Kendric contended with a figure carved into a door, with a man made of weepwaterwood, whose expression wept only resin and whose timberlike body remained rooted to the spot it warded.

'These Torlocs hoard their secrets,' Kendric grunted out, his eyes swimming in the rain of his sweat.

'I told you to use your magic,' the cat sang up from her secure spot on the floor.

Kendric braced his feet even farther apart and leaned into the door as into a killing wind. The wood facade buckled

231

suddenly, splinters driving outward like daggers. Kendric leaped back, then bowed stiffly to the cat, who preceded him regally over the open threshold.

'They will know we came this way,' the cat said, sighing, 'but I suppose you derive some satisfaction from expressing your more primitive powers.'

'Immense,' Kendric said unrepentantly.

They wound their way through yet another circuitous passage. Felabba led them deeper and deeper beneath the Citydell's extensive foundation. The old cat acted as if she knew where she was going, Kendric kept telling himself, but cats always acted like that — even the speechless, blessedly ignorant tabbies of lowly alleyways.

He had long since lost any sense of direction; in this tangle of unlit tunnels he was at the mercy of whatever should choose to claim him — death or a cranky talking cat. If only Irissa . . .

'She fares as well as can be expected,' the cat's voice imposed on Kendric's darkening thoughts. 'Which is less well than we. I would concentrate on our predicament, were I you.'

' "Our predicament" is your doing,' Kendric retorted.

'Here!' The cat's voice roughened with an underpurr of satisfaction. 'Here it is, the ancient Torloc spelling circlet.'

'I see nothing but a harshly hewn tunnel,' Kendric objected, but moments after light glittered ahead, at first in bright pinpricks, then in pendant festoons.

All glimmered cold and silver, but the warmth of gold, green, crimson, and azure touched the icy light. The array erupted into flamelike profusion so suddenly that Kendric straightened to view it and straightaway knocked his head on the passage's stony ceiling.

He and Felabba trod a pathway between dwarf trees laden with illuminated fruit and leaves. Some hung as heavy as amethyst grapes; others wafted slightly, as laden branches will cause their fruit to tremble just before harvest time. Icy, apple-round rubies suspended in the dark inner air. Twinkling assemblies of sapphires gathered like airy-boned birds on the ends of silver branches, bobbing up and down as if about to salute the underworld with a song. Tiny emeralds brighter than

232

foxberries grew low alongside the path, and all around trunks of twisted Iridesium reflected the jewels' rich colors in their bark-carved black depths.

Kendric heard water running like a delinquent melody through the farther darkness; the dank, stale smell of underground had evaporated into a clean, scoured odorlessness. Yet, the place sniffed of great age somehow, and the jewels seemed to have hung there for eons.

The path ended in a widening space that swallowed itself and became a circle. A map lay at his feet, every inch of it inset with gleaming gemstones. Its aquamarine seas churned with a cascading intimation of light and movement; emerald forests quivered as if to the weight of birds upon their airiest upper branches; topaz sands glimmered with lambent heat, and pools dark as black sapphires sunk their tiny selves deep in forest, desert, and city.

Felabba trod unhesitatingly over this enchanted surface, her familiar figure and ordinary scale looming large and almost blasphemously above it.

Kendric hesitated to step upon the begemmed map, though reason told him that many feet had preceded him. The glittering stones cast such an illusion of great depth that he feared he might sink beneath his own weight into them, his skin skimming their luminosity as he vanished.

Felabba paused amid an ocean of aquamarines and gave him the baleful glare of her emerald eyes. Kendric, great homespun thing that he was, moved onto the unreal shimmering world laid beneath his feet.

'What does it represent?' he wondered.

'Rule before it sank; Edanvant before it emptied; Rengarth before it hid itself,' the cat answered shortly.

'But a map can't show the lay of three lands.'

'This map can show anything it pleases — or that you please it to show. Call up vanished Clymerind if you want a sight for nostalgia's sake—'

'Clymerind?'

Kendric's awesomely whispered question became fact. A small purple-jeweled hummock of substance surfaced not far from his right boot and edged coyly around the archipelago of his foot before floating across the jeweled sea toward a blood-garnet sunfall.

Kendric jumped to evade the mobile illusion.

'Stop bounding like a tomcat on a sun-struck stone and follow me,' Felabba snapped. 'We have not time to dawdle.'

Three large strides took him well ahead of the cat. He put his hands on his knees and leaned down to question it.

'What do we do here of such importance? And how do we leave this city after?'

'That's my business,' the cat answered testily. 'Your business is to walk softly and keep quiet until I am done. Then we can get on with *your* journey.'

She minced past his skeptical features, the erect pennant of her tail tickling him delicately under the nose. Kendric sneezed.

'Hush!' the cat ordered, turning in what Kendric perceived to be the center of the far-flung circular map.

Iridesium inlay work marked the boundaries — a circle surrounding a six-pointed star whose center only had five sides. Kendric squinted to trace this impossible phenomenon to the point of anomaly but could find no place where lines ran awry. Yet a pentagram within a six-pronged shape represented impossibility . . .

The cat made a *tsk*ing sound. 'Impossible,' she complained. 'Too many careless spirits have stirred the surface. Ah.'

The pentagram darkened with a smoky mist. Felabba hung over its amorphous fumes as if to inhale them, her wedgelike face adding yet another geometric form to the scene.

Her whiskers trembled, then she seemed to blow upon the fog, which parted to reveal a slice of thin emerald glowing eerily bright.

'Yes, I know the touchstone of Finorian. I seek the true talismans, the ones bought or taken from others and other worlds — ah, now we shall see.'

Felabba crouched intently before the fog-veiled single eye of the pentagram. Kendric braced his hands on his knees and leaned over her. Before their unblinking gazes passed a parade

234

of objects — some plain, some garishly jeweled, most merely decorated.

There was a cup encircled with a serpent design in hammered silver. 'The flagon of bottomless borgia,' Felabba murmured over her shoulder at Kendric. 'From Rengarth originally, but late of . . . other places.'

Next a sinuous curve of linked brass wove into view.

'Jhandar's belt that weds itself to its wearer and confers an aura of invincible truth upon the prevaricator. A most useful thing . . . aha! So *this* is where it hides.'

Kendric stared numbly at the subsequent item, a great, dimpled, pear-shaped black pearl. 'I thought the Torloc men craved talismans, not jewels and wealth.'

'Such a talisman, my ignoble ninny!' The cat could hardly speak for purring. 'Tuck it under your tongue and you can speak all languages of all things and all worlds — speak fish even, or falgon. Speak Rengarthese or High Isselinian. Speak even cat.'

'An unnecessary facility,' Kendric judged. 'I converse too much with you already.'

The creature spat amiably in his direction and returned her sharp attention to the next image from the mist. A one-tongued flame whipped there, unattached to any object, simply fire of and by itself. It burned pure scarlet, as if untainted by the body of what it fed upon, as if self-feeding.

Kendric felt his face sear from within, felt a sudden sweat spring over his body. He had never looked upon a thing so hot, so boundlessly hungry. Beside him the cat sat silent, no descriptive phrase issuing from her thin pink lips.

'What is this thing?' Kendric found himself forced to inquire against his inclination. He didn't want to know that a thing so unnaturally disembodied had a name.

'It is . . . not to be named to its face.' Felabba stepped back, out of the star to the cool blue mosaic of sparkling water. 'It is enough to know they have it. We must go, and go quickly now.'

Kendric straightened. 'My thoughts exactly, all along. I presume you lead in this, as in all else?'

The cat was oddly quiet, her green eyes fixed — nay, almost impaled — on the reflection of twin flames that danced in them.

'You do know how to get out; you have all along, of course?'

No word came from the cat. She was dreaming again, of distance, of things even cats should not dream of. Kendric bent and scooped her up, making certain he was not tempted to eye the single flame that beat through a fog of smoke. The clean smell had gone from the underground chamber; a bright, burning scent replaced it, strong as distilled garlic.

Kendric tucked the limp cat under his arm and walked boldly across the other half of the floor-set map — islands and mountains, seas and forests winked richly beneath his hard-worn soles.

No magical garden of jeweled trees escorted them out. The way grew low, as before, and Kendric's sword hilt waxed warm and bright in answer to the sudden shadow. He hunched his way through the blackness, reasoning that a passage must lead to an exit, an exit to a pathway upward, a stair to hall, a hall to a doorway, a courtyard, a city street . . .

Nothing but endless, long-ago burrowed darkness and still, stale air met him. His hand, wrapped around Felabba's lean middle, felt the ripple of fragile ribs and feeble heartbeat, yet was warmed in the cold and the dark by a living mitten of fur.

She said nothing, the old cat, not even protesting the indignity of her transportation. Kendric's flame-inspired sweat dried dank upon his skin and stayed there, pressing upon him with the dark like a wet cloak.

Finally, a bit of ruddy torchflame lit the distance. At last. A trace of humanity. He was already planning how he would transfer Felabba to his left hand and carry the torch in his right when the thing ahead spread its red-veined wings, reached down the long expanse of tunnel, and enfolded Kendric in a deeper blackness bright with pulsing embers of blood.

236

CHAPTER FIFTEEN

Kendric dropped Felabba as gently as he could. In moments the cold weight of steel replaced the cat's limp warm form in his hand. He wrapped his other hand securely over both hand and hilt. Through the interweaving of his ten fingers the pommel blazed white-hot warning, its light bleeding through the thinner portions of his hands to make them appear prematurely bloodwashed.

The character of the passage in which they stood had altered utterly. Its rough stone surfaces had smoothened; against its new slickness ropy veins of red throbbed in turn. It resembled the surface of some curled green-black leaf, every vein engorged with the invisible ichor that fed it. The passage seemed alive in a remote, unreachable way. Pulsing ragged lines of red threw lurid flashing light over Kendric and the cat. Kendric sensed that the very walls yearned to collapse upon them, to squeeze themselves shut and wring their hapless contents dry, but were restrained by their nature if not their inclination.

At his feet, the cat spat, turning humpedback in a circle, her tail swollen to twice its natural size. He had expected more than ordinary feline rage from Felabba in a crisis.

'What happened?' he demanded, hoping for enlightenment and deprived of an object for the ready application of his sword.

'The flame commands a guardian,' a subdued Felabba answered. 'First my senses were befogged; then some trap sprung upon us. Are we still in the passage?'

Kendric hesitated before answering. 'Something loomed all around us — something crimson-eyed and red-taloned and

237

large as a keep tower. I think it — it overwhelmed us, passed us. I think that it . . . surrounds us now.'

'Then we cannot go forward.' The cat peered into the glaring red darkness.

'You misunderstand my meaning. I said *it* surrounds us — not a number of adversaries, but the thing itself. We are — inside — it. Whatever — it — is.'

'And we can go forward?'

'If we would wish to.'

'The single Tongue of Flame is a potent talisman and naturally was imbued with a secret guardian eons ago. How would you guard a tongue of magical flame, Wrathman?'

'With a mouth,' he answered promptly and sourly.

'A mouth . . . Very good indeed.' Felabba's green eyes made a striking sight in the bloodied darkness. 'Or would you say — a maw?'

'Say whatever you like; I don't see that speculation will get us anywhere.'

Kendric circled defensively, bereft of any individual foe to defend himself against. The newly fluid walls around them painted dizzying patterns of red on black as if moving subtly.

Where would one house a tongue of fire? In a lamp? Small licks of red flickered in the heaving darkness. The cat's ears pricked, and Kendric heard it, too — a bellowslike sound, regular and almost soulful, as if something gigantic were sighing.

And still it nagged at him, the stubborn, vein-freezing feeling that the thing that had yawned out of the common darkness had not so much passed them as encompassed them, so they were part of it even as they strove to define it and break free of it. This made a conundrum fit for a cat of Felabba's exacting temperament to decipher, he decided. It was mind work, not sword work, and Kendric had always complained of being unable to think properly in the dark.

Thinking was not much required in the next few hectic moments. Speeding from the unseen darkness ahead came whips of swirling fire, intertwining as they unraveled into one knotted snapping-flamed mass.

238

Kendric severed one knot with the upward slice of his sword; fiery threads sizzled to the black ground. More knots scattered from the belaboring of his sword, hissing wildly as the sword's edge honed itself on their heat.

Facing a dancing circle of severed flames, Felabba hissed back with her own feline fireworks. Kendric's booted feet stamped out the writhing filaments, but they always flared into fresh heat and new heights, weaving up in the air to knot with their fellows until they formed a hot and living bramble hedge that barred the passage from top to bottom and side to side.

Kendric, sweat-beaded and breath-shy, stepped back to study it, inadvertently stamping out the length of Felabba's tail.

'Ill-done, ill-done,' the cat remonstrated, leaping far away when released.

'What would you have me do but retreat when faced with so hot-blooded and serpentine a barrier?' Kendric asked.

'Use your head instead of your feet,' the cat snapped, bending to lick her tail assiduously — an activity, Kendric couldn't help noticing, that should have been applied long before to the ocher spine of dust that stained its length.

'By using my head you mean magic, I presume,' Kendric retorted.

He cast one last glance at the tail-tending cat, then regarded the writhing wall of interlocked flames. It reminded him of the pool Irissa had overheated with her eyes' ardent power when they had first arrived in Edanvant, using his sword blade as a kind of magical envoy between her gaze and the icy water.

Kendric eyed that poor, misused, mind-made blade. It had not long before served as a lowly conduit of heat, and did not heat and cold together help fashion the most ordinary sword? He concentrated his gaze upon it, upon the cool blue length of steel he knew so well he had evoked it into reality from memory alone. A blade was an aloof, icy thing in its way, cold-tempered enough to wield hot red death and remain indifferent to it. Knowing that was only a step away from *seeing* that. And when magic is one's medium, seeing is but a short remove from *being*.

The blade before him chilled until it seemed a fresh-forged

239

shaft of pure blue light. Frost feathered along the gleaming length and etched a facile tracery of design from pointed tip to broad hilt base.

Beneath his hot and nervous palm, Kendric felt leather binding tauten and crack, felt cold seep into his bone and blood as a fever does — swift and suddenly pervasive. His right arm became an extension of the sword's frigid length, stiffening in support of it.

Kendric's sigh of relief made his breath bloom briefly in a white rose of mist upon the blade. By the time it had vanished, the sword had raised and Kendric faced the flickering wall. The sword crashed down as if quenching itself in fire, and the conjoined hiss of flame and blade seared through the dark space like a sibilant scream; like many screams, repeated endlessly.

Flames shriveled to ashes and fell light as snow cinders; red leaped upward again, but cold blue lightning felled it. Kendric's arms sawed the smoky air; where he struck, the sword shattered lattices of flame. Only embers burned on the floor, paired like angry eyes, and blinking out one by one.

'Nicely done,' Felabba volunteered from the self-absorption of her grooming. 'Now invent a way for us to escape the thing that swallowed us.'

'Swallowed . . . So that's what we saw — a sweeping, oncoming maw, spread wide to devour us and closing shut soon after, locking us in this living darkness!'

He let the burden of the sword swing at last to ground, where it slowly paled to mortal metal again, before he resumed his reasoning.

'You asked where one would conceal a Single Tongue of Flame, and I said a mouth — only not quite a mouth, you answered, a maw. A colossal serpent's maw!' Kendric laughed his delight with his conclusion.

'Now that you have solved the mystery of our containment,' the cat said acidly. 'I suggest you apply yourself to releasing us from this pleasant place you describe — the belly of a giant guardian snake!' Her final hissed word sounded appallingly ophidian. 'Quickly!'

Kendric blanched.

It was one thing to decipher the form a spell took, another to overcome it. He carried no shield but his desire to be on straighter paths in more illuminated surroundings.

With that in mind, he started into the darkness, turning only once to see the cat trotting quietly behind him. If magic rained upon him again, he would dry it with the fires his sword could start, hard steel striking sparks upon the flint of whatever faced them. If only angry Torlocs waited in their path's end, he would use words first, then deeds and finally magic, if he must.

Perhaps the things that threatened in any world responded most to inner resolve. No further phenomena interrupted their progress. At last Kendric shouldered his way through a somewhat cramped doorway. Felabba slithered through his feet, taking the lead once they were in common tunnel again. But Kendric lingered at the exit.

'At first I thought these bowed pillars handsome.'

He gingerly touched one of the two ivory tusks that formed the doorway's upright members, glancing above the lintel to where a mottled portico raked back to a center-set obsidian eye on each side. At the pointed base of each oversized fang, a puddle of dried borgia shone virulently green.

'Is this a Torloc thing?' he asked the old cat. 'It weeps borgia.'

She turned and, seeing the serpentine likeness of the portal, hissed her violent distaste. For a moment Kendric traced a terrible similarity between the feline and ophidian face in striking posture, all paired white fangs and flattened skull.

'Nothing Torloc in it,' Felabba said, shaking her head as if a gnat had encamped in her ear, 'save that it was set here long ago by Torloc eyes to guard the Damen Circle.'

'That was a Circle place? Like that Irissa said Finorian convenes beneath the woodland castle?'

The cat was leaving, limping quickly along the earth-packed passage. 'Like all growing things, magic roots in Nursemaid Earth. It keeps best in cool, damp places,' she said over her shoulder.

'So do other venomous things,' he retorted, finally shouldering

241

his sword and following her faintly phosphorescent figure. Against these earthen halls, she looked like an ambulatory version of the white mushroom Irissa had called Fool's Cap, Kendric thought, savoring the comparison more than he had the mushroom. He amused himself by weaving many subtle and slightly disrespectful, although privately entertaining, variations upon it.

But soon the passageway ended, informally, with a leafy bower. He and the cat stood near the outer city wall, which loomed darker than the night sky. A moon kept one soulful eye on them, and the gatekeepers slept. Beyond the wall, a shrill shriek ended in a muffled gurgle.

'You wish to retrace your steps.' Felabba's statement served more as question.

Kendric shrugged. There had been a time when the idea of debating any course with a cat, however articulate it might be, would have seemed ludicrous. Now he had traversed two gates to as many worlds and had found the greatest wonders were not the magical ones, but the common stuff of everyday life that he had once known so well and scorned so freely.

'I think she bleeds,' he answered the cat, and did not answer her. 'And does not know it.'

'It is possible to do so?' For once Felabba sounded uncertain.

'More than possible,' he answered with authority. 'It is the lot of humankind.'

'Irissa is Torloc.'

'Worse, then, for her.'

'She can heal herself.'

'Not of this.'

The cat thought for a while. Kendric never questioned that her quiet, meditative stance indicated deep consideration. 'You seem sure of yourself,' Felabba finally conceded.

Kendric crouched beside her, smoothing back her whiskers with one forefinger. 'No . . . sure of Irissa's uncertainty.'

'Paradoxes, Sir Wrathman?' The cat sounded coy. 'Soon you will be weaving riddles and rhymes and be sure of nothing, including yourself.'

'Ah, that.' Kendric stood, giving the cat a parting pat on

242

the head from which she shrank distastefully, an effect Kendric loomed too lofty already to detect. He stared at the wall. 'That, too, is the lot of humankind. Be thankful you are feline and certain of everything.'

He didn't glance down again, but walked to the wall, bracing his hands on it.

The cat minced after him. 'You used the Shinestone for a key—'

'I know. But no sun shines now to melt this metal. I wonder what Irissa used . . . Here, stick close to my boots, old mousegrinder. I plan to try the Shunstone again and fear the wall will fall.'

He tipped the plainest stone in his ring, more discernible for its lack of visibility than its looks, until it chimed dully against the night-subdued Iridesium. This time pure black parted before them, curved away as if blown by a fierce wind. Kendric had never passed through such gloom, unleavened by any light. It did not even reflect the gently glowing hilt of his sword; his senses had to rely on logic to assume that the dark wall leaned away from him on all sides.

His mind became so anxious for orientation that it began to paint bright shadows on the darkness — shadows of his old grandmother's face, bramble-crowned; the tall form of Valodec, Wrathman of Rule, now entombed in sunken Clymerind; a lean, sinuous shape that could have been the Rulian sorceress Mauvedona or a moonweasel, also late of Rule; Delevant's icy, pillarlike shape, a cold candle of illusion burning into utter blackness; and there, beyond them all, the bright vague likeness of Irissa.

Knowing the wall and what he saw within it for mere imagining, Kendric hurried through. Nowhere in the white form-haunted passage did he see the reflection of a white cat.

'Orvath lives?'

Jalonia's collection of half-sliced mushrooms scattered like wet jewels from her fingers. Her face went as white and watery as an opal. 'Tell me about Orvath.'

Irissa, forced to account for herself as part of the price

Finorian charged for her return to the bosom of the Torloc dames, fought for further words. Articulating the name had been difficult enough; saying what its bearer had done would be unbearable.

'I told you he would do well enough through the gate,' Finorian interjected.

'I think Orvath survived *despite* the Inlands and the gate,' Irissa said coldly, wondering why Finorian's attempt to take credit for her father's safety struck her with such distaste.

Jalonia swept her mushrooms like chicks back under her wings again, absently turning and numbering their bright, decapitated heads. 'You did not see him in the central Eye of your Damen Circle, Finorian,' she said softly. 'I asked and asked, but you saw no sign.'

Finorian's garb rustled, but no one looked at her. 'When one goes beyond a gate, it is difficult,' she said. 'Besides, I assumed he would return when he could. And did he find his talisman?'

Irissa felt the question settle on her, heavy as a snow-season blanket around her shoulders, and remain hanging there.

'He found hardship and danger and the face of death itself,' she responded, not looking at Jalonia, not looking at Finorian. 'He found an ancient Torloc wizard.'

'Wizard!' The word undulated from mouth to mouth down the long trestle table, from Torloc dame to Torloc dame.

'There are no Torloc wizards.' It was left for Jalonia to state the obvious. 'Has he gone mad? Tell me.'

Irissa couldn't answer, hearing in her memory a voice that excused itself even as its possessor committed the inexcusable. But was it madness — or mere villainy — or something yet unnamed that could be forgiven still?

'Delevant.' Finorian sounded satisfied. 'He saw Delevant.'

Irissa looked up at last. 'As did I. And Kendric. We also wrestled with Delevant, only Orvath had no magic and suffered from the struggle. To this day, he—'

The image of Jalonia's wounded eyes hovered before her mind like great golden bees seeking some scent of sweetness and finding only the sour succor of gall.

'He escaped,' Irissa finished meticulously, 'with his life.'

'And Kendric.' Finorian had risen and paused behind Irissa, her gnarled hands curled into the young seeress's shoulders. 'Where is Kendric now?'

'Behind. There was no need for both of us to . . . to carry this news back.'

Finorian's hands tightened to talons. 'And you were not welcome there.'

'No. It's true. They consider themselves well served without us women.'

An 'ah' of insult wafted softly down the table and back again. Jalonia's small knife had resumed slicing mushrooms into luminous sickle shapes; its blade hit the hardwood tabletop with a rhythmic rapping sound.

'They have the folk of the city, you see,' Irissa added, 'to do the domestic work, among other things. For the rest, there are their magical talismans.'

'The talismans.' Finorian's hands wrung Irissa's shoulder. 'Did you see any?'

'They were secret. Guarded.' Irissa remembered a night of tale-telling and deep drinking, a night when she had sat as invisible as some truly kindred spirit among her Torloc kind, when even the one who was least like her and thus most dear to her seemed to have momentarily forgotten her . . . She sighed, at last knowing her sense of hurt for what it was, self-inflicted. 'Kendric had a certain, natural rapport with them. *He* may have seen some of their talismans—'

'A pity he did not accompany you back,' Finorian noted with heavy irony, her hands lifting from Irissa's shoulders so suddenly that Irissa spun to verify the Eldress's position in the room.

Finorian stood against the farthest wall, far too distant to have laid so much as a finger on Irissa. Irissa stiffened, knowing she had felt the invisible force of Finorian's will, a disembodied thing, yet more real perhaps than most people's physical presence — excepting possibly Kendric's, she thought with a wincing regret. To hear Finorian express Irissa's own deep chagrin at Kendric's absence was most galling of all.

'It was not necessary for Kendric to accompany me,' Irissa said at last, loath to admit that she had left him behind because she feared he might refuse to return with her. 'Edanvant is my native world. Why should I not move within it alone, freely, safely—?' she demanded defiantly.

'Why indeed?' was all Finorian would say of that. 'What's a mere war to so wise a seeress? Was there — did your Wrathman mention a stone talisman? Similar to the beringed ones you both wear but more individual, I think.'

In Finorian's voice, Irissa heard the avaricious echo of another, nearer one, though male. 'I told you; the men did not trust me with their talismans,' she said stiffly.

'You could have used your powers to discover these things.'

'I didn't — think of it.'

This time Finorian actually advanced on Irissa. Her hands fanned on either side of the Iridesium circlet, not quite touching it.

'The men oppose us utterly! They seek to drive us back through the gate to worlds that will not have us either. You must think of that, seeress! You must think of many more unpleasant things before Torloc is through with Torloc in this Edanvant of ours. And you will use your magic against Torlocs, against kin, before our contention ends; perhaps against Wrathman as well.'

Irissa's every impulse urged her to her feet. Finorian's hands hovered at her vision's very edge, keeping her seated through no more obvious force than the press of their presence. Between them the Iridesium band squeezed tight on Irissa's temples. She sensed a rising greenness in the metal, as if it hummed to the tune of the emerald touchstone slung around Finorian's neck.

'Let her be.' The tone came low and silent.

Irissa would not have been surprised to hear Kendric voice those words, or even a rather raggedy old cat. She glanced across the table to the speaker, startled by the searing golden fire in Jalonia's usually smothered eyes.

'She sought peace with us,' her mother said heatedly, 'as we sought it in Edanvant, and she has been betrayed enough.'

246

'By the men,' Finorian rejoined, but her hands dropped away, 'the men who guard their alien talismans so jealously, who deny the elder and the inner magic for the gewgaws of latter-day and outer magicks. The men who threaten us. The men who do not miss us,' she added forcefully.

Jalonia wavered, her face whitening.

'We are not welcome here,' Irissa agreed swiftly. 'Why not find another gate, then, to a land where Torlocs are unknown? We have lived without the men for as long as I have lived, and longer. Why force ourselves on those who will not have us?'

'We will lose our magic, our birthright,' said one of the women down the table, her voice dreary.

'Do you bear magic?' Irissa retorted. 'Or you? Or even odd-eyed Melyconial? No. You have lived a long time with a single source of what was once a mighty spring of magic.'

In her mind, and in her mind alone, Irissa rose from the bench and spun to face Finorian. 'Only one of us truly bears the name of seeress, the title of Eldress. I have magic, yes, gained since I left you, practiced by good luck and ill adventure, ebbing and flowing with my fortunes. I am no living talisman to steer a community by. Only Finorian can be said to lead you, and she is an old woman. Where is there future in that?'

The room wavered black in Irissa's senses. She was instantly blind to everything but the pale image of Finorian she confronted at the back of her mind. Her argument held logic enough to lull a Wrathman's suspicions. It was not proof against Finorian's awesome sense of survival.

'You bear magic,' the Eldress's voice invaded Irissa's consciousness, shaking at last, as Finorian was finally shaken.

In her mind Irissa saw a power-armed Finorian standing with her hands starfish-pale upon the emerald touchstone. The stone's rich surface had frosted over. It gleamed as bloodless as Finorian's face. Frightened, Irissa mentally clutched the Overstone at her breast. Finorian immediately perceived the nonphysical gesture. Her thin lips smiled scornfully.

'You bear magic and dare not use it — what greater pride, folly or faithlessness is there than this? Had *I* but one talisman

247

– the Overstone Orvath failed in claiming – I could reconcile this madness, we could rejoin our kind without loss to either of our natures.'

'Yet you would condemn the men for searching for talismans,' Irissa challenged, mind to mind. 'What of the emerald touchstone? You inveigh against talismanic magic, yet cling to that presence. You claim the men's talismans betray our kind of female magic, yet I have employed talismans in my travels. My ring came to me from a Torloc wizard who eons ago wed the seeresses' inbred magic to that of acquired talismans . . .'

The Finorian in Irissa's mind swelled to encompass it. She seemed to have inhaled the world and expanded into its globular shape. Irissa felt her spirits shrivel under a blast of icy-green mist.

She occupied no space or time but nothingness, barren even of gates. Irissa saw only the Eldress now, could only hear her voice crackling like angry lightning.

'*You* are the first Torloc seeress to employ talismans, Irissa of Rindell! The first and only. My emerald touchstone is no external talisman but an illusion, a spectral embodiment of my very breath, exhaled back to me from the Eye of the Damen Circle itself.

'As a young seeress undergoing Far Focus, I delved so deep in the well of powers that my very breath and body slowed nigh to the chill of death itself. I looked into the Eye so far I saw myself blinking shut. My last breath came as a green mist, then froze in that icy atmosphere of cold power into this form.'

Finorian's long forefingers tapped the emerald. 'When I touched the last warmth within me to it, I found my life pulsing again. My emerald touchstone is no talisman, despite its physical guise. It is Far Focus incarnate; a pledge that I will serve my kind and my calling even unto death.

'*You* are the anomaly, Irissa, and always were, not I. *You* are the flaw that shifts within my emerald touchstone. I know not to what purpose, nor to what ultimate good or ill for our Torloc kind, but it is my burden to bear the knowledge of your

248

importance even as I do not understand it and you betray it.'

'You do not need me! You simply need a genuine talisman to flourish at the men — my talisman!' Irissa cried, feeling her very being squeezed breathless within the vice of the Eldress's contempt and fury. Only the pulse of the Overstone within the tight clasp of her hand held Irissa to her shaken sense of self. 'You are no better, no less greedy than they are! Why?'

The Eldress's grip upon Irissa's senses slackened with the sudden, dry, cooling withdrawal of a breaking fever. Her form took physical shape in Irissa's mind again, and seemed smaller, stiller.

'Men respect talismans in this age, not foggy emanations of our race's instincts,' she admitted tonelessly. 'I cannot grip their minds, as once I did, as I can still encompass yours. With the Overstone borne by one willing to use it, I could meet the men upon equal footing, challenge them to parley and treaty, because with it I could open a gate to Outside. There we could jointly claim a world uncontaminated by our Torloc past and our separate roles, a world where inner and outer magic could meet.'

Irissa felt her own projected presence in the Eldress's mind grow clearer and stand straighter. 'You seek another false paradise, Finorian,' she said, compassionately. 'If we cannot solve our differences and resolve our separate strengths, our warring magics, here — in Edanvant — we will only import our weaknesses elsewhere. I have traveled too long in too many worlds to believe in the superiority of a new one.'

Finorian laughed. 'Ah, Irissa, you speak with a tongue borrowed from a born doubter, a man of marshes and magic swords, not instincts. If you but knew what worlds you will someday see . . .

'But I know and you do not, and that is my burden, and your flaw. I had hoped that your presence, your very existence and youth proving that seeresses are not lost to our kind, would force the men to realize their need of our magic. Instead you have proven . . . immaterial . . . to our Torloc stalemate.

'Instead we now stand ready to contend to the death: the

death of our peculiar magic, of our personal selves, of our particular kind — it does not matter. It has been coming for a long time, Irissa, and fate placed you as a key in the long-closed door between us, that I know. But you will . . . not . . . *turn!*'

The image of Finorian in Irissa's mind snuffed out candle-quick. Irissa heard the flap of the Eldress's withdrawing robes and watched all the Torloc faces turn to follow her going. To these mostly unmagicked women, only seconds had elapsed, and the tense dialogue had been unspoken. At Finorian's departure, Silence came and sat invisibly at the long table. Then one woman spoke shyly, her voice rusty from long reluctance to speak for itself.

'How many men were there at Citydell?'

Irissa dragged her mind back into her body, back to here and now questions of mere emotional importance. 'Twenty, perhaps a few more,' she answered absently.

'Three-and-forty left Rindell,' another woman noted, her voice listless.

Silence took its conversational turn as the toll of lost Torlocs sounded in each mind present.

Then, 'They are well?' another woman asked.

'Mostly well; most of them,' Irissa said brusquely.

'You had barely seen a Torloc man since your birth,' Jalonia reflected. 'What did you think of . . . them?'

Irissa considered it and was surprised to find she had formed an opinion separate from her personal sense of injury.

'I knew them no better than I knew all of you,' she answered truthfully enough. 'What could I think, except that they were my kind and it was a pity that we had all journeyed so far to reunite — or fight — with strangers.'

Dame Silence held the floor for an endless time, until — woman by woman — the Torloc dames slipped from the great empty hall, and Irissa was left sitting opposite her mother.

Jalonia's work-roughened hands suddenly swept Irissa's into their steel-tight grip. Her eyes bore intently into her

250

daughter's, direct as Kendric's, as they had never been before.

'Tell me,' she said again, pled again, 'about Orvath.'

Something long and low and dark stalked Kendric and Felabba through the thick vegetation between the walls. He sensed it as one would sense a shadow, not with his eyes or ears or nose so much as with every crawling inch of his skin.

It was not that his more traditional senses didn't have much to occupy them. The land between the walls reeked of raw, animal scent, especially at night. It writhed with the movements of hunting beasts, every leaf seeming to twitch from the coming or going of some large or small leaf- or flesh-consuming creature. Branches cracked and leaves rustled; stones shifted and sticks snapped; cries impossible to define as to whether of fear, attack, defense, or death echoed endlessly, reverberated between the inflexible metal drumskins of the encompassing walls.

Yet the thing that slithered alongside him, unseen, unheard, unsniffed, loomed more real, more lethal. The other creatures kept aloof from the crash of his coming, despite their all too real hungers. This thing hunted something less substantial; Kendric knew that with every strand of magic woven so agonizingly into the braid of his being. It hunted his soul.

Felabba paced his progress in the seemingly aimless, at-arm's length way of cats. Her lean white shape remained within eye-glimpse, though, as she stole beneath the underbrush, her white coat now dappled green. Occasionally her claws would rasp up a tree trunk and Kendric would watch a flying white form leap whip-thin upper branches to fall onto rather than jump across a bridge of insubstantial striplings.

At moments like that, Kendric felt more awe for Felabba's common feline talents than the anomaly of the cat's speech or even her seldom-displayed magic.

Both man and cat came to the second wall scratched, exertion-heated, and as wary as they were weary. Kendric reluctantly raised his ring with the Nightstone turned toward him. It seemed only logical to use the same stone that had unlocked the wall before, especially since the qualities of both

251

wall and ringstone remained so immutable — each gleaming blackly impassive in every respect.

Yet . . . the thing still hovered behind them in the light-obscured forest. All motion and sound had stopped save the harsh, slow breathing of something as large as the night.

Kendric faced the implacable wall, faced an emotion he had never encountered in all his warrior's lifetime — utter two-mindedness. Something told him the wall had become more than it was, or that he had become less than he was, and it was now dangerous to him in a way it had not been before. Yet behind lurked only the breathless watcher and a company of Torlocs whose harshness had driven away the one constant in his life of late.

He paused, knowing that to be a fatal flaw for a warrior, for anyone who traversed the unknown, knowing all that — and yet pausing.

A flash of white caught the corner of his eye, bounding into full view before he could do more than raise his hands to the hilt slanting above his shoulder. Before he drew the blade, the thing was confronting him.

An awesome beast crouched at his feet — large and white-furred, with an open, saw-toothed muzzle and coin-bright golden eyes. It was more wolf than Inlands fowlen, and it watched him with a wise, wary look. Despite its petlike position on its belly, Kendric knew that it could leap — before he delivered his blow — either away into the surrounding woods or to his throat.

Behind him lay woods he had no desire to turn and find again. Only dark impervious wall he did not trust loomed before him. In it he saw the faint reflection of himself, elbows elevated to strike.

Cautiously he lowered his arms. The lupine face relaxed into a grin, exposing a lolling length of tongue. The creature stood, stretched, then ambled into the wall, glancing once over its sharp-boned shoulder to see if he followed.

Kendric knew better than to try this passage unaided. He smiled skeptically and touched the Nightstone to the gently heaving flank of the metal wall.

252

CHAPTER SIXTEEN

The green-tongued torches that lit the great hall of the forest-shadowed castle never burned low. Except for the daily dimming and brightening rhythm of the coldstone windows high above, suns could fall and rise again eternally and still the torches would flame on.

Night darkened the high windows now, but Jalonia and Irissa still shared the long trestle table, alone save for the somber company of their evening-cast shadows.

The mushroom heads, sorted but unstored, had begun to dry; they left a clinging metallic dust on fingertips when handled — magenta, crimson, azure, or deep green, according to their native hue. They had been handled a good deal over the past hour, with as much idle calculation as Tolechian dice, by both Irissa and her mother, who seemed disposed to distract their eyes elsewhere when talking to each other.

Irissa's fingernail slowly pushed a snail-colored mushroom fragment across the wooden tabletop, studying the glittering bronze trail it left.

'He said . . . he said that you urged him to go,' she pointed out.

'He' could only be Orvath, of whom they still talked, much to Irissa's discomfiture.

Jalonia nodded, again without looking up, her voice reflective. 'It's true. I was younger then, very young, and devoted to our community needs. If Finorian said something must be—' She sighed and swept a company of dried mushrooms off the table into the palm of her hand, then crushed them to iridescent powder. 'I still do as Finorian says.'

'He said that you and Finorian *wished* him gone,' Irissa

went on diffidently. She had no desire to serve as inadvertent envoy for a man who would not welcome her speaking for him any more than she wished to do it, but she knew more than Jalonia and could not withhold that knowledge.

'He believes,' she added. 'that Finorian sent him into the gate unwarned, knowing he was as unlikely to find and secure the Overstone egg as he was to return safely. He thinks that she — and you — did not wish to contend with a father's influence, that you both wished to separate him from me, from the first Torloc seeress born in many ages.'

'I did not know what you were until you opened your eyes!' Jalonia's common amber irises blazed like topazes, full into the quicksilver pools that were her daughter's.

'When did I open my eyes?' Irissa asked. No one had ever regaled her with stories of her infant antics, so she had never asked before.

'Too soon.' Jalonia's gaze dropped back to her long-abandoned task. 'Barely had I grown strong enough to take you in my arms when Finorian stood beside the bed-curtains, declaring you a seeress born and ordering the mirrors and armor stripped from the walls . . . I, of course, assisted in this work of protecting you from yourself — as long as I was allowed to.

'But I missed the armor-hung walls, and I was vain enough to miss mirrors.' Jalonia looked up, to a vision only she saw impressed on the plain wall opposite. 'Such a glittering place the great hall in Rindell was, Irissa, when men still came and went there. Polished armor gleamed like sunfall-gilded windows along every wall and Iridesium mail chimed so constantly it seemed to tell the time. There were ballads sung and tales told; wine and borgia were quaffed as one. And there was much brave talk of us all coming together at last — in peace and safety — in Edanvant.'

Jalonia studied the bleak hall, her loss-armored bronze eyes a dull reflection of it. Irissa saw that even the one-horned bearing-beast prancing on the tapestry opposite had lost its luster, looking more of a dapple gray than its true gold and silver. She wondered if that meant something she was too dispirited to perceive.

254

'Citydell is a no-more-joyous place.' Irissa meant to comfort.

Jalonia nodded grimly. 'So we are both equally miserable, men and women. There is some triumph in that, I suppose, in the way of a losing war that permits small victories.'

'You talk of war, yet the opposing sides are only two camps of twenty-some people. How can so few wage anything that resembles war?'

'We are Torlocs, Irissa, and born to make more of less. This, our legacy, once was used to enrich ourselves and those around us. Now it impoverishes us — and those around us. Magic levies its own justice.'

'Did you never mind,' Irissa wondered curiously, 'not having magic yourself?'

'Not until Orvath was gone and could not return, when even Finorian said she could not recall him or seek him by Far Focus. She said he had died attempting to capture the talisman, as likely all the men had, further proof that we violated our natures when we sought them and that she should never have sent him for one.'

'Nonsense.' Irissa sat back to take a long look at her mother. 'Why can I wear the ring of Inlands Stones forced upon me to no ill effect — and some excellent ones? Why can the Torloc men wield talismanic magic? And they claim they can.'

'You ask questions more suitable for Finorian.'

'No! They are suitable for us all. Perhaps we have left too much to Finorian for too long.'

Jalonia's lips stretched ruefully. 'Perhaps I left you to Finorian too easily, but you seem to have slipped her teaching.'

'Or learned it too well.'

They both mulled that for a while; then Irissa looked up suddenly and smiled.

'You need not miss mirrors any longer,' she told Jalonia. 'My sometimes-mirror Kendric informs me that you are the exact image of myself, and I of you.'

'Are we?' Jalonia's pale face brightened as she studied Irissa. 'I had not thought to look for myself in you; I had not thought to look at myself for more than twenty years. Did — did . . . did Orvath see the resemblance?'

Irissa dropped her glance to the tabletop again. 'He said I was the very image of you. It seemed to anger him.'

'Orvath was not an angry man.'

'He is now.'

'Perhaps his wounds . . .'

'He wrestled with a demon, a Torloc demon,' Irissa said quickly, seeking to console herself as much as her mother. 'A terrible, icy-hearted being that would have taken his very life's breath and instead claimed a portion of his body and perhaps his soul. He seems well, save for his stiffness. But—'

'Yes?' Jalonia leaned forward, her braids softly brushing her face, her hands clasped upon the table rim, everything in her indicating eager interest barely dampened.

Into this clean-faced hope, how could Irissa cast the ugly words needed to describe what Orvath had become — an angry man cheated and therefore willing to take where he should give? Her own hands clasped the Overstone at her breast, warmed by its innate heat, its presence, its belongingness.

'Irissa . . .' Jalonia was looking discomfited in her turn. 'You left the Wrathman behind in Citydell. Kendric. He seemed a . . . decent man, despite Finorian's opinion of the sex. Did something happen between you?'

'No. Nothing.' Irissa wondered how she could speak so true and still taste a lie upon her lipe. Nothing between them . . . and everything. For the first time she pictured Kendric, occupied below with borgia and good fellowship when Overstone-hungry Orvath had stolen upon her like a wolf — like a lion, Irissa corrected herself. She must be kinder to wolves now that the white one had come to warn her.

Why then was Kendric somehow implicated in the Torloc men's betrayal? Perhaps simply because he was male, and hence more a part of their company than even she — than especially she — given how the Torlocs had fractured on the dividing line of sex. That was not his fault, her internal voice of fairness shouted. Was she not blaming Kendric for what the men had blamed her — was she not seeing him as a forest and not as the tree that towered far above it? Forest or city, her world emptied in his absence.

'We agreed to leave here together,' she finally hedged. 'The decision to return was mine alone. I could not ask him to return to a place where he was so . . . unwelcome. Everyone has a right to welcome somewhere.'

'And he did not ask after me?' Jalonia asked again.

Confused, Irissa stared into the sober golden eyes across from her. Did she herself look this troubled, this lost? Did Jalonia but mirror back Irissa's uncertainty, or had her own long-nursed supply contaminated her daughter? No wonder Kendric had been shocked by confronting the two of them. Kendric. The name brought a private pang, but he was not the 'he' of Jalonia's questions, which always came back to Orvath.

'I did not speak much to Orvath,' Irissa said in stiff evasion. 'He thought me only a tool of Finorian's.'

'He blames me,' Jalonia diagnosed regretfully. 'All your careful sidesteps cannot hide that. I should not have let him go. I should have used your coming birth as an anchor, but I was too proud. I should have gone with him, but I was too weak. I should have learned to forget, but I am too loyal. I should have kept Finorian from overseeing your every breath,' she said most bitterly of all, 'but I was too heartsick at Orvath's absence.

'Now,' said Jalonia, standing. 'I have lost you both, because I have found you both again too late.'

She left the room, leaving the mushrooms, their bright colors desiccated to powder, on the table.

Irissa remained alone in the hall, haunted by the great distances that rent the Torlocs even as they at last occupied the same world. She wished the cat, Felabba, was crouched beside her, ready to tap her lethargic hand with barely sheathed claws and launch a lecture the likes of which would leave Finorian breathless.

Great silly Torloc, the cat would say, would spit. See the ruin you have made of your world within and without. You have found a father and mother you never even sought and have lost the one who found you. You are tangled tight in the schemes and heartaches of your kind and yet sit more alone than you have ever sat. You are the most powerful seeress to direct her silver eyes to any goal, yet you are powerless to change the past and the ill it wreaks in the future. You are quite worthless, girl, and headstrong besides, and will regret it bitterly.

'Yes, Felabba,' Irissa agreed aloud, leaning heavily on the table to push herself up. 'You are right, as always.'

The Overstone egg weighed more than it had when Irissa first plucked it from a frozen beak in the Inlands. That night it dragged heavier than a millstone as she made her solitary way to the upper stories, to a chamber different from the one she had used before. It didn't matter which bed she slept upon, only that it be one new to the double weight of her regret and dread.

'We are not alone.' The cat's voice cracked when it spoke. It had been uncharacteristically silent for too long a time.

'As usual you carp about the obvious,' Kendric answered. He, too, had felt the altered atmosphere the instant he had stepped into the dissolving wall. Darkness stretched in all directions, silent and supple as a giant cat. No one direction called him, yet from every side something sinister pressed softly nearer.

'Keep close to my heels,' he instructed the cat and stepped in the direction in which he was pointed. An endless ribbon of gloom wrapped tighter around him; he could feel it hobbling his ankles, constricting his throat.

He wheeled, and moved against the current of his own direction. Oily, thick darkness muffled his senses with the mere fact of its presence.

'I feel like a village string-dancer,' Kendric growled to the cat. 'Someone far away toys with our actions, tugs at our wills with long black velvet ribbons.'

'You make malice sound more elegant than it is,' the cat replied.

'You should know,' Kendric said frankly.

The cat sniffed rudely in the dark, a cheering sound under the circumstances. 'Remember my warning.'

'Which one? In Rule it was that we would all come to a

bad end. Here . . . you said my life was endangered.'

'I did not *say* it; I implied it. And it was not your life I feared for.'

'What else have I to lose?' he demanded. 'Save for a few trinkets gathered in my travels?' Kendric shook his ringed fist at the swallowing, strangled darkness. 'Here!' he shouted. 'You want something of me, come and take it!'

But whatever presence settled doomfully around them had no need to resort to force. Rather, it applied the opposite. It simply existed, and by that fact sucked the confidence, the will, the sense of inner direction from them.

'You have nothing to offer, I suppose?' Kendric asked the cat, his hopeful tone of voice contrasting oddly with the surly phrasing.

Felabba sighed in the vacant midnight. 'It is not I the Hunter seeks.'

'Then what good are you? We put up with your blathering for more than the pure pleasure of hearing it. I would use my magic — any and all of it — but there is nothing concrete to direct it against.' Kendric glanced worriedly over his shoulder. 'Even my hilt-light pales under the impress of all this inimicable dark. It's as if this were not a wall of Edanvant at all anymore but a — a long, black bridge—'

Kendric's speculations were leading him down a path he recognized as the needle-narrow road of truth, and one that inevitably leads to a dead end.

'At least I can *see* in the dark better than you can think in it.' The cat sounded tart. 'Look around you, Wrathman-that-was, and view a sight that should please you more than my humble aspect.'

Kendric recognized gloating when he heard it. Peering into the endless corridors of night, he saw no stars, no moon, no limit to it. Then he discerned the vague white-gray fluttering of something nearing them in the murk. A furred face — pointed everywhere from ears to muzzle to eyes to teeth — loomed death's-head clear for a terrifying instant.

'The wolf that led us in! It leads us yet.'

As if the creature had understood his words, the white form

moved away, dimming instantly. Kendric stepped eagerly after it.

'Great clumsy gallumpher! Do you never look where your feet are planted?' Felabba wailed.

'You told me to look to the distance.' Kendric smiled in the dark, treading close behind the faint white blur bobbing just in sight. 'Follow me, then,' he instructed Felabba, 'and mind your tail.'

They swam through the blackness, Kendric feeling he walked underwater in the hidden depths of some marshy bog. Any moment he expected to meet a wailwraith.

'Good day,' he imagined himself saying to this legendary creature, bowing to it despite its reed-choked hair and rootlike limbs. 'And would you favor us with a serenade in a minor scale or two—'

A screech at his feet interrupted the reverie. He had stopped without warning, once again treating one of Felabba's extremities to an unexpected pressing.

But he had stopped for a reason, and it wasn't merely because the wolflike form had clarified a pace or two beyond where he stood, or that he knew as a man knows the name of his worst enemy that the wall ended but a foot or two to his left.

He stopped because he had finally seen something clearly in the clogged darkness. No wailwraith, but something nearly as tall as he, almost as human and in some ways more familiar.

The image of Irissa faced him, attired in the ebony velvet gown she had worn briefly in Rule — or was she wrapped solely in the night's impenetrable fabric up to her shoulders, so she seemed to float in the darkness as pale dead faces float in marshwater?

She hovered there before him, a disembodied head and neck, her eyes' silver softened by the sooty dark but still glimmering preciously. An alien necklace spilled over her collarbones, and an expression mixed of deep surprise and recognition masked her utterly familiar face.

'Irissa,' he numbly hailed the apparition, stopping.

'Now!' Felabba screamed with uncatlike fervor.

260

Something sharp leaped up his thigh and sliced deep.

His cry of outrage burst with Kendric through the wall's metallic edge. Irissa's likeness slid sideways, impaled in the hard dark he left behind. Ordinary Edanvant night threw its obscuring shadows over a woodland scene that ended abruptly in an impenetrable metal wall.

Kendric pounded it for good measure, for emphasis, for the form of it, ignoring the throbbing in his thigh where Felabba's primitive warning had plowed crimson furrows. His fists throbbed upon the metal until it seemed to pant from his blows.

'I was not ready to leave it yet,' he told the cat. Now his hilt-light beamed like a greedy merchant's grin over his shoulder. Kendric sought entry to a reflection of his own quizzical face.

'I saw her,' he insisted, stroking the wall in search of a seam.

Felabba paused in licking her bloodied forefeet long enough to cast Kendric a disdainful look with the reflective greens of her eyes. 'You saw an illusion sent by one whom it suits to deceive you. Are you not more eager to see Irissa in the flesh than in a dark and dubious wall?'

Kendric turned reluctantly to the woods, to the direction in which he was going, tucking the image of Irissa deep within his memory. The white wolf sat on its snowy haunches at the edge of a tapestry of lacy-leaved birches, its thick ruff haloing a face etched in sharp strokes of black skin for lips, nose, and eyes.

'It brought us through,' Kendric speculated. 'Of course it is merely a mute thing, but I would like to know how it manages to trot through a wall that bars passage to all living things, unabetted by magic—'

A voice from the woods interrupted to tell him.

'A creature is hardly mute when the mere glance of its eyes speaks well enough to guide you.'

Kendric twisted to view the speaker. 'You again! Who in Edanvant are you?'

Moonlight limned the form of the fair young man as he stepped from tree-strewn shadows into the clearing beside the wall. The wolf whimpered welcome and flung its lean length

261

at the newcomer, stretching human-high to rest its forepaws on the man's shoulders. The man laughed and evaded a doglike lick, stroking its thick fur as one would pet a cat. Yet he gave no answer.

'I'll tell you who I am, then,' Kendric offered. 'Kendric I was called from my birth, and see no reason to alter habit. This wisp of weather-beaten fur who has so recently etched my trouser leg is known as Felabba, though if that be her real or only name, I would be surprised. Now, what do you call yourself?'

'My name is like a good many things in this wood . . . lost,' the stranger answered resignedly. 'Sometimes I think a thick hedge has sprouted in my head, turning it to wood. And she is—' He glanced fondly at the wolf. 'She is nameless also, but she came to me from the first night I spent in this forest, and although she comes and goes, always comes back. She must have been tame once.'

'How do you know it is a "she"?' Kendric asked dubiously.

'That I know,' the young man said, regarding Kendric with solemn silver-gray eyes. 'I know that as well as I know that I ought to know you — and don't.'

'And the cat. I suppose you ought to know the cat, too?'

'The cat. No, I know nothing of the cat.'

Kendric tried to stare the fellow into admitting duplicity or at least secretiveness. But the steady gray eyes of man and the great gold eyes of wolf met his most businesslike glower with serene calm. He gave up with an oath.

'This Edanvant is a paradise fit for a moonweasel or a soul-leech! I see Irissas who don't know me within the glassy black depths of endless walls, and meet vague young men who don't know themselves in midnight forest strolls.'

Kendric stepped at last away from the wall, away from the mystery within it that he was ill-equipped to solve. 'We journey to the fortress of the Torloc dames, the — er — cat and I. You . . . two . . . are welcome to accompany us.'

'A castle in the forest,' the man mused. A small smile quirked his features. Kendric saw he was not simply gifted with the bland handsomeness of youth, but wiser than he looked. 'I believe I have looked on such before. No, we stay here, the wolf and I. We are' — he touched the fur feathering the ears; the creature's powerful jaws nipped lightly on his fingertips — 'friends,' the man finished.

'And you have no names, either of you?' Kendric could not imagine walking through a world without at least a word to call one's own, if not a sword.

The man regarded him soberly. 'What does your name mean to you?' he asked.

'Kendric,' he answered into the face of this chilling anonymity, 'means more than two mere syllables. It says "Kendric the Marshman, son of Halvag the Smith. Kendric who was once Wrathman of Rule. Kendric of the Far Keep."'

He paused. With every description he had memorialized conditions of his life more deeply buried in the past. What he named himself with, he interred himself with.

'Kendric,' he finished more softly. 'A journeyer in Edanvant, who is happy to meet friends whether they bear names or not.'

'And whether they wear . . . feathers or fur, say?' came a voice from the area of his feet.

He looked down. 'Or claws,' he added.

Felabba curled her lean torso past his boot, then disguised the possible gesture of affection with a luxurious stretch.

'At last you see sense, Wrathman,' the cat said, invoking the past deliberately. 'And there is a Far Keep still in your future, though it is not what you think it is.'

Kendric sighed, looking past the forms of the man and wolfish pet to the deeper lengths of forest.

'What is, old cat, what is?' he asked, setting out with a farewell wave to the two who stood like ghosts against the flat black framing of the wall.

They walked, companionably quiet, for some time. Kendric had scouted the forest on his first venture into its wilderness, and steadily led them closer to their goal.

'What will you do when you come again to Finorian's keep?' the cat finally asked when they had stopped to rest awhile under the moon's mellow glazing.

263

Kendric studied the four sharp projections of the old cat's legs as she hunched into her ragged fur coat on a rock pedestal.

'First . . . eat.' He laughed at the intensifying sour expression that carved itself into the furred face beside him. 'Then ask questions.' He thought awhile. 'Then speak to Irissa of things she may not want to hear.'

'She left you behind.'

'You grow unwise, Felabba. It must be the dire influence of Edanvant. She fled herself; she did not leave me. There is a difference.'

'To mortals. But the result is the same. You come again as one who must sue, must mend. And you are not a—'

'I know. I am a render, not a mender.' His hand slapped the sword that reclined against the rocks with him. Kendric flexed the hand as if he saw it anew. 'I was a maker and a breaker; all I had with which to accomplish either good or ill were these five fingers and five more on the other hand. Now I can make and break with magic, if I am lucky or wise — with my mind, my greed, my hopes, my fears. It is a heavy thing to carry, the burden of magic, and never so heavy as when one refrains from using it.'

'Kendric the Philosopher,' the cat mocked. 'You will need more than philosophy in the time ahead,' she predicted in her usual dour tones. 'You will be given a prize that many would claim and you will despise. You will walk the bridge that has grown together. You will fight one you do not hate for that which you do not love, and then you will hate that which you fight and fight for more than one you love and know not. Dire doings there will be, and it will not be in Edanvant.'

'What of Irissa? I will find her with Finorian surely?'

'I speak of the future.' The cat's vertically slit eyes narrowed horizontally as well. 'You must still live the past, for the bridge I spoke of is the Present and you have not got that far yet.'

Felabba's eyes had shut. Kendric studied the aged cat as he never had while she was watching him. Did she speak with oracular wisdom, like Valna in Rule? Or mutter senilities? Did she know something more than anyone else, or merely enjoy appearing to? Had she struck him dumb with skepticism —

264

or with foreboding? She had never spoken so portentously to him; that chilled Kendric to his deepest bones. He was an afterthought, a follower in a quest for someone else's world. What role could he play but that of guardian, helpmate, and, sometimes, fool?

'It is Irissa's quest,' he said suddenly.

The cat's eyes flickered open.

'It was. But pain and joy, striving and rest, love and hate weave all together on a larger loom than you or Irissa see, though you are woven into it.'

'And you?' he demanded almost angrily.

'I play my part, as always, when required. I am but a knot in one dim corner of the tapestry and seldom show myself. It is for the central figures to reflect the glory.'

'Glory!' Kendric stood, fastening on the long burden of his sword. 'I would give all the glory to be gotten through all the gates Within and Without for a plate of Dame Agneda's greens right now.' He paused, then spoke more measuredly. 'I make light where I am heavy and lie to myself in the bright face of honesty. I would give it all to see Irissa.'

'The bridge grows to its center,' Felabba said, rising arthritically. 'And there is nothing left to do but walk it.'

CHAPTER SEVENTEEN

Orvath sat in the same chair at noon as he had the preceding midnight and morning. His features assumed the starched composition of a magistrate's and the glass goblet his stiff fingers still supported had been empty for many hours.

Daylight poured icily through coldstone windowpanes, filling the goblet with brightness and casting bubbles of reflection across the white stone floors. Larger spheres than these threw their faint shadows at Orvath's feet — the delicate spawn of a single casting crystal — and hung like an oversized necklace between Ludborg's extended sleeves.

'You seem grim-minded, my lord Orvath,' Ludborg observed from behind the dazzle of his display.

Orvath's eyes flickered, as if discerning too much light.

'Break your crystals and let them speak for you.'

The shoulders of Ludborg's voluminous gown shrugged. Jeweled spheres plummeted to hard stone, breaking haphazardly. Only the mother crystal remained clear and whole, elevated between the supporting sleeves.

'Look then, Orvath, and see the future,' Ludborg intoned impressively.

But Orvath remained motionless, watching the still tremulous shards batter motes of light between their shattered surfaces. Finally he leaned forward, catching his own dangling sleeve back with his frozen hand. His other hand hovered mothlike over the glancing glass fragments — then one was in his grasp and elevated for reading.

Ludborg's hood tilted, the only indication that the wandering Rengarthian took anything other than bored interest in the affair.

Glass shattered to slivers between Orvath's fingers and was cast away. He snatched up another shard and flung it down as hastily. Shard chimed upon shard as Orvath's face grew paler and his fingertips bubbled tiny jewels of blood.

'They are fragile — and cutting — the casting crystals,' Ludborg intervened. 'If you do not want to read the future—'

'The future!' Orvath's bloodied hand shook a fragment of glass under the emptiness of Ludborg's hood. 'Show me the future and I will face it; these cursed pieces show only the past, wear only faces I have not seen for twenty years.'

'Sometimes, I daresay, our past is our future,' Ludborg noted humbly. 'The crystals seldom prevaricate.'

Orvath threw the last fragment to the floor and hurled himself from the chair. He ranged to the window, dragging his disability behind him as if it held the stiff dignity of a ceremonial cloak.

'Torlocs have no past and future, Traveler,' Orvath said. 'We live too long. Life for us is one endless present.'

'Perhaps, then, you see images of the present. If you would describe—'

'No! It is . . . indescribable. Take away your crystal, caster. It, too, toys with those who would believe in it. I have seen more truth in the bottom of my empty drinking glass than I have discerned within the broken patterns of your illusions.'

'As you will,' Ludborg agreed, bowing himself out of the chamber and thus making himself as round as one of his spheres.

He nearly bowed himself into the arriving form of Medoc, who stepped aside to let the visitor pass and then carefully approached Orvath.

'You are unhappy with the visions of the crystal? They offer no guidance?'

'What guidance is to be found in the face of Jalonia — or Irissa, whichever one haunted the crystal shards?' Orvath demanded. His hand reached out to brush away a shaft of gold-dusted sunlight as if it were a cobweb. 'I haunt myself,' he concluded, 'for I have seen myself truer in a slick green mirror of borgia than in any scrying device.'

'And there was nothing in the crystals?' Medoc insisted. 'Ludborg always delivers enlightenment.'

'He delivers our own gullibility to us in an empty globe. Have you not seen the grin of the glass before it breaks?'

'What did you see in the shards that you want so badly to unsee?' Medoc's tone held no curiosity, rather a stern demand.

Orvath spun to face him.

'First my eyes turn traitor, now my ears. Do you question my perception, my truthfulness?'

'I question your judgment.'

Orvath swooped an arm to the floor, handing his father a curved glass fragment. 'Here, see for yourself.' He tucked his much-pricked fingertips between his arms and body, as if a chill claimed him.

'It would not hold its image so long, nor offer it to outside eyes.' Medoc handled the thing delicately, shifting its position until the daylight strained obliquely through it. 'There is something, though . . .'

Orvath's eyebrow raised skeptically. He looked like a carven pillar of a man, with his arms wrapped around him and his demeanor solidified into a kind of encasing indifference.

The crystal piece fell from Medoc's releasing fingers, chiming to destruction among its fellows.

'Orvath! I saw—'

His son straightened, if that were possible in so erect a figure. 'Saw what?' he said, careless bravado a thin patina over his fear.

'I saw you take the Overstone, saw Irissa wither with its absence, saw you leave her—'

'Enough.' Orvath cast himself in the chair again, perhaps seeking concealment in its shadowy depths. 'I did not see . . . that . . . at the time,' he added in a different voice. 'I saw nothing but the fact that the talisman for which I had given so much had been given to another.'

'Your daughter,' Medoc clarified, but Orvath went on as if, now seeing so clearly, he could not hear.

'I saw only the Overstone egg, the *possibility* of it. I never saw what taking it took from her; never saw that it claimed her now. I did not perceive that the past was past — a Torloc flaw perhaps, in a world where we grow rarer by the day.' His hands spread wide, helplessly. 'So another saw it, and stopped me. I might even have stopped myself, I think, had I seen myself.'

Medoc's boot-toe shifted a sprinkling of glass. 'Now you have. Does it make a difference?'

'Yes.' Orvath's dark eyes burned black from within the shadowed frame of his chair. 'It makes me regret that Finorian and the women have driven us men to this extremity, that to claim what is our own, we must be willing to destroy what is part of us. Forget sentiment, Medoc. It comes down to who will rule Edanvant — and how. Shall it be centuries more under the thumb of Finorian, the talismans you men bled to procure extracted from us one by one as claws from a cat?

'You harbor a soft spot for Irissa, don't deny it. She is young and seems innocent. Yet would you want your every action debated by her silver eyes if she were the sole seeress? Whatever . . . regret . . . I may feel for my action is moot; Irissa has fled to Finorian. We cannot be certain our safeguards have held. She has personal reason now to hate us, and when have you known a seeress wronged — or who thinks herself wronged — to temper her power? We must act now to regain the forest, to subdue those within the forest.'

'You have always advocated outright attack, but I admit it troubles me, Orvath. Finorian is old, even for our kind, and Irissa is indeed young. She seemed eager to meet us at first. Perhaps she is too uncertain to bear the grudges against us the Eldress does.'

Orvath shot his father a sharp look. 'Will she not? She is woman, like the rest of them, and does not forgive easily. And you forget my assault upon the Overstone; she will not.' He brooded, his closed face bolted fast against even his sire. 'Then there is the cursed cat. Felabba. It is more than it seems. Who knows how it may meddle now that it is here again? And Kendric—' Orvath's every thought named a potential foe.

'The Wrathman would not work his half-breed magic against

us,' argued Medoc. 'For one non-Torloc, he sits among us more easily than any mortal man.'

'Together they are formidable, he and she, and we know not what they may do,' Orvath insisted, 'nor how she has bespelled him, as women ever do. And what has changed? The women still refuse to recognize our right to rule in Edanvant; they refuse to obey to the bitter end. We are still barred from our forest paths, from hunting the beasts within it. We are still walled like eggbirds crated for market within double bands of Iridesium wall by that unrepentant Eldress. Do you think she will soften now that she finally has empowered allies to draw upon? I shudder to imagine what sorcery she bestirs even as we debate.'

Orvath's fingertips steepled before his face, neither hand looking weaker than the other in that light. Perhaps he pressed his hands together to halt the bleeding from his casting session; perhaps he prayed to a distant god for protection or intervention; perhaps he simply thought deeply.

'You brought the Single Tongue of Flame to Edanvant,' he told Medoc at length. 'We found afterward the risk we took in introducing so alien a talisman to our midst. Now we must risk more and use it fully.'

'It is a demonic thing!' Dread and vivid memory brightened Medoc's dark eyes. 'I do not know if it fell into my grasp or I into the talons of its power. It came so tamely to my possession, as if possessing me, a gift from the good-as-dead, wrapped in this medallion.' He tapped the gold circle upon his chest. 'The medallion I wear daily, but I use the dagger lightly. It burns too hot and wild—'

'It will burn our land back to us − and herd the beasts in a wave before our gate, force the women from their forest refuge into our hands and under our . . . protection. It will melt Finorian's iron will and Iridesium walls.'

'And Irissa and Jalonia?'

'They will be driven here, two among many, and receive the same consideration we tend the others.'

Medoc read his meaning and shook his head. 'The other women you might cow, as Finorian does, but Irissa will fight you for her freedom, as she would not — could not — for the Overstone egg. She will not concede that the past entitles you to take that.'

Orvath sat silent.

'She is the most powerful seeress in generations, perhaps greater even than Finorian,' Medoc reminded him. Orvath's hand waved dismissively, a gesture oddly offhand for a man of his temper.

'And the marshman, the Wrathman of Rule — Kendric. If you attack, he most certainly will add his peculiar magic to their forces. He has left our company to follow Irissa.'

'I remember some insolent person shaking me by my tunic collar . . .' Orvath smiled savagely. 'What kind of man would fight with a pack of women? I fear him no more than a dissident daughter. We Torlocs — I — have faced more formidable foes than they on our journeys — and survived.'

'So have they, than us.' Medoc's tones were grim. 'Orvath, will you not consider subduing the women by less violent measures? Even we do not know the full power of the Tongue of Flame.'

'Treating with the likes of Finorian becomes more *en*treaty than anything else. No doubt she sent . . . the girl . . . here to disarm us, to weaken me, as well as to steal the keys to our talismans. Well, it has not worked, not if we strike. We will attack them before they send some dread magic against us.'

Medoc looked down at the glittering crystal shards. 'You saw no rumor of war in these bits of shattered glass, only the faces you once loved.'

'Face,' Orvath corrected savagely. 'Irissa is naught to me but a stranger — as I was kind enough to tell her from the first — and worse, a spy, as I was not so foolish to tell her. I saw only the past in Ludborg's crystals; so there is only the past tense to what was loved, whatever name she bears, wherever she is and however she braids past, present, and future together in her own mind.'

Medoc recognized the wisdom underlying Orvath's willfulness. Only dire measures would shake the women from their high-handed path and give the men some security. Medoc had

271

always feared the contention would come to overt warfare, by one means or another. He had simply hoped it would not be necessary to loose so unknown a weapon as the Tongue of Flame.

He stepped away finally, away from argument, from dissent, from his son. He wished he could sidestep the future as easily.

'It is good to see some furred thing moving within this sleeping, scentless forest.'

Kendric sat on a stump in a clearing, watching Felabba sip daintily from a small spring. His tunic neck still showed a dampened dark spot from his less neat hand-to-mouth method of imbibing woodland water.

The cat looked up, her eyes as startled as a wild thing's.

'Compliments, Marshman? Soon you will be singing my praises and I shall have to flee in self-defense.'

'Oho, so that's what it takes to be rid of you — honey, not gall. I might have known a Torloc thing would exhibit the same contrary nature as the rest of the breed. With certain exceptions, of course; Irissa, for one. And perhaps on a good day, Medoc.'

'Your mind resides in two places, neither of them where you are at the moment,' the cat cautioned.

Kendric reclined against a tree trunk, his sword beside him. He rolled his head upward, to see the sky.

'My mind resides in many places, none of them entirely comfortable, but that is the way of the world.'

'Which world?'

'Any world, old one, as you know better than I . . .' Kendric sat up, alert but not reaching for his sword. He cast away a stem of grass he had been mauling. 'Look, through those branches, a bright winking.'

He scrabbled to his feet, his eyes squinted to read the dappled shade as he slung on his sword.

'The hide of the bearing-beast!' he concluded excitedly. 'See it flickering through the greenery in quick silver-and-gold turn! 'Tis the creature I would have tamed when we first came to Edanvant, which Irissa netted with her Iridesium circlet.'

Kendric edged into the leaves himself, his voice lowering to mimic their hushed susurration. 'Perhaps now I can capture it. Perhaps Irissa would see some good omen in it. She is in dire need of happy talismans now, I fear. I will bring her a gift from the forest.'

Felabba had frozen at the spring's rocky lip, her hair bristling into a slightly knotted halo.

'Wrathman, wait! This forest offers no gifts to you!'

But he had melted into the leaves as thoroughly as the form of his desired beast.

The cat looked left, then right, then into the tree-shadowed water below. The spring pooled round as a shield, a string of bubbles placidly breaking its surface.

Her eyes pinned one lordling-sized bubble in the water. It expanded as if to escape her stare until it burst its perimeter against the encompassing rocks. The motion shook the pool, which slowly calmed. Its waters dappled silver, then grew gold, and finally light, bright green.

Within the spring's watery green eye Kendric's moving figure stirred in miniature. Only his back was visible, but one thing was clear; he moved away from the clearing and Felabba. Beyond him, unseen by him, the elusive bearing-beast waited behind a wall of trembling leaves.

'Oh, the fool!' Felabba hissed, whether speaking of herself or Kendric was uncertain. The aged cat hunched stiffly into the cold comfort of her bones to watch.

Had there been birds among the forest branches, they could have hung over the water to observe a scene develop as precisely, in as intriguing yet inevitable miniature, as in one of Ludborg's crystal shards. But no birds claimed the woods, beyond the once-seen owl, and it was daylight now, when owls sleep deeply.

Nothing shared the view with Felabba, nothing overlooked the dance about to be begun by man and beast, unknowing partners in an improvised pattern as eternal as death.

Felabba's ancient eyes pierced the doubly green shade of the spring's mirrored surface. They focused not on Kendric, a form only too well known to her, were anyone to ask, but

273

upon the glittering bearing-beast. She stared harder, until the water seemed to tremble, until the image shook — and in that reflected shaking, altered.

To the old cat's eyes the bearing-beast stood tall and narrow, like a man, a golden man who bore a single golden dagger in a clenched fist; a man who raised that dagger to strike, so it poised at the level of his forehead like a single gilt horn; a man who waited in concealing shade and shadow, whose booted foot impatiently stamped the ground.

Felabba stood abruptly, hissing equal impatience. Her paw struck the image from the water. Then she turned and trotted briskly through the undergrowth, away from where Kendric had last been seen, away from a spring that would keep its secrets.

Kendric congratulated himself on his stealth. Not six lance throws before him the tranquil bearing-beast grazed on a hock-high patch of grasses.

Kendric edged nearer, a loop of vine wrested from a broad oak trunk curled in his hands. He rummaged his mind for magic to confine the mount — that's what he called it in his optimism — but decided to rely on older skills first. Once having sighted the creature, there was little time to think, and magic required more thinking than Kendric had ever dreamed it would.

He circled his prey, stepping closer with every leafy crackle beneath his boots. The bearing-beast gathered its greens, apparently too rapt to hear or scent him. In a moment he had flung the vine wide and watched it wrap the muscle-arched neck as perfectly as if aided by an invisible hand. He came nearer, tightening his tough nature-woven rope, exerting the force of his frame against the certain bucking of the beast.

The creature stood waiting for him, polished sides heaving, nostrils funneled wide as its breath gushed through in invisible bursts. The ears pricked, then flattened. Four gilt hooves struck sparks of reflected sunlight from the ground they pawed.

Kendric, certain of triumph, inched his hands up the vine, came closer, reached to pat the nervously retreating body.

Kendric stood eye to eye with the frozen beast, captor and captive both momentarily surprised into inaction.

The beast recovered first, as is the way of beasts. It wheeled to run, then paused to plant four gold hooves atop the broken grasses. With a snort and a motion too quick to sense, much less see, it tossed its head, using its single horn like a saw to sever the entangling vine.

Kendric, braced with all his might against the beast's anticipated struggle, fell to the ground with the separated vine. Golden hooves reared above him, churning toward his torso. Beneath him, the long, unsheathed welt of his sword bruised his spine from neck to tailbone.

Kendric lifted an arm in feeble defense. As if that gesture were a signal, something white and furred bounded across his vision.

'Felabba!' He shouted despairing, too-late warning, rolling away from the flashing hooves into the green grasses, then spinning again to see only blue sky.

Around him the earth pounded as if the sky-born Shield-Shakers of Rule stalked again. The grasses around him quivered. His bones vibrated.

He struggled upright, fumbling for the sword hilt at his shoulder, his mind dwelling on the sick certainty that the gift he should bring Irissa from this encounter would be the limp, lifeless form of Felabba — should he live to bring to Irissa any offering at all.

Standing, knees flexed, the sword in his fists at last, focusing his mind and body on the task of exerting force, Kendric saw the bearing-beast savagely thrusting its curved horn at an energetic white form.

'Felabba,' he breathed in disbelief. He thought the wiry old feline too wise to play inevitable meat for any creature, and certainly not in the defense of a humble marshman from Rule . . .

But the thing that fought the bearing-beast wasn't Felabba, unless she had grown recently.

A golden beak grasped the deadly spiraling horn in its tenacious maw. An agile wolfish torso twisted away from the

275

slicing hooves. The Rynx reared to its hind feet and challenged the beast head-to-head.

Even a Wrathman who'd knocked his hard skull on earth not much harder knew the contest futile. The Rynx was ill-armed to meet such a foe; however relentlessly it clung to the twisting horn, it was doomed to death or failure.

Failure came first. The bearing-beast spun in a dust-whipping circle. With a cry between a whine and a caw, the Rynx's muscular form was hurled against the surrounding tree trunks. The sound of its impact made Kendric wince even as he kept his eyes fixed on the horned one exhaling puffs of dust and breath between effort-widened nostrils.

No blood painted the horn's graceful spiraled length. Kendric only had time to notice that hopeful sign before the creature lowered its mane-whipped head and charged. Foreshortened, the equine face wore a malevolent, chillingly human look.

Kendric raised his blade, hating to mar the shining horn advancing in a scimitarlike sweep. Steel rang on rock-hard bone. The blow sent a stinging shudder up Kendric's arms. His hands tingled as if burned.

The beast backed off, its horn unnotched, and sprung its powerful form into another forward rush. Again Kendric turned it with the conjoined wrench of his arms and sword. Such a blow should have shaved the horn from tip to root; instead it disengaged from the singing steel, whole and deadly still.

His feet edging always to the side of the creature instead of its death-dealing forefront, Kendric contemplated a cruel blow across the rear hamstrings. His unimaginative mind already painted the scene crimson as the crushed grasses sipped up flowing blood like straws and the beast's muscular hindquarters collapsed to the turf.

Such an ignoble way to stop a noble beast, Kendric's very nature protested. And then one more craven blow would be required — a hack to the heart or to the neck, to end the disabled life as decently as possible.

He saw himself bringing Irissa a great, grisly blood-dripping

276

head, the horn untouched, to hang upon the Torloc keep walls like the head of a lorryk stag.

Kendric winced from the inevitable end to an ill-begun venture. His gorge rose to picture the ugliness to which his quest for beauty bound had brought him.

He lifted the sword again in aching arms, the muscles trembling but quite capable of the distasteful task at hand, more butcher-work than swordplay. The creature cooperated too easily, snorting as it spun away from him, turning its delicately corded hocks to his easy aim.

Kendric drew back for the blow, putting all his strength into it, knowing that only if the swing was unstoppable could he be sure of not tempering it at the last moment.

Kendric's arms lifted the heavy weapon over his right shoulder. His body twisted, spiraled like a horn. His torso lengthened with the effort, exposing a tunic of simple cloth. He had not worn mail since Rule.

The beast paused, a look of almost-human cunning dawning in its eyes. It wheeled in a moment, lowered its gorgeous head, and drove straight into the striking marshman, impaling its thick, smooth scimitar of horn in Kendric's exact middle.

Only the beast's quick retreat released Kendric — to the ground, to the ebb of his own blood, to the surprise that sang like birds all around him before the dark closed in — slowly — from every side.

The woods were still. No birds sang. Not even distant water rushed. The wind soundlessly combed the tangled green hair of the long grasses.

Hoofbeats came. Wild, drumming. The earth echoed the dull thudding so like a quickened heartbeat.

A white cat, its body low among the thick ferns, stole snake-smooth among the young rootlings.

The bearing-beast flashed through the still branches, its brocaded coat glimmering. Reaching the ferns, it reared, stabbing its red-tipped horn into the golden birch leaves.

The cat, low and quick, scrambled squirrellike up the birch

trunk and clung to a branch, her rough white fur blending with the pale bark.

She hissed for attention, then spoke. 'Begone, Hunter.'

The beast stopped prancing, suddenly still in every sinew and limb.

'You know me?' Its voice gleamed as golden as its aspect, yet faint as the barely rustling leaves.

'I know your purpose.'

'Do I . . . know you?'

'You know me,' the cat replied sardonically, 'from more worlds than this, but not by name.'

There was silence in the empty woods, where two speaking beasts confronted each other.

'Go,' the cat iterated. 'Little remains in you of the guardian bearing-beast born to these woods. Go to your new master, who is an old foe to me and mine. You are no longer a thing of Edanvant. Your magic ranges far from your new home, and your odious deed here is done.'

The animal's head lowered; for a moment its dark eyes gleamed triumphantly blue. Its scarlet-drenched horn jabbed the air playfully.

'You can make me leave?' it asked.

'Yes,' the cat said wearily. 'But it would be better if I did not have to. Seek a gate to where your meddling master waits. I will speed you off this world in which you have been so tidily corrupted. Only the upheaval of the Torloc disunity would have permitted the pure spirit of Edanvant itself to be turned to another's murderous purpose.'

The creature tossed a mane glossier than silken thread-of-gold. For a moment it posed — hooves raised, neck arched, the image of its tapestry-woven duplicate before its gilt had tarnished, then whirled and galloped away. Each hoofbeat lifted farther from the ground, until they soundlessly pounded air. The beast rose among the treetops, wraithlike, its dappled form dissolving into the shadow-freckled leaves.

'I brought you some fresh-baked spinach muffins.'

Dame Agneda hesitated at the threshold to Irissa's chamber.

278

She was a dumpling of a woman, unusual among the long-limbed Torlocs. Sometimes she reminded Irissa of Ludborg.

Irissa pushed herself off the windowsill where she watched nothing but the mirror of her own thoughts and came to inspect the basket. Steam rose in tempting tendrils.

'I thought we had no flour.'

'Finorian — er — summoned a batch when we first arrived, before it became apparent that her powers were better applied to defense than appetite. I always say the best defense is a good appetite — and yours has been scanty of late.'

Irissa smiled and selected one of the green-tinged muffins, biting it to prove her appreciation. It tasted succulent, hot and moist, though she couldn't help reflecting that Kendric would have eyed a green muffin askance, no matter how tasty. She dearly missed his natural skepticism. Without it, daily life seemed unseasoned, and she found herself viewing the world with a careless, uncritical eye.

'Wonderful,' she told Dame Agneda, sighing deeply.

The woman laid her basket on a large trunk and boosted herself up beside it.

'First Jalonia becomes good for nothing but deep thinking, and then you return to live among us as a hermit. What happened in Citydell?'

'You are blunt,' Irissa evaded, laughing.

The woman folded chubby hands on her equally plump lap. 'I have no power,' she answered simply. 'Bluntness is all that is left to me. Power makes one subtle; power separates,' she mused. 'Finorian is too proud to ask you; Jalonia too ashamed. I have no such reservations. I am but a gardener and cook. I make things into better things. Perhaps I have some small similar facility with people.'

'You make magic with people,' Irissa conceded, relaxing suddenly. She sat beside Dame Agneda and munched the muffin, the first food she had enjoyed in many days, perhaps because she consumed it in the presence of someone she need not fear or worry about.

'Ah, what is to become of us?' Dame Agneda's hands rolled into the apron that shielded her full skirts. 'Finorian keeps half of us chained to the Damen Circle; the other half spend their days consumed by domestic chores that were no great matter in Rindell. The only rumors we women hear of the men are that they despise us, deny our right to Edanvant, and must be fought.'

'Perhaps we are not despicable, but they,' Irissa said, something darkening in her eyes.

Dame Agneda shrugged. 'Who is to say who is the more despicable, or the less, so long as we never meet to debate the issue? Some of us talk' — she glanced at Irissa — 'when Finorian gives us berth to do so. We tire of our lot. We weary of opposing abstractions. We wonder if the way we are is the way we must be.'

'Then change your ways.'

'Easier said. Did you — when you were living among us?'

'No . . .' Irissa conceded. 'Not until events forced me to. But I was feeling restive even in Rindell—'

'So were we all!'

Irissa stared at the older woman, one of her few Torloc sisters who looked comfortably past the bloom of youth. 'But you were all so — so—'

'Docile?' Dame Agneda's wise brown eyes had bittered. 'We did as we were told, without question. That may appear docile, but it bears rank, hidden fruit. We envy you, Irissa, who can return to us as casually as a wayward bearing-beast, who can take a Wrathman of Rule as a for-granted companion, wear a sword and bare your seeress's eyes. Who can say no, even to Finorian.'

'We all can say no.'

'What if there is nothing to say yes to?' Dame Agneda's plain hands tucked the linens closed on the empty basket. 'Edanvant is not what we expected. To find ourselves still women without men is not what we dared gates for. To find our men unwilling to reunite with us is not what we severed ourselves from our kind for. We Torlocs, who used to direct our own fates, seem cast deeper into disarray. Perhaps we should go back . . .'

'It has changed, Rule, as we change Edanvant by our

presence,' Irissa warned. 'I think we have journeyed enough; the farther we go the more damage we wreak — to others and ourselves. We must make our stand somewhere.'

Dame Agneda squinted skeptically. 'If you are so certain of this, why are you so troubled?'

Irissa's lips quirked as she licked up the last crumbs. 'These days, certainty troubles me as much as uncertainty. It must be the human side of me.'

'No.' Dame Agneda's well-padded posterior eased down the trunk's curve as she stood. 'That is a pure Torloc trait. The mortals acquired it from us.'

Certainty. Uncertainty. Irissa balanced the two states in her palms after the woman left. One weighed heavier than the other, and it was not the one she had been discussing — certainty.

She returned to the window, her eyes searching the sky, the multicolored struts of the rainbow arch, the ground far below. Searching for a sign. She recalled the wounded, bloodless woman who had become a wolf. The shock of Orvath's attack had beaten that wonder from her mind. But now she thought of it. Perhaps the white wolf would come bounding up the treacherous rooftop road below, bringing news.

What news did she crave? Of Kendric, of course. He must have wondered, be wondering even at this very moment, why she had bolted. She wondered herself now, having found no peace within the safety of Finorian's rule.

And a deeper uncertainty stirred her, tugged at her mind's placid calm from fathoms far below. Suppose Kendric was not safe within Citydell, welcomed by his new Torloc comrades as she assured herself? Suppose he was no longer safe? No longer in Citydell? Why she thought that, she couldn't say. She thought it. And thought it again, until thoughts became worry, and worry . . . uncertainty. And uncertainty. . . fear.

Irissa put her hands to her temples, to the body-warmed circlet of Iridesium. It thrummed at her touch, like the throat of a cat. Felabba, she thought despairingly, though the cat seldom purred and never encouraged touching. Felabba.

The wound was mortal. The steam of his own hot, spilling

blood brought the scent of death to his nostrils even as he lay on his back; the sword he had finally fallen upon made a narrow bier beneath him, bound once again between him and earth.

Kendric's eyes rolled behind his shut lids. He saw the trap of it now, saw how he had lured himself into it, heard even the cat's distant warning cry as if it floated to the forefront of his mind now that so much blood welled at the back of it. He felt he drowned in his own blood.

In those red visions, he saw the Rynx torn in twain — a limp lifeless owl and wolf shattered at the foot of the forbidding tree trunks. From their fallen forms a pale mist wove into two separate shapes. One wore kind eyes; the other shook its head. Its human head. Madness! He dreamed death and conjured ghosts.

Opening his eyes, surprised, he found leaves dappling like water far above him. He almost expected to see his own face forming in their shifting pattern.

But nothing came except the certainty of death, and the uncertainty of his reaction to it.

His head turned to the tree where the Rynx had lain. The grass, crushed, was vacant. No creature lingered in the clearing at all, even the bearing-beast had deserted him, certain of its prey's fading mortality.

Kendric's hand, slowly, by itself it seemed, moved to his middle, to the sticky tender lake of fire his middle had become. There. There death had encamped to eat its luxurious way through his vitals — the slow, deliberate death of spilling blood.

There. There his magic must work and work hard to save him. Magic. It had seemed an alien thing, an addition, a burden as apart from himself as his clothing, really. Something he wore, like a sword, and seldom used, unlike a sword. A foreign accoutrement.

Now it was the only part of himself that could keep life in his body. He would have to heal himself, trying not to laugh at the idea. Laughing would be too literally painful, would quicken the spurt of draining lifeblood. Kendric raised his head to view the wound; movement turned his muscles to water. He must sew this chasm from within, blind stitch by blind stitch.

Kendric explored the crimson dark behind his eyes, diving into the blackness below it. A golden glow lurked yet, perhaps some fugitive reflection from the gilded beast that had gored him, he mused bitterly. The distraction — or the bitterness — pulled him back to a simple state of fatality. Blood pounded slackly in his neck, his wrists, spending itself in rhythmic surges, in waves of easy leaving. He muffled the nettled skepticism that was his inward armor. What did he need with such armor now? It only made an Iridesium wall to keep the Healer out.

Hunter, then Healer. 'There is a Hunter in the woods,' said she, who — bleeding — had whitened before his eyes to paler stuff than human. *There is a Healer in the woods*, his thought answered hopefully.

Not Irissa, he knew, although Irissa could have stemmed even such a mortal flow as this. Irissa hemorrhaged herself, in secret, unseen ways. Irissa was not in the woods. He was alone. Except for . . .

The Healer came, small as a remote spark of thought, distant as yesterday. It moved within him, skimmed down his veins, and was sucked at last into the maelstrom of his ebbing mortality.

The Healer *was* he, a lost and striving figure standing under a sky raining blood amid a world awash in wounds. Band by band, a scarlet rainbow arched the scarlet sky. Pink to rose to crimson to clotted black it ran, and in the darkest stripe he saw his name written with a fingertip.

This was too large a world with too much awry for one small Healer. Everything towered over him, he who was accustomed to towering. He would have to . . . stretch, stretch, stretch—

His arms reached from horizon to horizon, only in the wracked perspective of his inner eye, but it was a beginning. His palms pushed back the rain, drop by bloody drop. Even the rainbow began to collapse between his fingers, squeezing through them in gruesome clots, dewing the ringstones with companion rubystones, squeezing, squeezing. He felt he held his heart in his hand and choked the life rhythm from it.

Yet the inner sky paled to a sunfall shade of pearly pink, then reddened again as it reflected the rise of ruddy water all around him. To the knees it came, thick as marshwater, sluggish and murky. It boiled around his boot-tops, extending as far as his eye could see, red as a murderer's midnight.

This, too, was himself, and he bent to it, pausing, some shred of still-distant self urging withdrawal, rebellion — he bent to it sipping, taking the bloody water drop by drop by swallow by swallow by pool by pond by swamp by marsh by lake by sea back into himself.

The distant self objected, and rolled offended eyes away. The Healer knew no nicety but survival. It swallowed self in greedy gulps. In time the gory water ebbed, drying along the land, which showed rutted channels of its passing, driven deep into the packed soil.

But the earth no longer blushed and the sky grew becomingly blue again. The Healer straightened as if from under an invisible burden, wearing a crimson velvet robe with silver stars studding the hem and a circlet of stars girding his temples. He straightened until his crown touched the stars, the first pale stars tearing through the blue-silk sky. His hands reached for the horizon edges to either side and pulled them neatly shut upon himself, as a blanket upon a sleeper.

It was all dark again. The Healer slept, wrapped in his dark bloody self; and unleashed magic, working out its appointed task, cut the clotted knots.

CHAPTER EIGHTEEN

Finorian had convened a Damen Circle consisting of two —
herself and Irissa.

The underground chamber, emptied of its ritual band of
occupants, seemed doleful and a trifle ridiculous. Irissa noticed
for the first time the deeply scribed star-shaped channel at the
Circle's center and the pentagramic eye of age-darkened
malachite that made its iris. Obsidian formed its pupil.

'You have returned to us in body but not in spirit,' Finorian
noted. She seemed, like the chamber, older and more worn.

Irissa refused to explain herself, 'I have returned,' she
pointed out, 'which adds to the Circle's pool of power.'

'We shall need it.' Finorian sat wearily on a carved rock
bench. 'I have seen some potent talisman stirring in the calm
of my touchstone, scalding and yet unshaped. I fear Orvath
and the men ready a weapon whose weight they are too slight
to wield.'

'So much the worse for them,' Irissa commented.

'You misunderstand. Such a thing, once unleashed, hurls
itself wherever it finds those to break under it. It becomes an
undirected magic unto itself, lethal from every direction.'

'We Torlocs have splintered in every direction; why should
we not be attacked as universally?'

Finorian's gnarled hands knotted over her knees. Her pale
eyes, though not quite cast Irissa's way, grew piercing with
an inner light.

'This new indifference does not become you,' she snapped.

'What is left to me?' Irissa demanded. 'To have searched
for you all so faithfully, to have sought Edanvant so hopefully,
and then to find you squabbling here like — like Felabba's

great silly children — only far worse, with walls between you erected from old resentments and new perfidy!'

Irissa sat, too, on another rocky outcropping, setting her sword aside. 'I am here because what I am is not welcome there. But I find you women no fairer or kinder than Orvath and the men, simply more familiar.'

'There is no comparison between us!' Finorian bridled like an offended falcon and edged her body away down the stone. 'Orvath has become mad with imagined wrongs. I merely try to right what has gone awry.'

'Why did you send Orvath for so perilous a talisman — you, who had despised talismans? Did you know his return was unlikely? Did you intend his failure, as he suspects?'

Finorian unfurled her hands, maps of veined and cratered flesh, and dropped her gaze as if to read them.

'I intended nothing but the obvious. It is true I pleaded — nay, ordered — the men to remain, to forgo their quests for talismans. The Torloc foothold on Rule was eroding; alien trinkets were not enough to buttress us — except for the Overstone egg. Delevant knew it for a thing of elder power, made Without and meant to remain there. He tried to bring it through a gate and thus brought his own downfall. But not before he had succeeded to this measure: the Overstone egg lay hidden in the Inland's deepest Cincture, waiting for one wise enough and strong enough to claim it.'

'You chose Orvath. Even though Jalonia—'

'Jalonia! What was one Torloc when the fate of all was at stake? I chose Orvath, yes.' Finorian's wrinkled face smoothed into rueful merriment. 'Of course the only Torloc man left in Rindell, who happened to be the most well equipped to grapple with an alien world, would be Orvath, whose heart was in thrall to domestic drama rather than an intergate epic. But I persuaded him, and he went.' Finorian's memories chilled. 'And survived. He gives me no credit for that. He survived what many have not, what only a few Torloc seeresses have faced and lived to tell of — the icy wrath of Delevant.'

'Have you seen Orvath since?'

286

'Only in the Eye.' Finorian indicated the malachite pentagram, where black swirls of veining sidled serpentlike through the rock's grain. 'At first, after we women arrived here in our forest citadel, we had some — distant — communication, he and I. Until it became apparent that there was no communicating with a madman.'

'Or an angry woman.' Irissa frowned. 'What power of the Overstone egg makes it desirable across so many centuries of greed?'

'Not greed — need. But we argue when there is little time. The Overstone is a thing from Without. It passes gates.'

'So do I.'

Finorian's look sharpened on a distance her evasive seeress's eyes would not view. 'Not merely ordinary magical gates, Irissa, but extraordinary ones — ones leading to worlds Outside our own.'

'To . . . Rengarth?'

'Ah, Rengarth, that lovely, absentminded place that keeps losing itself. Yes, Rengarth. But much more than Rengarth. To the very places of Those Ouside.'

'Were you not afraid that Orvath would keep his hard-won talisman for himself if he returned to Rindell?'

'It works only for the magic-born.' Finorian answered shortly.

'But Torloc men have latent powers, else they would not be able to wield even talismans.'

'Trivial.' She frowned. 'True power cannot be won with magical cups and swords and jewels. It is won within, and men have ever been inferior at quests to their own inner landscapes.'

'Yet you would have had me wed a Torloc — Thrangar, who was lost in Rule.'

Finorian shrugged. 'You had a gift to bestow with your maidenhood. Better it be upon one of our own.'

'I bestowed it in ignorance upon another, but of my will.'

'Great ignorance it took to drag such a one into our doings,' Finorian said heavily. 'A fearful waste of magic.'

'Kendric — inherited — my powers, nevertheless.'

Finorian reared back until the rock stopped her head.

'And so he has grown truculent since first I knew him, when I saw in him a guide for your journey out of Rule and no more. That is what your bestowal of magic has achieved. Such is the weakness of seeresses, Irissa; best study the example of Finorian and learn. Was it he, then, who spied my true self at the door to this castle? There was an unknown feel to that seeking, but I thought you had changed in your travels.'

'I have,' Irissa said serenely. 'And so has Kendric. He took the powers I gave so ignorantly with even more reluctance, yet they grow in him. How is that possible if he is of such unmagicked stock?'

'Perhaps he is more than he seems, but I doubt it. He is lucky, Irissa, that is all, and that is not enough to survive in such worlds as we Torlocs make.'

'Survive? Why would you say that?' Irissa was on her feet. 'Is there something wrong with Kendric? Have you seen a sign in the roving Eye of your Damen Circle?'

'Calm youself. No. I see nothing but the doom Orvath evokes for us all. I see the men move toward some violent magic, though what it is . . . You must see with me. Irissa, join me in Far Focus.'

Irissa mulled the idea, her silence prodding Finorian to more and grander words.

'We will make such a Circle that casts itself so far and deep that even Delevant himself could not see the end of it. It will disperse any magical enmity, display once and for all the power tended to Torloc seeresses, convince the men to return to their natural role . . .'

Irissa had risen and Finorian paused, as if sensing the weight of Irissa's shadow upon her face. She continued to look up, blind and beseeching. It was not enough.

'What powers I have were born in me, as you have said, Finorian, and have been honed by trials you have not seen. I will use my magic, when I do, only when I believe it will do more good than ill, for all magic carries sorrow, even when it succeeds.'

'You have not learned this philosophy at *my* knee! You

forget all I taught you.' Finorian rose as well, standing as straight and frozen as an ice dagger.

'No. But I have not been at your knee for some time, and that is what *you* forget. Yet I am one of you and cannot overlook my obligations. I will consider it and tell you this evening.'

Irissa turned then and left, knowing with her purely physical senses that her back lay open to the magical onslaught of Finorian's balked will.

Some phenomenon tugged for attention at the very edges of her awareness — indecisive and ultimately impotent. Irissa followed the rock-hewn path upward, the beam of her invoked pommelstone casting watery reflection on the rugged walls.

In the deserted great hall, she found the cat, Felabba, ravaging the remains of their most recent meal.

'Cabbages!' The cat sounded as if she cursed. She leaped to the floor to meet Irissa. 'The Hunter has been in the woods and left his prey for dead.'

Irissa stood so still she seemed a statue of herself. 'Kendric?' she asked finally, through shocked lips as stiff as Orvath's.

'Hurry along. I don't want that old woman to see me. There will be such questions . . .! Well, come then! I am not young and must move while the notion is upon me, or will stop completely.'

Irissa broke into a run to follow the cat's loping figure, the unease that had dogged her empty idleness at the women's keep taking quick and all-too-concrete shape — Kendric wounded to death in the woods he had come to because she had sought Edanvant.

Irissa came toward him, in the dark, in the dream. Her eyes were green, not silver, but otherwise she looked the same, if Irissa had ever looked the same to him.

He wandered some endless tunnel or path or hall. Confused, he had thought himself healed, yet his inner self seemed cast adrift.

Irissa's hand opened like a flower and moved to his side. She pulled on his arm, tugging him aside into a dark solid wall of forest or earth or stone. Her hair hung jet black, as black as the shadowy Iridesium circlet at her brow. Her face was pale and held a vacant concern.

He tried to indicate his wholeness now. His hand went to his middle and pressed upon a chasm. Surprised, he looked down with dream-deadened eyes. His palm bloomed open, red as any rose.

But he was healed! Perhaps he slept, weakened; perhaps he dreamed. But he was healed. He had felt the forces move within him, his own forces, aided by other, small, cumulative things. There was the conjoined potency of Inlands Stones, the sword's tenacious stake upon him, the aftertaste of Irissa's shared magic, and a last, slim, recalcitrant ingredient that blended well with any mixture of magic — his own stubborn will.

Yet now Irissa — silent, beseeching — pulled upon him, urged him into the darkness that stalked alongside. Weariness warred with his natural suspicion of shadowy places. Night brought peace and slumber, healing and renewal. It also harbored things that did not care for daylight.

Torn in both body and mind, Kendric hesitated. Irissa's face was vanishing into the wall, and he reached after it with his bloody palm, forgetful of the dreadful sight he must make. She seemed unaware of that and melted backward into distance, her features pleading all the while.

He moved; though in a dream, movement is more a shifting than a walking or a willing. He moved after her. Another white ovoid of face drew near in the dark wall, then broke through it — long muzzle first, dark eyes and cocked white ears last.

A great wolf's head nuzzled him from the dark, as if drinking his reflection in a stagnant pool. Kendric wrenched himself back — his mind, his dream form, his wounded being — startled by the lupine threat hovering just beyond his reach. The world spun. He lay on his back, and the wolfish face breathed hot upon him, pink tongue lolling down like a ladder to a fang-lined cave.

Kendric recoiled further, but in an instant the muzzle had misted into a great curved beak. Eyes of owlish yellow changed to wolfish gray and studied him implacably. Confused, Kendric shut his dreaming eyes, expecting to have them plucked from his head by a digging beak.

When nothing happened in the dark behind his eyes he opened them. Golden eyes stared sadly into his — great golden eyes wet with weeping . . . No, gray! The eyes were kind and gray and quite human.

A parade of eyes hung over him, changing faces with the moments. At first man, then woman. Once human, then animal and back again — lupine, then avarian. Wolf, then owl. Gold, then gray. Kendric reached for the white mist suffusing his darkness in such myriad forms. It seemed to fracture within his clutching hands, like one of Ludborg's crystals, its many images spinning into teasing fragments from past and present and unseen future.

Then the vision was gone and a gauzy haze of leaves arched over him. Air brushed his temples. His hand, curling and uncurling at his side, felt stiff and sticky. Pain wakened in his center, stretched, and began prowling the limits of his limbs, looking for some cozy place to settle.

Kendric felt half dead, which is to say, he felt half alive. That was, he considered with uncustomary optimism, a most promising condition and worth investigation. His toes stirred within the hard confines of his boots, his shoulders shifted on a crackling bed of broken grasses and fallen leaves. Pain smote him in the middle with a white-hot sword and he fell back into passivity with a grunt.

'I hear his dulcet tones,' came a distant voice so familiar it made him wince.

Soon another white animal face, whiskered and fanged, but in reassuring miniature, hung over him. His arm reached up to confirm the reality of the vision, but the feline visage was shoved ungently aside by a second newcomer.

Irissa's features replaced it, mirroring and expanding upon the concerned expression that had roamed his dream, only now her eyes shone unallayed silver.

'Copper,' he murmured. 'Copper turns green with age. Must have been copper I saw, gone green.'

Her hair, hanging tentlike over his face, shading it, tickled his neck; but he was too weak to isolate the irritation and complain of it.

'You're fortunate,' he told her with great seriousness, 'that silver does not tarnish with use, you must have to polish your eyes constantly.'

She seemed to be taking his whispered advice quite seriously, for the sheen that intensified over her eyes gathered into droplets and came crashing down upon his unshielded face, brittle as hail but somewhat warmer.

Kendric shut his eyes. It was a great feat, a great trial, to heal oneself. But it was as nothing to what fuss came after.

'You are wounded,' Irissa said severely, as if the statement were an accusation.

'No,' he denied, trying to sit up, aware that he had slept for some time and now had awakened.

Her hand impeded him. First in dreams she urged him on; now, in person, she pushed him back. Will Torlocs never be consistent? he wondered.

Yet Kendric rested and savored the silence. He lay half-propped against a broad weepwater tree, whose sinuous branches trailed the water of a still stream, as did Irissa's hand, idly trolling the dark water.

Her motion disproved idleness as she lifted her hand and the soaked bit of silk it held to his head.

'I'm not fevered, I tell you,' he insisted. 'I saw you, walking beside me with green eyes and pulling me into the wall. And then there was a white wolf, leading me away — to safety, it seemed. But it was really an owl, or actually a gentlewoman. Who was a gentle man. But you offered me no harm. Or was it you I saw?'

Irissa glanced sideways.

'He wanders.' Felabba's voice came from somewhere near but unseen. 'Not unexpected for one who teetered on the threshold of that overeager host, Death, not hours ago.'

'I wander,' Kendric confirmed happily. 'I wander through worlds, through gates, through walls even, into woods, into—'

His features wrinkled in sudden memory. 'Into . . . trouble.'

'This trouble wore a golden horn, Felabba tells me,' Irissa interjected, 'and a shape not its own for walking a world not its own. It came to kill you and nearly did.'

'Who would kill me?' he said dismissively, 'besides rogue Wrathmen and Torlocs?'

'No Torloc, Felabba says, but the bearing-beast you lusted after. Are we all cursed to be destroyed by that we quest for?' Irissa asked unhappily. 'Torlocs in general, Orvath in particular. I . . . now you as well? What fell thing seeks you in these peaceful woods? A misguided sending of my father's willfulness?'

He managed to lift a hand and pat the top of hers. 'It was just a wild beast, Irissa, wont to turn on that which would tame it. Haven't you experienced that?'

She remembered the green fox that had returned her succor with the gash of its teeth. Irissa sat back, sighing. 'Yes, but not with such a mortal fury.'

'And I wasn't seeking the creature so much, or it me, as—' Kendric frowned in sudden recollection. 'The Rynx—'

'Lie back and rest,' Irissa ordered pleadingly. 'What of the Rynx?'

'The Rynx was dueling the bearing-beast; that's why I took my sword to the horned one. The last I saw, the Rynx fell hard against a nearby tree—' He strained to raise his head, finding the movement whipped pain to every extremity.

'Lie back, I beg you! There is no Rynx here. Felabba and I saw none. It must have recovered before you did and left. 'Tis only a beast; you cannot expect it to be faithful to the fallen.'

'Exactly,' Kendric grunted as he allowed himself to be pushed supine again, eyeing Felabba.

'Now, hush and rest,' Irissa urged soothingly. 'You have plumbed deeper within yourself than even I to cure so deadly a wound, and you wear the marks of it still.'

A rain of warmish stream water trickled over Kendric's face, itching unbearably, and his hands weighed too heavy to brush it away.

'Enough nursing. I am healed.'

Irissa sat back on her heels, the wet piece torn off her tunic hem spreading damp darkness over her trouser knee.

'Healed, you can call it.' She leaned over him again to do something to his tunic, possibly to unleash a colony of smart-ants over his stomach. 'Such ragged work I have never seen, save in some of my earliest tapestry experiments as a child. I think your healing very nearly was the end of you.'

'I breathe, do I not? I see. See too much.' He turned his head to the side. 'Where were you, brave brittlebones, when I was dancing my way into Death's very doorway? Turned tail — what there is of it that one could call a tail — and fled.'

'I sought help,' the animal answered smugly. 'Some of us must use our cool heads instead of our hot impulses. Those of us so blessed tend to be small in size to the degree that we are large in wisdom.'

Kendric sighed, a sound so diminished from its former gusty proportions that Irissa, concerned, caught his hand in both of hers. He shrugged himself higher against the tree.

'They don't call this a weepwater for nothing,' he growled. 'It was under one I recovered from my first wound, I recall, from Fiforn's lance blow in Rule. Now I bleed again and again I—'

'Again you will need my succor,' Irissa said. 'I must restitch nearly all.'

'Leave it,' he insisted. 'If I live I am good enough.'

But she shook her head. 'Then, in Rule, you ordered me to heal you, when I didn't even know such power resided in me as a seeress of my Torloc kind. Today you order me to leave you, and I am no more capable of obeying you now than I was of disobeying you then.'

Her eyes, head, ebony veil of hair bent to him. Kendric found himself drifting in silken solitude, found puckers in his flesh and spirit smoothing. He no longer felt he must feign irritation as the ruling after-emotion of his narrow joust with death.

His second sigh was louder than the first, and openly relieved. Before it finished slipping from his lips, he plunged

294

into a dreamless sleep unpopulated by wraiths of any eye color whatever.

He awoke, hale and hungry, much later. Sunlight poured obliquely through the interlacing weepwillow strands above. The cat, Felabba, sat outside the natural tent of softly swaying greenery, looking annoyed.

'Well?' Kendric asked, his voice still hushed, for Irissa lay beside him in a sleep so deep she had not felt him stir.

The cat folded herself more morosely into her patient posture. 'I hunger,' she complained.

'Then hunt.'

'What, I pray?'

'Oh, I see. No beasties in the forest save that which speared me, a white owl and a — wolf — all overlarge, I think, for your dainty appetite. Perhaps I could conjure some delicacy. I feel refreshed.'

'The Hunter has been banished from this world forever, thanks to me. You owe me at least a banquet.'

'A banquet it shall be then.'

The cat waited for results, apparently unimpressed by promises.

A certain belated craftiness overtook Kendric's expression. 'You say you are hungry. So am I. For news. What of this Hunter whose sting I felt? Is he the bearing-beast who vanquished me?'

The cat's weight shifted from forefoot to forefoot before she spoke, reluctantly.

'The beast is what it seemed — one last wonder of this wonder-bereft world; like an Empress Falgon, the last of its dappled kind to embody magic. It held what remains of the pure, native magic of Edanvant in its horn, and the spirit of every creature that walks, flies, crawls under this skydome within its heart. But it was subverted.'

'Subverted?'

'Taken by another. Influenced from Without by one with much power and more will to use it. It then became the Hunter and it became dangerous.'

'To me.'

Felabba's head inclined. 'To you, yes, as I told you.'

Kendric glanced at Irissa's sleeping face, brushing back a loop of braid with his fingertip while he thought. 'Will it come again for me?'

The cat consulted her inner self with an absent gaze. 'For you, no,' she answered. 'I was forced to banish this last physical trace of Edanvant's soul from this world, though it was contaminated through no flaw of its own. This sorry chore is why I came to Edanvant, when I had business elsewhere.'

Kendric's lips quirked, 'For once I'm glad Finorian's schemes were successful.'

The cat snorted, or sneezed. 'You've never overestimated Finorian before; don't begin now. I came because I came, and will leave because I leave.'

'Who is the Hunter, Felabba? Is it the sorcerer Geronfrey? And why does he wish me dead?'

'Consult the crystal-caster,' the cat said flatly. 'I do not dabble in foretellings on demand.'

'But you are hungry?'

'Not that hungry.'

Kendric nodded thoughtfully. 'If it *is* Geronfrey, Irissa could be—'

'If it is Geronfrey, you will find out soon enough,' Felabba interrupted impatiently. 'Now that your curiosity is satisfied, what about me?'

Kendric puckered his brow to concentrate on the promised birds' remembered form, the first step toward evoking a thing in person. His expression cleared, but not his perplexity.

'Yet I would not − make − a thing, by any means, merely to have it destroyed,' he temporized, wondering if he could coerce more information from the cat. Felabba's jaded gaze grew disgusted. 'I know! I'll call it cooked and whisker-ready!' In moments a small roasted bird appeared, basted brown by an unseen campfire and still steaming.

Felabba lifted herself on her front paws and settled for demolishing it down to the bones while Kendric watched.

'Don't thank me,' he said finally. 'I myself am famished, but will wait for some of Dame Agneda's best garden greens.'

The cat favored him with a possessive glint and dragged her meal a bit away, as if she were an ordinary household tabby fearing food-nappers in human form.

Kendric shook his head and glanced again at Irissa. She slept like the wounded woman in white, like, as she had described another, a bespelled princess in a ballad. Her head had fallen on his shoulder, her white face buoyed by a ripple of tangled hair, her lashes and brows black as soot on snow. His arm cradled her spine, turning numb, but she had not moved since he'd awakened.

'I must have been stubborn stitchwork,' he mused. 'She seems more fatigued than from any healing before.'

The cat shot him a look that implied incredible stupidity on his part, but kept on munching birdflesh until bones crunched. Kendric, concerned in his turn, leaned to look closer, until his breath agitated the fine hair escaping the circlet and Irissa stirred at last.

She sat up hastily, rubbing her eyes and smoothing her hair.

'You are—?'

'As good as I ever was,' he said, spreading his freed arm wide. 'More's the pity. At least you could have improved things.'

She smiled. 'I think not.' Then she did not smile. 'Kendric, you were coming back to the forest keep to find me—?' He nodded neutrally. 'I must explain; I never meant to desert you in Citydell, but was so bitterly — wounded by my reception there, by what happened — or didn't happen, that I could think of nothing but fleeing the place, fleeing myself—'

'I know,' he said. 'And what's more, Orvath now knows what great wrong he did.'

'Oh. Is he—?'

'He is unshaken in his enmity. He is afraid, Irissa. Because he faced a thing greater than himself once, he fears that everything he faces is greater than himself. He meant you no special harm, but he offered you no special exemption, either.'

'I would I could say I took no special hurt from it.' She looked away into a sudden veil of unshed tears as thick as glass. 'But I have spent too much time among mortals for that.'

297

'Orvath's unhappiness roots in himself, not in you,' Kendric consoled, his arm round her shoulders. 'And he knows it. Perhaps that's punishment enough.'

She shrugged tentatively. 'I left Citydell without a glance back for more than Orvath. I thought I had lost something dearer even than the breath of my body, that you—' Bluntness served best. 'I thought you had found a new company whose presence you preferred,' she admitted.

'You thought I had betrayed you for your Torloc kin?'

'Not me, so much as . . . I thought you had found a new way to be true to yourself. There is no betrayal in that.'

'Irissa . . .' His eyes radiated aggrieved sincerity. 'There is no longer any way for me to be true to myself and false to you.'

They stared at each other for a long time, until Felabba took it upon herself to yawn noisily.

'We must be about our business,' the cat announced when she snagged their attention. 'Night comes and with it other elements. If you return to the keep to aid Finorian . . .'

Kendric rose first. 'I have seen with my own eyes the dire talismans the men cage. They are not likely to refrain from using them forever. You are right, Irissa, the men would not be so bad — if they did not think as they do, and if thinking were not what makes a man. So I'll add whatever I can to the Damen Circle's power. After what Orvath did to Irissa, I see that Finorian's cause is defense. I cannot argue with that however much I disavow her goals.'

Irissa caught his hand and pulled herself up. 'I can hardly move,' she apologized. 'Your wound must have been both broad and deep, the final healing of it reached so far and wide within me—'

'It was no dagger-nick,' the cat noted impatiently, 'and your powers wane even more under the additional burden you bear.'

Irissa's hand went to the gentle bulge of Overstone pouch at her breast. 'You mean this — the heavy Inlands talisman?'

The cat snorted. 'I mean we had best be on our way. It's poor time we will make of it between my old bones and the weight of the child slowing your spirits.'

'The child?' Irissa asked politely.

For once the cat was speechless, perhaps realizing that much of what she considered common knowledge had been uncommonly attained.

'Felabba, there is no child here,' Irissa explained as to one senile. The cat remained silent.

'Cat got your tongue?' Kendric couldn't help joking.

Felabba blinked and looked away.

'Perhaps the white man and lady have spawned a white child,' Irissa speculated lightly. No one answered her.

Irissa stopped talking and stood silent, seeing the motionless cat and sensing the stillness that had crept over Kendric as well. Even the water seemed to have frozen in the nearby streambed.

Comprehension came in stages, like awakening. Kendric watched flickers of shock, skittish understanding, denial, bemusement, refusal and disbelief dapple Irissa's features. His own amazement ran rin-deep, but he had never doubted the facts for a moment.

Irissa's head jerked back, as Kendric had seen an untamed bearing-beast shy when the alien bridle first touches its muzzle. Then Irissa turned and bolted through the whipping weepwater branches, vanishing into the forest.

Kendric turned on the cat. 'Waggle-tongue!' he spat with Felabba-like disdain. 'Have your wits grown senile, to break such news so callously? You make Orvath seem a master of subtlety.'

If it was possible for a white cat to blanch, Felabba paled to her bloodless ears. 'I did not think, a rare failing of mine.' The cat's look turned sly. 'At least *you* take it well,' she noted.

'What choice have I?' he ground out in frustration.

Kendric looked after Irissa, his features mirroring as much uncertainty as hers had, then slowly sat again, feeling the effects of a blow of purely aural nature, as if his ears had been boxed by truth.

'Do you not follow her?' Felabba inquired.

'Not — now. Not for this.'

'But we have little time.'

299

'You and the Torlocs have little time.' He settled gingerly against the tree trunk again. 'For this, Irissa must take all the time she needs. I do not know much, but that I would stake my life on.'

Among the grasses, the glimmer of Irissa's earlier-shed tears attracted his eye. He selected one, lifting its coldstone-hard shape to the soft light.

'I am no connoisseur of tears,' he said, recalling first using those words long ago in Rule.

The statement was no longer true. He studied the tear, which shone as clear and fresh as when it had fallen and still tasted sweet, not bitter, when he touched it to his tongue. It tasted, in fact, oddly sugared. And then he knew that Irissa's entire body, even her magic, had turned fecund. Her tears, once a salable commodity in Rule, were now pure sustenance for all but she who shed them.

She ran, the undergrowth snapping past her face and body, the windless forest seeming gale-wracked simply by the force of her own passing.

She ran until a knife-sharp stitch pierced her side, and she stopped, doubling over. Was the pain that racked her indeed hers — or . . . its? Her flight had brought her to a small clearing bordered by thick trunks. Irissa paced their perimeter as if caged, as if to outwalk the condition that claimed her and leave the fact of it dragging behind her like a train, like some shed skin of herself.

Around and around she went, to the same mad rhythm that her mind whirled. Of course she had known the possibility of it — the how and when of it. Only, not for *her*. Not the must and have-to of it.

She felt trapped as any beast in any cage whose waiting jaws it had not seen until they were shut. She had altered unknowingly, altered irrevocably, and with it changed everything about her. So much had come to her through magic, through her willing — nay, her struggling — participation. This came unasked for, silent, on nature's stealthy, unretreating feet, without so much as a by-your-leave.

It came, and having come, would not depart.

She shuddered, wrapping her arms around herself in the deeper shade of the forest. So had Kendric felt, feeling within him the alien presence of another's magic, feeling . . . visited . . . by that he had never consciously ached to have.

Faced with the fact of it, and told he must accommodate himself to it by an inflexible Torloc seeress — now she knew why he so resisted what to her was natural, and more, a boon. It was a thing that had come unwilling, from outside oneself, and that was the heart of any change. What to one might be a gift, to another might be a burden unbearable. One mortal's magic was another Torloc's misery.

It was as if she held a fierce, silent debate with herself in the woods. Neither side of herself won, but both at least had their say, and perhaps she could then spare others the burden of it. Certainly she had a fine example of stoicism in Kendric. Smiling grimly, Irissa brushed the branch-combed hair from her face with the heels of her hands.

She returned through forest paths, following the trail of snapped branches and trampled grasses. She could not outrun her own inevitability, any more than Kendric could evade his magic. They were both caught in traps of the other's making and unique nature, and had nothing left to do but make the best of it.

CHAPTER NINETEEN

Medoc lifted the horned-man medallion over his head, laying it on a samite-covered table. Around the ancient Torloc Damen Circle rim inside Citydell the men gathered, solemn-faced and silent.

Orvath stared into the Circle's clouded central Eye, watching vague images resolve and dissolve in rhythmic turn. To one who was not a seer they meant nothing.

Medoc paused before lifting a dagger with a blade of blood-red metal from the table.

'This has been as much a curse as a talisman, and was given me by a dying woman from a world that had turned its back on death,' he cautioned.

'The Single Tongue of Flame is the only pervasive talisman we have, which runs upon its own tight-wound will,' Orvath answered. 'If we send it seeking, it will fan wide through the central forest; its effects will diversify and its harm will dissipate.'

'You speak as if an unleashed demon were mere flood or fire, Orvath. It becomes its own insanity and will do what it can in the way of evil.'

'You are older than I, Medoc, and have listened overlong to Finorian's theories, which serve herself most. You saw her power quail before the smallest manifestation of this instrument more than twenty years ago. She has grown no stronger since. We must demonstrate our magical superiority. Then the other women will have no reason to resist reunion with us. Our kind was never meant to be parted by power as by a comb. Do it.'

Medoc knelt then and plunged the alien dagger into the foggy Eye of the Star. Smoke boiled out, followed by a crimson mist.

Finally a narrow filament of fire, spark-bright from one end to the other, sizzled onto the damp stones.

It streaked across the inlaid aquamarine sea heading straight for the emerald mosaic of forest that took shape even as the talismanic demon sped toward it. A likeness of Citydell and the habitations around it sprung under the men's feet, so they stepped back in superstitious dread of treading on something so near and dear to them.

Shade by shade, shape by shape, the floor-inset map molded itself to the likeness of Edanvant. But among its multicolored expanses, a grayness stole over the woodland greenery. At that mist's dull center wove a narrow tongue of fiery venom.

Finorian's scanty white hair floated around her face as she peered into the malachite Eye of the Damen Circle. She crouched upon the floor like some sharp-boned cat, looking uncharacteristically disheveled.

'Where is Irissa, now that our need is urgent?' she wailed, again producing an uncharacteristic effect.

'Perhaps Irissa has needs of her own.' Jalonia seemed to have acquired some of Finorian's missing composure.

'Her needs and ours have ever been the same, only she is too ignorant to know it.' Finorian rose from regarding the eternally clouded Eye and lifted her hands. 'Make our Circle as strong as you can, Torlocs, for at last we face a foe it will be difficult to keep out.'

Jalonia lent her hands to her companions, but her mind and heart yearned in two directions. One harped, as it always had, on the absence of Orvath, no matter what he had done. The other reached blindly but instinctively into a direction too new to be named. It called, softly and unself-consciously, for Irissa.

Kendric waited, and while waiting, thought. Thought became a shield of sorts, muffling all his senses.

'What are you thinking of?'

He managed not to move, as if he feared startling a wild thing he hoped to tame. 'The Rynx,' he answered Irissa's subdued voice behind him. 'I wondered why we had not seen the beast of late.'

'Perhaps it wanders, as do we, between one impossibility and another.'

She parted the lachrymose weepwater strands and came to sit beside him, or rather, at an angle to him, so all he saw was the edge of her face and the intermittent flicker of eyelashes.

'Nothing is impossible,' he said hopefully.

'Apparently not.' Her silence fell like tears, in hard bitter beads between her words, separating her sentences. 'I was surprised.' Silence. 'Where is Felabba?'

'I, too,' Kendric answered. And paused. 'She has withdrawn, ashamed of herself.'

'I suppose it is no great matter to a cat.'

'No. Likely not.'

'Nor should it be to me.'

'Or me,' he agreed.

They were both silent. Then Irissa spoke.

'When, do you suppose, did it happen?'

His sigh exploded more bombastically than he meant it to. 'These things do not announce themselves at the time! I could count on one hand the occasions.' He fanned his fingers. 'Twice, in Rule—'

'Once in the Inlands,' she interjected.

'Does it matter?' Her silence goaded him to further calculations. 'Twice here . . . or three times.'

'You are on the second hand,' she noted scrupulously. 'I hope it wasn't at Geronfrey's under-mountain tower in Rule.' An unleashed shudder rippled through her voice.

'When you came to me,' he said, his voice warming with remembrance.

'You like that I came to you,' she accused.

'It was a — pleasant — surprise in a world too full of unpleasant ones.'

'If you were so surprised, what of the inn in Rule?' she asked. 'You seemed aware of the possibilities then.'

'I was a soldier then,' he said impatiently. 'I knew nothing of love other than the quick taking of it.'

He had invoked the forbidden word, which they had avoided through two worlds and as many gates.

'What are you now?' she inquired softly.

'I don't know, but it doesn't seem to matter.' Kendric's bootheel kicked a clump of grassy turf away. 'Perhaps Felabba is wrong.'

Her eyes turned to him. 'Has she ever been?'

He shrugged, then plunged into a secret thought. 'Perhaps . . . some magical method of revocation exists—'

'It is a purely natural thing; magic would go against its grain.'

'So are death and deep wounds natural things,' Kendric said logically, 'but we have turned their blades before on the shield of magic.'

'The long-gone seeresses might have known.'

'What of Finorian, then?'

'I don't know.' Irissa turned to him, her shoulder touching his. 'Kendric, how is it you are calm; that you do not speak of your stake in this — state — of mine?'

'I, too, have borne the unexpected. It is a grimmer burden than the soft, smothering weight of daily hardship or kindred betrayal or even loneliness.'

Kendric's finger on Irissa's chin rotated her face to parallel his. Her headlong retreat through unclipped woodland had drawn red veins of injury on the anxious whiteness of her skin, he noticed with fond chagrin, his eyes tracing the shallow wounds. Beneath their gaze, the lines vanished.

He blinked, amazed, then realized that his wish to restore her, his baffled need to soothe an inner injury, had smoothed some smaller outer ones. Had his unsought magic become so unthinking then, so interwoven a part of him?

Unthinkingly still, he leaned toward her and brought his lips to hers. It was not an unheard of gesture between them, but now it rang loud with resonances of grave responsibility. His hand in her hair trembled.

'It is the source of both our unwanted burdens,' Irissa said, as if forced to remind him.

'It is our consolation,' he replied.

Later, she drew back from him a moment, her eyes unwavering. 'Kendric, I'm afraid,' she confessed.

His only answer was an echo.

'Revolting indolence,' came the abrasive tone of the old cat, Felabba, who had returned to lave her feet — and ultimately her face by proxy — with the thistled side of her tongue, thus imbuing her voice with a double burr.

Irissa and Kendric bowed their way out of what had become a sheltered bower for too brief a time.

'I am no younger than I was an hour ago, though you two may feel so,' Felabba went on sarcastically. 'Now, if you would be kind enough to provide me a perch, Wrathman, it will speed the journey back to Finorian. I sense our presence would be . . . welcome.'

'Your ambition aims high,' he commented as he bent to scoop up the cat's featherweight form and install it on his shoulder. 'Be wary of bumping the hilt.'

'I have ridden the apex of a bearing-beast's withers through half of Rule. Your shoulder is not so much more elevated than that, though you may think it so.'

Kendric forbore to answer, beginning the march through the woods.

'At least,' he remarked to Irissa, 'you could have run in the right direction; then we'd have a start on getting there.'

'At least you could have saved your breath and strength for when you really needed it,' the cat riding his shoulder added testily. 'Then we'd have a chance of aiding in whatever enterprise Finorian considers so vital.'

Their uneasy jests fell on still-raw sensibilities. To prove them wrong, Irissa increased her pace to stalk ahead of Kendric in manner that would have been flight had she not known so clearly where she was going.

Perhaps Felabba had exaggerated, or perhaps being told she should weary easily prevented that very thing. Irissa arrived first at the castle courtyard and stopped dead still, her breath barely hurried. Behind her the undergrowth groaned as all seven feet of Kendric crashed through the last circle of choked foliage into the clearing.

'Release me,' Felabba demanded in put-upon tones. 'Fifteen times I was whisker-whipped by vagrant branches. I had no inkling the upper airs were so crowded.'

Kendric happily stooped to rid himself of his passenger, then straightened to look around.

'It seems quiet enough.'

' "Seems" is a word meant to be seen through,' Irissa noted. 'Finorian must be occupied elsewhere; all the doorways hang open and empty.'

Through one of these unhinged portals the old cat walked, tail rampant, its very tip nodding regally from side to side. Irissa and Kendric trod the ghost of Felabba's silent-footed path, amused to find her leading them all the way down, through the rock-hewn tunnel to the chamber that housed the Damen Circle.

'I know where we go, though I have never trod these tunnels,' Kendric whispered, running his hand along the rough rock. 'Citydell had such a passage under it, and a vast stone room where a Damen Circle had convened long ago. Now it functions as a talisman treasury.'

'No talismans here,' Irissa guessed, 'other than ours.'

The green-flamed torches, lit at last, leaped high in flame as the two passed; fiery motion made it seem the tongues of light licked their fire-rinsed chops. Kendric and Irissa moved single file through the tunnel, avoiding the snapping flames.

Where the passage swelled into a cave the illumination grew vivid. Kendric, the cat, and Irissa passed, as from the neck of a long green bottle, into a fire-flickered room crowded with a full complement of Torloc women. They made two circles now — one inner, one outer — and in their midst, at the very pupil of the pentagram's Eye, her pale garments rinsed garishly green, stood Finorian.

'My compliments, man of Rule, for returning our seeress to us,' Finorian hailed him. 'You have a stronger sense of duty than some who are called Torloc.'

'My sense of duty is finer than a Torloc's,' he answered,

307

'and no one returned Irissa to you but Irissa herself. You overestimate me.'

Something in Finorian's pale, inward-turned eyes flickered. 'A natural mistake,' she said, her voice sounding strong and sure again. 'I have spent so long underestimating you.'

Kendric knew it was as much apology as he would ever get from the Eldress; its very existence stunned him.

'And you.' Finorian crossed passing glances with the white cat at the newcomers' feet. The opaline surfaces of her eyes flashed silver. 'Felabba,' she accused silkenly, as if addressing an old friend, an old enemy. 'Creature of my optimism and her own contrariness. You come at last.'

'And I will go sooner,' the cat answered. 'I am not here at your behest.'

'Perhaps not. But you have picked up bad habits from Irissa. You come with too little, and perhaps too late.'

'We are late,' Irissa admitted briskly, her use of the plural forging them into a party of three again. 'My fault. I am, it seems, to bear a child, and already the unseen inner drag of it has its way.'

She had meant to drop this new, undigested reality into the Damen Circle like a crumb, casually, then step over it to more urgent business. Instead, her news rippled across the circling ears, stirring waves that grew louder with each passing second.

Jalonia broke from the rest, her face alive with surprise. Finorian, if possible, grew gray first, then whiter than ever. Her infallibly evasive eyes glanced past Kendric with an expression of − barely veiled triumph, he would call it. And approval.

'A child,' the Eldress mused. 'Well. Well indeed. The seed of another seeress among us takes root. A Torloc seeress has not conceived for ages past − and you, Irissa, were the first born in some generations. We have had to rely on fluke, not breeding, for our silver-eyed ones.' Her posture straightened with resolve.

Finorian brushed her way through the double circles of women, carelessly striking clasped hands apart. She stopped before Irissa.

'You must wed.'

'Bed-bond sufficed for my parents!' Irissa objected hotly, already stricken by the attention, the focus of every eye upon her, upon her obvious ambiguity. 'Besides, we had thought you might even know of some . . . revocation.'

Finorian's smile spread grimly. 'Nature is no magic spell to be countered on anyone's say-so. No, you have made your bed, girl, as I said before, and shall lie in it. Bed-bond may suffice for common Torlocs, but you bear the last thin thread linked to the long-woven tapestry of our kind, Irissa, and cannot escape ceremony. Besides, you would have wed Thrangar, had he come to Rindell, and what happens now was my very hope for that union.'

'I would *not* have wed him! You never thought to seek my say-so on it, Finorian. And I will not wed on your word now.'

'This may be the hope of our reconciliation,' Finorian said obliquely.

'You forget I have seen my father, Orvath, and my father's father, Medoc. If you think such men will let one unborn babe weave sentimental ties to bind them . . .! Besides, the men have dispensed with seeresses. They are self-sufficient now.'

'No one is ever self-sufficient but he who is deluded,' Finorian answered.

'You sent Orvath away when he would have stayed for my birth; why do you seek to force yourself — and ourselves — upon the Torloc men now?'

'Before reunion, there must be separation,' Finorian insisted stoically. 'Before good, bad; before resolution, confusion. And, in most cases—' Finorian's icy eyes glimmered with amusement. 'In most cases, before birth, union. You have taken a step crucial to your kind, Irissa, and must admit to it. To wed is only to put a name on the past. Encourage her, Wrathman.' Finorian's silver-white eyes lifted to aim unerringly toward Kendric.

'I am no longer a Wrathman, and my encouragement seems to pull Irissa in directions she would not choose,' he noted calmly. 'This is between you seeresses.'

Irissa turned to him so quickly strands of her long hair

snapped like myriad whips. 'You mean you do not care one way or the other?' she demanded incredulously.

'I mean that what I think will have little bearing on the matter.'

'But you are as concerned in it as I!'

'One would think so,' he said, smiling.

Irissa pursed her lips, perplexed. She ached to confront Finorian further; it was a most liberating emotion. She savored the heady power of having fulfilled the Eldress's wishes without knowing it, thereby holding even more power over one who had directed her merest action in an earlier life. She sought a means to make Finorian writhe even more — and found it in the man beside her.

'Two steps into the ceremonial star to wed,' Irissa said with a trace of smugness, drawing her arm through Kendric's. 'I will abide by his decision on this matter.'

'Kendric.' Finorian's dry voice choked on a name she knew too well. She drew herself up, as if tasting defeat already. 'What does a man from the Marshlands of Rule know of Torloc custom?'

'Little,' he admitted. 'But we had a few of our own. Among them were weddings. If Irissa wishes to follow my wishes, we will wed.'

Irissa's hand drew back from him as if confronted with fire. '*You* wish—? But we have never sought to interweave our freedoms in any conventional way. I thought you of all men would—'

'We have never willfully sought to free ourselves of each other, either,' he pointed out. 'Besides, what harm can it do to humor the old crosspatch?' he whispered, bending near. 'No doubt Felabba approves as well, speaking of crosspatches.'

Irissa looked around for support, and saw herself surrounded by expectant faces: feline, Torloc, and mortal. Kendric's amber eyes twinkled, like topaz set in sober ebony — not meant to be noticed but winking suddenly into golden fire.

She had been trapped, by her own body, by his unforeseen willingness to make formal what had been so informally successful. She didn't resent being a captive of circumstance in this instance, but one last evasion awaited her.

'What of the necessary ceremonial artifacts?'

'They always reside here, near the Circle,' Finorian answered, bowing to a small hooped chest and opening it on an array of items.

Shrugging a surrender she felt far less casually than she showed, Irissa stepped toward the central star-shape, double circles parting quickly for her, for Kendric, for Finorian, for the old cat, Felabba, who was not about to be left out at so deliciously unforeseen a moment as this.

Irissa glanced to the complacent cat at their feet. Perhaps this step was not wholly unforeseen. Perhaps Felabba and Kendric had conspired while Irissa had plunged into the forest, attempting to outsprint her fate.

So now Irissa finally stood where Finorian had always wanted her, in the ceremonial star beside a Wrathman of Rule, save that he was not Torloc, which must have discomforted Finorian as much as it comforted Kendric.

The couple ritually faced one another, their feet planted on opposing spokes of the design, their hands extended between them and clasped over the last two pointed triangles of star-arms. Around them, the circle of Torloc women had sealed again.

Kendric looked solemnly down at Irissa, his eyes still dancing as if he saw himself as the creator of an unapprehended jest rather than the victim of fate's ironic long way around the simplest matters.

Beside them, Finorian draped her desiccated voice in the same heavy seriousness that seemed to swath her meager body, pronouncing rituals to confirm what had become natural to them through many trials and travels, when they had acted as one despite the many splinterings on the road to that always negotiable reality.

'This Cup of Tears I spill between you, that you may know the sorrow of living and contain it.' Finorian tipped a chalice shaped of green gold, spilling hard, gemlike Torloc tears of many clarities and vintages to their feet.

'This Veil of Division I pass between your faces, that you may see your differences and surmount them.' A wisp of silk greened their mutual images for a moment, then wafted away.

'This Horn of Hope I fill with comet wine that you may know change and the peace that comes after.'

They sipped in turn from a hollow coldstone horn brimming with a heady scarlet brew neither had encountered before. The offering's shape and color reminded Kendric of his less optimistic encounter with a bearing-beast horn, and his eyes evaded Irissa's for a moment. They were still fixed on him when he looked up again, luminous with unspoken understanding.

At last Finorian extended circlets of green flowers blooming bright against blue leaves.

'This Wreath of Enamorment I bestow upon each, to remind you both that love waxes evergreen but blooms in some seasons and withers in others, that you may discern its true face behind the masks.'

Already the wreaths showed their fragility; one flower fell from Irissa's brow to come to ludicrous rest behind Felabba's right ear.

'Who catches the first fallen evergreen blossom shall wed next,' Jalonia announced as Felabba shook the offending posy from its position with flattened ears.

So ceremony ended in laughter, and a cat far old enough to know better found herself caught in the folklore-woven web of a wedding. She minced from the star pattern just as its outline blazed golden for a fleeting moment, connecting angle to angle, inner pentagram to six-armed star.

They all glanced down to study this seal upon the ancient ceremony and frowned to see a faint mist obscuring the phenomenon already.

'Is it a bad omen?' Jalonia asked, worried.

'An omen of worsening danger,' Finorian said harshly, bowing to study the Eye.

The Eldress crouched there for a long while, hands braced on bent knees. When she finally straightened, she didn't quite unbend to her full height, as if dire news still weighed her down.

'While we dallied for a wedding, the men gathered for a grimmer ceremony,' she said. 'The clouding of the central Eye shows that they have succeeded fully in releasing a talismanic blight. Even now, Citydell's sending reaches hungry tendrils toward us,' Finorian warned. 'Quickly, Irissa, take a place in the circle and join us to repel it!'

As Irissa moved to obey the urgency in Finorian's voice, Kendric caught the Eldress's always-wandering eye. She smiled. Finorian smiled. Broadly.

'And you, Kendric of Rule, be so kind as to step aside. This will be overtaxing work for a bridegroom.'

He bowed out of the Circle to join Felabba in the shadows.

'Mumbo jumbo,' he grumbled under his breath, impressed nevertheless by the women's mutual concentration, by the almost visible pulse of power throbbing through Irissa to the rest of them. He could gauge that growing force by the intensifying rainbow shades of her Iridesium circlet.

'It will take more than far-cast Circle magic to defeat anything like that which swallowed us under Citydell,' he predicted dourly.

'For once we agree,' the cat murmured into her scanty whiskers. 'Let them lay their flimsy nets. Others will tread the rope-dancers' path above them.'

Kendric glanced piercingly to the cat. 'I will not stand aside at Finorian's asking again. Irissa must be spared too much risk in battling for Edanvant; I bring full mortal and magic powers to my endeavors now.'

'Aye,' Felabba said. 'But we are little more than watchers now, you and I, for all it is a role you wear with rue.'

'What of the grandiose fate you fortold for me? The prize unwanted I will be given? The battle I will fight?'

The cat's eyes blinked as evergreen as emeralds.

'I can speak no plainer. The Present builds its bridge even as we stand here. First that must be crossed. Then there will be Future enough for even a Wrathman to meet it with teeth-to-teeth and throat-to-throat relish.'

CHAPTER TWENTY

It seared through the Iridesium walling the civilized city from the ring of woodlands beyond it. It drove a hot, weaving path through the beast-crowded narrow tangle of forest pressed between the two walls. When it breached the second wall, the metal melted from its path as if cloven by a huge, fire-sharpened blade. Wild creatures flowed to either side of its forceful passage; it cut through their massed, panicked ranks as an Iridesium-prowed ship parts waves of storm-whipped water.

Toothless, it gnawed upon trees. Legless, it walked over and through the second wall of Iridesium, leaving a melted cradle of metal in its wake. In the foggy train of its passage, wary beasts edged over the wall's broken threshold and picked their way by hoof and by paw into the larger, outer woodland. Birds, fluttering cautiously from branch to empty branch, broke into nervous chatter.

Beyond the animals' careful reclamation of what had once been theirs, far ahead, the sending sizzled through nature-raised walls of ichor-plump leaves and grasses, wringing green growing things dry as it went, charring tree trunks and leaving an ever-thickening smudge of smoke as a misty train. The smoke separated into thinner tendrils, and then it wove higher . . . and wider . . . and longer, interlacing the forest with its gray choking presence, instilling at last a scent where none had been before — the stench of smoldering earth and green hope gone gray with ashes.

Amorphous, the thing slithered among deserted Torloc edifices, dulling the Iridesium, veiling their bright coldstone windows. It wrapped itself bandagelike around the tall black

Torloc tower where Irissa and Kendric had glimpsed endless selves. It wafted upward like wind and crept among the softly murmuring treetop leaves like a conspirator, coarsening their blithe voices as it mingled with them. It surrounded the Torloc women's keep and seeped under doors and through keyholes, in between chinks and into crannies. It had lost its color, its redness, and left only leaden grayness in its trail.

It slunk through the green-flamed passage beneath the keep, choking the eternal tongues of the torches in their sockets until they begrudgingly guttered out.

It stole into the cave and intermingled with the impromptu bridal party itself, soundlessly wreathing their eyes and ears and noses in the underground twilight, muffling the glow of Kendric's hilt, the joint green lambency of Irissa's pommel-stone and Finorian's great emerald touchstone.

Even Felabba's eyes winced momentarily shut.

'What is this . . . thing?' Kendric turned as if to engage the sudden new presence that lay upon them as invisibly as a curse.

'Orvath's sending,' Finorian said shortly, her voice dead. 'It travels faster than our means to contain it. Our Circle strength wanes as fast as it waxes, despite Irissa amongst us. It contaminates our land and our strongholds — perhaps ourselves if we remain long under its weightless burden. It could even taint the babe within Irissa's body.'

In the dark, Irissa froze indignantly at that invasive idea, feeling oddly protective of a possibility she had only just recognized and a burden she had never foreseen bearing.

'And none of our magic will suffice to repel it?' she asked.

'Once it might have,' Finorian said darkly. 'Had we joined our hands soon enough, wholeheartedly enough.'

Kendric, tiring of talk when action, any action, seemed needed and guided by the hilt light that came unbidden from his sword when darkness or defeat threatened, broke into the Damen Circle. He bent to grasp Irissa by one hand and Jalonia by the other.

The women gasped at the surge of foreign male magic among them. Irissa, smiling quick understanding, matched his firm handclasp. Her magical inner weaving swiftly braided the rough, thick, emotionally tangled threads of his power into a silken skein to pass through her and round the Circle.

Kendric felt his own outpouring return through Jalonia's soft grasp — a stronger, softer, yet more inflexible thing — and marveled at the pull of yoked powers through him, cleaving his physical presence like a silent mental sword stroke.

The mist faded over the malachite Eye, and for long moments abated. Then the Eye reddened, aswirl in a furiously lethal fog that obscured it completely. The bloody miasma boiled up, hissing with heat, forming a cloud that swelled in the Circle's midst. Amorphously it pressed against the linked forms, somehow pushing their arms backward, challenging their contact.

Kendric, who had never bothered to kneel on more than one knee, braced himself as if he were anchorman in an invisible tug of war. The Circle leaned left, then right. The women moaned as the glowing cloud pushed their fingers apart and they clung to each other by the drag of fingernails on flesh.

A sound like wind rasped in the still place, the rush of air fanning flames. Irissa's fingers were slipping like flax through Kendric's encompassing grasp, oiled by sweat that felt slick as blood. On his other side, he held Jalonia by three ebbing fingertips. Across the Circle, the women's teeth drew blood from their lower lips as they fought to remain linked.

'Finorian!' It was too dim to see her clearly amid the cloud, but Kendric openly called upon the Eldress's aid.

'I cannot. I cannot,' finally came the broken answer. 'I am Circle mistress and cannot act alone once I stand in your midst. Save yourselves!'

In the increasingly lurid red glow, they saw the Eldress caught center-Circle, mist erupting into flames on the hem of her gown and surging up her narrow figure like tongues from a huge, panting mouth.

'Felabba!'

The voice was Irissa's, and the tone was as commanding as Finorian's had ever been and as beseeching as ever Irissa's had.

316

'I cannot.' The faint, echoing answer came from a distance away. 'This sending was begun by Torloc and Torloc, and must be undone by Torloc and Torloc.'

Even as the cat spoke Kendric felt the reins of power abrading his grasp upon them. Magic bucked through him, coarse and unheeding, threatening to unseat his grip upon himself.

'Irissa, I must . . . let go.'

'All of us must,' came Jalonia's gasping voice.

'Then—' Irissa's one word struck some common note and they held together, despite the strain. 'As we stand together, so we separate together — now!'

Hands dropped apart around the Circle. The steaming cloud, freed, rushed over their overheated faces, wringing exhausted coughs from every throat. It was sucked into the distance of the cavern, turning rock-gray as it sped away.

Finorian remained in the middle of the broken Circle, her garments singed and hanging as limply about her as her hair. The emerald touchstone at her breast shone so pale a green it seemed drowned in milk.

'We are lost,' wailed someone.

'No! But we must confront this sending at its source,' Irissa urged the Circle. 'If we try to use the Damen Circle now that its purity has been contaminated by an antipathetic spell, we could choke on our own magic turned back at us. We must—' Leadership was clearly hers now, and she had no path to propose . . . 'We must leave this keep where we are trapped like mice in a maze and march to the city.'

'Into Orvath's hands?' Dame Agneda's voice wavered from the darkness. 'We do not know what he wants of us.'

'What do men always want of women? Surrender,' Finorian croaked, inflexible even in extremity. 'You must not go to the city.'

Silence greeted her words. All were used to heeding them, and none yet had summoned reason enough to debate them.

In the continuing silence, the red mist continued to disperse. Dimness snuffed the Circle chamber again, as well as any optimism left alive in it.

Kendric and Irissa's hands had met in quick tandem resolve to guide one another at the falling of the new darkness. Now their clasp tightened in mutual recognition of the danger the leaderless women faced with Finorian proven to be, for the first time in her unreasonably long life, inadequate.

'I will not surrender,' Jalonia spoke from darkness, her voice as firm as any Wrathman's. A bitter resolve underlined her words in iron. 'I would have walked with Orvath to the Gate of Death itself, but I will not walk to his servitude.'

'Not to servitude or surrender, but to confrontation,' Irissa argued. 'Surrender claims those who wait here passive.'

A course, one she would not have chosen, etched itself more clearly in her mind and heart. 'Running away from the men, running away from anything is never a solution,' Irissa heard herself telling that self along with the others.

'We must take this battle to them, to the gate to Citydell,' she said. 'We must bring our Damen Circle to where our walls have been breached and there stand to talk and make peace between us — or to fight . . . eye to eye, magic to magic, woman to man — inner power to outer talisman,' Irissa concluded, naming their differences.

'Sword to sword, if it comes to it,' Kendric added, underlining the realities he knew so well.

'Torloc to Torloc,' came a sharp warning voice from the dark, 'for the people of Edanvant want no part of either your return or your disaffection and the fuss it causes. But you will learn only by doing, and sometimes dying, as is the way of all human beasts, even Torlocs.'

'Who spoke?' Jalonia interrogated the darkness. 'Finorian?'

'Not I.' The Eldress's voice, unbuttressed by her physical presence, quavered like an ancient, frayed harpstring.

Irissa and Kendric recognized the doomsayer for Felabba, and in each other sensed foreboding like a tangible thing, a silent third party made real and come between them. The old cat kept mute now, taking no credit for her meddling.

Finorian spoke at last, bestirring her raw, throaty voice. 'All my plans since coming to Edanvant have turned to smoke of another's weaving. I can no longer command so much as a cat. Do what you will if you can summon will to do it. A Circle, once broken, cannot be restored, and land, once lost, cannot be reclaimed. I . . . abjure you. I am of you but not with you. Look elsewhere for guidance now.'

This concession brought every eye to the earth, to the mute Eye of Edanvant so open and staring and uncommitted beneath them. Finally, reluctantly, they looked to Irissa, one by one, Kendric last, as if he feared facing the inevitable conclusion of his gesture.

She rose and picked up each of their gazes in turn — Kendric's first. Finorian's last.

'We go to the city — for the reasons most people go,' Irissa said calmly. 'Because we have no place else to go; we have nothing else to do.'

The company began to rise, turn, and to feel their way along the rough walls to daylight, every woman speechless now and bone-chilled by the future that had fallen like an icy mantle over their shoulders. Finorian joined Kendric and Irissa and Jalonia at their forefront, but kept as silent, and seemed as little-regarded as Felabba at their feet.

Once they had regained the keep's daylight-touched ground-floor rooms, the outlook appeared little better. They wandered a maze of smoky chambers, everything in them dampened by the gray haze. The chairs seemed draped in tatters of twilight. Fireplace mouths exhaled huge rolling clouds of ashes. Even the bestiary tapestry's glittering threads lay flat and muted beneath soot-begrimed coldstone windows.

'The bearing-beast!' Irissa caught Kendric's hand as well as his attention. 'It's gone! The tapestry reflects Felabba's banishing of it.'

They stopped to stare, still discerning the figures of a man and woman in the drab thread-work. But between the couple lay a blank, pallid space occupied only by an anemic array of embroidered grasses and flowers.

'Good,' Kendric said defiantly. 'If that's the last I see of that beast and his bloody horn the better.'

In the meager light of the great hall windows, they confronted one another's outer semblance at last. They all seemed

319

draped with a pall of foggy hue, as if their spirits had faded. Jalonia brushed at the dust coating her clothes and hair. Felabba's fur, never pristine, now wore a jaundiced, yellow-gray cast.

Outside the forest keep, the atmosphere but echoed their own drab aspects. It seemed as if the sun had drawn a decent distance away; some midafternoon twilight rolled from horizon to horizon. Dishwater-murky light squeezed almost visibly from between the trees to cast a soft penumbra on the ground, as mud between dirty fingers.

Above them, the sun indeed seemed half its normal size, so fog-swathed it was easy enough to regard directly in its blazing bloodshot eye. Around it ran a fiery ring of vermilion color, a skyborne noose intent on throttling the sunlight itself.

'There hangs the true Torloc eye,' Finorian said sadly, infallibly raising her self-blinded gaze to it. 'When even the sun dims, fell magic prowls our Edanvant.'

'I see a direr thing — or, rather, don't see it,' Kendric pointed out from the loftier vantage point provided by sheer height. 'Where is the distant rainbow that perpetually arched this wood? Has it, too, been swallowed by the Single Tongue of Flame Orvath loosed?'

'The rainbow is a sign of our hope in ourselves.' The light, insistent hand of sudden intuition prodded Irissa to speak. 'It fades from sight now that our enmity has been made magically visible. Who are we Torlocs to merit sky-set signs when all can see what a morass we have made of our earth, our Edanvant. Perhaps it does not wish to be fought over, and makes itself into a thing no one will desire.'

'The magic the men have called forth does that, Irissa,' Jalonia objected, her voice heavy with sadness. 'We can all take blame for our division, our pride, our unworthiness. But Orvath, your father, has led them to this final doom, and neither you nor I can hide from that.'

'It is odd to hear one counsel against hiding from the truth who has hid from it so successfully herself.' Finorian's voice stung with some of its old sharpness. For a moment the fog surrounding them seemed to wither at its acerbic force.

320

Jalonia said nothing in answer, but Kendric leaned down to confide in Irissa. 'Finorian feels her control slipping on all sides; at least we are no longer the sole targets of her ill humor.'

'Control.' Irissa laughed a bit emptily. 'That is the greatest illusion of all. Well, do we make our pilgrimage to Citydell or not?' she demanded of the others in a rallying voice.

'You still seek to outrun your Present,' the cat observed from her immobile post at her feet, 'and are in no condition to do it, since you carry the Future.'

Irissa tossed her braids back over her shoulders. 'I feel splendid,' she insisted. 'You have swallowed some unsettling senile illusion, Felabba, and now try to regurgitate it upon our doorsteps. I have walked this way before and can again!'

So Irissa became the first to plunge into the ashen forest, to step under the sickly shadow that coated everything with dreariness — not from any desire to lead, but from a stubborn intention to remain unlead by the subtle inward leash of her own body.

The others followed — first the Torloc women, then Kendric as rear guard. He guessed there would be no more sendings until Torloc faced Torloc at the city gates.

Beside him ambled the cat, whether from desire for his taciturn company or because she was indeed as slow-footed as Irissa had implied, Kendric could not guess.

'An eventful day,' the creature mentioned slyly after they'd walked in solemn silence through a long, foggy stretch of wood. 'First you marry, then you march. An ideal day for a warrior.'

He ignored the bait of its taunts, keeping an eye on the flickering signal of Irissa's pommelstone gleaming cat's-eye green ahead.

'A splendid day for a prophetic cat, no doubt, too,' he rejoined. 'You have seen us dragged from pillar to post — or wall to keep — and back again, doubtless merely for your own entertainment. Perhaps you will declare the entire affair a sand-dream and vanish like a desert-wraith once we confront

321

the men and find no one on either side has anything to say and no wherewithal to win any kind of battle.'

'You wax uncharacteristically optimistic, Wrathman,' Felabba snapped back. 'Wax rather your scabbard and your brains, for you may find need of drawing both quickly.'

The dream-wood unfolded around them, tree after tree, clearing following clearing, clogged trail leading to paths even more clogged. In time, the gray-draped shapes echoed one another endlessly. Kendric's eyes passed, deadened, over scenes so like those just viewed that he almost could believe himself to be slogging in place. But always ahead he saw the flutter of the women's pale robes; if they could march through uncertainty incarnate into certain, albeit foggy, danger, so could he.

Yet time wound slowly, a thin, ragged skein making the same monotonous round of a spindle. His thoughts had settled into a similar vague sameness. When he saw Irissa sitting on a fallen branch ahead of him, alone and waiting, he realized he hadn't been watching where he was — and where he was going — for some time.

'Where are the others?' he wondered.

'Ahead,' she answered, mumbled really, as if she had hoped he would not notice her and even now would stumble on past.

'What is the matter?'

Her eyes had dulled, like the wood, and her face was waxen-looking. Her breath came in rueful bursts.

'The cat was right,' Irissa finally admitted, 'I tire.' She sighed. 'And tire more because I tried so hard not to tire.' Her boot-toe kicked up a cloud of noxious smoke. 'I feel someone has strapped a sword to my back, without asking my leave. I try to go on as always, but . . .'

Her hand jerked suddenly to the Overstone pouch beneath her tunic neck. 'And this, this Inlands souvenir. It hangs heavy as — as an Empress Falgon's liver about my neck and seems about as useful at magical things. What good did it do us when the smoke shattered our Circle? Perhaps I should rid myself of it—'

Her hand moved to wrench the cord off her neck. In that

moment the cat hissed wildly and Kendric bent to sweep Irissa off the log.

She viewed the world from his level, horizontal in his arms, and forgot the talisman.

'We cannot lose sight of the others,' he said, moving after them.

'You cannot carry me.'

'Apparently I can.' He grinned and then shrugged for good measure, as yet unimpeded by her weight.

'I am the most powerful seeress of my kind, Finorian's most precious weapon in her war with the men. I cannot be carted to a confrontation with them like a sack of cabbages! Better I should crawl and arrive late.'

'Lateness only becomes Felabba. I'll put you down before we reach the city,' he promised. 'What is the point of being strong if I cannot use it now and then without fear of somehow stealing strength from you? And leave the Overstone alone. You chose it; now it chooses you. You can tamper with such matters no more than Orvath.'

Irissa's fingers laced reluctantly around his neck. She thought for a while, lulled by the languorous, rhythmic motion that marks a mere passenger. Fatigue had overtaken her swiftly, like a lorryk that had let her outrun it only to show its supremacy in racing past her later. She had walked until weariness had seemed a physical thing slung over her shoulders, until her every step had raised less high and went less long, until her very breath had come languid and shallow.

She rested her chin on Kendric's shoulder and watched the veiled wood behind them slip into gray obscurity. That is how she saw her life now that an unexpected force had gripped her in its unrelenting talons. Confusion behind and even thicker confusion ahead. She had expected to grapple with magic, daily, to the death even. That was her fate.

But there was nothing magical about the common act of conception — a scullery maid or a queen could do it with equal ease. Why then should a Torloc seeress be so burdened, when there were so few of her kind and so many other women eager to fasten onto the demanding magic of a commonplace thing?

323

Kendric's long, even strides through the unsettling murk never flagged from the moment he had added her weight to his — her weight and that other, invisible weight that would make itself known slowly, ounce by ounce and day by day.

She longed to ask him her unanswerable questions, but dare not. He seemed to be taking the unseen change in her well, but of course he had to go on as if unaffected, Irissa ruminated. How could Kendric express joy in her confusion, or rail his own dismay when hers could always be the greater?

And so he had wed her, for he would never feel as betrayed by circumstance as she could feel betrayed by herself. She had robbed him even of the right to share her bewilderment, she reflected, and that made another kind of burden, neither magical nor natural but equally as heavy.

Tears ran down her cheeks, hardening into coldstone as they went, and resting on her lips, sweet and pendant as flower dew. They fell at last, like all things left behind that day, into the mist and the thick, smoky morass below it. They fell without a sound.

Kendric walked on, seemingly unhampered by his passenger or anything she bore, or even by a fear of the future that lay beyond the mist-smothered woods, beyond tomorrow. Irissa found a growing comfort in that fact.

Above them, an ashy rainbow cut monotone striations of gray into a wan, sun-bereft sky.

'When does sunfall come?'

Everyone had paused to rest. Kendric's practical question disturbed what peace they could find reclining on mist-soaked ground in a wood that had become a ghost of itself.

Water dripped disconsolately off the tips of leaves and beads of mist mixed with the fine filigree of sweat on every sober face.

Irissa, despite her sudden spell of weakness, was far from the weariest looking of the company.

'We near the walls,' Kendric went on, 'and must decide whether to confront those behind them now; whether the dark of night be in their favor or no.'

'What is our alternative?' Jalonia's voice had sunk to worn huskiness.

Kendric's face, lit by the shoulder-high light of the hilt, grew grimmer than the woods around them. 'Wait for sunfall, pass the night here and make ourselves known at daylight.'

'If the light of day will ever come to this wilderness again,' said a cynic.

It was impossible to tell which woman had spoken, save that it was none Kendric knew by face or voice. They looked depressingly alike now, he thought, these once-exotic Torlocs — more resembling lanky, rain-drenched weepwater trees encircling a particularly doleful spot than women.

Finorian stood, the oldest, most dampened, and yet dryest weepwater of all.

'Sunfall or sunbreak; they are the same — irrelevant to our struggle. This dire magic lays waste to what once was wonderful. We cannot suffer it any longer than we must. And if we wait, we tire. Our strength is not such that we can afford to see it ebb.'

Irissa looked up, raising mist-dewed eyelashes.

'Felabba is gone.'

Finorian was silent, so no one could tell whether the news struck her as good or bad.

'When?' Kendric wanted to know.

Irissa shrugged. 'Somewhere between here and where we were. Who would notice one soft-footed old cat treading into the fog? Our cause shall miss her.'

'Nonsense!' the Eldress burst out, speaking as if to convince herself as much as anyone else. 'She is but a cat at base, and a crotchety one at that. What has she ever done for us when we have called upon her; she would not even come at our Circle command. We must not let the loss — or lessening — of one weapon consume our courage.' Finorian seemed to lash her own spirits. 'Rouse yourselves, Torlocs, and make a Circle behind us that Irissa and I can draw upon when we meet the men.'

'What of me?' Kendric crossed his arms and looked down at Finorian, amusement and irritation blending bizarrely on

325

his hawkish features. 'Or am I too awkwardly alien to play any role but that of onlooker at this tragedy?'

If Finorian had an answer, if was forever silenced by a movement among the white-barked birches. Trunk-tall, it stirred again, then broke through the miasma into the crowded clearing.

The women gasped nervously. It was a man, a man who seemed as cloudy in mind and body as the air surrounding them.

Every Torloc and one who was not Torloc started at his unannounced approach. He hardly regarded them, but wandered into their midst as if they were senseless as trees, shaking his white-and-gilt head and staring from side to side without truly seeing anything.

'A poaching townsman caught in the woods and the path of Orvath's sending?' Jalonia wondered.

Irissa shook off her lethargy to approach him.

'It is the man Kendric and I met in the midnight woods, who shimmered as softly as moonlight in our sight and offered us mushrooms,' she discerned, looking at Kendric as if he could not only confirm her diagnosis, but offer some remedy for it.

He stepped forward. 'True enough. I saw him again, briefly, when I came through these woods in search of you. Stranger, our paths cross more often than chance permits,' he confronted the man. 'At least you owe us a name — for yourself if not for your errands.'

'Errands.' The man laughed self-mockingly. 'Errands indeed. Has a . . . forgotten memory . . . errands?' His face puckered into new puzzlement. 'As for my name, it is Ilvanis . . . Ilvanis!' he repeated, as if discovering the word. His gray eyes took full count of the company.

'Ilvanis of Rengarth,' he added, pronouncing the second word as if he spoke it for the first time. 'I am—' He laughed lightly once more. 'Lost. My turgid thoughts swirl and separate like cream in milk, but I do believe' — his eyes focused on Irissa and Kendric in turn — 'I've seen your like before. Especially you, dark man of Rengarth.'

Kendric stepped back as from a pit that yawned unannounced before him. 'You dream and wander, as you always have in these woods,' he said. 'You aided us on our journeys, that is all, and now you do not recall us. There is no Rengarth except in the memories of those who have left it. At least so Ludborg says.'

'Ludborg.' The man's silver hair shook in misty disarray. 'The name is not familiar. But you are, you two.' He looked beyond Kendric to the somber, circling women. 'And you women. I have seen your kind before, but not in such profusion. My thoughts tangle like skeins of silken thread. I stand in many places, in more than one self.'

'You have always stood before me in this very self you wear now,' Kendric accused. 'When last I saw you, your shoulders wore living epaulets of wolf's paws. But that is the only difference.'

'A wolf, a snow-white wolf with huge, citrine-colored eyes?' Irissa asked eagerly.

'Aye, golden eyes.' Kendric recalled, softening despite himself. 'One white wolf seems much like another, although this one appeared to be uncommonly tame.'

Irissa went to one knee, her hand at her forehead. Kendric, concerned, mirrored her motion.

'What is it? You are ill?'

She laughed reassuringly. 'No, I think, and it seems harder to do that standing upright now.' Her eyes probed the unfocused space before them, evoking the images of other days upon the ribbons of drifting fog, much as Ludborg called pictures into his casting crystal shards.

'Kendric, I think I see . . . everything!' Irissa's hand caught his forearm. At that instant a snapping in the underbrush caused every head but Irissa's to jerk up. Kendric's entire body would have followed suit, but Irissa's grip tightened to an Iridesium-hard band on his arm.

'Tell me,' she whispered without looking to see. 'Who comes?'

'Someone does come! It is—'

'The woman from the woods and from the rooftop whose

327

limbs and life you saved. The maiden in white who accompanies the dawn,' Irissa declared.

Spectacular as was the appearance of this very apparition in the dim archway of the opposite trees, it was not enough to keep Kendric from returning his dazed attention to Irissa's concentration-bowed head. She had named the woman without seeing her.

'What magic is this?'

'Mine? Or theirs?'

'Either or both, but tell me *something!*'

She looked up, excitement rampant in her quicksilver eyes. 'No magic but riddle-solving. Whose company have we missed?'

Kendric looked around as if to find the answer in absence. 'Felabba, you said, had vanished.'

Irissa shook his arm. 'Not only now — almost from the moment we arrived! Who — or should I say what? — is gone?'

'The Rynx! Or course . . .' He dubiously surveyed the pair in white. 'And these — people — are its emissaries?'

'These are some of its lost parts.' Kendric stared at Irissa as if she were mad while she went on. 'The woman you retrieved from the rooftop; the one I half-healed but could succor no more!' she reminded him. 'I never told you. She — she became a white wolf whose leg I mended.'

Irissa's pleasure at having solved a mystery darkened as unwelcome remembrance stole into her face. 'She bounded down over the roofspines — whole, her golden eyes mellow — just as Orvath came to . . . to take the Overstone. I had forgotten the wonder of that in what came after, in what I felt after.'

'It is a pity,' Kendric sympathized with a rare tinge of bitterness, 'that we can unravel the nature of a creature so tangled as the Rynx and not that of simple paternity. Although it chafed me in Rule, I have seen enough of higher placed folk now to be glad of being only Halvag the Smith's son and a simple marshman. That is magic enough for me.' He shook his head and began reexamining the recent arrivals.

'So some magic joined these two in the form of the Rynx

— I always thought its royal "we" and two-throated ways a bit overbearing — and it set them to guard the chained wizard, Delevant, in the Inlands of Ten. But when you and I released Delevant to his long-delayed dissolution—'

'Their purpose ended, so they came with us to fabled Edanvant — a Torloc land of green and growing wizardry, ripe with suspended spells and ancient, long-unpracticed magicks!' Irissa said. 'And here the Rynx found, as we did — dissension, division, enmity.

'It — they — found Torloc against Torloc, variety of magic opposing magic. Men battling women. Ilvanis and the woman were warp and woof of the Rynx, but the threads of their joint ensorcelment began unraveling with the tear of this disintegrating tapestry we Torlocs wove so long ago and now call Edanvant and our own.'

He smiled and considered their position. 'Deep sentiments, but the past is costly to consider when danger lies in wait ahead. Are you through thinking and can we stand now?'

'I think so.' Irissa grimaced gamely, but kept hold of Kendric's arm so his rising helped lever her upright. The scene they surveyed had grown as confused as the two who had joined it.

Other Torlocs were mingling their speculations and voices into a gossipy buzz that hummed through the forest. The visitors' white figures wafted vaguely among the grayer forms of the women like ghosts seeking roost in an old but sadly altered haunt.

Finorian, in their midst and already lessened somehow by the night's revelations, stood silent. The unnamed woman in white, being last to arrive, wore the most misplaced look of all upon her face. She studied them one by one, coming finally to Irissa. Her arm extended, unfurling a furred wing of fabric as her gilt eyes melted into mute question.

Irissa nodded recognition of her handiwork. 'Your wound has ebbed with your memory of it?'

'Yes,' the woman marveled. 'Thank you.' Her eyes, as remarkably limpid as the wolf's, studied Kendric. 'And you, tall man of the woods, helped me down from the stony hilltop,' she remembered with rising confidence.

He bowed. 'And later you risked hurt to warn us of the Hunter. I'm afraid I did not heed you well enough. I, too, have felt the fire of his curved lance.'

Her features sharpened with wisdom. 'Oh, well. The Hunter touches all. Yes, the Hunter wounded me because I would warn you, but his power springs from elsewhere and he has but one blow to each body he aims at.'

She turned at last to Ilvanis; perhaps in having found two faces she knew, she could confront the one so like, and not like, hers.

They stared at each other, the white-garbed man and woman, so oddly old yet young, confused but certain, alike but different. Even the evil fog could not dampen the sheer alabaster shimmer of their garments and blanched hair, the vibrant sparkle of their jewel-bright eyes.

'My name is Ilvanis,' he said politely, as if introducing himself to himself as well as the woman.

She looked away, seeing nothing, searching for something. 'Ilvanis. And I am − am—' Her features, terrified, twisted back to Kendric and Irissa in silent beseeching.

They shook their heads and spread empty, helpless hands. Irissa, who had healed her twice in two separate forms, had no balm for ordinary forgetfulness.

'I am lost,' said the woman . . . confessed the woman. 'And have been lost for a time as long as memory.'

'This is Edanvant.' Finorian's voice came out a croak; it had been so long since she had spoken.

The woman spun to face her, her airy garb weaving around her form like a gossamer cocoon. 'Edanvant. Yes, I have . . . heard of it. Remarkable folk live there. Tor . . . Torlocs, I believe. I come from Rengarth,' she explained without sensing what she said, 'and we are all widely read there. I have − read − of Edanvant in a great violet silk-velvet book buckled in green gold.'

Silence pitched its pervasive tent in the fog-swirled glen. All who had heard of Rengarth mulled the meaning of finding two such lost beings from one so lost a place.

The woman turned back to the man, as if the act of remembering one thing had led unerringly to another stepping stone of memory.

'And my name is — Neva.' Its sound delighted her as unselfconsciously as would rediscovering a favorite toy from long-ago nursery days.

Ilvanis embraced the name equally. He neared her step by tentative step.

'We must talk of Rengarth,' he said, extending a hand.

She placed her frost-white fingers in his; they withdrew from the clearing's center with the grace of great-hall dancers.

'Should we not stop them?' Dame Agneda's voice was as dazed as Ilvanis's or Neva's. 'They might be some ill sending from the men.'

'Would you stop fog?' Jalonia scoffed. 'Irissa, what are they?'

Her mother had never deferred to her as seeress, Irissa realized, never thinking that she was being asked in Finorian's place.

'They seem half here, although they're human enough,' she answered. 'We saw Ilvanis eat — and with great relish, too. Now that I think of it, mushrooms would be a treat to a man forced to range for rend-worthy food as an owl. They may be the separating strands of a spell cast long ago and far away.'

Finorian came to the spot where they had stood, and then only because she needed to consult Kendric and Irissa.

'What makes you doubt that they are magical personifications Orvath has raised?' she demanded. 'You know something of them.'

'No more than anyone may,' Kendric said impatiently. 'You misplace your suspicions; Orvath had no more to do with them than a mite has to do with an Empress Falgon. Are you Torlocs so sunk in your own spats and small spells that you cannot see a larger one for what it is?'

'Orvath *couldn't* have evoked these two,' Irissa said. 'Talismans are too clumsy to breathe forth whole beings.' Her glance crossed Kendric's. 'But I think I know what they are and why they wander in and out of our path so mysteriously.

331

What do you think Kendric? They are not make-magic,' she speculated, referring to the Inlands brand of positive sorcery, 'but are they *break*-magic?'

He understood instantly, nodding agreement and causing Finorian's face to set. Events had made her once-indispensible presence virtually redundant to all but herself.

'The Rynx, plural beast that it always was, has fractured under the strain of the dissenting Torlocs,' Kendric suggested. 'It divided temporarily into man, woman . . .'

'Bird . . .' suggested Irissa.

'Wolf!' Kendric realized suddenly. 'Neva was the white wolf during my healing vision! It pushed me from the wall as I would have wandered back into its spell when your absent self seemed mirrored in it. So the Rynx becomes bird and wolf, by day and night, one or the other — but it is too difficult a sum to tote!'

'She was wolf by night, woman by day; he man by night, owl by day.'

Kendric's fingers snapped triumphantly. 'The wall! In one form or other they've been slipping through from the beginning. The Rynx caught the fox in the wood between the walls. They were the pale wolf and owl we saw by turns in the dark world within the wall. They guided us through. But why all this shape-slipping? It must confuse even them.'

Irissa nodded somberly. 'It would not have happened had we not come here. Edanvant separated them, and separated Edanvant called forth their native forms by alternating turns. Now we see them both, separately. Perhaps they could never come together again until they had come totally apart. One good at least the Torloc severance has caused,' Irissa finished, 'one spell at least has broken for the better.'

Kendric mulled it. 'You are sure it is better to be human and separate and uncertain of oneself than to be a magical beast? You ever were an optimist.'

She glanced to the murmuring couple barely visible through the fog, who looked like figures on an alabaster frieze come to life.

'Perhaps their magic will aid us,' Finorian said, her pale eyes narrowed.

'Perhaps our magic can aid them,' Kendric suggested quietly.

The look Finorian flashed past his face was one of such sudden shame that he recoiled from its searing after-shimmer.

'At least they can accompany us to the wall,' Irissa proposed. 'Perhaps the men will permit them safety in Citydell while we Torlocs debate our rights — and wrongs.'

That settled, the new pair were gently surrounded by the Torloc women and borne off in their midst. Kendric's new-found solicitude slowed Irissa to a pace that kept them from following on the party's heels.

'It is not my quarrel,' he said, 'this Torloc division, except with Orvath. If he could stand on two equal legs and wield a weapon with both arms, I would call him to a duel and decide the entire matter there.'

Irissa paused. 'I would not . . . like that.'

'Why? Orvath bears no nicety for you, no fatherly sentiments. He tried to bereft you of what was yours and even the one thing you would not have without him — life. Talismanless or not, he leads their side, Irissa, and single combat is the way of men and war. You have seen me raise sword before — and against greater odds.'

She shook her head until her Iridesium circlet mustered a small flush of color in its fog-smoked metallic surface.

'I cannot put it into words. It is too close to what I carry now, you and Orvath fighting. Besides, swords have never been our way amongst ourselves. Let Finorian manage it with spell and Far Focus, if she can; let the men rattle their talismans and sharpen their wits. I will repel their attacks with whatever powers I have.'

'You will be on the defensive! That was ever a way to lose anything and everything. Finorian scorns my easily come by and hard-learned magic,' Kendric complained. 'Like you, she will let me do no more than play witness.'

'Edanvant is not your world,' Irissa pointed out.

'No, but my stake in any world, in the burdens you carry,

333

is no less because Circumstance shoulders between us and forces me to the side. I cannot speak for what I will do if it comes to that which I cannot tolerate. I stand the same earth, breathe the same spell-choked air as any Torloc in our company. And as Orvath is your father and would forget it, so I am father to what you bear and cannot forget it. Otherwise, we are much the same, I suppose.'

Irissa's five-stoned ring smote the fog with the quick flash of its passing as her hand moved hastily to stopper his mouth from further words, further comparisons.

'Not in the slightest,' she whispered, her eyes and mouth alarmed but smiling. 'Not in the slightest.'

CHAPTER TWENTY-ONE

They stood at last where the paired Iridesium walls had forged the fact of the Torloc division into reality. Little remained to testify to that reality.

Eternal twilight smoked between the ruins of once-impregnable walls. The men's sending had scorched the foliage within the walls to blackened ashes. Skeletal trees loomed stark, naked as nails. Smoke mingled with the forest-sent mist to produce a constant hissing, as if myriad unseen serpents boiled around the desolated ring of earth.

Beyond the fallen walls, behind the melted sag of Iridesium nearest Citydell's ten proud white towers, stood a dark, indistinguishable clot of Torloc men.

'They await us.' Finorian stiffened.

'Would not you?' Kendric said.

Irissa remained silent, unsure which distressed her more — the sight of the desolation, or that of the distance between the surviving halves of her people.

'It is time.' Finorian turned briskly to Irissa. 'I feel revived. We must show the men a sign of our resistance, our power. They know mine of old and respect it not. You, whose silver eyes have passed the severest of tests to see directly what generation of seeresses have dared not look upon in person, you must be the vessel of our victory.'

'Or your revenge?' Kendric interjected.

'What do you want of me?' Irissa asked quietly.

'Look behind you, Torloc, see how the vile, alien smoke and stinking fog have defiled the forest, have bled white the very green heart of our Torloc spirit. You must employ your silver eyes and whatever other knowledge or instinct you can command — yes, even any talisman in your possession — to show these men with their magic toys that naught can contest the will of a true-born Torloc seeress.'

Irissa's pallid smile matched her almost inaudible sigh for ruefulness.

'Much can contest a Torloc seeress's will, including an old cat of my acquaintance, an Eldress, a man of Rule—'

'Enough! Will you do it?'

'I will do what I can,' she promised finally.

Irissa gathered herself, her eyes lost in that inward looking that draws magic outward before Kendric could catch their glance and . . . And what? he asked himself.

It was not, he reminded himself again, his affair. Yet every fiber of his being screamed to take some part in it and his palm itched for the slap of a leather-bound hilt. Even his deep-buried magic stirred uneasily, rising to the bait of battle-lust. He quelled it angrily.

Finorian's eager gaze flitted from a deceptively motionless Irissa to the city towering through wisps of mist. 'Strike them!' she urged herself as much as Irissa. 'Show them that their sending has not harmed us, that we resist.'

'What will she do?' Kendric quietly asked Finorian. 'I have never seen Irissa use her powers with calculation and a cold heart. It seems against their nature.'

'She will do as I say,' Finorian answered in an undertone. 'You forget I had the training of her. She knows that her kind's survival depends upon it, especially now that she carries the possibility of yet another seeress within her.'

'The men are her kind, too. But . . . I had not thought of that . . . other.' Kendric shifted weight from one foot to another, as if the ground had arched its back beneath his feet of a sudden.

Finorian smiled without bothering to turn her head to display her satisfaction. 'I had.'

'I am . . . not a Torloc.'

'No.'

'And no true . . . adept at what magic I do command.'

'Most certainly not.'

336

'Then . . . how can I father a pure-born Torloc seeress?'

'All things are possible, even with a flawed instrument.'

'I am my father Halvag's first and only born. I will — Irissa will — bear a son,' he asserted stoutly.

Finorian's smile remained. 'Yes. And no.'

Before Kendric could investigate that cryptic answer, Irissa stirred behind them. Everyone in the clearing stiffened, all watching her, all waiting for Irissa to send the thud of her magic hammering on the doors of Edanvant city.

Irissa herself no longer saw anything or anyone beyond her set-upon task. Her face was utterly severe, or rather utterly composed, so it seemed carved of stone. Even her silver-shaded eyes had muted to the dead gray that gazes from the faces of granite statues. She had never looked more beautiful in a purely external sense, Kendric thought, and she had never looked less human.

He pivoted to view the declivity's opposite bank, where the men stood. Irissa twisted momentarily to look back to the forest, then faced again the arc of black destruction that was the wall, faced the small tangle of men and the hulking parchment-pale silhouette of city beyond them.

Where the sun stood now could only be guessed. An overcast wiped the sky clean of rainbows and other overseers — be they high-hung sun or moon or stars. Nothing witnessed what transpired but the divided Torlocs themselves, the city folk huddled behind their shutters, and the pair who had been the Rynx and now stood — aloofly puzzled — apart from these doings.

There was one last witness as well — Kendric, man of Rule, Wrathman, reluctant sorcerer, who had as great a stake in this inter-Torloc enmity as anyone could and still stand outside it, as shackled by apartness as he was bound by likeness.

Irissa's ringed hand mindlessly clutched the Overstone egg. The pouch's velvet warmth soothed her. Surely, she thought, so powerful a talisman, no matter how unknown, remained a weapon of last resort. Only if he— The name of her father prowled outside the circle of her serenity and stayed there. Her grip eased as the throbbing in her hand, her heart, ebbed.

Her mind smoothed. She would call on no external talismans; they were the root of this uncivil war. The Overstone egg sprang from Outside, she realized, and this — of all possible conflicts — was most Inside.

A mass indrawn breath made her pause. To the side, breaking through the last ring of trees to stand alongside the demolished wall, pressed hordes of oncoming animals — hot-breathed beasts tall and squat, long and short, furred and dappled, scaled and feathered. At their fore, already seated as if waiting remained its principal fate, was the old white cat, Felabba.

'What do you do here?' Finorian demanded.

'We wait and see,' the cat replied.

'Lend us your aid, then.'

'We are merely another weight to be thrown in the scale, perhaps to balance the man of Rule,' the cat returned, glancing to Kendric. 'We wait to see who will win, and what the winner will make of us.

'Between you quarreling camps of Torlocs we beasts have been held fast by two iron bands of wall, we have been pursued in our woodlands and banned from them. Our voices have been silent, but our anger stretches as long as the trail of our hunted bodies. We come to watch and make our own judgment.'

'You are animal, but you are also a Torloc thing!' Finorian reproved. 'You must help us.'

'I am Felabba and I am Guardian,' the ancient cat hissed back, her wiry whiskers trembling. 'In Rule I watched a Sword because the last of that world's magic resided in it. In Edanvant the wordless beasts are my charges — these creatures you have penned and hunted and driven and killed.

'Have you not seen the anger and enmity that every creature under every sun bears toward you, even the mildest? If I have moved among you, it was not because I was of you; it was . . . mere coincidence. You Torlocs think yourselves the centerpiece of whatever world you walk, when you are merely its fringe,' the cat finished sharply. 'More magic abides among these silent ones than in all your bickering and boasts.'

There was no answer to give. Irissa, gathering the far-flung reins of her magic, barely listened, though she had understood. To her, it remained irrelevant. She had committed to doing what Finorian had commanded of her: impress the men with her magic. The only thing that remained Irissa's in this long-inevitable act was *how* she would do it.

Her senses, swelling, seemed to encompass all of Edanvant, forest and city. Like a rainbow her mind arched it, spanning the ugly miasma that had defaced the forest for both Torloc and beast. Her self-set task was to revoke this most recent ugliness, nothing less than eradicating the immediate past. It seemed worthwhile work.

Draw, she told her inner self, draw away the cloud of ill-sent magic and destruction. Irissa's hands clasped; her forefinger pressed the Drawstone in her ring as if to take its pulse. Draw, as Chaundre of the Inlands had proven nature could do as well as magic. Will wove itself into a tangible thing and bowed to her bidding.

She drew her powers together next, into one taut ball — every strand of seeing, each fragile filament of wish and will and ungoverned force that interwove her nature. It became denser than the moon, brighter than the sun. It swelled with possibility. It burst within her, seeking expansion without.

And there, outside of her, it exploded — up to the slate-faced heavens. Her eyes followed its invisible progress and pinned it to a cloud somewhere halfway between Citydell's towers and the ashen lintel of the sky.

Behind her, a long train of mist and fog and smoke wreathed into a braid and drifted up; over treetops; over tilted, gawking heads; over expressionless, watching beasts.

Tendrils came from every side behind her, starting wide and then snaking narrow and narrower. They twisted into a tight black rope, then curled into a ball, filament by filament. The blot spread in the sky until it seemed a midnight-black sun hung there, then added width, depth, circumference. It expanded and expanded and expanded.

Irissa's eyes grew with it, wide and staring blind as Finorian's, her black pupils the eye of the needle through which all this spell-made mass was drawn.

'What does she do?' Finorian's eyes batted nervously, but Kendric watched Irissa with dawning relief.

'She is cleansing the forest, withdrawing the destructive results of the Single Tongue of Flame, turning back the men's wrath upon them and showing it empty of threat.'

'Reclamation is no display of power!' Finorian cried. 'This shows only weakness!'

'Only to the weak. Irissa is—' Kendric said deliberately, his voice unable to mask intense satisfaction, 'a mender, not a render. If you would use a weapon, you should be sure of its strengths, Eldress.'

Something in Finorian snapped. Kendric could almost hear it give — a timeworn, half-rotten tendril of magic. Sudden regret washed him, dampening that speechless, utterly selfless pride in another that was thickening his throat. He turned, worried, to the old woman.

Her shoulders had slumped. The emerald touchstone on her breast lay lifeless, the flaw within frozen on the verge of cracking it in half.

'So about Irissa I am wrong and you are right,' Finorian finally conceded. 'We have long battled over that and you have won. In . . . other things I am more often right. Know that in her mercy and your pride there is a price to pay that even I would not have asked of her.'

Kendric felt himself pale for the first time in his danger-edged life. A tide of icy dread oozed up his limbs to his eyes, which kept vigil on Finorian's expressionless face.

'What?' His voice was flat.

'That . . . black . . . magic she holds above us with all the strength that is in her and a bit more. It still retains all the ill it ever did — and, taken from our ravaged earth to another element, to the sky, it has become a gate for any unanchored darkness that cares to strike through it.'

'Why should any Outside evil meddle here?'

'You can ask that, when the Hunter has tipped his horn to you? Yes, I know of that. The Eye of Edanvant sees much.'

Kendric's hands squeezed Finorian's reedy arms in their overzealous custody. 'What can I do?'

'Wait,' Finorian said tonelessly. 'Wait and see. I may be wrong. A second time.'

Balked, he turned horror-drowned eyes on Irissa. She looked unmoved, unmoveable, even impregnable — though he knew that not be true in every sense.

Yet her magic was working. The Torloc women alongside Irissa glanced frequently beyond her to a forest that now lay green and moist under departing skirts of mist, trembling in every leaf. Across the chasm separating Torloc from Torloc the men could be seen standing still, staring up at the huge ball of black suspended over them.

'At least they have no magic to match this,' Finorian noted ironically, 'and they appear suitably impressed. Irissa of Rindell . . . always literal in her waywardness—' She began a bitter smile.

As if in answer to a boast of magic — or as if struck by some cataclysmic lightning bolt — the snarl of black cloud spread like suddenly spilled ink against the sky. It churned into charcoal thunderheads and cloaked half the horizon, dimming already dampened daylight to night.

Around them, the ring of animals tightened. Growls rose from lupine throats and hackles raised visibly. Bearing-beast hooves churned turf. A strong scent of beastly enmity mingled with the airborne sniff of storm-tang.

And as that swift, tenebrous cloud took on darker definition, watchers on both sides of the ravine saw it lengthen into the likeness of a Torloc — into the semblance of a Torloc seeress with streaming black hair and white empty holes for eyes, inky garments whipping around her though there was no wind.

On the women's side, a wolf howled as if its heart were being torn out through its throat. Smaller creatures huddled, whimpering, against their larger natural enemies.

Irissa paled as the phenomenon darkened; her eyes fastened upon it as if they could never break free. Inwardly, an icy, intruding blackness smeared the surface of her magical isolation. She felt poised to drown in it as in her own image glimpsed on still, shadowed water — and reached out warding hands.

Then Kendric was beside her, shouting into the sudden tempest that howled abroad. The bands of his encircling arms upheld Irissa's sinking senses, just as the Iridesium circlet clenched her temples as if to keep her head upon her shoulders, to keep her face from drifting upward to impress its swollen features upon the dark, clouded figure that strode the sky in her semblance.

'You are right,' Kendric shouted into the new wind, toward the white, watching face of Finorian. 'This black figure is not animated by Irissa's magic. It is alien!'

'Or too familiar — some new sending of the men?' Finorian suggested.

Kendric shook his head. 'I have seen this image before, and wished I had not. You are right again — Irissa's mercy risks her magic. The sorcerer Geronfrey reaches into your Torloc world, as he has many others, using his stolen, mirror-bound link to Irissa as a bridge. This vision is a dark reflection of her powers, of Irissa herself. In the hands of another, it can destroy her . . . perhaps destroy us all!'

On the opposite bank, the men were seen to motion madly, to brandish artifacts that sparkled in the dim, hot daytime evening like faraway stars.

Feeble sparks of magic danced around their talismans. A particularly bright flash launched an arrow of light at the heart of darkness overhead. It sped skyward like a reversed lightning-bolt, tearing a jagged rent in an ebony flounce of cloud.

Irissa cried out like a sleepwalker and flailed in Kendric's arms. He glanced down to see the earth scorched at her feet.

'Their talismans only strike at *her* through the clouds!' he raged, for the first time finding his physical being a trap. His eyes searched the ranks of restless yet transfixed animals, and found the smallest, whitest among them. 'Felabba!' Kendric demanded urgently.

For the first time, the grass-green eyes flinched from his.

'Felabba,' he urged, 'you know these Torloc forces above dangle from another's perverted grasp. You saved us from

342

Geronfrey's wrath once before. Surely now, when Irissa's very self hangs in doubt, for her sake—'

'We weigh even in the balance, you and I,' the cat replied, sounding genuinely sorrowful. 'If I act, you cannot, and that may weigh heavier upon you in the future than any burden you know, including magic or mortality. I cannot interfere with the weaving of your two fates — for her sake . . . or your sake. Not even for my own.'

Kendric knew the bitterness of those who hold the future in their hands and are helpless to shape it. His strength contained Irissa as a bezel holds a jewel safe from outer harm while the inner facets shatter.

Kendric glanced again to Irissa's face, then rounded on the Eldress. He said her name only, but there was in that one word more of pleading than he had believed himself to possess.

Finorian ignored her victory, watching the battle. 'The men are foolish. Their feeble talismans will not abate that overborn magic,' she predicted with contempt.

The Eldress's sightless eyes pierced the hovering darkness. She sighed, a bland reaction to such imminent doom.

'I see what you say, Wrathman . . . Irissa was never the whole answer, as I thought, but only a piece, and this piece we see above is of Irissa, but not willingly. It is called by Torloc magic but infected with another's malady. It is a thing of our found Edanvant — and from a place more lost than any we know. It comes to devour us all—!'

Finorian's face reflected sudden, insight-illuminated despair. 'Hold Irissa, help her,' she ordered Kendric with new authority, 'and I will, I will . . . I can, I must—'

The Eldress's voice howled, blending briefly with the wailing of the wolves, as if she addressed the wind in its own words. Already the emerald touchstone gleamed green again between her parchment fingers, a jeweled breastplate of shining magical armor.

'*I* will walk the breaking bridge, cast my powers and myself into the ethers! Irissa is not to be sacrificed to her own willingness.'

'We agree on that, old woman,' Kendric said grimly.

Finorian was beyond heeding anything of earth or Edanvant. Her whole aspect faced the sky above. But though her will and magic interwove to make a ladder to the storm-lashed heavens, nothing stirred except the hovering cloud figure of a dark Torloc seeress striding the sky on devouring winds.

Finorian's touchstone gleamed the heavy lurid green that paints the world before a storm. It shone beacon-bright. Some of its color seeped into the blanks of Finorian's eyes. The flaw split the stone with a crack that reverberated thunderously in Kendric's inner consciousness and brought Irissa to struggling awareness in his arms.

Irissa heard first the discordant keening of the anxious beasts, smelled the lightning's after-odor, felt her senses reassemble. Finally the bright, newly twin gleams of the shattered emerald snared her attention. She regarded the cloven touchstone for disbelieving seconds.

'Kendric! She'll destroy herself!' she warned desperately, 'Stop her!'

'We cannot even stop ourselves, much less each other,' he muttered, knowing that only his grip withheld Irissa from a similar and as impulsive self-destruction. His arms tightened to hold Irissa powerless, but his eyes watched Finorian.

The Eldress uplifted the sundered touchstone in her hands and did not seem to hear, not even when Felabba broke from the forefront of the animals and came to address her.

'You are old, seeress, and have wrought much ill in your latter days in service of a greater good seen only by yourself. You called me to Edanvant for reasons other than parting, but I have come, for reasons of my own, and can aid you in your last task as I could not in the others, and as I cannot aid those who are to remain. Go. Leave this tainted element of Edanvant. Undo what you have done. Take the sky as you wish.'

They all watched, stunned, as the touchstone melted from Finorian's fingers into a green mist, a mere exhalation that veiled the Eldress's face and became a writhing mask across its lower portions. The old woman took a deep, battle-ready breath and the tendrils vanished as if inhaled. Finorian began striding up an invisible stair of air, each step taking her higher above their heads. In moments, they could no longer distinguish her pale form against that colorless sky.

Finorian was gone, gone with the last, pale tail of rising smoke. White clouds bubbled above the forest, piling higher and higher.

Irissa's fingers clawed into the muscles of Kendric's arms. 'She cannot . . . Finorian cannot walk on air. Only the dead can defy an earth element's essence. Hariantha of the Inlands did — remember? But Finorian . . .'

'She is dead,' Kendric answered, for he had seen the Eldress's eyes last. For once no guarded double message lay in them, but only blank white resignation.

'Not gone,' a voice announced. Melyconial focused her mismatched eyes on the black seething tapestry above.

Even as they looked, Finorian's spare form reshaped itself large within the paler thunderheads. She boiled whitewater-rapid across the sky, as though riding a whirlwind, her unfocused eyes sweeping the dark image of Irissa that even now flashed lightning to the city towers below — deadly black bolts striking from the emptiness of the holes that were her eyes and smoldering into the earth near the embattled Torloc men.

The men shrank to their knees, smoke spiraling around them, their talismans winking out in a smudge of fog. The dark seeress of the sky gathered her airy image around her. Power glowed behind her midnight exterior, like the sheen of many colors in the black of Iridesium, ready to explode forth in full force.

Every Torloc on either side of the declivity froze in equal fear — except Irissa, who had lapsed into an absent state again, as if drained by her own airborne image.

Before the dark magic could unleash its bright victory, Finorian's cloud figure retaliated in kind. This was no Torloc spat, but sky-high war between the very distilled spirits of the power Within and Without. Brilliant green lightning plowed the swarthy clouds, cutting into the smoky darkness like living knife blades. Thunder growled at the feet of the contending cloud seeresses, mimicking a guardian pet held on a leash not to its liking.

On the land below, the assembled animals hissed and bayed in discordant concert, milling beneath the trees until it seemed they would trample themselves and all Edanvant to death.

On opposite banks, awed Torlocs abandoned their grievances and stared upward, waiting mute as trees for the storm to finish its preliminary buffeting and break the back of the sky, as a farm wife would crack an egg into a bowl, to pour its power down upon them.

In the circle of Kendric's arms, Irissa sagged, abruptly released from linkage to her usurped magic. Her closed eyelids and pale face reflected the jagged scars of green and sable lightbolts ripping the fabric of the heavens. Kendric kept one eye on her and one on the battle above. He strained in the simple task of holding her, of holding her upright — not from any lack of physical strength, but because some unseen force seemed intent on sucking her away in every sense but the physical.

Linked, his hands enfolded each other around her. His fingertips felt the pebbled surface of his ring, felt the cool stones dewing it. Shunstone, Sandstone, Lunestone, Gladestone and Nightstone. The bits of Inlands magic he bore gathered into a mass as his befogged mind renamed the five stones. Plainstone, Copperstone, Silverstone, Greenstone, Blackstone.

His inner eye recounted their colors in turn. Green Gladestone for the Torlocs' fecund forest magic. Lunestone — a hopeful talisman to bear in a world where the sun had fled the sky. Shunstone, plain as honesty, might keep evil from reaching Irissa, docile cousin to unconsciousness as she was at the moment. And copper-colored Sandstone — perhaps it would raise the earth at their feet into a dusty shield to obscure them from the force above.

His thought merged with magic to become fact. Kendric coughed into the gritty result of his own effectiveness, a shield of agitated earth.

That half-hidden skyforce wanted Irissa, he knew. It dreamed of Irissa, named her, called her. It had seeped into the white emanation of her magic, had infused the cloud of

346

herself she had projected upward. It had taken that part of her that even now Finorian fought with her own white expanded image.

And it craved more. Kendric felt that ambition in the trembling of his arms and legs, which seemed so heavy he was tempted to relinquish his hold upon Irissa so he could contend with the agony of upholding his own self. Sweat rained like coldstone tears down his face, although he knew the air around them swirled icily since Finorian had sprung into the sky.

Someone, he decided, had to stop it once and for all.

He glanced about for aid. Ilvanis and Neva stood white and shocked, holding each other as he held Irissa, but mutually. Magic cloaked their very existence, as it had the Rynx when its divided nature had walked as one, but these two were victims of magic, not its wielders, and of no use to him.

The cat, Felabba, sat small and undistinguished before the wall of restive beasts again. She, too, watched; as he looked her green glance crossed his − and looked away. No aid there, for whatever reason. Felabba seemed all beast now − implacably apart from human or Torloc. Her ways had sundered from theirs. Her meddling in their lives seemed a mere memory. She was cat, and a man was a fool to expect succor from a cat, Kendric, the marshman of Rule, reminded himself.

He had been a fool, and he had been aided more than once by a cat, answered the reluctant man of magic within him. Kendric glanced at Irissa again. Inner senses roused by the snap of Finorian's touchstone had faded to outer senselessness again. The wind that plied them all whipped her languorous dark hair around her face until it seemed to weave a fence over her features. Otherwise nothing of Irissa moved. His eye fell at last to the subtle swell of the Overstone pouch under her tunic.

If this was so powerful a talisman, why did no one turn to it? he wondered. The protective cloud of dust the Sandstone had evoked still whirled around them, obscuring them from the others. Perhaps he could reach for the Overstone, find some way to crack its mystery and use it as a shield. That was all he sought — defense.

His arm hurt — the left arm against which Irissa's weight most sagged. That was all. That was why he shifted her suddenly to the tight custody of his right arm and reached with his free, left hand, for the Overstone.

Some instinct told him the act was risky beyond his understanding of the word. Yet what other weapon had he — with his sword strapped to his back, with at least one arm holding Irissa from being utterly subsumed into her darker sky-self, and his grasp on magic shackled by his grip upon the reality of merely holding on?

The ring flashed sullenly on his finger as his hand lifted; he had never read warning so plain. His hand felt lead-weighted, as if the ring bore every pound of doubt-laden mental ore he had ever mined, and more.

The ring. And the stones. And the one last stone he had not considered evoking, the one he would not name, even to himself. The Nightstone of Reygand, of Geronfrey — black as unworked Iridesium; dark as deep, dead water that has never reflected light; sable as the center of every eye on every earth, the very pinprick of night itself.

Reygand. Geronfrey. The words echoed like half-comprehended spelling syllables in his mind. Rengarth. Ilvanis. Neva. They made some pattern, yet ungrasped, some shape larger even than the dueling seeresses etched in the clouds above.

And the Nightstone. In the iris of a slick, black surface, Kendric had seen the shadows dance, and they had worn names too near to bestow on them. All was linked, more finely than a coat of Iridesium mail. He was but one mortal ring of worn metal in the overall scheme, but he would not break.

He called upon the Nightstone then, much as he loathed it, as he loathed his unwilling caretakership of it. He amplified the small puddle of black upon the ring into a lozenge of lengthening darkness until it hovered before him as a glossy shield. Every bit of magic inner and outer he possessed met in that deep, darkly reflective surface, in that hard, nocturnal sliver of shadowed magic. Other things moved in it, things unguessed at, things tenebrously distant.

It expanded, a thing of opaque, thin ebony air, yet as solid as self. It rose, casting a widening shadow, protecting not only himself and Irissa, but the Torlocs on either side of the devastated ravine. It grew as it ascended. Lightning crashed harmlessly to its sheltering surface and rebounded into the clouds from which it had been hurled.

In the sky, bolts of crimson seared Finorian's heaped white figure; greenish streaks slashed into the boiling dark form that had begun as a misty Irissa. This self-stabbing forced the cloudy forms apart enough to form a rift of placid sky. Into that sudden, sky-blue niche the Nightstone shield slowly floated, between the clouds' separate shapes, larger even than the dueling seeresses etched there.

It hovered while Kendric straightened his burden-bent figure, as if spared some weight, as if all weight in Edanvant had levitated to the level of the clouds.

Then the slice of black spun, so swiftly Kendric only glimpsed the bright silver underside it presented to the banks of dark clouds shaped into the semblance of a Torloc seeress. Its black outer side faced the white form that was Finorian.

Together, while every eye except Irissa's watched, the two cloud images hurled as if haunted at the shield, cast themselves into it as ships dash themselves on rocks. A clap of thunder and clash of lightning echoed from every eye and ear in Edanvant. Darkness shattered on a shield of sky-hung silver; lightness pierced a wall of gleaming black. Animals keened as if mourning the passage of death itself.

They were gone, the warring sky seeresses. The sky was blank again. Empty. Innocent. A moment after, the shield spun to present its narrowest edge like a long, black vertical seam in the sky, and vanished, too.

A thread of animal whimpers twined with the retreating wail of wind and softened to a hush. Everything human, animal, or vegetable paused, as if having momentarily forgotten how to go about being itself.

Then Irissa stirred in the crook of Kendric's arm. On his

349

hand the Nightstone shone newly dull, as if he had breathed on it too closely and veiled it with his breath.

He rubbed the ring against his trouser leg and lifted the jewel again. The stone looked permanently dimmed; perhaps calling upon it had skimmed the luster of its magic. Still, everything was as it had been. The forest lay clean with no scum of smoke overshadowing its green expanse. Torlocs stood on the opposite banks of a waterless river of broken woodland and eyed each other at a distance. The silver-touched man and woman from Rengarth wore new wonder on their ever-wondrous expressions. Irissa opened her quicksilver eyes and blinked into Kendric's anxious expression.

Finorian was gone for good. He looked up to a clearing sky and thought he glimpsed a phantom rainbow lurking behind the thinning clouds. The blue benevolence of an ordinary midday radiated down upon Edanvant. No trace of the Eldress lingered either on earth or in the sky, not even a faintly green wisp of wind-driven cloud.

Kendric, disbelieving, looked to the place Finorian had stood when he had last seen her — exactly there, against a backdrop of ominously gathered animals who had sat in silent judgment.

At woods' edge the calming animals watched with newly shy, wild eyes, but Felabba was no longer anywhere to be seen.

CHAPTER TWENTY-TWO

'I have been somewhere,' Irissa said vaguely, shaking off Kendric's custody to lean on her own weight.

'Perhaps there,' he answered, pointing to the empty sky. 'In the clouded Dark Mirror.'

She regarded him for what seemed silent eons. 'No . . .' She spoke with sober slowness, as if only then realizing the possible truth. 'I think the Dark Mirror was in me.'

Brushing tangled hair back from her face, Irissa frowned as she sought to recall what had happened. 'Finorian . . . she strode aloft to confront something when I — faded.'

'In the end, she faded, too.'

Irissa read the rest with her eyes, studying his until she seemed to have memorized their contents. 'She saved us, then, from something we do not comprehend and at a cost we cannot guess.'

'So did Kendric.' Jalonia stepped forward, came to them. 'His was the shield that broke the spell.'

Irissa turned to him, amazed. 'How?'

He shrugged dismissively. 'Sheer luck, I think. I bore a shield when I was a Wrathman. Perhaps I was the only one who thought to use such a simple thing.'

Irissa turned to the place where the passive animals waited.

'Felabba is . . . missing again as well,' Kendric announced before she could discern it for herself.

'Missing? Dissolved like Finorian? Does everything we knew fade away?' she lamented.

'I don't know, but doubt it. There was nothing in that old pricklepuss that would deign to merely dissolve. Perhaps she has matters elsewhere to divert her. I fear we are not so lucky as to have seen the last of her.'

Irissa stared back at him, her silver eyes polished mirror-bright. 'Finorian . . . saved me by her intervention?' He nodded. 'And you by a magically evoked shield?' He nodded again.

She spread her hands wide as if to touch the unfamiliar feelings that invisibly surrounded her, as if to recall the familiar things that had vanished in the past few minutes.

'I would not have thought it of Finorian, that she would fight for me — or that I would hang helpless in the crux of my powers and you would weave the spell that saves me.' Irissa smiled ruefully. 'What use am I, then, who cannot save myself when I would save a people? And now I am the only seeress of my kind in truth,' she added pensively.

'You drew the results of the evil sending to the clouds and saved the land, saved Edanvant,' Kendric consoled her. 'You cannot be expected to save yourself as well. Leave something for me and the Eldress to accomplish,' he added lightly.

She nodded, then sobered again. 'It knew my name, that outer darkness. I hope Finorian destroyed it as it destroyed her, otherwise—'

'Otherwise, like Felabba, it waits.'

Memory made a leap forward. He saw its progress reflected in the sudden blanching of her face.

'Kendric . . . I remember now! And I fear more than one irrevocable phenomenon has laid uninvited hands upon me — one of known evil rather than merely an unknown possibility. For an instant, I saw— There is a darker side of myself kept someplace else.'

He nodded calmly, again. 'I felt the breath of Outside, too. But we have rebuffed it for now. What else can we do but that and hope for the best?'

At last Irissa nodded acquiescence and began taking inventory of the surviving faces around her, trying not to search for Finorian among them, and failing.

The scene looked the same, and yet not the same. Everyone there seemed spiritually disheveled, as if returned from a long and uncomfortable journey without having stirred from the spot. Irissa counted herself as not the least of these unsettled beings, whether they were beasts or Torlocs, men or women. Finorian's absence had torn a great hole in the fabric of the community.

'I wonder what Jalonia does,' Kendric said. 'She seems intent on something.'

His words drew Irissa's dispersed attention to a single point — to Jalonia's figure moving hesitantly to the very rim of the broken wall. As Irissa watched, Jalonia picked her way across great boulders of melted metal until she stood where the wilds fell away to a wide gash of twisted and charred foliage.

'Orvath,' Jalonia offered to the empty abyss, the word half question, half statement and spoken only loud enough for those on her side of the declivity to hear it.

Irissa and Kendric neared the ravine. On the opposite shore of what served as an immense waterless riverbed separating the two camps, small figures moved also — slowly, painfully, as if the men, too, moved in an unhappy dream, devastated by the ill power their talismans had unleashed.

It was impossible to tell which dark figure was Orvath's, not even by some telltale stuttering of movement.

Nevertheless, Jalonia stood and gazed, looking as woodenly faithful as a figurehead on a ship's prow. She raised a hand to shadow her eyes and stared as if she would pierce distance itself with her vision.

Irissa sighed wearily and turned to go back to the forest keep. Kendric caught her tunic sleeve.

'Look!'

She paused. There, opposite them, where the men stood, one figure stepped apart from the many. One small, dark man grew infinitesimally larger in their view as he made his clumsy way to the brink of the broken wall where the land plummeted before him.

'Likely Medoc,' Irissa guessed with reviving interest. Her emotions were seeping back to her from some dark and cold distant exile. 'I always sensed he felt inclined toward reconciliation.'

Kendric demurred. 'Some things call more strongly even than magic, and there are more things you have not named than that darkness in the sky. That is Orvath himself; I know it.'

'Your magic becomes omniscient,' she mocked gently. 'But what's the use, Kendric? What if it is Orvath? It's too late for reconciliation. We Torlocs have truly driven ourselves to our own extremes. Not even Finorian could save us were she here.'

'No, not Finorian . . .' Kendric was silent then, his posture as vigilant as a guardbeast's.

Apparently his interest had a reason. The far figure that he had named as Orvath made a small leap, then knelt. After a long moment it stood, then overstepped the last ridge of fallen wall and moved ahead, toward the abyss — actually *over* the abyss.

'No—!' Irissa stepped forward with the distant figure despite herself. 'He seeks to destroy himself! We must stop him!'

But Orvath — if it indeed was Orvath — did not fall. Yet he clearly stood above where the land had naturally eroded centuries before. Kendric kept quiet, so long that Irissa regarded him suspiciously.

'He stands on air,' she finally complained with narrowed eyes. 'What delusion is this, what new talisman has he found?'

'No talisman. No delusion.' Kendric spoke evenly, as if fearing the mere rise and fall of his breath could disturb something immensely delicate.

'It is magic,' he continued, grinning cautiously. 'A piece of . . . stonework . . . has appeared before Orvath's feet, and he has stepped forward to test it.'

'How can you see that far? Nothing but darkness and death looms beneath Orvath if he would walk on air.'

'That, and now there are the first, inlaid stones of a bridge.' Kendric grimaced. 'Not coldstones, I fear, or other Torloc fancywork, but quite serviceable simple gray stone, as made many bridges in Rule and brought more ordinary folk than Torlocs across less steep gulfs.'

'You! You build bridges now that you cannot see!'

'Aye. I draw upon the bridge within, between my mortal self and Torloc gifts. I feel the pull even from here; something of myself is stretched thin and strong all the way across the gulf.'

Kendric held himself stiffly, as one who performs some terrifying precarious trick. For a mere instant, his eyes flickered to Irissa's.

'If you would begin your own bridge, from our side, it might persuade Jalonia to advance a step or two.'

Stunned by the suggestion, Irissa regarded the tiny figure of Orvath floating at the gulf's opposite edge. She next studied the back of the woman she had been told mirrored her own image. Stubbornness shaped it, and a familiar mute pride that made Jalonia seem like a queen expecting tribute rather than an empty-handed woman examining the depth of the break between herself and her past.

'No,' Irissa harshly counseled herself. 'Let them build their own bridges as they broke them to begin with — by themselves.'

'You grow hard, Torloc,' said a steady voice nearby, 'and that is the last thing that will aid you.'

Irissa's head jerked around. The words were as familiar as the voice, but not the two in tandem. She looked again to Kendric, whose dark eyes narrowed in concentration as she watched, as if the act of speaking just then had dislodged his grip on the frail reins of his magic.

Across the gulf, the small figure that was Orvath — or perhaps was not — stepped the merest bit closer on the foggy semblance of stonework arching up from the ground like a ghostly plow impaled in it.

'I only sought to rejoin those I had been severed from,' Irissa said unhappily. 'That goal has cost me — us — dearer than we know. Torlocs were solely women, as I knew them, and all who remain stand here beside us now. What need have we for more than that?'

'Perhaps *we* do not need more, but *they* do.' Kendric glanced to the cluster of watching women. 'They, too, sought what was lost — each other and both sides of their kind.'

'This was not my quest! Nor yours!' Irissa retorted passionately, feeling a begrudging pity for those who had been pitiless toward her and resenting it. 'How can you tell me where my duty lies? Why should I help them? Why should I become a bridge laid at the feet of their failures? Why should you? Torlocs have brought you only grief.'

She expected a response reeking of grandiose sentiments, appeals to mercy and other noble qualities, including the ignoble one of guilt.

'Not always,' Kendric said quietly, 'although one brings me grief now. Finorian's fondest hope was that your power would resolve the Torloc rift — save she expected a forced reunion with all the cards falling face up. Now, with her gone, and gone for good, your powers balance on the very brink of Torloc reunion, through truce. Had you not come to Edanvant, do you think we would be debating duty on a chasm lip at this moment?'

The speech was long for Kendric's taste. He blew out a gust of breath and grimaced. Sweat dewed his forehead with a circlet of effort. 'It is not simple for one of my limited magical attainments to build on nothing,' he added frankly, 'particularly when it stretches over so much additional nothing. If you will not help them, help me.'

A hiss of exasperation escaped Irissa's lips.

But at the ravine's brink, Jalonia suddenly forsook her frozen position to glance down. Before her eyes, before all their gazes, clear golden blocks of stone popped into being, leading to a meeting with air.

Jalonia's tentative foot reached out, then planted itself on the amber surface. It held. She balanced statue-still on a pedestal of honeyed stone overlooking the desolate land.

The stone, multiplying, probed forward another foot or so. Jalonia's feet followed the abuilding bridge's lead, moving farther out over emptiness.

Step by step, stone by conjured stone, the bridge erected itself on air. The two who had committed to treading it moved forward with every segment as it became visible, each growing larger in the other's eyes and smaller in the sight of those on the more solid ground they left farther and farther behind them.

'It *is* Orvath,' Kendric noted smugly as he etched another reach of gray stone and the man's figure stepped near enough to identify.

Irissa remained silent, and Kendric did not dare take his eyes from his magical construction. But the golden blocks piled up before Jalonia, leading her along a gilded road.

Kendric's construction arched between the spans; Irissa's met sharply, leaving an airy pyramid. This design discrepancy seemed not to hamper the destiny of the bridge, which now had spanned two-thirds of the ravine. Some foresight — or perhaps a touch of overvaulting ambition — had cast the bridge as wide as a road many could walk. Irissa's version matched Kendric's — both in width and the way it aimed straight for the oncoming selvage edge of its opposite span.

With their next, mirroring steps, the two who walked the span stood closer to each other than those they had left behind. They still moved slowly, dependent on the stones that sprung into place before their feet, trusting the phenomenon more than they could possibly trust each other even now.

At last they stood nearly face to face, though no watcher could discern the expressions on their faces. They stood but half a body length apart and would take no further steps.

Kendric wrinkled his brow and clenched his fists and drew on magic old and new and unheard of. Yet no more gray stones would attach themselves to those he had evoked. A gap remained.

Irissa needed no gestures of magical striving. But her silver eyes could stare at the interrupted span until they, too, turned golden. No more amber building blocks appeared, as if from air, to bridge the narrow gulf.

'Ah!' Kendric relinquished his grasp on the bridge with an impatient sound. 'They shall have to overcome the rest themselves. Is that enough adversity for you?' he asked Irissa.

She, too, felt magic tension ebb within her. 'It will have to be. I wonder what they talk of.'

357

'Of things that are not our business for the moment, thank Finorian, wherever she has gone.' He shifted the set of the sword upon his back. 'Your choice of stonework looks suspiciously like the fiery blocks from which a certain sorceress of Rule constructed her forest castle,' he added.

'You would have a bridge,' Irissa returned demurely. 'I cannot be responsible for what well my magic dipped its bucket into. I fear I never did see much of the common gray stones of Rule.'

'Then you shall see them now if your golden stones do not let us down. I've a yen to examine my handiwork closer up.'

'Not yet.' Irissa watched the two in the middle of the bridge. Even as she spoke, Jalonia turned and raised a gesturing arm.

'It appears we are invited to cross.' Kendric took a first step toward the chasm. Irissa hung back.

'How can we be sure the men will not greet us with enmity?'

'We cannot,' said Kendric, putting a hand to the sword upon his back.

'Besides, how will we all cross the gap?' Irissa asked, eyeing the distance that still separated the reunited Orvath and Jalonia.

'We will employ the oldest magic,' Kendric replied promptly, leading her onto the first span of air-supported stones. 'We will use our feet — and jump.'

They were the first from the forest side to set foot upon the bridge, but behind them came all the women, Dame Agneda panting at their rear. Last of all came Ilvanis and Neva, holding hands and wandering like two enchanted children into a world of greater enchantment.

'The animals!' Irissa stopped as they neared midbridge and turned to face the forest. Far behind them loomed a solid wall of green, each leaf nodding breezy sylvan farewell. Not a creature was to be seen. All had melted back into their woodland retreats, each and every one. At some time while the bridge was growing, the unnatural link between beast and humankind had broken. The beasts no longer judged, and the people no longer deserved their mute judgment.

'Felabba was wrong for once,' Kendric said abruptly.

The raven wings of Irissa's raised eyebrows requested plainer speech.

'Reunions are *not* overrated,' he explained, then smiled broadly. 'But I had already learned that in the Inlands of Ten.'

No reunion with Orvath and Jalonia awaited the company when they reached the end of the bridge.

'They have withdrawn to Citydell,' Medoc explained as he came to greet Kendric and Irissa, the last two to set foot again on solid, unensorcelled ground since they had helped the women leap the longish gap and now came as rear guard.

Irissa's face reflected sheer relief. Separately, Jalonia and Orvath provided her with enough conundrums of a personal nature; united, the strain would double. Relief fled as she reconsidered. If reuniting one Torloc man and woman was a thorny proposition, reconciling forty-some would be thumb-stabbing work — and who was to attempt it now, with Finorian gone?

Two uneasy clusters of Torlocs — the women near the bridge and the men near the open city gates — eyed each other uncertainly. The men were well armed, but looked shamefaced for that very fact as they surveyed the unarmed women they were so set on opposing and defeating. The women answered with mute suspicion, the anger in their eyes tempered by an edge of curiosity.

Irissa, Kendric, and Medoc had learned enough of each other to speak civilly despite the recent struggle.

'A formidable construction,' Medoc began uneasily, admiring the incomplete bridge. 'How wide is the gap?'

'A stride,' said Kendric.

'Two strides,' Irissa had guessed at the same time.

'A good sword's length — three feet.' Kendric clarified his inborn overestimation of distance. 'Orvath and Jalonia would step no closer, it seemed, and even magic cannot bridge such a natural gap.'

'Perhaps they make their own bridges now,' Medoc speculated, twinkling with what would have been grandfatherly glee had he not so resembled a man in his late youth.

'I hope so.' Kendric frowned. 'Even a leapable gap is an inconvenience. I had no idea so many Torloc dames made up our party until I served as the recipient of their bounding forms at the city side of the gulf.' He stretched his long arms achingly. 'I feel I've gone a round in the practice yard.'

'A festy thing indeed — an unexpected hole.' Ludborg, plump as a pumpkin, had amiably rolled into their midst. ' 'Twas how I lost Rengarth — or Rengarth lost me — to begin with. Welcome back, my attenuated friends, to the city of Edanvant. I trust your reception shall be more hospitable now that all have recognized the folly of this feud.'

'We saw our own folly writ large in the sky,' Medoc admitted for the rest. 'Our very blood turned to coldstone in our veins.' His inquiring glance drew nods of agreement from the gathered Torloc men, who managed to look sheepish despite their Iridesium-mailed dignity.

'Was it truly Irissa in the clouds?' Medoc went on eagerly. 'We who never thought to see seeresses again stood stone-still to see them sky-high and dueling some murky evil beyond our ken and certainly our evoking. Outside knows we meant only to dismay the women, not destroy them . . . or ourselves. And where is Finorian, who fought for us all in the end? Perhaps she deems herself unwelcome here, as she has been before, but a truce seems called for and cannot be made without her.'

'It will have to be,' Kendric said. 'The Eldress did indeed drive back an Outside evil, as you suspected. We won its absence at the price of hers.'

'Ah.' Medoc seemed lost for words. He glanced around. 'Well, the rest are all safe, sound, and rejoined at last.' Medoc regarded the silent, huddled women. 'I doubt we will harbor enmity of this ilk again, or worse — act upon it.'

His voice lowered as he turned Irissa and Kendric with him to face the city. 'I used the dagger only at Orvath's insistence. Now that I have seen what it can do, I would employ it again at the urging of no man, woman, or demon. Were a wailwraith to rise from my basin-water dripping blood and demanding that I draw the dagger, I would refuse.'

'Where is it?' Irissa asked, 'the thing that caused the fire and fog?'

Medoc pointed shamefacedly to the ground at his feet.

'It will not stay put in a chest, but appears atop it mere moments later. I locked it in an Iridesium casket wound round with chains of that metal as thick as my small finger.' He waggled that sturdy appendage. 'By dinnertime, it had appeared beside my plate. The only way I've found to keep it dormant is to impale it in something living.'

Irissa shuddered.

'Hence, the earth.' Medoc's long forefinger pointed downward where the dagger drove deep into the grasses. 'Apparently what we walk upon is more sentient than we realize, although deeply so. I would be rid of it, but know not how.'

Ludborg squatted — if one so equidistant from top to bottom and side to side as he could be said to squat — and regarded the talisman.

'Ah . . . the haft is Rengarthian, did you know that, my height-racked friend? Rengarthian enamel-work set in copper. The blade, of course, must have been forged in the Salamander Tewel of the Paramount Athanor near the Spectral City.'

Ludborg straightened, or simply expanded. His sleeve ends wriggled, as if agile, boneless fingers were tapping consideringly inside them. His hood lifted to aim its disconcerting emptiness at Kendric.

'Yes, forged there, I think, at the place called the Far Keep, for short. Where the sword our tall friend here carries was fired — in its original incarnation, of course, not this version.'

The sight of a seven-foot-tall Wrathman with his jaw dropped would have been amusing had it not been so serious a matter. Ludborg ignored the effect his incantation of names both familiar and utterly alien had made upon the former residents of Rule. He bent to touch dagger haft with the end of his sleeve, then rose and spun again to face Medoc.

'How came you by this toy?'

For once Medoc looked abashed. 'I . . . I found it in the gate as I departed Rule upon my quest for a talisman. It was . . . given to me by a woman—'

'A lady's dagger? Indeed. The only ladies in Rengarth who bear arms— But go on. Your tale is most intriguing.'

'I was about to say . . . it was given to me by a woman who was dying, I think. She was pale beyond parchment; even the whirling colors of the gate left her untouched. Her face wore the mask of pain and fear and flight concealed by will alone. She was — nearly as round as you, Ludborg — so great with child it was as if the babe bore her rather than the other way around. I feared for her, but not for myself, oddly enough, though she warned me I might go where she had come from — and mislike it.

'She gave me that dagger, pulling it from her cloak where it acted as a pin, and added this medallion to it.' Medoc lifted the gold circle on his chest. 'She said the dagger's magic weighed against her now and she could not cross the gate while it pinned her spirit to where she had been. She said it was difficult enough to bear a Willing One through the gate — those were her words, as if there was something marvelous in it — and she could not afford the millstone of magic.

'I, of course, regarded this as a happy omen — a talisman so easily won — and when I took it, the rainbow swirled her away. I always assumed she went to Rule, although I don't know why. I came, without any trouble, directly to Edanvant, the only one of our wandering company to have had so soft a time of it.' Medoc sighed deeply. 'Orvath fared infinitely worse and came away empty and half-handed for it.'

Ludborg clapped his sleeves together and performed a rolling dance that made Irissa and Kendric step back in polite amazement.

'You left Rule long before Orvath, did you not?' Ludborg asked Medoc, giggling.

'Not very long before, a matter of five or ten years as mortals count it.'

Ludborg's giggles had risen in pitch to cackling. 'Long

362

enough! Long enough. So that is where Phoenicia fled! Phoenicia, Reginatrix of Rengarth, until the Usurper came and poisoned Ajaxtus the Heirlord. So she escaped through a gate, a gate to Rule!'

'She escaped to death,' Medoc interrupted dryly. 'I have never seen a face so filled with it.'

Ludborg was suddenly subdued. 'Perhaps . . . perhaps. I would have to consult the crystals to be sure. In the meantine . . .' He spun quickly to Kendric. 'In the meantime, Sir Wrathman of the Far Keep, perhaps you would care to dispose of this festy talisman of Rengarth for us. I think you are the only one of us who can by right do so.'

'By might or by magic?'

'By any means you can.'

Kendric bent smoothly to draw the dagger from the earth. He weighed it experimentally upon his palm.

'Those are − er − runes, the figures on the handle,' Ludborg instructed delicately. 'Rengarthian runes.'

'Deviltry,' Kendric dismissed it. He thought for a moment while Irissa watched, wondering how he would rid himself of a thing that clearly intended to haunt its holder.

He answered her unspoken speculation with action instead of words, taking the blade tip between his fingers, pulling back his arm and casting it hard and high into the endless clear sky. So simple a solution should not have worked with such a fell talisman, but it did.

End over end the Rengarthian dagger flew effortlessly upward, as if propelled by will as well as skill. It seemed to penetrate even the reassembling rainbow itself, not seen over the city until this day. It flashed and turned, casting its enamel-work runes to face forward and back as it rolled through empty air.

It stabbed the rainbow and sent a different shade earthward the farther skyward it went − crimson first, then gold, green, and finally silver. On the last quick, silver note, it winked out, never having met the apex of its own flight.

The others looked amazed to Kendric, who shrugged his ignorance. 'It seems to be my lucky day,' he explained.

'Methinks the thing eager to flee you, friend Kendric,' Ludborg noted. 'I will ask the crystals what they make of this.'

'Ask your crystals what you will,' Kendric said caustically. 'That does not mean I will swallow their answers.'

But Irissa was silent beyond the weariness of her state and trailed the party back to the Citydell like a burr swept up mindlessly in an endless train of self-congratulation.

Through the city gates, the common people of Edanvant gathered, wary of the reunion of more Torlocs but hopeful for having seen the clouds swallow the smoke-beast. Eyes narrowed anxiously in worried faces; their mouths folded into taut silence.

Only Irissa of all of that relieved and suddenly celebratory company echoed the city folks' aspects in her own. Only Irissa kept silent, and thought.

Habit breaks hard.

Twenty-odd Torloc men lounged on one side of the trestle table in the great hall of Citydell. Twenty-some Torloc women sat stiffly on the other.

The Iridesium-veined peach glass ceiling high above warmed the daylight like Spicemullen wine before melting it down upon them, but even that mellow radiance could not illuminate shadows formed of suspicion and long severance.

The men, nervous, toyed with their talismans and daggers, shifting uneasily so that the chime of mail rang constantly. The women, worried, sat stiller and stiffer, their white faces freezing into a multiplicity of Finorian's forbidding aspect.

Irissa and Kendric had settled between the two groups at the table's abandoned head — or foot, depending on one's point of view.

No one spoke.

'Finorian, at least, would not have allowed a lull in the conversation,' Kendric at last said to Irissa.

She sighed. 'Felabba, at least, would have carped at us until both sides felt too shamed to keep tongue-tied. I will miss her.'

'Ludborg—' they started to say together, then laughed. Kendric resumed speaking first.

'He at least would have entertained us with his crystal-casting during what will apparently be a truce as silent as the Torloc disaffection was long.'

Before Irissa could agree, a figure rustled into the too-silent hall. Jalonia, her smooth brow fretted, stopped before them both.

'Your father wishes to see you,' she told Irissa a bit breathlessly.

Something in Irissa gathered itself. 'Have you become his messenger now?'

Jalonia's white skin flushed. 'The message is mine. Orvath is . . . unwell. The events, the long walk across the bridge and back—' Her amber eyes flashed an emotion Irissa had never glimpsed in Jalonia before — parental impatience. 'The reasons are unimportant. Will you come or no?'

Irissa's glance interrogated Kendric's, but Jalonia spoke again before he could.

'Do you think I would invite my daughter into danger?' she demanded. 'This is something she must do alone.'

Kendric studied the depths of Jalonia's eyes until she moved restively. 'You are not the same, selfless woman I met in the forest keep. I don't know if I can trust Irissa to you.'

'You must, man of Rule. She was mine first, and I lost her, as will you if you do not let her resolve her past.'

'You were Orvath's before Irissa was yours,' he answered. 'Whose good do you serve first?'

'No one's — and all's.'

'It is my choice,' Irissa interjected. 'I will go with her,' she told Kendric. 'I know too much now for Orvath to hurt me.'

He snorted impolitely in answer, but let the two women leave unescorted.

Irissa found herself rushing to keep pace with her mother across the unnaturally silent expanse of the great hall and down a high, shadow-choked passage.

There were stairs to climb, chambers to cross, towers to

corkscrew around, and tapestries to brush by, although no Citydell embroidery showed a single-horned bearing-beast dappled with gold and silver thread.

Jalonia hurried forward, glancing over her shoulder repeatedly to mark Irissa's presence. They moved too rapidly to speak, and Irissa began to dread confronting what waited at the end of this long, dark hurtle to reunion.

An aperture, curtained in night-black brocade, gaped before them. Jalonia raised the fabric and ducked under it into the reassuring brightness beyond. Irissa, her palms fast upon her sword pommel and the Overstone pouch, followed.

There was no missing Orvath. He sat in a throne-high chair in a chamber so lit with candelabras it appeared feverish. Flames danced spark-quick, casting spasmodic shadows on the pale, surrounding stones.

In his chair, half-lounging, half-lying, Orvath remained still, only his dark eyes moving, and then only because the reflections of the flames cavorted on their opaque surface.

'Pardon my not greeting you upright,' he said on seeing Irissa. 'My one leg tells me it has had enough of standing this day, and the other supports it. Welcome to Citydell, daughter.'

'Do you mean that?' Irissa asked curiously.

His lips folded. 'As much as I ever did, to anyone. I am not a welcoming man, Irissa. I do not welcome even life — or have not for many years. As I told you when you first came to Citydell, my regard for you was no more — or no less — than my regard for any other. Including myself.'

Jalonia went to stand beside him in mute distress, her hand molding itself to the stiff contour of his damaged shoulder.

'It is the side my heart sits on, Jalonia,' Orvath said wearily, 'which was frozen in my encounter with the Inlands wizard. I feel your touch, but it does not truly touch me. Too much water has gone under the bridge, no matter how magically it is erected now, for Torlocs to mend the rents that have torn them apart — whether as Torlocs in general, as men and women, or as you and I.'

Despite brave words to Kendric, Irissa felt dangerously

366

abandoned to see Jalonia physically align herself with Orvath in the face of his inflexible words. Irissa forced herself to regard the man and woman confronting her as possibly hostile strangers.

'Then you did not truly wish to see me?' she asked Orvath politely, seeking release.

His head shook before Jalonia could contradict him. 'No. What is there to discuss between you and I, between a marshal of talismanic magic and a seeress of Far Focus? We are still as opposed as ever — we men's talismans against the women's pride, for the women have no power left to them now that Finorian's gone, except for you. Had you not been born, had you not been born a seeress, this contention would be over. The women would do as we wish — what other recourse have they? You alone can prolong this division. So I see in you a future I do not truly wish to see. You are inevitable to me — inevitably my daughter, inevitably a stranger, an enemy—'

'Irissa multiplies your fatherhood,' Jalonia broke in, seeking to bridge bottomless chasms with the spidersilk of sentiment. 'She carries another.'

'Mother!' Irissa reproved for the first time in her life, half in annoyance, half in embarrassment.

Orvath stared from one woman to the other — so alike and yet so different in themselves and their relationship to him.

'Women always fancy generation answers all. Should I rejoice that I am once again responsible for the spawning of a seeress?'

Both women, repudiated by the same blow, stood silent as Orvath twisted his head to look up at Irissa's mother. His eyes softened slightly.

'But it is not your fault, Jalonia. Now that we have talked I know that you never wished me to leave Rindell, that Finorian ill-served us both in the belief that our separation would better serve some distant reunion of our kind. Yet you must see that your loyalties were already divided. It was easy to bid me your farewell when you would soon be welcoming another to your existence!'

'No!' Jalonia's strong hands strangled the high finials atop

367

Orvath's chair. 'Irissa was never your rival. I was young, and terrified to bear a child alone — yet men's missions were mysteries not to be gainsayed, like Finorian's magic. I thought it my — duty — to subjugate my lone desires to the needs of all. Surely you can understand that?'

'Finorian wanted me gone!' Orvath argued forcefully. 'Not for the excuse of a talisman, but because she foresaw Irissa's seeresshood. She would not have shaped my daughter unopposed had I been there.'

'Perhaps that's true,' Jalonia admitted, 'but—'

'I don't think Finorian was that afraid of you, Orvath,' Irissa broke in.

'What?' He looked at her, his brows fiercely knit.

'I don't think Finorian sent you deliberately to your destruction, that's all,' she added, knowing what a blow to his pride she dealt; but then, his opinion of her was not lightly felt. 'She truly wanted the talisman and thought you the one to fetch it. Thrangar was the only remaining Torloc warrior, but a Wrathman couldn't undertake a Torloc mission. Besides, carrying one of the Six Swords would have enhanced his latent magic, and Finorian certainly wouldn't have wanted an empowered male to find so potent a talisman as the Overstone.' Irissa was beginning to understand the devious ways of power. 'But her motives were good. She told me the Overstone egg could unlock a gate to the Outside and hoped that we all — men and women — would find another Edanvant there, a place without a past for us to quarrel over.'

'Then take us there yourself, Seeress!' he challenged.

Irissa couldn't help smiling as her hand rhythmically loosened and tightened upon the Overstone. Her body heat had warmed the pouch until her palm was damp.

'You are impatient to traverse a gate when a similar journey brought you to so ill a state. This is our Edanvant, Orvath. We must make the best of it, as we are.'

'Then I am the worst of it,' he said, his right foot shifting harshly on the stones. 'And I worsen. This — contention in the sky, it seems to have shaken even the feeble grip I kept upon my diminished self. I can hardly walk — or move — at all now. But my weakness does not affect my ability to lead. We men will not relinquish what we have gained. We will not bow to the will of a seeress again.'

An expression of peace touched Orvath's harsh features. 'I am not sorry my last steps were taken to Jalonia. If you were unwelcome in my eyes, Irissa, it was partly because you impressed them with the memory of her and all I would forget. That is not your fault, nor that you wear the eyes of Finorian. But it is there between us.'

She shivered and nodded, feeling again the pitiless draining of self that had come when Orvath had taken the Overstone.

Behind him, Jalonia spoke again, her face set.

'I thought that there could be no greater wrong done than that Orvath did when he left me—'

'Or you did when you let me leave,' he interjected.

'But even as I found our common misunderstanding melting in the crucible of time, I have learned today of a greater wrong. Orvath, when you confessed how you tried to wrest the Inlands talisman from your own child—'

'I had never seen her! She was child only to accident. And the talisman was promised *me*—!'

'And not only from your child, but your child's child, although unknown, and as unborn to Irissa as she was to me when you left . . . Orvath, no matter how we Torlocs quarrel over public issues, you must undo your private misdeed—'

'Has this not occurred to me in my sleepless nights and dreamless days? But how?' he demanded, burying his face in the cradle of his good hand. 'Nothing undoes in this world but death, and that is a long time coming to a Torloc.'

The two women were silent over Orvath's bowed head, their eyes meeting for many moments.

'You talk of death so much I would take you for a mortal,' Irissa finally said, the cool control of a seeress edging into her demeanor. 'Perhaps you contracted your melancholy in the Inlands, grappling with the deathless wizard Delevant.'

'Only a seeress could name the unnameable,' Orvath answered thickly.

'Oh, Delevant was nameable. There was great will — and great greed in what remained of him. By embracing him, even to contend, you embraced all that evil and contracted some of it. It froze half your heart as well as your body, I think.'

'Now you sound like Finorian,' Orvath sneered with deliberate effort, 'full of high theory and magical mysteries.' Still his face remained hidden in his hands.

Irissa stepped nearer to the chair, to the man crouched within it like some beast contemplating a spring. She knew his strength ebbed, but approaching him took more courage than she was sure remained in her.

Behind him, Jalonia held her breath, watching her daughter take yet another risk with a father who had not proven himself worthy of any.

'So we must be what we must be.' Irissa drew herself up, her fingers as instinctively moving to the Overstone pouch under her tunic, as Finorian's had once clung to the emerald touchstone. 'That is all the more reason for us to resolve what differences we can. Below us the long-separated Torlocs eye each other across a table. We have no such convenient barrier. I speak to you eye to eye, Orvath, as seeress to unempowered Torloc. I tell you that I will try my utmost to do as Finorian ultimately wanted — to negotiate a truce between our severed people. I will speak for the women, if you will speak for the men.'

Orvath did not move, his eyes hidden behind the screen of his fingers, his left hand jerking slightly where the stiff fingers curled into the carven armrest.

'But first,' Irissa said, taking a deep breath, 'we must speak to each other, as each other; see each other as each other. Then it will not be so easy to hate.'

Orvath remained motionless, almost as though afraid to move or speak.

Cautiously, Irissa knelt before her father, as she would to a sulking child. She dredged the thong holding the

Overstone pouch from inside her tunic and stretched open the drawstring.

Even the sound of breathing deserted the chamber as Irissa turned the pouch's contents onto her palm. A pale stone, egg-shaped, balanced in the curve of her hand, its bright ruby veining glowing in the dimness.

'The dead stone lives,' Irissa told Orvath. 'Life within death; death within life. It is always a choice. Here. You may not have it — it contains the life in me. This stone is the most dangerous thing I bear because it is the most precious. But you may . . . share it. For a moment.'

'No!' His good hand waved the object away before masking his eyes again. 'Cursed thing of pain and separation, and most cursed for separating me from myself above all! I am not worth finding, as you told Medoc—'

'He told you that?'

Orvath glanced at Irissa. 'He is my father,' he said ironically. 'A father can say many unpleasant things. And I tell you one now, daughter of my darkness. I was wrong, and in that wrong lies more of myself than I can ever find in rightness. Some things cannot be redeemed, not even by mercy. There is nothing left for us to do but continue playing the parts destiny has cast us in — enemies to the death.'

Above them came the raw echo of Jalonia's sob.

Irissa, her face reflecting the Overstone's vivid pulsing, was still a moment. Her hand extended, slowly, until the Overstone shone into her father's face.

He cringed from that small, magical light, as if something within him wished to be well away. His hand made a fist. The fist could have pushed Irissa's arm away, could have sent the Overstone egg rolling across the hard stone floor and Irissa sinking into instant oblivion. There would be no redeeming the past or any form of future then.

'Leave me to my misery,' Orvath begged. 'It is easier. I understand it.'

'So do I,' Irissa said, surprised to find that was true.

His hand lowered. 'You risk much for little.'

'I risk much for much — the slender hope of a Torloc

371

reconciliation must begin somewhere. Finorian always said I came with too little too late. She is gone, and perhaps meant better than any of us guessed, but there is that in me that would like, for once, to prove her utterly wrong.'

Orvath's self-disgust softened in his eyes. 'You forgive me . . .?'

'You deserve it.'

He caught the double-edged import of her comment and chuckled bitterly. 'You sounded, for a moment, like your father's daughter.'

'Thank you.'

'That is no compliment — yet.'

Irissa wordlessly proffered the Overstone.

Orvath stared into its shifting surface. 'A fell thing, magic,' he said, licking his lips. 'I was mad to covet it. I would be madder to trust a seeress. Take it away! Your human forgiveness is more than I deserve.' He finally met her eyes without wincing. 'I am sorry, Irissa, that I fathered only fear in you. Perhaps someday we can begin again, but not now, not with this . . . talisman. It is not necessary.'

'I insist,' Irissa said gently. 'I insist you have it for a moment. I am my father's daughter, and I insist. Who can gainsay that?'

Orvath's iron heart, lightening within him, sank again at her words. He saw the face of force and it wore his own flesh. Much as he now loathed the Overstone, so that he shrank at the notion of touching it, he recognized her inherent right to make him do so.

Trembling with effort and mocking himself even more, he lifted his useless left arm, braced it on his right, and brought the time-curled fingers to the ember-bright egg.

Irissa's silver eyes flashed satisfaction. Orvath knew a mixed moment of dread and self-reproach. He seemed to be drowning in a silver sea. Nothing of the room remained but light — burning, blazing, sizzling light. His fingertips seared. Fire streaked up his arm to his shoulder. If flared down one side of his chest and branded itself along the length of his leg.

He jerked his head so hard it resounded on the wooden

chairback, further confusing him. His body burned as if alight on a pyre, and death no longer seemed a welcome friend. His eyes, rolling up, saw Jalonia hovering above him. For a moment he thought himself a wailwraith in a pool of flames and saw her face through burning water. He raised a hand, toward it, to reach out and touch it.

He reached a hand through buoyant, cooling water, through the still pond above him. He reached up a hand, his left hand, and found the flaming in his bones had faded. He found he could name the fire that had coursed through him from the Overstone, for now it inhabited half his body, the frozen half. The name of the fire was . . . feeling. Unfrozen feeling.

His fingertips grazed the side of Jalonia's face, setting one of her braids swinging. Orvath looked down quickly. The same face, or very like, looked up at him. For a moment he saw not the seeress. His child knelt by his knee, by his easily flexed left knee, holding some clever toy upon her open palm and smiling.

His pliant fingers stretched, then reached to touch the now-muted Overstone.

'Today,' said Orvath, 'I've come at last to Edanvant. Tomorrow,' he added, promising nothing, 'will see what we shall make of it.'

CHAPTER TWENTY-THREE

Twelve ice-carved empress falgons sat the long banquet table in the great hall at Citydell that night.

Forty-six Torlocs, a man of Rule, a lost Rengarthian, and two recently found strangers dallied along the benches. No one sat at either head or foot of the endless table, and no center seat served as informal throne for any ruling couple.

Yet couples there were, as there had not been before. Irissa and Kendric, as at first; Ilvanis and Neva, as once long before; and, at last — again — Jalonia and Orvath.

Irissa had left her father with Jalonia, and it had been many hours before they rejoined the rest in the great hall. What the two Torlocs had said, for how long, or where, no one in the hall save they knew. But they had emerged from their closeting with one, reunited mind and apparently determined to spread such similar accord among all other Torlocs.

Orvath's formerly icy demeanor had fled to some unnamed corner of the fortress. The Torloc men noticed the absence of the physical stiffness that infected his figure, but seemed too awestricken to comment.

To the Torloc women, Jalonia, in turn, could be seen to have shed her dull passivity. She walked with a firmer step, spoke with a louder voice, and smiled with a brighter eye than she had before.

'We shall see how long *this* lasts,' Kendric the Skeptic murmured as he passed the saltcellar to Irissa and surveyed the subdued, but peaceable Torlocs.

Irissa smiled but remained thoughtful. 'I wish them all they have not had, and — with time — I think they'll have it. Yet I hardly knew them before, and I only begin to know them now. My quest was not for my past, but my future.'

'Perhaps they are the same,' Kendric returned.

She regarded him quickly, finding his face sober despite the buffing effect of softening candlelight, its warrior's angles sharpened by a touch of the same malaise she felt. Dispersing the forest devastation and healing her father through the Overstone had been exhausting work.

'Kendric, we must talk—'

But Ludborg stepped forward then, into the hot exhalation of air shimmering before the great roaring lion's mouth of the fireplace.

'Your attention, Torloc gentlemen and Torloc damen, illustrious visitors . . .' Here he bowed, or mostly rolled, in the direction of Ilvanis and Neva.

'And Kendric — man of . . .' Ludborg's sleeve tips tied themselves into an ambiguous gesture. 'Man of — mystery. You seem no longer a man of Rule,' Ludborg added hastily as Kendric shifted to express his disagreement with that characterization.

The sleeves fluttered ingratiatingly as the exiled Rengarthian went on.

'We gather to celebrate the end to old mysteries and the beginning of new ones. Behold the crystal, moon of my delectation.' A gleaming translucent ball popped into the space between Ludborg's encompassing wings of cloth.

Once again the globe spun in his tenuous grasp, creating illusive selves that stretched Ludborg's short limbs wide. They fell in the wholesale way of a deck of cards, the lucent spheres — at once and everywhere. The chime of their shattering rang like windblown tinsel in the vast chamber, a sound delicate and exquisitely musical for a brief, destructive moment.

'Who will read the shards?' Ludborg intoned. 'Who wishes to stare the future in the face?'

'Not I.'

'Nor I.'

First Jalonia had spoken, then Orvath. They turned to each other, surprised by their common choice.

'We will make our future, not read it,' Jalonia said at last.

375

A murmur of agreement raced up and down each side of the table.

'Then you, who — born again — have no past,' Ludborg suggested, his faceless hood rotating to the dazzling white forms of Ilvanis and Neva.

They rose as one and came to stand among the shards, the long, fur-drenched sleeves of Neva's gown stirring the scattered bits.

She bent suddenly, graceful as a lily nodding to its image in the waiting water below, and cradled a great, barely broken shard in her hands. It sat their curve like a crystal ladle while she gazed into its empty translucent bowl, almost as though to read the lines of her palm through it.

Her expression darkened even as her light skin whitened seemingly beyond possibility. Ilvanis, alarmed, bent to retrieve a smaller shard and studied it as if to share the same volume that Neva consulted.

But Neva, oblivious to him for once, rose at last and, step by breathless step, as if the broken orb contained some invisible fluid she feared to spill a drop of, made her way back to the table. She sat there and balanced the shard before her, still sipping from it with her eyes.

'It is Rengarth,' she said, in mixed tones of recognition and first acquaintance. 'My home. Our home. The home of our father, the Heirlord Brenhall; of myself, Neva. And of him. Ilvanis.'

The last word fell from her lips like a pearl; if the shard had contained water, it would have rippled at her breathing of the name. Then she frowned.

'Then came the Usurper. Then came death, Brenhall's death. Magic. Despair. Envy. We are the rightful heirs, we deserve better than this — this — exile. Ah, death comes and with it another kind of death. I feel light, lighter than air — and then I feel no more. Neva is no more. Ilvanis is no more. Eternal Neva; eternal Ilvanis. Now we are . . . Rynx.'

Neva's golden eyes flashed wider yet. 'Rynx, set upon an alien land to fulfill an alien destiny and guard an alien entity

376

at a gate to an alien place. Lonely . . . lonely as our prisoner, our partner in exile. Delevant.'

She lifted the shard as she would a wassail, then smashed it to the tabletop. It splintered on the rough wooden boards. Slivers trembled into still silence.

Ilvanis held the shard he'd chosen but never read. Now his fingers pinched it into disregarded dust. 'She saw the past, Conjuror, that we have not recalled these hundreds of years!'

'Hundreds!' Kendric's exclamation only echoed the astonishment of even the long-lived Torlocs. Millennia lay between the distant scenes Neva had recalled and her present form.

She nodded her dazed belief, looking down at her silken white gown. 'It is what I wore the day the Usurper called Ilvanis and myself to him. He was young for an heirlord, too young for heirs of his own, although he had been old enough in magic to defeat our father. Usurpers were always challenging any ruler of Rengarth. So he was wise beyond years — and foolish beyond wisdom. He would not slay the brother and sister who could contest his rulership, but banish them beyond even the recall of physical form.' Her hands fluttered to her face, covering the golden eyes.

Ilvanis stepped behind her, his shard-dusted fingers riding on her shoulders. He addressed the company fiercely, like one forced to make certain harsh realities clear to them.

'I see now, too. We stood between the Usurper and his unbegotten heirs. The rulership could have gone to any promising contender — Neva, myself. The sorcerer-Usurper spelled us there, in his throne room, in the light of midday. He joined us eternally — we were twins, after all — in the shared form of a misbegotten beast, half wolf, half owl. Only the gift of speech was left us. That, and some magic that fell to us upon our father's death, when some — other — force set us down in the Cincture and put us as guard on fallen Delevant. We had no memory of our former personages until we unaccountably . . . separated . . . on our arrival here in Edanvant. I know not why—'

'I do.'

They all looked to Ludborg, but Irissa had spoken. She paused to brush her forebraids over her shoulders.

'Edanvant separated you, and Edanvant now unites you, as it reunites itself. That is why you read no future in the crystal shards; the future begins for you now, as you begin to know yourselves and your own history. You begin at the beginning — here and now.'

Kendric's attention was drawn from contemplating Irissa and the disparate parts of the Rynx in turn by a subtle pull upon his sleeve.

Ludborg lurked obsequiously at his elbow.

'Kind sir, Lord of the Short Phrase and the Long Sword, he who once called the Far Keep his unseen home, please glance into my shard. Someone must see his future, or my credibility as a scryer is shattered, so to speak.'

'My future is in my hands, not my eyes,' Kendric objected.

'One glance,' Ludborg begged, proffering a shard pincered in his puckered sleeves.

'What can I see in such a skinny slip of crystal as that? Oh, very well. One glance, but that is all.'

Kendric held the sharp sliver of glass at arm's length, squinting as he would at a particularly repulsive specimen of insecthood that he was loath to display his disgust for.

'I see the table through the glass. I see a few traceries of color — rose and azure, the same wan shades that arch the heavens here and bowed over Rule after a rain. My future is a rainbow, Ludborg; or is it another gate?'

'Do not jest of gates; they have a way of snapping up disbelievers in their jaws.' Ludborg stirred anxiously. 'You see nothing else?'

Kendric frowned, then settled forward to study the remnant as he would a book written in an alien language. 'A plain, a vast plain of sorts, with three mountains rising from it. No! Not three peaks, three peaked cities . . . the distances must be vast, then—' He chuckled. 'Or the cities small enough for mice.' Kendric elevated the shard to return it. 'That is all, a piece of geography and probably most of it a mere reflection of oddments within this chamber.'

Ludborg pocketed the piece in his capacious robes. 'No,' he said quite authoritatively, 'all who look into the crystals see first their origins. That is the root of all futures.'

'My origins?'

'Unwrap the hilt from the well-worn leather that obscures the runes you hide — and hide from — and then read them. They are pure Rengarthian.'

'What need I of Rengarthian runes? I am of Rule! Halvag the Smith fathered me and his mother mothered me on the untimely death of my own. My human span is brief. It permits me the luxury of knowing my antecedents, and respecting them. Deny not this most basic truth.'

'You see Rengarth in the crystal and bear the shadow of a sword of Rengarth on your back, as you once, unknowing, bore its reality,' Ludborg said. 'Your future is, as is no one else's in this chamber round, out of your own hands. And the sooner you recognize that, the sooner you will be able to leave your unwanted future as you wish it — well behind you.'

'Now you see.'

Irissa stood by the same upper-story window of the Citydell where Orvath had tried to wrest away the Overstone. Her palm cradled the talisman, but she was oblivious to its weight or warmth except in the remotest sense.

Behind her paced another man — as tall as her father, perhaps stronger both in an outer physical and an inner moral sense. At this moment, he was no less disturbed than Orvath had been the night he had come to take the Overstone.

Now Kendric spoke almost as bitterly.

'I see the past is held out to humankind as a sheaf of sweet grass to a wild bearing-beast; so that we, in hopes of devouring it to sustain ourselves in future, are led step by shackled step into someone else's pasture.

'If Ludborg thinks his revelations in broken crystal will lead me to trace the patterns of another's dance, he is mistaken,' he added savagely, still pacing.

'Why is it that when we seek our own future path we always must tread upon someone else's past?' Irissa answered him

379

with a question of her own, then sighed and regarded the moonlit rooftops of Edanvant.

'We Torlocs returned to Edanvant and found that the ordinary people whose existence we require for us to be our extraordinary selves had lived here contentedly without us for generations; our self-sacred future threatens their past happiness.'

'The townspeople seem more reconciled now that the Torlocs are settling their own differences.'

' "Seem." No one bows to a future one has not elected.' She turned from the open window, circular coldstone reflections dotting her garments and mottling her expression so Kendric could not quite read it. 'A child, even a grown one, should welcome new knowledge of lost parents, save a child looks toward the future and parents always guard the past.

'Now you see,' she repeated, 'why I wished to eschew the affairs of Jalonia and Orvath; they pulled me back into the fruitless lands of What-Never-Was and Should-Have-Been.'

Kendric suddenly sat upon the bedchest, his troubled expression seeking the relief of concealment in his hands.

'Curse Rengarth!' he said feelingly. 'Curse crystal-casters. Curse all elusive things that taunt us with their distance. What do I care for their mysteries . . .?'

Irissa approached him, smiling. 'Mysteries are the foundation of magic. You have always borne, unknowingly, some shards of it. Now perhaps you understand why you were so . . . receptive . . . to sharing a measure of my magical talents. I would like to see Rengarth someday.'

Kendric looked up, aghast. 'This Rengarth sounds a deadly place,' he warned.

'Unkind to rulers and heirs, certainly,' she agreed.

'Yet you wish to go there?'

'I wish nothing now, but safety. However much you may berate the tear of the past at your trouser legs, I bear the future, or at least that part of it that will shape ours whether we wish it or not.'

He studied her, for the first time in a long while, without

flinching from the fact of her condition for which he felt so unwillingly responsible.

'You have negotiated a truce with yourself and your unasked-for burden. How?'

'By looking at the lives of others, which are so twisted by the things they cannot help.'

His hands reached out, to her waist. 'You have changed — a bit, but your body has not.'

'Not . . . yet.' She smiled with roguish rue. 'Don't expect a Torloc to become clumsy and vaporish; we are a long-lived kind. We steep an endless time in the making and manifest ourselves with subtlety over many years—'

'Subtlety is not my virtue. Do you mean to imply that you don't know . . . how long until . . .?'

She shrugged. 'I have never seen a child of my kind born. We are few and far between, perhaps for a reason. Perhaps too many Torlocs would ruin a world.'

'Perhaps,' he agreed heartily. Kendric contradicted himself by pulling Irissa down beside him into an embrace as much intended to take as to give comfort. 'What shall we do in this mysterious future of ours we cannot evade? That we cannot meet with a sword or magic? You. And I. The . . . three . . . of us?'

'I don't know, although Ludborg pretends to and Felabba, were she here, would make no bones about telling us what we *should* do. Finorian no longer plays upon the strings of our past. We are cut loose at least, yet bound more tightly than ever by our own hands. Rengarth — well, it is a place that hides from strangers as well as citizens, and besides, I cannot cross a gate with a child within me. Unless I unraveled Phoenicia's secret—'

'Not her probable fate, though,' he swore, his arms tightening.

'Then let us do as Neva and Ilvanis — accept this world that we have found, although it is not ours. There is much need here.'

'Aye, the Torlocs need shepherding,' Kendric said with brisk relish. 'The forest is a ruin and its beasts run wilder

381

than they were meant to; the city folk glower. These are matters that need more careful cultivation than the magical, arrogant glance of a Torloc lordling or dame.'

'You see now,' Irissa repeated playfully. 'You have a new role, Wrathman warrior. Peacemaker. It should be a source of some satisfaction to put an entire company of Torlocs in their proper places.'

'There is only one Torloc whose place I have any interest in,' Kendric swore, his amber eyes waxing more golden than Neva's for a moment.

'And only one Torloc who knows that at the bottom of her too-human heart,' Irissa answered, answering thus all the questions they could not settle until present became past and future present.

In the morning Kendric rose early and left without words — not because they were harsh or unhappy, but because they were extraneous.

Irissa swept the coldstone windows open on a clean-washed sky, on flights of forest-bound birds caroling past the city towers as they had not in years, on an unclouded view of both the thick green knot of central forest and the colorful surrounding tapestry of city life.

She even saw as far as the charcoal-dark slice of ravine and the undulating, thin threads of unnecessary Iridesium walls raggedly stitched all the way to the horizon.

And she saw a bridge — a long, two-minded bridge that changed the color of its building blocks halfway across.

A small, dark figure walked the breadth of that bridge alone, a slant of sword across its back. Irissa leaned dangerously far out to study it, her braids and the Overstone pouch swaying over the long drop below.

Where was Kendric going? she wondered. To inspect Torloc ruins? To hunt for animals both tame and feral? To seek the dimensions of a land that had been diminished by strife and now stretched wide and free and uncontaminated again?

Irissa didn't know what Kendric did, and found the morning more interesting for that fact.

382

She watched him reach the bridge's halfway point — then looked beyond. The bridge was whole! Gray stone met gold stone, interlocked, mingled, made one solid link in a chain of magic that spanned the ruined lands from city to forest.

Kendric walked on, his eyes on the world around him, before he paused and glanced down. Stunned, he stared, then stepped back from the grown-together gap. He studied it, as Irissa studied it from her distant perch, wondering whose magic or what force had finished the task of mending the Torloc bridge.

For a moment she thought it was to be the last straw, that he would turn and retrace his steps, back away from the bridge that should not be, that should not by rights be expected to heal itself unseen and unannounced.

At last Kendric moved again, recoiling from the gap, as Irissa had feared. Her fingernails pressed worry like an invisible white handkerchief into her palms.

Kendric paused to plant one stubborn foot, then another, and confronted the anomaly, hands on hips, the long, invisible but everpresent blade of his skepticism unsheathed.

In a moment his long legs had bounded over the mended stone, over the gap that no longer existed in any sense. Once beyond what to him must seem more of a barrier than empty space, having once again outfeinted magic on its own ground, Kendric continued at his usual brisk pace across the remainder of the bridge and on into the forest.

Irissa watched until she could see nothing more of him to watch. She released a deep breath, unconsciously hoarded until it was as empty of sustenance as yesterday, and smiled.

A SELECTED LIST OF TITLES
AVAILABLE FROM CORGI BOOKS

THE PRICES SHOWN BELOW WERE CORRECT AT THE TIME OF GOING
TO PRESS. HOWEVER TRANSWORLD PUBLISHERS RESERVE THE
RIGHT TO SHOW NEW RETAIL PRICES ON COVERS WHICH MAY
DIFFER FROM THOSE PREVIOUSLY ADVERTISED IN THE TEXT OR
ELSEWHERE.

All Corgi/Bantam Books are available at your bookshop or newsagent, or can be ordered from the following address:

Corgi/Bantam Books,
Cash Sales Department,
P.O. Box 11, Falmouth, Cornwall TR10 9EN

Please send a cheque or postal order (no currency) and allow 60p for postage and packing for the first book plus 25p for the second book and 15p for each additional book ordered up to a maximum charge of £1.90 in UK.

B.F.P.O. customers please allow 60p for the first book, 25p for the second book plus 15p per copy for the next 7 books, thereafter 9p per book.

Overseas customers, including Eire, please allow £1.25 for postage and packing for the first book, 75p for the second book, and 28p for each subsequent title ordered.